2004

A ROYAL WELCOME

There! A shadow moved under the water. Long and dark, it glided beneath the surface. Cam almost swallowed her heart.

Powerful arms propelled the bounty hunter through the water as easily as a fish. As he stopped to search the boulders along the rim of the pool, his long black hair fanned out, undulating with his movements. He pushed off again, his stomach flexing. A set of six-pack abs warned Cam that he'd be no easy man to overpower. All the more reason to cork him on the first try. A head start was going to be very important in this match.

She readied her rock for striking. *Closer, sugar, come a little closer to me*. The second his head came above water, she'd whack it like a coconut and run like hell.

THE SCARLET EMPRESS

SUSAN GRANT

LOVE SPELL

NEW YORK CITY

LOVE SPELL®

December 2004

Published by

Dorchester Publishing Co., Inc.
200 Madison Avenue
New York, NY 10016

ISBN 0-505-52597-6

The name "Love Spell" and its logo are trademarks of Dorchester Publishing Co., Inc.

Printed in the United States of America.

Visit us on the web at www.dorchesterpub.com.

My heartfelt thanks to authors Patti O'Shea, Liz Maverick, and Kathleen Nance for agreeing to be part of the 2176 project; to Chris Keeslar for the hard work in helping make it happen; to Dorchester Publishing for going with my idea in the first place; to Susan Squires, Ronda Thompson, and Pamela Britton for their equine expertise; to Cindy Holby and Patti O for spur-of-the-moment reads; to Mary Jo Putney for her lovely quote; and to Màili/Holly for coming up with a fantastic title for this finale book. Finally, my deepest gratitude goes to all the readers who came along on this wild ride. Your support and enthusiasm mean the world to me.

THE SCARLET EMPRESS

Life will throw you a ninety-degree left turn when you least expect it, but that's no excuse to travel along riding the brakes, I always say. If you live too carefully, you risk losing the thrill of the journey. I know. I had two chances to navigate life's path, and each time the ride got wilder.

My name is Maguire, Bree Maguire. Most know me as "Banzai," my fighter-pilot call sign, the earning of which is a story in itself. My gutsy Japanese-American great-grandmother's actions may have won me the label, but my flying was the reason it stuck. Debate all you want about the fine line between "insane" and "fearless," but me, I laughed at danger. As a pilot I pushed the limits; I skated on the edge. The more risk involved, the more eager I was to tackle the mission. I was everything I wasn't in my personal life, where I preferred to proceed with caution, yellow warning lights flashing.

Then everything changed.

One long-ago wintry morning, my wingmate and I took off from our airbase on a United Nations–sanctioned patrol sortie

1

known as Operation Keep the Peace. We expected the usual drill: a flyover of the North Korean side of the border, then of the Southern side, a few easy hours carving racetrack patterns in the sky. As flight lead of a pair of F-16s, a position I'd earned through rank and experience, I'd oversee the overall handling of the mission—a routine mission. In the spirit of sudden sharp turns, it turned out to be anything but.

Shot down and captured by a mad scientist, my wingmate and I slept through almost two centuries imprisoned in biostasis deep in a cave before anyone figured out we were there. When I woke, the year was 2176 and everyone I knew and loved was dead.

Or was missing. My wingmate was gone, and no one knew what had happened to her. I vowed to find out, no matter how long it took. Not only was I the flight leader and responsible for her safety, Lt. Cameron "Scarlet" Tucker was my closest friend.

Cam was a top gun soaked with Southern charm. With a Southern-belle mother and an army-general father, she was supposed to have gone straight from charm school to hosting soirees for a West Point–grad husband. Instead, she set her sights on the U.S. Air Force Academy, pilot training, and fighter school, taking distinguished grad honors at all three. Few seemed to grasp Cam's potential, and I loved nothing more than watching her smash expectations. She was never one to give up. She'd fight until the end. That was why, no matter what anyone told me about the hopeless odds of finding her, I knew she was alive and looking for me, too.

Complications—big ones—kept us apart. Our new world was nothing like the one we'd known. I was the "guest" of Prince Kyber, the acting emperor of Asia. Gone was the United States, the country we'd served and loved, swallowed up by a meganation called the United Colonies of Earth that for all its foibles had actually delivered on the promise of stability and world peace. It stretched across the globe, with "colonies" of Mexico, Antarctica, South America, and the Middle East. The cost? Liberty, free speech, and a government elected by the people.

Someone wanted to change all that, though. A mysterious freedom fighter I knew in those days only as the Shadow Voice, or the Voice of Freedom, was a defiant advocate for liberty who seemingly granted me none of my own by sweeping me into the heart of a revolution.

A revolution that began as a tax revolt, like four hundred years before.

But this wasn't just any tax; nor was it just any revolt. Like everywhere else on Earth, in the UCE the Interweb was the main source of communication, entertainment, education— everything. In dire need of funds, the overextended nation's bureaucrats had slapped a tax on the Interweb to squeeze money from its most powerful colony, Central—what had once been the contiguous United States. Like the British in pre-revolutionary America, the bureaucrats seemed indifferent to the almost universal resentment the new tax created.

That was where the Shadow Voice, or the Voice of Freedom, came in. Its goal? To make sure the events of 1776 repeated themselves: a full-fledged rebellion in Central, leading to independence and democracy as envisioned by the Founding Fathers. But to accomplish that, the Voice claimed to need me.

I was the equivalent of Paul Revere's ride, the Boston Tea Party, and Yankee Doodle all rolled into one. I stood for freedom and democracy, Uncle Sam and apple pie—everything that had been lost when the USA became part of the UCE. If you think I saw myself in those terms, rest assured I did not. I didn't want to be the revolution's mascot any more than I wanted to be the Voice of Freedom's muse. This wasn't my world. It wasn't my war. My duty was to find Cam, and that was all.

The Voice was patient, though. Or perhaps it knew me better than I wanted to admit. Using quotes by the Founding Fathers, it grabbed my attention. Playing on my patriotism and my inbred sense of duty, honor, and country, it lured me closer. " 'The summer soldier and the sunshine patriot will, in this crisis, shrink from the service of his country; but he that stands now deserves the love and thanks of men and women.' "

It worked. I took the bait. That was how I ended up in the middle of the Indian Ocean, waiting to make contact with a nameless, faceless rebel instead of searching for Cam, all while praying that the guilt of that decision didn't eat me from the inside out. Yet, given the chance to save my country and everything it stood for from extinction, how could I refuse? I sure as hell couldn't. Neither, it turned out, could Cam.

Those earlier adventures I recounted in The Legend of Banzai Maguire, but what you know is far from the final chapter. I am an old woman now; it has been over seventy years since Cam and I began our journeys, and high time, she says, that I finish telling the rest: how in a world turned upside down, two men vied for our trust—and more. One was supposed to be an enemy; the other an ally. Both gentlemen, we soon learned, were a little bit of each. Their love for us and ours for them proved essential to the destiny we were born to fulfill. Our exploits, they say, are legendary. But more than that, they are true.

Now, sit back and let me tell you a story, a story of the heart. Four hearts, to be exact . . .

"I am well aware of the toil and blood it will cost you to come to me, Banzai Maguire, but come to me you must. Hear my words; heed my call. I am waiting for you."
—The Voice of Freedom, heard on the Trans-Malaysian Interweb, October 2176

Chapter One

Rocks pelted a sleek black sedan making halting progress through the streets of New Washington, DC. Hastily erected electronic barriers restrained an angry mob. Black-clad UCE police were too overwhelmed trying to keep the protestors in one place to worry about the few who got free.

A small group ran onto the road and emptied their arsenal of rocks at the approaching sedan. A proximity alarm beeped inside the vehicle, and the driver braked.

"Go!" UCE Supreme Commander General Aaron Armstrong rapped his knuckles on the clear barrier separating him from his driver. *Do not stop*, he mouthed to the sergeant, who floored the accelerator. There was a thud, a jerk of the steering wheel. A body tumbled over the bumper, striking a corner of the windshield before rolling off into the street.

How am I to avoid hitting them when they throw themselves

at the car? Once more, he pressed the phone to his ear. "Back with you, Mr. President—"

A flaming pipe glanced off the hood and whacked the shatterproof windshield.

"Yes, yes, I know," Armstrong grumbled. "Next time I'll take a heli-jet."

The sedan accelerated. Armstrong could no longer see the individuals in the crowd or read the slogans on the signs they carried. The gaudy American flags—it seemed every protester brandished such an artifact now—became a broad, neutral blur. Speed had canceled out the fury of the mob.

The general relaxed against the rear passenger seat. It was recently upholstered in UCE blue; he could smell the new leather. He lifted the phone back to his ear. Before he could speak, a communicator resting in his other hand vibrated: once, twice, three times. His fingers flexed convulsively around the unit. It repeated the code, as he'd hoped. *Finally.* He had waited long enough for this moment. Too long, he often feared of late.

"Hello? Are you there, Aaron?" the president was shouting into the phone.

"Indeed I am." A smile curved the general's mouth. "And with news. Good news."

There was silence on the other end of the phone line. It was the closest he'd ever heard Julius Beauchamp come to breathless anticipation.

"We found her," Armstrong told him.

"Banzai Maguire . . ."

"Yes. We've a positive location. The team is in place."

"Grab her! Despite our every effort to stop those broadcasts, the damage done, Aaron . . . it is incalculable. Banzai's ability to escape us has reached mythical proportions amongst our citizenry. They say she turns to air to slip out of any trap, that she catches bullets with her teeth! She can change the minds of men with a single look."

"Surely you don't believe that, Mr. President."

Beauchamp growled. "I want her heart on a platter."

"A bit medieval, that, but it can be done."

"Banzai is the worst threat we've faced in two centuries. Her weapons? Passion. Inspiration," the president spat. "That's my job, Aaron—*my* job to inspire the people, not this outsider's. She doesn't know jack about our world. Her actions prove it. She doesn't understand how only we, the UCE, stand between world peace and chaos. I want her silenced. I want her *gone*."

Armstrong smiled. "All but done, Mr. President. All but done."

"And the second pilot? Lieutenant Tucker? Could she have been raised, too, like the legends suggest? Any sign that she survived?"

"None yet. She wasn't in the cave where Banzai first surfaced, though they were said to be buried there together."

"A paradox. How do you explain it?"

"Interference by an outside party is my hunch. Someone wants her as badly as we do. If Cameron Tucker's alive, Mr. President, I'll find her. Meanwhile, we soon will have Banzai."

Ahead, several hundred protesters broke through a barrier and surged into the street, setting off the black sedan's proximity alarm once more. A soft computerized voice repeated the warning: "*Stop. Obstruction in roadway. Stop.*"

The general exchanged a sharp glance with his driver. The car didn't slow.

"Don't let Banzai get away, Aaron," the president warned.

"Have no worries." The general flicked a speck of dust off the steel toe of his boot. "The team is moving in. There's nowhere for her to go."

They say she turns to air to slip out of any trap, that she catches bullets with her teeth! She can change the minds of men with a single look. . . .

The president might very well fret the growing legend, but Armstrong had an advantage no one else did: he knew Banzai's Achilles' heel, her one weakness. The chink in her armor was his son.

By the time the first of the rocks began hitting the windshield, the general had ended the encrypted call. Crossing one leg over the other, he settled in for a turbulent ride to the White House. Nothing could affect his mood now. At long last, Banzai Maguire was his.

Chapter Two

The Raft Cities were the kind of place you ran to when you needed to hide. The region belonged to no nation, no world order. Sea gangsters lived alongside former Maldivian islanders and the scrappy ancestors of the Lucky Ones, survivors of the unintended nuclear war between India and Pakistan a century ago. In this cobbled-together hive of bandits, mercenaries, and lost souls, U.S. Air Force Captain Bree "Banzai" Maguire sought refuge from the assassins on her trail.

Temporary refuge. She was willing to bet on that. After inadvertently managing to piss off nearly every world leader to the point that either they'd ordered her killed on sight or issued warrants for her arrest, she had the feeling it would take more than a game of hide-and-seek to make them change their minds.

At the controls of a speedboat, she raced over choppy seas. Thunderheads sprouted on the horizon like spunglass mushrooms: rain to soak the lush grounds of pirate-lord Ahmed's estate, which weren't grounds at all, but structures and landscaping sunk deep in dirt hauled generations ago, shipload by painstaking shipload, to this nameless, town-sized raft, one of thousands anchored over submerged islands once known as the Maldives.

Bree could almost taste the thunder in the air, the crackling anticipation, the humidity. It was going to pour good and hard—a real toad-strangler, her friend Cam would have predicted—and before nightfall, by the looks of it.

She'd arrived at the pirate's stronghold just in time. Then again, timing—*good* timing—was everything, wasn't it? It was the only reason she was still alive.

Infamy was a bitch.

To the sound of distant thunder, she yanked back on the throttle of the speedboat and decelerated in a wide arc as her partner watched for threats through the enhanced sights on his rifle. Tyler Armstrong. Protector, confidant, lover. The top UCE general's son, he no longer acted the part. With over a week's worth of scratchy growth on his jaw, he resembled a UCE SEAL commander even less.

Ex-SEAL commander. His military career was finished. He'd jettisoned his bright future the day he helped her evade the charge of treason his country had foisted on her—that same nation for which his father, Aaron "Ax" Armstrong, ran the military under the telling and chillingly accurate job title of supreme commander.

Bree alone knew that hidden under Ty's shirt was a scar from the bullet that had almost killed him—put there by an assassin on the UCE's payroll, a soldier whom Ty feared the Ax himself had dispatched with orders to kill anyone standing in the way of taking her out. Ty had been half-dead from blood loss when he voiced that opinion, and since recovering, he'd never mentioned it again. She hadn't forgotten, though. Was that all he was to his father—collateral damage? It was clear where the general's loyalties lay, and they were not, to her disgust, with his son.

Bree turned more sharply than she needed to and opened the throttle. Water sprayed over the bow. The raft town looming ahead was huge. Beyond-imagination huge. Ty had described it to her, but she hadn't expected a man-made island.

They'd been in the Raft Cities for about a week now, quietly learning the lay of the land—and the water— until they deemed it safe to contact Ahmed. Lying low, they'd restocked supplies, anchoring out at sea, never on one of the rafts. Much of the region was poor; she'd seen a lot of squalor. But this raft? All she could say was that the pirate biz must be good.

Coasting up to their assigned rendezvous spot, Bree killed the engine and deployed the autoanchor. The speedboat looked like a gnat sidling up to a dinosaur. The boat pitched precariously, throwing salt water onto the deck, splashing Bree's boots. "Holy Christmas, Ty." Wiping damp strands of off her forehead with the back of her arm, she lifted her gaze higher and higher until she found the top of the structure towering over her. "This thing is huge." Shiny black pontoons bristled with parasitic flotsam, jetsam, and guns—big guns, resembling cannon. Except these puppies glittered with LED lights and sensors. If the great sea captains of the past were looking down from heaven, it was in a fit of must-have envy.

"I was impressed the first time I saw it, too. For different reasons. I'd come here to infiltrate."

She turned slightly, met his bracing blue eyes. "I bet *that* was exciting."

"No more so than today."

He'd fought in the Pirate Wars, a prolonged campaign to combat sea terrorism. It had been his first command. He'd lost men there. Lost them *here*.

"It must feel strange coming back," she said, quieter.

"It does," he admitted. "But the circumstances . . . they couldn't be more different. Then, I fought to keep my country from harm. Now, it's to keep my country from doing harm to me." *So that I can stay alive to protect you*, he left unspoken. Ty was a career soldier. His life came second to the mission. His mission, he said, was her.

Ty secured the safety on his rifle before stowing it in a holster slung over his back. The wind rippled across the fabric of his faded, olive-green T-shirt, which he wore tucked into equally bleached-out camouflage pants, secured at the waist by a weapons belt from which a variety of killing devices dangled. It hit her how hard and battle-ready he appeared. Bree doubted that he had an ounce of body fat left on him. Any smidgen of softness had turned rock-hard the past few weeks with the brutal physical training program he'd put them both through. She would have liked to say that she, too, was now the proud owner of buns of steel, but no. Biology (or was it heredity?) had played a cruel trick on her. But hey, a girl couldn't have everything.

"It's far from being the largest of the rafts," Ty said. "But it is among the best protected."

"It had better be." She gave the raft another once-over. "Or we're screwed." *Again* . . .

More thunder rumbled, a hollow sound. Wind ruffled strands of hair that had come loose from her ponytail, drawing Bree's attention away from the raft to the sea, where the sun rode ever lower in the sky. Sunsets at the equator seemed to last forever: long, drawn-out, and utterly gorgeous spectacles. When night finally fell, it'd be blacker than any she'd ever known. Her scalp crawled as she imagined a rifle scope trained on her head.

Assassins are like roaches; for every one you kill, there are ten more to take its place.

Or at least it seemed that way. The first person to take a crack at killing her was a guard at Prince Kyber's palace; the second tried doing her in by dropping acid from a plane; and the third shot at her while she slept—and very nearly was successful.

Bree scanned the horizon, half expecting something dark and formless to appear on the edge of the world and swallow the peace she'd hoped to find here. *If this is supposed to be a safe haven, then why is my gut screaming at me to run, to get the hell away from this place?*

It defied all logic, the sense of dread dogging her all day. But she couldn't shake it, couldn't help wondering if someone had followed her here.

Like Ty's father. Her gut told her that the elder Armstrong wouldn't stop until he pinpointed their location. The general's back was to the wall. With the UCE rushing headlong toward revolution, everything he'd worked for all his life hung in the balance. With Bree as that revolution's inspiration, if she lived, he lost; it was that simple. She knew a military man of Ax's reputation would see only one way out: her immediate and efficient execution, along with the deaths of all those in her company. Hadn't that hypothesis been substantiated by the past few weeks?

Which, of course, meant Ahmed the pirate and his merry men were as good as dead. Dead like almost everyone else who helped her and Ty.

Bree squeezed her eyes shut and swallowed. Personal danger didn't scare her as much as the consequences of her actions—or lack thereof—on the innocents in all this. Or on the guilty. How many lives would be saved based on her decision to help the Voice achieve its goals? How many would be lost? Would it all be worth it in the end—if there was indeed ever an end?

She often wondered if this was the kind of torture world leaders and their generals went through when contemplating whether to involve their countries in conflicts. And if it haunted them as much as it did her, not knowing what would be the outcome of those decisions.

"Bree . . ." Ty brushed a warm, work-roughened finger down her cheek, making her aware of the jaw she hadn't realized she'd clenched. "You okay?"

The speedboat bobbed on the choppy seas. She held on to the wheel to keep her balance. "Peachy."

"Peachy, my ass." Her slang often threw him, but it never fooled him; he saw inside her head as no man ever had. But hell if letting him inside her heart wasn't scarier than hand-to-hand combat.

"Am I going to have to wrestle it out of you?" The edges of his wide mouth twitched. "I'm certain you remember what happened the last time."

To her surprise, a laugh burst out of her. Ty had a way about him that undercut all her defenses. "Vividly."

She glimpsed Ty's private and very male satisfied smile as he bent his head to taste her lips with each word: "If we were still at sea, I'd take you right here on the deck. You'd be wearing a different expression when I was done with you. In fact, you'd be wearing nothing at all. . . ."

She could almost feel the images his words left in her mind, because she'd lived them these past few weeks. They had been the only high points of the flight to freedom: the unexpected, easy playfulness between her and Ty; the way he kissed; bare, sun-warmed skin; the shocking heat of their passion, and afterward, always afterward, a sea breeze cooling the dampness left on their bodies. They'd passed many an hour that way, making love to forget the rest of the world was out there, hunting them.

Relentlessly hunting them.

If you let fear rule you, girl, they've won. She'd never let the bastards claim victory. Never. She was in too deep. No turning back. She'd come too far.

Now that you have won your liberty, Banzai Maguire, you must win freedom for us all! She winced at the remembered words of the Shadow Voice.

"Bree . . ."

She glanced up sheepishly.

Ty's thumbs circled over her upper arms, a small movement that was nothing short of miraculous in the way it soothed her. But then he was good with his hands. Very good. "I lost you again," he said.

"I can't help it." Wearily, she sighed. "Any chance I can trade this job for what's behind door number two?"

"I've got you covered, Bree. I'll keep you safe."

17

But what if he can't? What if I can't promise the same? A thread of ice coiled up her spine, raising the hair on the back of her neck.

Ty felt her tremble, a frisson of fear she tried to hide. "Help me out here, Bree. What's eating you?"

"It's nothing concrete. Just a hunch."

"If I'm going to protect you properly, I need to know what's going on in your head. Gut feelings included."

She swallowed. "I've had them before. These hunches."

"Yeah, and they've been damn accurate."

For a moment the only sound was the wind whistling through the nooks and crannies on the speedboat.

"I think we've been followed," she admitted finally.

Ty didn't say anything at first. His eyes narrowed slightly, freezing into chips of blue ice. Whenever she saw that glacial look of his, she considered herself lucky that she'd never ended up on the business end of his rifle; his coldness was that scary. Yet that expression was all Ty. The man never showed fear, though she knew he often felt it. Instead, he revealed his apprehension with subzero aloofness. "By whom, Bree?" he asked. "Who's on our tail?"

Your father. She thought about vocalizing her opinion but changed her mind. He knew. And family, she decided, was best left out of this. "Does it make a difference? If the UCE finds us, I'll likely be killed. And if it's Kyber, probably you will. Now that we've involved Ahmed, your pirate friend, he's fair game, too."

"We sailed here under the radar, Bree. Total radio silence until making contact with Ahmed. Even with satellite surveillance looking down at us, we would have

18

been but one boat out of millions. It's unlikely that any-one knows we're here."

"Unlikely. But still possible. We left a string of dead bodies behind us that stretches all the way back to the Han Empire. Bread crumbs on the trail."

"Those are some grisly bread crumbs."

"Even so, it's a trail for anyone able to spot it."

Ty shook his head. "If someone wanted us, why wait until we came under a third party's protection before striking?"

"Because they haven't caught up to us yet?"

"Bree . . ." He sighed. "Sweetheart."

"You asked what I thought, and I gave it to you. Hey, how about this? It'll be the best of both worlds. We'll board as planned, restock our supplies, stretch our legs a little, but that's it. We could launch again by midnight."

Ty folded his arms over his chest. "And go where?"

"Someplace . . . less populated. I don't know. What's to the south?"

"Antarctica." His expression didn't change.

She rolled her eyes. "I mean between here and there."

"Not Australia. It's back to its eighteenth-century colonial roots as a dumping ground for criminals—Earth's human refuse. The country lies in the hands of an opiate-addicted parliament run by a group of self-indulgent dandies who model themselves on nineteenth-century Regency England society."

"You never know . . . it may not be as bad as it sounds."

He made a clipped, strangled sound. "Newgate? Not as bad as it sounds?" He rubbed his forehead, a sign of irrita-tion. "Bree, the longer we run in the open, the more likely someone will spot us. Ahmed's raft is our best shot at making contact with the Voice of Freedom without calling attention to ourselves. We're safer here than anywhere else. Look at the guns, the warning systems—and those are only the ones we can see. What about the rest of the arsenal? It's considerable, let me tell you. I've seen it. It's going to take more than a simple knock on the door to get inside. Even if that were to happen—I won't rule it out—we'll have warning, something we didn't have the last time an assassin found us."

In that hotel bedroom in New Seoul. They'd almost died that night. Assassins, assassins everywhere. Again, unease filtered through her.

"This raft is a fortress. We'll be no safer anywhere else. Trust me on this. Is that possible?" He smoothed a hand over her hair tenderly, as if she were the most important thing in the world to him. Her chest squeezed tight. "You always want to be the one to take the fire," he murmured. "But you don't need to prove anything, Bree. Not with me."

Her desire to act flippant was crumbling. She wiped sweat off her brow and tried to act more laid-back than she felt. Ty took hold of her chin between his thumb and the crook of his index finger. Dipping his head, he looked her straight in the eye. "Would this have anything to do with your aversion to putting others in dangerous situations?" He held tight to her chin so that she couldn't turn away from his scrutiny. "Well? Does it?"

She was overprotective. She knew it. It was why losing Cam cut so deep. But she sidestepped Ty's question with one of her own. "Does it matter? Is it fair to force ourselves on Ahmed without telling him the whole story?"

"That you're a soldier from the past? Or that you incapacitated the most powerful dictator on Earth with a neuron fryer?"

"After I got you out of his jail."

"Dungeon," Ty put in with deadpan humor. "It was definitely a dungeon."

"Sure, laugh about it now. It wasn't so funny then." For most of her stay in Prince Kyber's palace, she hadn't known the truth about the deplorable conditions Ty had endured. When she did find out, she had been shocked. The emperor of Asia had been so kind to her. Well, while she had agreed to be his guest. "I don't know if Kyber ever intended to let you go."

"Or you, for that matter," Ty said woodenly. Prince Kyber was a touchy subject for him. He probably still wondered what sort of feelings she'd developed for the prince over the course of her stay at the palace. She wasn't sure herself sometimes, but it absolutely wasn't what she felt for Ty. More, she doubted Kyber was capable of feeling anything resembling adult love for her. Even if she had accepted his numerous invitations to be his lover, his doting affection would have made her feel more like a special house pet than a real woman.

"Look Ty, by now my face has been on every monitor—personal and public—all over the world, from the Mars station to Newgate, along with a handy downloadable catalog of my crimes against humanity—too many offenses to count, the last time I checked—but if I remember right, 'armed and dangerous' and 'guilty of inciting rebellion' are on the list." *Dangerous*, she thought with a snort. *Get real.* The only thing she'd ever considered treacherous about herself was her mood when she went too long between chocolate fixes.

21

Suddenly she was battling a bone-shaking craving for M&M's. Of all the things she missed about her old life, junk food was nearly tops. She used to think nothing of downing a Coke and candy bar for breakfast. Ever since she'd woken up in this world, however, her snacking had been pitifully nonexistent. Some of the old goodies were still available in the UCE, Ty told her, but life as Public Enemy Number One had a way of putting a damper on her hopes of getting any.

"It makes no difference, Bree. Ahmed won't turn us away. Not with an open blood debt." An obligation on which she knew he would never have tried to collect if it weren't for his desire to keep her safe. "He already knows everything you just mentioned."

"How?"

"The Interweb. Even in this far-flung region, they have access to it. They would have learned about you, the Voice of Freedom—all of it. If they're inviting us aboard, it's because they want to. And we have nowhere else to go."

His expression was so to-the-point, so frank and penetrating, that it emptied the air from her argument in one fell swoop. Frowning, she turned away, reaching for her travel pack. Ty snatched her back. "Wait a second, Sleeping Beauty. What about our promise?"

Sleeping Beauty—it was his nickname for her, and the very first thing he'd said to her, ever, when he woke her in the cave. Caught off guard by the sudden shift in atmosphere, she would have smiled if she were a little bit more confident about his question. "I don't recall any promise."

" 'No more secrets.' Does that ring a bell?"

"Oh." She wrinkled her nose. "That one."

"Yeah, that one." His mouth twitched with exasperation and amusement. "Something was eating you, and I had to spend the last twenty minutes digging it out of you."

Blushing, she regarded him with a caught-with-her-hand-in-the-cookie-jar feeling.

"I can't believe you didn't remember that conversation."

"I did remember."

"I had to remind you."

"I just . . . well, I forgot. Damn it, Ty. You know I'm better at flying than I am at long-term relationships."

Instantly the curve of his mouth softened. "Ah. So you admit this is a long-term relationship."

Her cheeks grew hotter. "Isn't it?"

"I asked you first, Maguire." A mix of amusement and emotional intensity glowed in his eyes.

"Yes."

"Yes *what?*"

She pushed her fists against his solid chest. He grabbed her hands and held them there. His heart thumped powerfully under the heels of her palms. "Yes, Ty, we're in a relationship. Me and you. A big, fat relationship with a capital R. How's that? Clear enough?"

Ty threw his head back and laughed. Then he swept her close. "Long-term?" he asked against her mouth.

"Long-term," she mumbled back.

Ty made a gruff, satisfied sound, teasing her with small, nipping kisses until she wound her arms around his neck and pulled his head down. His lips were warm, his mouth moist and hot as his tongue found hers. Her knees went weak with a rush of desire. Ty's kiss was fierce and possessive, tender and loving at the same time. No one made her respond like Ty did. He'd spoiled her for anyone else.

"A relationship," he murmured, lifting his head. "Heaven help us."

"It had better," she whispered back. "We're going to need all the help we can get."

They shared a look that in its tenderness bared all they'd been through together.

"Just think," she said in a lighter tone, "tonight we're going to have a real bed to sleep in." After weeks on a small boat, fleeing their attackers across the southern reaches of Asia and the Indian Ocean—a grueling journey by anyone's standards—having Ty between the sheets on a real mattress was what she looked forward to the most.

The press of warm lips to the side of her throat sent a shiver of anticipation straight to her belly. "I have quite a few plans for that bed," he said. "None involve sleeping."

She laughed; she couldn't help it. He could make her smile when happiness seemed farthest from her mind.

She pulled back to gaze up at him, as if trying to remember his face for all eternity. The setting sun had turned his suntanned skin a deeper bronze. Amber light glinted on the prickles of his beard and the ends of his brown hair. The wind whipped around them, carrying smells from the raft that brought back memories of tidal pools and shell hunting—childhood vacations to the beach and all the happiness associated with those days. The familiar smells, the good memories, the "rightness" of this man; it was as if her past and her future had come together.

If she indeed had a future . . .

She met Ty's clear blue eyes with an odd sense of

hyperawareness that the moment was a turning point she'd remember the rest of her life. For what reason, exactly, she didn't know. A shower of tingles made her shiver. Not the good kind this time. It was a scared-shitless shiver—fear of losing someone who had become so important to her only months after finding out that everyone else who'd ever mattered was gone forever. "Just don't ever die on me, Tyler Armstrong."

His jaw moved. "I'll do my best. You do the same."

"Fine. I will."

The morbid humor seemed to defuse the emotional intensity of the moment. If she wasn't mistaken, Ty appeared as relieved as she was.

"Ahoy!"

She lifted her head, then used the boat's viewer to zoom in on who'd called down. A number of men were high above, leaning over the edge of the raft. Big, tough, scruffy-looking men. They looked like a gang of bikers. Bree couldn't be happier. If anyone came searching for her, she had the feeling Ahmed and this gang of rough-if-not-merry men could defend themselves. "Ahoy?" She smiled. "Do people actually still use that word?"

"These pirates do."

Getting into the spirit, she waved back. "Ahoy!"

Someone threw a rope ladder over the side; it slapped against the mussel- and seaweed-encrusted pontoon as it unrolled. Then a man cupped his hands around his mouth and shouted down, "Armstrong—send your woman up first! Then, if she falls, you will be able to grab her before the sharks do."

"I guess I'm your woman now," Bree said out the corner of her mouth.

Ty hauled her toward him and brought his mouth to her ear. "You sure as hell are." His breath was hot, his voice low.

They'd barely begun to kiss when reality intruded in the form of wolf whistles from the raft above.

They jumped apart. After so long alone, it was easy to forget they had an audience.

Ty lifted his eyes to the laughing men on top of the raft, but his hands were slow in leaving her waist. At that, the pirates exchanged amused glances. "She's on her way!" he shouted up to them.

Bree used the viewer again to focus on the top of the raft. Deftly, she zoomed in. As pirates went—not that she'd ever met any in person—their leader Ahmed's appearance was both expected and not. A neatly trimmed goatee was a striking contrast to his head of long and wild black hair, which he wore knotted with shells and what Bree was sure were bones. Human or animal? Maybe it was better not to ask the question and to accept the refuge he offered.

Ahmed cupped his hands around his mouth. "It's about time, Armstrong! Not that I expected any less from the UCE's most famous lover."

"*Former* most famous lover," Ty bellowed back. He appeared to take his fabricated reputation as a playboy bachelor in stride. In reality he was a private man, a dedicated, decorated military officer who got his thrills from participating in extreme sports, not hopping from bed to bed, as the UCE media seemed to want to believe in their relentless quest to solidify the more sensational reputation they'd assigned to him.

It also explained why so few knew that over the years,

Ty had become a respected figure in treasure-hunting circles. Well, they'd all know now, she thought. When he'd come in search of her, it was as a tomb raider inspired by a too-short biography buried in a military history text; a mention of her disappearance, along with her wingmate.

"You're freedom and democracy, Uncle Sam and apple pie," he'd told her much later, after they'd escaped from Kyber's palace. "You're everything lost when the USA became part of the UCE."

He'd wanted to bring her back to the UCE in hopes that her presence would replace something intangible that he felt his country now lacked. His intentions were above reproach; unfortunately, when he'd tried to spirit her out of the Kingdom of Asia, not only was he violating nearly every international law still on record, he'd earned Prince Kyber's wrath. Justifiably furious, the prince had thrown Ty in prison and staked his claim on Bree. The tug-of-war had been going on ever since.

Ty twisted Bree's ponytail around his finger. "Playboy no longer," he shouted up to Ahmed. "This one's for keeps."

"I can well see why!" The pirate lord grinned, binoculars held to his eyes as he evidently inspected her.

Bree made a noise in her throat. She didn't know if she wanted to sink into the ocean or kiss the daylights out of Ty, whose eyes danced with mischief. She had never seen him this lighthearted. Was it because they'd just lifted their relationship to the next level? Or was he simply happy to be disembarking onto something resembling dry land? Regardless, she decided to take his cheerfulness as a good sign. If he didn't feel they were out of harm's way, he wouldn't be goofing around. And if he thought they were safe, then maybe she could convince herself, too.

They gathered their meager possessions and slung their travel packs over their shoulders. Thunder boomed. Lightning sparked. The seas were getting rougher, making it hard to keep her footing. Ty hustled her onto the ladder. "It's going to rain, and Ahmed's getting impatient."

Bree let her gaze travel up the swinging ladder. It seemed a long climb to the top. The sight made her blood rush crazily. Making the haul wouldn't be as much of a kick as flying an F-16, but it'd be fun nonetheless.

"Go on," Ty coaxed. "Ahmed won't bite."

"Yeah, but I might." To the sound of Ty's laughter, she grabbed hold of the swaying ladder, took a breath, and pushed away from the speedboat.

The huge raft rose and fell on the swells, movement that hadn't been so apparent from the speedboat. Bree's stomach flipped with each pitch of the structure. For a second or two she felt as if she were losing her grip; then she started climbing, rung by rung. There was a clicking noise, a faint hiss. Then the entire ladder jerked upward.

Ah! Shock made her hands clamp closed. She swore, barely holding on as the contraption flew upward. The barnacles on the surface of the pontoon sped by so fast that they blurred. The thing was motorized! And whether she liked it or not, she was on a light-speed, one-way trip to the top.

Chapter Three

"Whoo!" Bree whooped as the ocean fell away from her. By the time she reached the top of the raft, her heart was racing and she tingled all over.

The ladder stopped, jerked, nearly threw her off. Before she did fall, someone reached for her hands and pulled her onto the raft proper. Her boots thudded onto . . . grass? Bree straightened, then froze in wonder at the scene spread out before her. It was a tropical paradise. An Eden.

A sweep of manicured lawn studded with palms and mangoes led to a grand estate, a mansion surrounded by more gardens and groves of trees. Flamingos struck poses in a pond shot through with fountains ejecting water high into the air; monkeys chattered in the tops of the trees, noisy but unseen, unlike the parrots that swooped low, preparing to roost with the coming darkness and thunder. The sight was a visual feast for her starving eyes, almost blocking her feelings of unease. Almost, but not quite.

"It is beautiful, yes?"

Breathless, Bree whirled on the pirate she'd almost forgotten was standing next to her, the man she'd decided was Ahmed. "Yes, it is. It's an amazing place."

The man's teeth were white and straight. A diamond glinted in his left canine. A pierced tooth. She gathered her wits and stuck out her hand in greeting. "Pirate lord Ahmed, I presume."

"At your service." He bowed low, his braids making tinkling noises. "Welcome, Banzai Maguire."

"So, you do know who I am." She wasn't sure how to feel about it, either.

"Who doesn't know of you—the figurehead of the upcoming Central revolt? Or of your crimes against the Kingdom of Asia."

Bree made an exasperated sound. "Yeah, yeah. Evasion and escape. Intimidation with a deadly weapon. Knocking an emperor on his ass."

Ahmed laughed with hearty delight, and with no small amount of respect.

A whizzing noise cut short their conversation: the mechanical ladder. Ty landed on the raft next. Ahmed barreled toward him. "At long last—the commander returns!" After a moment of back pounding and general embracing, the men stood, gripping each other at arm's length. In their eyes were a thousand memories, most of them brutal, Bree was sure.

The spray-laden wind whipped her hair across her eyes. She pushed the strands aside to find the several dozen sweaty, brawny pirates not quite leering at her but staring pretty hard. "Yo," she said under her breath, waving.

She wouldn't have thought it possible, but now they stared even harder. "Back to work!" someone shouted at them. "The sooner the goods are unloaded, the sooner you'll get your money." Grumbling, the men dispersed to their duties.

"Cino, my new second-in-command," Ahmed explained. A lean, hard-looking soul paused in his ordering the others around to acknowledge Bree and Ty with a crisp nod.

Several manservants arrived to take Bree's and Ty's travel bags. The weapons, though, they were allowed to keep. The days of walking around unarmed were gone. Ahmed, of course, recognized that. It showed just how much he trusted them to let them hold on to their arsenal.

"Come, come," Ahmed said, ushering them along. "A feast awaits us."

Bree felt a surge of gratitude. "You know we'll never be able to properly repay you."

"Repay me? Bah! Your man saved my life when he had every reason to take it. I tried to give him my eldest daughter in thanks, but he refused me."

"Tactfully," Ty put in, grinning.

"Tactfully, yes," Ahmed agreed, with a hint of grudging disappointment. "But firmly. The bachelor was not yet interested in settling down. But now, it seems, he is! Let us celebrate that as well as your arrival. Come!"

Ty gave Bree a smug smile and took her hand. "Capital R," he reminded her under his breath, and gave her fingers a squeeze.

Under a billowing red-and-white-striped awning, five women sat around a table, waiting for them: two older women, two more in their very young twenties, and one teenager. "My wives and daughters," Ahmed announced with pride.

Bree's heart hit her stomach. Wives? Daughters? "He has his family here?" she whispered out the side of her mouth to Ty. "And he's invited fugitives marked for death aboard?" Was he insane? Bree's stomach knotted up, a feeling she hated, but with which she was very familiar.

Ty took her hand, but she could tell that he, too, was surprised to see Ahmed's family. The women called out greetings, but Bree could barely acknowledge them, she was so shaken by their presence. The wind brought their perfume to her nose as Ty pulled out her chair. Sandalwood and jasmine, she thought, sitting down.

Conversation whirled around her as the women began passing around platters of food that must have taken all day to prepare. By Ahmed's cooks, Bree assumed. These women looked calm and rested, not like they'd been slaving all day over boiling pots.

Ahmed's second-in-command sat on one side of the women, and Ahmed on the other. With a nervous tic in his cheek at odds with his mean features, Cino appeared wary, watchful, much more so than Ahmed. His suspicion undoubtedly stemmed from not being able to convince his boss not to honor this crazy thing called a blood debt, and the risk that posed to his family.

Anger hammered at Bree, making her head hurt. She reached for a goblet of ale someone had set in front of her, and took a healthy swallow. It was pirate's brew, sharp, but good. A couple more deep swallows and she'd gained enough buzz to soothe her frayed nerve endings the way an electrician's plastic caps sealed off hot wires. Then she shoved the goblet away. More ale and she'd lose her edge. She had to stay sharp. Just in case.

Thunder rumbled. The awnings rippled in the breeze. The rain was getting closer; she could smell it. Something else was coming closer, too, but she didn't know what it was.

A shiver of fear and dread raced along her spine.

Screw staying sharp. The idea of numbness was sounding better and better. "I'll make you a deal, Ahmed. I'll watch out for your ale if you watch out for my enemies."

The conversation died down. Ty turned to her, frowning.

She frowned back. "I have to be honest, Ty. His *family* is here," she said, as if Ahmed and crew weren't listening to every word she said. Or perhaps because they were. No one seemed to be taking their danger seriously. "His wives and daughters. You didn't tell me that."

"I didn't know!"

She turned to Ahmed. "We appreciate all you've done for us—you can't imagine how much—but we can't stay here. After dinner, we have to go."

"Go?" the pirate all but bellowed. "But why? Is it my food? My hospitality?" He lifted the hand of the wife to his right and brought her palm to his mouth, kissing it. "Surely it cannot be the beautiful women at this table. You are one of them, Bree Maguire." His dark, sparkling gaze challenged her to defy him.

The guy was a charmer for sure. "Ahmed," she tried again. He knew her situation, but, "I have enemies . . . ."

"Who doesn't?"

"I'm worried that mine will come here. And you know

33

there might not only be UCE forces, but possibly Han troops, too."

Ahmed bristled. "Yes, yes. Let them come! Let all of them find their way to my raft. They will not survive the day!" Lifting his goblet of ale, he sang out, "To our enemies and all their minions! How lonely our lives would be without them!"

A chorus of something resembling "hear, hear," went around the table, and everyone tossed back the contents of their glasses.

Bree called out above the noise of laughter and conversation, "I don't think you realize how serious my enemies are about taking me out of the equation."

"Bah! I am used to fending off the UCE." The pirate lord's mouth thinned disdainfully. Since the Pirate Wars, that long and bloody crackdown on sea terrorism, there had been no love lost between the inhabitants of the Raft Cities and the UCE.

"Those were pirate hunters."

"I know." Ahmed exchanged a brief glance with Ty that was dark with shared memories.

"This won't be a frontal assault. There'll be highly trained Special Forces trained in covert operations. And Prince Kyber has every reason to come after me, too. Not only did I leave without his permission, I sprang Ty out of jail—the son of his mortal enemy!"

Ahmed's youngest daughter let out a sigh. "Prince Kyber . . ."

Until now, the teenager had appeared somewhat bored by the conversation. One mention of Prince Kyber, though, and she'd thrown her hair behind one shoulder with a tinkling of jewelry, her eyes wide and begging for gossip. Few knew much about the secretive and isolation-ist Kingdom of Asia, making everyone hungry for details about the man who ruled it with an iron fist in his coma-tose father's place. "He is said to be as brutal as he is handsome. Is it true?"

Actually, Kyber was too hot-looking for his own good, but Bree decided to let pass the opportunity for that remark. "The prince is brutal with those he considers enemies. I don't deny that. I saw how he treated Ty and others who he believed were a threat to his kingdom. But to me, he showed only kindness." *In a self-absorbed, over-bearing sort of way.* "I'm grateful for his care. It was top-notch. If not for his physicians, my recovery from the biostasis would have taken much longer."

Ahmed's daughter sighed again. No doubt she found the entire idea of a stay in the dictator's palace romantic. Maybe Bree would have, too, if the killings in the wake of her escape weren't so fresh in her mind that she could still smell the blood: the rebel chauffeur shot driving them to New Seoul, the assassin in the bedroom. . . .

Bree made fists on the table. A fat raindrop splashed onto the knuckle of her right hand. "The fact is, it doesn't matter how kind Prince Kyber was to me then. I doubt he will be now. I made him look like an idiot. The ruler of the Kingdom of Asia! I left him lying out cold in a sleazy hotel room in a bad part of town."

Admiration sparkled in Ahmed's dark eyes. "Yes. Many wish to see you dead, Banzai Maguire."

"Yeah." She swallowed. "With cause. All the more rea-son for Ty and me to get under way in the morning, and—"

"Enough!" Ahmed sliced his hand through the air. A

few stray drops of ale glittered on his lips, which he dashed away with the back of his hand. "No one can get within ten kilometers of this raft without my knowing."

"He's right, Bree."

She swiveled on Ty. "You're siding with him?"

"I'm not discounting your worries, but you're exhausted. I am, too." He rubbed her back. "We'll revisit this in the morning. Things will look better after a good night's sleep."

And some great sex. She saw that particular guarantee reflected in his eyes.

She shut her mouth. Boy, she could be bought cheap, couldn't she? She stared down at her plate of fresh-farmed seafood and bioengineered tropical fruit. *You sure fell down the rabbit hole, Banzai, baby.*

Stabbing at a piece of flaky fish, she stifled a snort. Fell? She didn't think so. Maybe that plucky little blond kid from *Alice in Wonderland* fell down the rabbit hole into her adventures, but the word wasn't anywhere strong enough or descriptive enough to convey what had happened to *her*: Once upon a time, she was Bree Ann Maguire, daughter of an auto mechanic and a stay-at-home mom, a small-town tomboy with a keen sense of competition and a heart full of patriotism, a kid who'd dreamed of following in her Marine Corps grandfather's footsteps and who had done so, winning an appointment to the U.S. Air Force Academy and then a slot flying F-16 fighter jets. And now? She was a fugitive dining al fresco on a supersized houseboat roughly 170 years after her twenty-eighth birthday, with two pirates, a pair of wives, three daughters, and a navy commando for company.

That didn't equate to "falling," in her opinion. Not even close. When it came to the proverbial rabbit hole, she'd been sucked in, chewed up, and spit out—facedown and headfirst.

Conversation continued, Bree listening more than contributing; she wanted to learn as much as she could about the people willing to risk so much to shelter her. And Ty . . . he seemed happy. He needed this. She realized this was the first time she'd seen him in a social setting. He was warm, easygoing, a teller of colorful war stories. She'd expected him to be more reserved, but that wasn't the case at all, as it wasn't with her. He opened up to the people he trusted, and she took that as a good sign.

The group consumed their food with gusto, the ale, too. And finally the rains arrived.

A nanobarrier—an invisible shield formed by microscopic computers—kept them dry, but the air flowed freely though it, thick with moisture and electricity.

"The dinner has ended," Ahmed announced. He turned to Bree and addressed her in a tone that told her he knew she remained unhappy about the presence of his family. "We will revisit all open issues in the morn. After we have had our rest."

"Which will happen only after I scour every cubic centimeter of our quarters for assassins," Ty said, folding his napkin next to his empty plate.

"Intruders?" Ahmed appeared indignant. "Impossible."

"And any security breaches."

The pirate growled. "I'll eat the heart of anyone who dares try." Delicately, he shelled the last of the tender prawns and directed a sharp glance at Cino. "But to make you feel better, Cino will inspect the guest quarters."

"Done," Cino said.

"Do it again," Ty demanded.

Ahmed hesitated, appearing to change his mind about something. He threw down his napkin on the table and stood. "I will go with you." To a tropical symphony of rain and thunder, everyone exchanged good-nights.

Bree went with the men, walking along a twisting path through a grove of palms. Here the rain fell freely, warm and soaking. The trees did little to shelter her from the downpour. She wanted to lift her face to it; she wanted to lift her arms high and let it wash away all the tension, all the fear. She wanted the rain to make it all better again.

Right. And all she had to do was click her combat boots together and she'd be home again.

Ahmed and Cino split up when they reached the guesthouse, one walking the grounds, the other checking the inside. Ty backed them up. In any other circumstances, three battle-hardened warriors prowling an area that couldn't be more than fifteen hundred square feet would be overkill. With three attempts on her life in as many weeks, Bree figured it was probably okay to have too much of a good thing.

The men finished up and joined her just inside the guesthouse. The pirate lord aimed a sharp, questioning frown in Cino's direction. "Everything is good?"

The man squared his shoulders. "All is as it should be."

"No one can ask for more than that," Bree admitted.

Ahmed acknowledged her gratitude with a slight dip of his head. Ty saluted the men and closed the door behind them, then walked over to the bed and sat heavily on the edge of the mattress. First he dropped his head in his hands and scrubbed his fingers through his wet hair. Then, one by one, he took off and stored his weapons in the quick and efficient way that marked a man as a career soldier.

Bree lifted the strap of her automatic rifle over her head and leaned it against the wall near the bed. "It's gotten to the point that I feel naked without this."

"Not naked enough."

Grinning, she turned around. Ty had stretched out on the bed. His loose-fitting pants rode low on his waist. "Yeah?"

He wedged his hands behind his head. "Yeah."

A heated stare went back and forth between them.

Anticipation shimmered through her. They'd waited a long time for this. With one tug, she pulled out the band holding her hair in a ponytail and shook her head. Heavy and wet, the black-brown strands swung around her shoulders.

Dripping, she stepped toward the bed. "Wait," Ty said. "The fryer. Get rid of it."

"Picky, picky." To the floor dropped a belt laden with the neuron fryer and other assorted futuristic devices designed to debilitate and kill.

"And the dagger."

"That? It's just a little knife."

"Drop it."

"Yes, sir." Grinning, she discarded the dagger and its scabbard with a stripper's flourish. Then she brought her hands to the hem of her shirt.

"No."

She quirked a disbelieving brow. "No?"

"The clothes I'll remove myself." His smile was distinctly male. Swaying her hips, she came to bed. He reached for her and pulled her down the rest of the way.

"Hey—unfair advantage," she pretended to protest, almost giggling as he kissed his way down her neck. "I'm unarmed."

He rolled her onto her back. "Don't worry. I've got you covered."

Their lips met hungrily, canceling out their laughter.

Ty kissed her as if he couldn't get enough. Well, that made two of them. If Ty was good with his hands, he was even better with his tongue. Sometimes they'd lie on the deck of the boat and kiss, just kiss, for what seemed like hours—long, lazy, languid kisses. But not tonight. There was an urgency she couldn't quite decipher. A stronger need.

Playfulness changed to sharp desire when his warm, work-worn hands slid under her shirt and over her bare skin. Those amazing hands smoothed up and over her rib cage to her breasts, which seemed hot-wired to her more private parts, firing off sensations that made her catch her breath. Then, when he bent over her and didthings with his mouth that made her forget all about his hands, she moaned, bunching her fingers in his hair.

"Do it again, Sleeping Beauty. That little sigh you make. When I'm inside you, it drives me crazy. *You* drive me crazy, Bree." He made her tremble again with the feel of his fingers trailing down her belly. Her muscles contracted. He noticed, smiling wickedly with his eyes as that dangerous hand moved lower. He focused on her pleasure then, and brought her to a climax before she took another dozen panting breaths.

She grabbed his wrist before he could do it again. Their

eyes locked. Under her fingers, his pulse beat hard and determined. "My God, Ty . . ."

"Finished already, Maguire?" he teased. "You'd better catch your breath. I plan to accomplish a lot more than that."

Still gasping, she laughed. How could he make her so happy when so much else was wrong?

Because he's the one. The one you've waited for.

Yeah. He was. The weeks alone with him on the speedboat had confirmed what her heart had told her from the beginning.

She reached up and ran a finger along his cheek, her laughing smile melting slowly into one of wonder. "Well, I love a soldier with a plan." He turned his head and kissed her fingertip. Heart pounding, she cupped his hard jaw in her palms. "And . . . I think I love this soldier."

It took less than a heartbeat for Ty's expression to change dramatically. She dashed the back of her hand across her eyes. "Damn you for making me cry."

"Nothing else seems to have been able to."

"Except you," she whispered.

His eyes had turned so vividly blue that she thought he might cry himself. Her throat ached with his open emotion. If she'd had any doubts left about his feelings for her, whether they were genuine or based on long-ago fantasies, they were erased in that moment. With that one look, she knew she'd captured his heart. *I've thought of you since I was ten*, he'd admitted the first time they made love. *I kept your picture in a place of honor for all the years I lived at home. I went to Harvard and then to medical school for a year. When the war started, I joined up. But I never forgot you. . . .*

41

It was the most amazing story. Hearing him tell it to her that night when they were hiding out in New Seoul had made her feel even more displaced in time. For once, though, she hadn't minded.

A sweet shiver went through her at the caress of Ty's fingertips on the underside of her jaw. "When this is over, I want to marry you."

Her heart almost jumped out of her chest. She would have liked to say something in reply, but her vocal cords didn't seem to be working.

Say yes, you idiot! The laughing rebuke came in her friend Cam's voice. Bree's thoughts rewound to that day in Life Support when she and Cam had dressed for their last mission. The subject of men had come up. It wasn't the first time the saucy Southern belle had accused her of serial dating, of trading men in whenever they started to get too close. *Admit it, Maguire. You're afraid,* Cam had teased that day in her usual refrain. *Afraid to let a man get too close.* Then she'd turned away to finish preparing for the mission, a familiar prove-me-wrong expression on her face.

It was the last time they ever saw each other.

And now there was Ty, sweet, incredible Ty. *Cam, I want to make a future with this man.*

If they survived long enough to try.

Ty took her silence as uncertainty. "I love you, Bree. I loved the legend, and now I love the woman. As for marriage, you don't have to answer yet. I only wanted to make my intentions known. In case . . ." He stopped himself. "I wanted to make my intentions known, that's all."

"I know full well what 'in case' means. You were going to say, 'In case one of us doesn't make it.'" She ran her thumb over the curves and hollows of his handsome and suddenly oh-so-serious face. "Do . . . you think it will ever be over?"

"Yes, Bree, I do." His conviction put hope in a place deep down inside her where little was left. "You'll be the spark to set the revolution ablaze. Just a little push and we'll be there. Beauchamp's regime will fall, and a democracy will take its place. It'll happen all at once, the way the Iron Curtain fell centuries ago in Eastern Europe. And then, our mission complete, we'll slip away into obscurity and"—he patted her on the stomach—"have an enormous squealing brood."

She coughed out a laugh, and he joined her, grinning. "Hey, Ty, give me time to get used to 'brood' first, before you start throwing out words like 'squealing' and 'enormous.'"

His smile gentled. "We'll have a life together. I swear it. I'll do whatever I have to do to make it happen."

"It all sounds so optimistic. Maybe too optimistic."

"It's more than a pipe dream, Bree. If it weren't, I wouldn't be here with you."

She shook her head. "I don't even want to consider the baggage we'll bring to this, or how your family will see me."

"I don't know if I have a family anymore."

Awkward silence filled the sudden void.

Bree tried to lighten the mood. "'No fear' used to be my motto. I can do this. I can. I can marry you, baggage and all."

"*We* can do this," he corrected. "We're in this together. All the way to the finish line."

His expression was incredibly tender for such a hard-looking man. "This is meant to be, Bree. We are meant to be. I've known it my whole life. Now you have to believe it, too."

"Then help me." She felt her eyes stinging all over again. "I want to believe. . . ."

He splayed his hand behind her head, lifting her to his mouth before he forced her back down to the pillow with a crushing kiss. Their embrace blazed with hunger, with possession, and the fear neither of them wanted to bring up—that they'd better make every moment count, because neither of them knew how many were left. And when Ty buried himself inside her, she rode the tidal wave that was her response to him, losing herself in the intense, almost rough lovemaking, until nothing mattered but Ty and the sensations he roused in her that never failed to make the world fall away.

Afterward, when they lay dressed in dry, clean clothes in bed—Ty in boxers and her in panties and a T-shirt, ready for a quick escape should it be necessary—Ty held her for a while, kissing her tenderly before he inevitably, dutifully packed several pillows behind his back and settled in for the night in a semisitting position. "You're not going to sleep?" she asked.

"I will. After a bit." He leaned his rifle against the wall by the bed. "You go ahead."

She snuggled against him as much as his sentry posture would allow. His stance tonight made him even more remote than his usual habit of rolling onto his side, his face to the door, his body serving as a shield. It would be nice, she mused drowsily, to be able to sleep facing him, or spooned against his stomach, instead of curled up against his broad back. But there were a lot of things that would be nice to have, like anonymity and world peace and rescuing Cam, things she'd best not ponder if she wanted to get any sleep.

"You're thinking too hard," Ty murmured.

She smiled in the dark. "How'd you know?"

"I know."

"Guilty as charged."

"Sleep, Bree."

"Yes, sir."

His teeth shone white in the darkness. Bree had just closed her eyes when she felt Ty jerk away. For a second she wondered if he'd fallen asleep and was dreaming. Then she saw shadows moving just outside the windows.

Bree's heart lurched as her senses tried to process what was happening. Intruders? *Not again.*

Not here.

Four huge figures crashed through the front door. Ty fired, but his bullets did nothing to stop them. Wreckers!

They wore no insignia, no visible rank. Wreckers were cybernetically enhanced mercenaries. That much she knew, thanks to Ty. They were known to soldiers of all sides as hard-core badasses, having earned their nickname when one particularly brazen example bragged on the Interweb about how badly he could "wreck" human bodies.

Other men appeared behind the wall of wreckers. These arrivals were ragtag—normal, not supersized. And standing dead center in the middle of them was Ahmed's right-hand man.

The pirate lord himself was nowhere to be seen, but Cino shouted instructions, his voice all but drowned in the chaos as he orchestrated the surprise attack, strutting as if he were some sort of god.

Hatred like she'd never known welled up inside Bree, black and thick, and tinged with utter terror. *You bastard.* Cino had betrayed them—and had brought wreckers along for insurance! Barring a miracle, it meant she was as good as dead.

Chapter Four

A hand landed on the back of Bree's head. "Go!" Ty commanded.

"Wait, I need my—" She was going to say rifle, but it was out of reach, hanging from the hook by the bed.

"No," Ty barked, and shoved her. Her nose bounced off the mattress, making her eyes water. A smudge of blood proved just how forcefully in his fear Ty had shoved her to safety.

After using all his ammo, he tossed his empty rifle to his left hand, reaiming with a loaded pistol with the right while Bree scrambled to find a weapon, any weapon.

Ty's pistol shots rang out. A couple of sharp, abbreviated screams told her he'd scored hits on pirates. There wasn't much he could do about the wreckers. More shots blasted all around. Chunks of plaster exploded and shards of wood whistled past. Another grunt of pain signaled a hit.

On her belly in the midst of it all, and against every

sane cell in her body, Bree combat-crawled off the bed. It was exactly what they'd planned, if this were to happen: Ty would cover her escape. *You're too important to lose, Bree.* No matter how many times they'd argued over it, Ty's reasons won out. But hell if it didn't go against everything in her training to leave him. She knew he could take care of himself; he was an ex-SEAL, smart and physically powerful, but she hated it, both from the heart as a woman who feared for her guy, and as a warrior who didn't believe in turning tail and running.

Your plan had better work, Ty, because every time we talked this through, I was supposed to have had a freaking weapon in my hand! Instead she was under attack and unarmed. And there were wreckers in the game. Of all the potential consequences she'd expected to befall her, this one was the worst.

Bree slithered over the floor. Her weapons belt lay where she'd thrown it in her little striptease. Her hand closed over it. A huge shadow appeared over her, and a wrecker's black boot kicked the belt from her fingers.

Then the monster tossed her out of its way like so much trash as it made its way toward Ty and the center of the fight.

Shock delayed the onset of pain for a couple of blessed seconds, but when it hit, she almost passed out. The heavy, armored boot had snapped her wrist bones like toothpicks. The fracture launched sensory explosions up her arm. Agony dizzied her for a moment; then the exquisite burn brought extreme mental clarity. The wreckers' cybernetic body armor, matte black plates covering their bodies and half their faces, was surgically attached. What kind of person chose to permanently damage their bodies this way? No one with any humanity left; she was certain of that.

They don't care if they hurt you or not. It was bad news. Real bad. Soldiers, at least, had a code of honor. Brigands—and mercenaries—were in it for the profit.

The question was: Who was doing the paying?

Thunder raged outside. Wind blew in the rain. It splashed through the window and pelted everything. The floor was slippery, and her knees slid sideways. She swung her head around, searching for another weapon, and found her dagger almost by accident. She dove for it. Razor blades of pain sliced up her arm from her wrist. She couldn't feel the hand. It had gone numb. The wrist was already horribly swollen, the skin darkening from the pooling blood underneath. She grimaced, her stomach rolling. *Don't look at it.* There was a reason she'd never considered med school.

She gripped the dagger left-handed and started climbing through the open window. She'd make a run for it, get Ahmed—if he was still alive—and his loyalists to help. Reinforcements were essential.

The fight raged on behind her. "Save yourself, Bree."

She swallowed hard. *Sorry, Ty, but I just can't do that.* It went against everything she was.

She turned around in time to see him, clearly out of ammo, leaping off the bed to take on his attackers. Viciously he whipped the butt of his weapon upward. Struck under the chin, a pirate flew backward. The next in line got the rifle butt in the gut and doubled over. Spinning about, Ty took out the man lunging at his back. He was putting up a good fight, but with four wreckers waiting for a piece of him, how much longer could he last? From behind a pirate lunged at Ty, an iron bar in his raised hand. Bree didn't think. She reacted. She hurled her dagger, and it sank deep between the pirate's ribs.

The man screamed and went down, pulling out the knife as he fell. Blood spurted onto the wet teak floor. Boots smeared the gore around like some kind of macabre watercolor painting. A wrecker grabbed Bree by the hair, yanking her backward, then propelling her forward to the floor. Her kneecaps skidded over the grass mats, abrading her skin. She tried to cushion her fall with her injured arm before remembering to tuck it close to her chest.

"Bree!" Ty's expression was raw. Two attackers jumped him before he could get to her. He took out the first with a roundhouse kick. Then the huge shadow of a wrecker loomed over him. The hulk punched Ty in the jaw and sent him flying backward. He landed hard, skidding across the floor. And he didn't get back up.

"No!" Bree fought to reach him, but the wrecker holding her like a pull toy dragged her backward.

Ty stared at her, his eyes dazed, half-open slits. Blood dribbled from his slack mouth. Then his eyes began to slowly close. The promises they'd made tonight, all the good things they'd hoped for in their future, winked out in his eyes one by one like fading stars. Then his body shuddered and went limp.

"Ty," she whispered on a choked sob. It felt as if her heart had been ripped in half. "Help him!" she screamed. "God, someone help him, please."

The pirates turned to her then, their expressions terrifying. A wrecker stood behind her, fist wrapped in her hair. Forced to bow in her T-shirt and panties, she quivered with grief and shock and rage. Pain from her injured wrist slammed her in relentless waves of agony. Would they rape her before beating her to death? Or would it happen the easy way: a bullet in the back of the head?

Yet none moved toward her. Several pirates lifted Ty's limp body and carried him from the room. The cottage smelled of sweat and alcohol. Men milled around her, acting in their wandering inefficiency more like the brigands they were than an organized military force. But it didn't matter who'd paid them for this; she blamed the UCE. Every event in the long chain that led them to this point had originated there. She and Ty never would have been on this raft if not for Central's imminent rebellion. She'd hoped to figure out from the Voice of Freedom if she could help the cause the way he thought she could. Now, in one horrific instant, everything changed. Ty was hurt, maybe dead. The revolution had just become personal.

She was part of it now, part of the rebellion, ready to fight for as long as it took, even if she never heard another word from the Voice or anyone else. If Ty had sacrificed his life for freedom, by God, she'd spend every last minute of hers making sure it wasn't in vain.

A pair of black-clad legs stepped in front of her. "Look at me!"

The wrecker with his fist wrapped in her hair jerked her head back, exposing Bree's face to Cino's harsh glare. "You bastard," she choked out.

Cino backhanded her. Fire exploded in her head, for a moment rivaling the agony in her wrist and hand.

With blood dripping from her nose, she regarded him almost serenely. She felt different inside. Not dead. Different. When Ty went down, it had changed something deep inside her. She'd become confident. Strong. She'd become Banzai Maguire.

Cino broke eye contact first, as if she frightened him. "Get her to Elliot—now," he ordered his men.

She searched her brain for the name and came up empty. "Who's Elliot?"

Cino stared at her as if he couldn't believe she'd dared ask him another question. "You might say he's somewhat familiar to most here in these seas."

The men guffawed.

"The only thing that matters to you is that Elliot plans to trade you to the UCE."

The UCE. *Good.* That was where she needed to be. The heart of the revolution. They were handing her over—alive. On the downside, it meant that somewhere, someone had their hopes set on handing her a fate *worse* than death.

Cino smirked at her. "One pilot down. One to go." Then he walked out into the night.

The chill inside her turned to ice. *One to go?* Now that they were finished hunting her, they were going after Cam.

Chapter Five

Demon hands plucked at Lt. Cam Tucker's body. Merciless, relentless, they jabbed and pulled her muscles and bones until she reverberated with agony.

"Cameron . . ."

The demons paused in their work. Someone had called her name. Who?

"Mama?" The voice was broken, whispery, like a very old woman's. Cam didn't recognize it as belonging to her mother, but she knew better.

"Cameron."

"Here," she whispered. *Yes, I'm here. I'm alive.*

Only she wasn't sure she wanted to be. The demons were back at work, this time attacking her skin, their nails scraping and slicing while they played tug-of-war with her hamstrings. Cam pressed her lips together to keep from howling.

Someone stroked her hand. There was compassion in that touch, understanding of the pain ripping through her. "I'm sorry I'm not your mama." The high, sweet voice faded in and out. "But I will take care of you. I promise."

"Who . . . ?" Cam couldn't remember who the person was, couldn't even finish the sentence.

The hand squeezed gently. "They call me Zhurihe. . . ."

Zhurihe. Sure-ruh-hey. She remembered now. It was the voice Cam had heard since the darkness had lifted— and even before she was fully aware, floating . . . floating in nothingness until gut-wrenching pain had thrown her ashore. *If that was what it felt like to be born, I'm glad I don't remember the first time.*

Cam made the mistake of trying to shift positions in bed. Needles pricked her body through the mattress, joining forces with the demons that battered her day and night with their sharp, cloven little hooves. She forced her eyelids open with all the smoothness of prying a top off a rusted can. "Hay . . ." she croaked.

"Zhurihe," the girl corrected patiently.

No. Hay, Cam wanted to tell her. *Straw.* Where was she that there was so much hay? High over her head motes of hay dust floated in the sunshine pouring through cracks in the wooden tepee. A yurt, Zhurihe had called it. So many questions. How would she ask them all? "Tell me," Cam croaked. "Tell me what happened." She wanted to hear it again, to hear what had happened to her. Maybe this time it would make sense; maybe this time the tears would stay dammed up until Zhurihe finished with her explanation, telling of unspeakable horrors in that high, lilting, English-accented voice of hers. "It is 2176," the woman began. "The world has changed. . . ."

Cam closed her eyes, trying to absorb it all.

"Nuclear war destroyed everything you knew. It's been fifty years. There is no modern communication, no electronics. No motorized travel."

"America, too?"

"Yes, everything is gone," Zhurihe confirmed in a gentle voice. "There is no America, no Europe. No Asia. Only this place. Mongolia. You are here now. You live with us on a farm—a cooperative, a collective farm. These people, they're my family, though not by blood. We grow many things here. Raise livestock. And we maintain a shrine, a religious shrine, where travelers come to pray and partake of the hot springs. You will share in the work when you are well. We are your family now. . . ."

We are your family now.

Zhurihe had told her that over and over. That they were family, that this was her home. That nothing else existed. If Cam could scream, she would. If she could make fists without convulsing in agony, she would. All she could do was close her eyes to slow the falling tears, to get a grip on the pain, the anguish inside and out that held her in a relentless grip. Mongolia . . . It was a long way from Korea. How did she get here? And why alone? *Bree, what ever happened to you?*

The ball of sorrow in her chest expanded. The last she'd heard from Bree was on the radio after they'd been shot down. Then Cam had been captured. After that, her captor had done the answering for her, using Cam's radio to answer Bree with clicks of the mike button, luring Bree closer, to Cam's outraged, gagged-and-bound horror. They'd been brought to a cave, tied up, and drugged. The next thing Cam knew, she'd woken in this world of pain blunted by a haze of confusion.

She struggled to make her lips form words. "Must find other pilot," she whispered. Bree would know what to do.

"No." Zhurihe's answer was sharp. "There are gangs, dangerous gangs. They roam the less civilized areas, which encompass most of the world. Yet here, on our little farm, we are safe, free of radiation."

Safe . . .

Free . . .

This is your home now. . . .

A rooster squawked, warning the world of sunrise. Prying one eye open, and then the other, Cam blinked up at a dark, conical, smoke-filled ceiling above her bed. It always took a few minutes to distance herself from the dreams she had of the long, painful days of her recovery. Why did the dreams come every night? Maybe it was her mind's way of analyzing everything Zhurihe told her. Yet if that was the case, then why hadn't anything worthwhile come of that analysis?

Feeling like a ninety-year-old grandma, Cam rolled from her side to her back. Mercy, she hurt. All over. Her bones, her muscles . . . shoot, her damn eyelashes were killing her. She wished she could blame the hay-stuffed mattress, but she knew her daily morning pain was a consequence of more than that.

It was only bad like this the first few minutes after waking, when she was fixing to get out of bed, not all the time like it used to be. Over the course of the day exercise worked out most of the kinks, but at night the pain settled in again as she slept.

The bed made crunching noises and sent puffs of dust into the air that tickled her nose and made her sneeze.

Hay. It was everywhere in the yurt. Cam wrinkled her nose at the powdery sweet odor, the first scent she'd recognized after being revived, and the first thing she'd tasted, felt, and seen after becoming aware. Straw cushioned the dirt floor; it fed the horses and served as bedding. The cloyingly sweet smell filled her nostrils from dawn until dusk, making her nose itch. It found its way into her homespun wool undies, pricking and itching, and it tangled in her hair. *If I never see, feel, smell, or taste another piece of hay for the rest of my life, I'll be the luckiest woman alive.*

More roosters crowed. Dawn meant it was time to accomplish her first chore of the day: milking the goats.

And she used to complain about early flight briefings? At least no one required her to be mentally alert while tugging on goat nipples. It had gotten to the point where she could milk the herd in her sleep—which was likely to be the case this morning. Her body was not happy after the physical exertion she'd put it through yesterday. Not happy at all. She'd be lucky if she could walk. The people who sheltered her understood little about physical therapy. Yet Cam knew that if she wanted to heal, if she wanted to get strong again, she'd have to force herself through the daily torture disguised as training. She looked at her hands: scratched, chapped, swollen in spots from frequent falls. Those hands had once held the throttle of an F-16. Those hands now milked goats. What would her hands be doing in five years? Ten? Fifty? Did people live that long anymore? Did they want to?

Once, her hopes and dreams for her life had stretched out like a wide-open country road in front of her. She'd known exactly where she was going, and how she was going to get there; all she had to do was follow the path.

Now she couldn't see much past the tip of her nose. She hated driving blind.

"Well," she whispered to herself, emphasizing her Southern accent, which in truth she'd been losing slowly over time, "it sure don't matter now, Miss Scarlet, does it?" Scarlet was spelled with a single T because the guys in her fighter squadron who'd given her the call sign and written the name on her helmet hadn't known *Gone with the Wind* from the Weather Channel. "Now you milk goats."

A one-way ticket to hell—that was what she'd surely bought that day the missile slammed into her F-16. One minute she was running for her life through thick North Korean forests; the next she was here, in a cold, remote, postapocalyptic no-man's-land. Everything else was one big, fat, useless chunk missing from her memory.

"I can always tell when you're thinking about the past."

Cam rolled over. A pretty seventeen-year-old girl smiled at her from the adjacent bed. "Zhurihe! When did you get home?"

"A few hours ago." Zhurihe gave a distinctive tiny sneeze that ended in a squeak.

Cam smiled. "Allergies again."

Eyes watering, Zhurihe smiled. "They stay with me after I visit certain places."

Cam knew better than to ask just where those *certain places* were, or what she'd done while there. The girl disappeared with no warning for days, and once for weeks at a time. "Mushroom picking again?"

"Uh-huh," Zhurihe replied.

Yeah, right. The girl's response brought back Cam's

childhood memories of sneaking off to find her brothers behind the old tumbledown tobacco barn. They'd bribed her with Krispy Kremes so she wouldn't make a peep about catching them chewing and smoking when they were supposed to be off picking blackberries. Cam had a strong feeling that Zhurihe hadn't been picking mushrooms, that she never was. The girl was a pretty teenager with a baby face and braids that made her look even younger, but something about that face looked mischievous. Cam had no proof, only a nagging feeling that there was a missing piece in the puzzle. Yet it was on one of her supposed mushroom-picking missions that Zhurihe claimed she'd discovered Cam buried under the permafrost, snug in her high-tech casket.

At the same time, despite her sporadic tenancy here and Cam's moments of doubt, Zhurihe remained an emotional anchor, and had been ever since Cam had been set adrift in this world she no longer recognized. Zhurihe was a Mongol name that translated to *heart* in English, a fitting label for this teenager who was, bless her heart, equal parts instructor, guide, cheerleader, and a shoulder to cry on. That Zhurihe—and everyone else in Mongolia—spoke perfect English was a mystery in itself, something about a long-dead king who'd unified all of Asia under one flag and one language before the war. But English? In Asia? It was hard to believe that any one person could have had that much power, charisma—and trust. Cam had thought the modern world incapable of producing leaders like that anymore. A tragedy that that the extraordinary man was now dead. His successors, too.

Cam reached across the space dividing their two small beds and gave the girl's hand a welcome-home squeeze.

"It's good to see you back. I missed your company. And you're right—I was thinking about the past. Bree, specifically."

"Surely she wasn't as good a friend as me!"

Cam smirked at the ceiling. Zhurihe seemed at times to have the simple mind of a child. And yet Cam had witnessed too many examples of her feisty cleverness to believe it to be true. She was an enigma. "We couldn't have come from more different backgrounds. It didn't matter. Bree was the sister I always wished I had."

"You had five brothers."

"Five older, overprotective brothers." Zhurihe never seemed to tire of Cam's descriptions of her family. "I miss them." A persistent ache, much faded now, clutched at her chest. She let her hand drop. "They're dead now, all of them, and no matter how much I think of them, they're not coming back. I know that. I've accepted that. But not when it comes to Bree." Cam searched Zhurihe's shadowed, earnest face. "She could be alive, you know. She's the one person who could have followed me into the future. I'm going to find out what happened to her, Zhurihe." It was why she battled her clumsy, aching body every day, desperate to be strong again, so she could take charge of her fate—and Bree's.

Zhurihe pursed her lips and shook her head. "It's too dangerous outside of the valley."

"All my life people have been telling me to give up. I'm used to it."

"Listen to me, Cam. Do *not* try. You won't get far. Maybe not even past these mountains."

It was always the same story. Zhurihe underestimated her. Everyone did. Even when dressed in a flight suit and combat boots, a .45 strapped to her thigh and an against-the-regulations switchblade wedged in her pocket, Cam knew her blond rich-girl looks and bred-in grace screamed that she was something else, that she was a woman like her mother, a Southern belle from a wealthy Georgia family, raised in a world of old money, cotillions, and rigid expectations. No one could believe it when she pursued an appointment to the Air Force Academy, and that she actually graduated. No one had thought she could do it. They never said it aloud, though, they were too well mannered for that, but she'd seen it in their faces. It made her victories all the sweeter. Defying expectations every step of the way, she was one of the few females accepted into Euro-NATO Joint Jet Pilot Training at Sheppard Air Force Base in Texas, finishing as a distinguished graduate, and at F-16 training, too. One by one by one she'd shut the cynics up. But there were always more of them, fixing to doubt her wherever she went, even after she'd received the coveted Gabreski Award for being the top air-to-air student in the USAF. It seemed if you were shapely, blond, and soft-spoken, no one figured you could kick ass. But not Bree Maguire. Never Bree. When Cam had gotten to her assignment in Korea, the infamous Banzai had, after flying a single mission with her, told the squadron at the bar that night that "If Chuck Yeager had made a kid with Scarlett O'Hara, it would have been Cam."

It was the finest compliment anyone had ever given her.

The roosters crowed some more. Outside, the tinkling of cowbells rang in the morning calm. Cam pushed to a sitting position. "Enough lolling around in bed. I can hear the goats calling my name." She grabbed for one of the two crutches leaning against the wall by the bed and used it to push off the mattress. The floor was icy cold under her bare feet. "Want me to fix you breakfast?"

Zhurihe shook her head. She was never very hungry after coming home from her absences.

"How about I take the goats up to the pasture this morning? Then you can stay in bed."

"Oh, would you, Cam? How can I make it up to you?"

"Tell me you're staying around for a while this time."

Zhurihe looked coy. "I would like that."

A typically vague answer. It saddened Cam more than angered her. She enjoyed Zhurihe's company, and missed her when she was gone. She had so little else to cling to in this world.

Zhurihe threw a blanket over her head and disappeared from sight, only a muffled squeak of a sneeze giving away who lay under the lump of brown wool. Cam wished she could stay in bed, too, but the ladies awaited her, udders filled to bursting.

The first challenge of the day was not stumbling and falling into the hole outside in the dirt that served as a toilet. If that meant sacrificing her pride and completing the task with the help of a crutch, that was fine with her.

Cam rinsed her face and brushed her teeth using a bowl of cold water. Then she fixed her wheat-colored hair in the same style as Zhurihe's, but her braids were mere stubs no longer than the back of her neck. Cam studied herself critically in the small mirror. Somehow the style didn't have the hoped-for youthful effect it did on Zhurihe. She was only twenty-five, but her eyes were prematurely old. Hollow, they reflected her devastating loss. While she no longer wept big buckets of tears when she pondered what she'd lost, grief had left a permanent stain.

Cam turned away from the sad face in the mirror. After stripping and changing into soft layers of brightly colored wool and a pair of cowhide boots lined with the wooly undercoat of a yak, she fixed herself a plate of bread and goat cheese and ate standing up in the kitchen. Her leg muscles were so stiff and painful today that she feared not being able to leave a chair once she sat in it.

She was wiping her hands clean of crumbs when she heard a strange noise from outside. The sound wavered, as if it were traveling from a great distance. In a city she wouldn't have noticed the sound, and it wouldn't have woken her if she were sleeping, but in the utter quiet of the countryside the rumble stood out.

Cam ran to the window. Her heart hammered, threatening to drown out the distant roar, and the aches in her muscles were no longer noticeable. She knew that sound!

She shambled to the front door, throwing it open. Cold, dry air slapped her in the face. The sky looked like steel wool. And yet she knew what was behind the clouds.

It was an airplane, too high to see any detail, only a sliver of metal at the tip of a contrail. It was high and moving fast.

She jumped up, thrusting her fist in the air. "Oh, baby, oh, yeah!" Somewhere, someone still had the technological knowledge to maintain and fly a plane!

Before Cam realized what she was doing, she was running, lurching along in an unsteady gait out past the pens of animals and piles of manure, past a few early-riser locals heading out into the fields. Ahead, there was an opening where the strands of clouds had separated. Cam limped to a halt on the rutted dirt road, her face turned to the sky. Where was the aircraft? Then she saw it: a minuscule sliver, glinting high up in the rarified, raw sunshine that only pilots and eagles knew.

Every cell in her body seemed to soar skyward, taking her trampled spirit with them. "Y'all, I'm here. Don't go. . . ."

Even without knowing who sat behind the controls, friend or foe, she knew she was calling out to one of her own kind—another pilot.

Just then, a ray of sunlight hit her square in the face, and she laughed, truly laughed, for the first time since crash-landing in the year 2176.

Something slammed into her from behind. A wool blanket fell over her as the ground rushed up to meet her. All she had to break her fall was a long, thin arm she'd sprained once already during her endless, ongoing recovery. Her ankle twisted, sending a spear of pain up her calf, but she rolled her weight to the side, landing on her back in a cold puddle of mud, but saving her leg from another injury. The question wasn't what hurt, but what didn't hurt; her body had turned into a war zone with the enemy winning. Blindly she threw a fist, bringing up a knee. It impacted something solid, and she heard a muffled, "Oomph."

"Ow! Cam! Be still!"

Cam stopped fighting. "Zhurihe?" She tried to throw off the blanket, but the girl kept it in place over her head. "God almighty," Cam mumbled, tasting sour wool. "Will you tell me what's going on? I'm fixing to suffocate in here!"

The blanket moved back slightly. Zhurihe sat on top of her, straddling her hips. "This," Cam told her in a tight voice, "does not feel good."

But the girl was not listening to her. Her head was tipped and she was peering at the sky. Cam listened, too, but she no longer heard the distant, droning noise of the aircraft. It took everything she had not to let disappointment overwhelm her. "Did you hear it, Zhurihe? It was an aircraft. An aircraft!"

Zhurihe's dark eyes were wild with alarm. "You ran outside to see it."

"Of course I did." Cam hesitated at the girl's obvious alarm. "Why wouldn't I?"

"Because you do not know about anything!" Zhurihe's small fists grabbed the blanket draped around Cam's shoulder and tugged, half raising Cam's head off the dirt. For such a petite person, Zhurihe had amazing strength. "If you see it, it may have seen you. Never let them see you. Never! It's why I have told you always to wear a veil when outside." She took Cam by the shoulders and shook her.

Teeth chattering, Cam grabbed her hands and stopped her. "I thought it was local custom, the veil."

"It was for your protection! To keep you safe here." Her expression grew even more intense. Her apprehension was contagious. Although Cam didn't understand the threat, the very real fear Zhurihe felt launched straight into her gut and turned it cold. "Zhurihe, how did you find me? Did you by chance steal me from someone?"

For the first time, the girl broke eye contact. "I told you."

"Tell me again."

"It was far to the north, a remote place few know."

"You were picking mushrooms and tripped over my pod." The story was becoming harder and harder to believe, especially now with the bolt from the blue of seeing the airplane. And if the story of her discovery was a lie, what else was, too? The nuclear war? The lack of technology? Bree's whereabouts? "You asked your family for help, and they brought me here on an oxcart."

"Yes." Zhurihe's wild eyes swung back to Cam. "Promise me that you will never go with them if they come for you. Promise me!"

The girl, it seemed, had but one thing on her mind. "If *who* comes for me?"

"Anyone!"

"Can we be a little more specific?"

"The emperor's Rim Riders."

Ah, so that was it. The vicious barbarian warlord whose stronghold was thousands of miles away. The monster who, according to Zhurihe, ate peasants alive and made overcoats from their dried flesh. He sounded a little like Genghis Khan crossed with Count Dracula, but since neither he nor his minions had ever been seen in this remote place, she hadn't much worried about it. "He has jet aircraft, Zhurihe. Do you know what that means? He has computers. And if he has computers . . ." The possibilities were mind-boggling. Suddenly Cam was extremely interested in the emperor, despite his rather gross-sounding wardrobe and eating habits.

But Zhurihe didn't share her enthusiasm at all. "Promise me. Please."

"Okay, okay. I won't go with him."

"The Rim Riders!"

"I promise I won't go with them. What are Rim Riders, anyway?"

"They're the emperor's bounty hunters. You'll know them when you see them. They wear only black. Even their horses are black."

The image that came to mind was something resembling Grim Reapers on coal-black steeds. Not pretty.

"If they come here, you must run to the springs. Do you understand? Hide there, under the water. Remain there until they go. Do you understand?"

"Run. Springs. Hide. Got it."

The girl bounded to her feet, checking the sky once more. "I'll be leaving for a while."

"What? You just got here." Cam sat up, slowly and painfully. Speech was impossible until the spasm in her back passed. "I thought you weren't going off again right away."

But Zhurihe was already running back down the road toward the farmhouse, her long braids spinning.

Promise me, Cam!

Sitting, legs sprawled on the dirt road, Cam watched Zhurihe go, an oddly terrifying mix of dread and fear and hope filling her. The world she'd thought she was beginning to understand had just taken a 180-degree turn.

Chapter Six

General Armstrong's black sedan skidded to a stop in front of the rear entrance to the White House. Neither its VIP passenger nor the driver said anything for a few moments.

Finally the sergeant shifted her gaze to the rearview mirror. "Hell of a ride, sir."

It was that, thought the general. "Are you injured, Merrick?"

"No, sir."

She answered a little too quickly. Pride, he decided. Too many females on the military staff wanted to be seen as invincible. Didn't she know? No one was. Not even him.

"And you, sir?" Suddenly worried eyes gazed back at him. "Are you hurt?"

"It'll take far more than that to put down this old warhorse, Sergeant." General Armstrong shoved on his hat and pushed open the rear passenger door. Wet, fluorescent orange paint splashed down onto the toe of his shiny black boot. Drawing his trenchcoat around him, he stalked around to the front of the vehicle. In the slanting light of late afternoon, the pieces of eggshell littering the windshield looked like golden confetti. More goo pooled in fist-sized dents on the hood. The rocks had done their damage. A shallower, wider indentation resembled a mold of a human torso where one of the protestors had rolled over the bumper. A smear of blood was almost indistinguishable from the stains left from the hurled rubbish.

Standing quietly at his side, the driver pondered the sight. Then, taking off her cap, she dragged the back of her arm across her forehead. "I'll put a call in to dispatch for another vehicle, sir."

"Consider yourself off duty, Merrick."

"Sir?"

"I'll take a heli-jet from now on." He retrieved an attaché case from the backseat. The loaded weapon he'd stuffed deep in the pocket of his trench coat thumped against his thigh.

"General. A question, sir."

The driver looked shaken; he noticed that now. She hadn't uttered a sound after striking down the protester who'd thrown himself at the moving car, hadn't said anything at all until now, when they'd pulled up to the White House. But then, he expected—required— the soldiers he maintained as personal aides to be stalwart creatures. "What is it, Merrick?"

"Do you think it will get worse?" The driver cleared her throat. "Sir."

She was worried, perhaps even frightened. And she

had every right to be. He turned his attention back to the damaged car. Gusts of wind swept in the from the east, where the original Washington, DC, lay, abandoned after rising seas had rendered it too often flooded. The breeze brought the smell of salt and the equally muted roar of the demonstrations, cordoned off some five city blocks away. "Do you hear them, Merrick?"

The woman fell quiet for a moment. "Yes, sir. I do."

"Remember the sound," he said tersely, "for soon it will be a thing of the past. I know so, especially after some news I received today. Soon, very soon now, all will be as it once was. The government will restore order."

"Yes, sir. Of course. Thank you, sir."

The general left the driver behind, his leather trench coat whipping around his boots. At the security checkpoint, he handed over his attaché case for inspection and submitted to retinal and DNA scans before beginning the trek across the marble foyer to the Unity Office.

The door slammed shut behind him. His eardrums popped. A pressure seal. The air he breathed was now from a separate source from that in the rest of the White House. Clasping his hands behind his back, he watched a circle of the carpet waver and open. A platform in the same shape as the cutout rose slowly from the depths beneath the floor, accompanied by a faint whirring noise. Armstrong stepped onto it and rode down to President Beauchamp's briefing room.

It was several degrees warmer there than the upper limit of the general's comfort level. He preferred the chill of the north; the president, the cloying heat of the Central colony's Louisiana district. Rich velvet wallpaper and similarly upholstered seating added to the thick, choking atmosphere. Armstrong smelled cigar smoke in the air—and leather?

He whirled around as a soldier clad in body armor emerged from the shadows. The young man wore new boots; that explained the leather smell. "Who are you?"

"Lt. Col. Christian Bow. Presidential Special Ops," he answered at the same time Beauchamp said, "For God's sake, don't frighten the boy with that scowl, Aaron."

Armstrong swerved his glare to Beauchamp, sitting, hands folded, at his massive desk. "It's better to be safe than sorry, Aaron. You know that."

"Your weapon, General." Bow held out a gloved hand. "Please."

"What the hell is going on?" Armstrong growled.

"We continue to be in a state of national emergency. I cannot take any chances, not even with my most trusted associates."

"So, I'm your *associate* now? Is that the new, politically correct term for supreme commander? How droll." The general thrust his weapon into Bow's hand. The man inclined his head with respect and left, retreating somewhere into the bowels of the White House—with Armstrong's pistol, a family heirloom! "This associate happens to command your military, your entire armed forces—"

"And I intend for it to stay that way."

The men exchanged dark glances. The deteriorating, volatile situation had made doubters of them all. "Do you suspect me of plotting a military coup, Julius?"

"Don't look so insulted, Aaron. These are times of tremendous unrest in our great land. My greatest and most difficult duty is maintaining the integrity of the

71

United Colonies of Earth. Even at the risk of insulting those I trust the most. Especially when they pay me an unexpected visit."

Armstrong didn't give him the pleasure of an acknowledgment. "We got her," he said simply.

Beauchamp's only outward reaction was the fanning of his fingers on the burled surface of his desk. He was, after all, a master politician. No one else could have steered the UCE on an unwavering course for as many years. "Banzai Maguire. In custody." He closed his beefy fists, as if eager to get a piece of her himself. "Congratulations are due, General."

He acknowledged the compliment with a nod. "She's on the way to Fort Powell, estimated time of arrival"—he glanced at his wristwatch—"nineteen thirty. Tonight."

Beauchamp pushed himself out an arm's length from the desk. "It will soon be over, this terrible moment in our history." He seemed overcome by emotion. "We need a trial. Quickly."

"After I've gotten what information I can out of her."

"Interrogation . . ."

"Yes. No holds barred. Those are the orders I will give my interrogators and their guards."

The president frowned.

"Don't act so worried! I thought it was you who wanted her heart on a platter. I won't kill her before you have your trial. Or at least I'll endeavor not to."

"Oh, I'll see her dead; don't doubt me on that. Just beware of turning her into a martyr, Aaron. She's enough of a legend, unwarranted as it is."

Armstrong nodded. "Agreed. But she's more dangerous alive. As long as she lives, it gives the rebels hope that they will succeed. She provides a link to the past, a past without a United Colonies of Earth. We must sever that connection—and quickly."

"Arresting her, silencing her, isn't enough, General. Execution for high treason is the only answer."

"After a full military tribunal, of course."

"Of course."

The men paused to contemplate the trial and its inevitable findings.

"We need that trial, Aaron. Don't forget. The citizens will expect it."

"You'll have your trial. I promise you that."

"With Banzai Maguire in the courtroom, not watching the proceedings from the intensive-care ward."

Armstrong inclined his head. "I would say that gives me quite a bit of latitude."

The men smiled at each other.

Beauchamp's chair swiveled around and he cast his gaze out the window that faced east—faced the Han Empire. "It troubles me that the second pilot eludes us. We know both were shot down together. Air force archives speak of witnesses who saw both captured by the same individual, who died, presumably, when the underground lab was destroyed in the war. If one pilot was there, it follows that the other should be, too. And yet we haven't found her."

"We will." Armstrong was sure of it. "No word from our man in the royal palace?"

"Hong? No, the minister has had nothing for me," Beauchamp snarled. "And so we wait. Kyber had better not be hiding her. He's played his game of one-upmanship too many times. It could very well bring us to war."

"It would not be wise to open another front until we've secured this one, here in our own land. Let the unrest in the Kingdom of Asia and around the world do the job for us until we're ready to finish it."

Beauchamp grabbed a cigar and bit off the tip, spitting it onto the floor. "The barbarian bastard. He makes me appear the fool."

"And I no less of one."

Beauchamp turned abruptly, the cigar clamped between his teeth. "How is your boy?"

Armstrong's fists clenched and unclenched. "To be frank, I expected him to arrive home in a flag-draped box. Tyler has more lives than a cat, it seems."

"So I hear."

The men scrutinized each other. Neither wanted to touch the incident with the covert operative who'd died trying to put a bullet through Banzai Maguire's head—after falling short of doing the same to Ty. Armstrong thrust his hands behind his coat, where he could make fists with impunity. With a powerful effort, he transferred his anger to his words. "I will find the second pilot and bring her here."

Beauchamp clamped his teeth around his cigar. "And if Kyber has Cameron Tucker?"

"If the charming prince couldn't hold on to the first pilot, how will he keep the second?"

Beauchamp's smile bloomed behind a cloud of smoke. "Indeed, General. Indeed."

Chapter Seven

"Your Highness. The pilot has been located."

Prince Kyber, ruler of the Han Empire, lifted his gaze from the shapely woman soaking his feet in a bowl of hot water to meet the gaze of his chief of security. Nikolai Kabul appeared somewhat breathless. It wasn't at all typical of the all-business, ascetic man he'd known since they both were boys—a friendship between a child of royal blood and a streetwise commoner that had somehow survived the years. "Excellent, Niko. The news pleases me. I'll read the full report tomorrow at the morning briefing."

A single sapphire on Nikolai's fez glittered in the war room's cold overhead light, but the man said nothing.

"Your silence tells me that I did not give you the response you expected, Niko."

"I assumed you'd be . . . more surprised."

"I'm simply glad the situation is over."

Nikolai pressed his lips together in another gesture of frustration.

"But of course it displeased me greatly, losing a top fighter pilot in a midair collision caused by human error. And over the Himalayas, no less, making it difficult for search and recovery to do their job. Difficult but not impossible. It's why I appear more relieved than surprised by this swift conclusion to the affair. Pass along my praise to the team for a job well done. And as soon as the pilot is healed, have him sent to me for a little career counseling. He is due for a change of vocation, perhaps as a street-sweep driver in Macao. Fighter craft are tools of defense, not playtoys."

Speaking of playtoys . . . Kyber exchanged a smile with the pretty woman massaging his right hand and forearm with fragrant oils. She had a way with her fingers. Had he invited her to his chambers before? He couldn't recall. He pulled her down for a kiss. No, she didn't taste familiar, but it was hard to be sure. There had been a parade of females warming his bed—and his dining table, swimming pool, and baths—since Banzai had disappeared into the ether.

Kyber set the woman back on her feet to find Nikolai watching him, his eyes ablaze. "What is it, Niko? You appear fairly ready to explode."

"Not the downed YR-55 pilot. The one who has evaded us. You know of whom I speak. I cannot say more until we are alone."

Banzai Maguire! Prince Kyber heard a thud to his right, accompanied by a small whoosh of wind and tinkling jewelry. He realized that in his shock, he'd thrown the manicurist to the floor.

Grabbing the woman's hand, he tugged her to her feet. "Are you certain?" Quickly he locked his jaw. He

76

despised the anger in his tone as much as he did the hope. Banzai . . . She'd routed him, that one, knocked him out with a nerve stunner. And then she'd disappeared with that imperialist jackass pig Armstrong.

Kyber rubbed the back of his neck. Perhaps it was best that his memory was wiped clean of the encounter itself. All he remembered of that day was waking back in the palace with an aching head and double vision, surrounded by attentive servants and a very angry Nikolai. Rebels had gotten Banzai out of the kingdom, he'd learned that much, but where she had gone after that, he didn't know. She'd been missing ever since, but, thank goodness, hadn't shown up in the UCE. It would be a mistake, a deadly mistake, if she defied his advice and did so.

"Off with you." Kyber waved the servants away. Suddenly the company of a female, any female, felt like a sliver under his skin.

As soon as the servants were gone, Kyber turned his attention to his security chief. "So you found the wayward American. Where was our Banzai hiding?"

"No, Your Highness, the *wingmate* has been located. First Lt. Cameron Tucker. Scarlet."

Kyber recoiled. "These woman legends from the past who seem to be infesting abandoned underwater caves, they're a plague, I tell you. A plague!"

Nikolai started to say something and then stopped.

"What, Niko? You have never held back your opinion from me. Don't start now."

The chief stiffened his back. "I thought you would have been more excited by the news."

"Why, so I can repeat what was an unpleasant experience? Banzai took advantage of my generosity, only to cast me aside with little more than a few hollow words of thanks. Prince Kyber of the mighty Han Empire, ruler of all Asia, does not offer favors for nothing, Nikolai. From Banzai, that is exactly what I received." He spat out a curse. It was a weakness on his part, forming an attachment to Banzai Maguire. A foolish error. He never should have allowed himself to feel affection for her. One thing he could say, however, was that he never made the same mistake twice.

"I do have some intelligence images I would like to show you in more secure quarters, my lord. Minister Hong will join us in the war room." The security chief's eyes tracked down to Kyber's feet. "Will you be soaking much longer?"

That was when Kyber realized he was standing in a shallow bowl of steaming water with rose petals whirling on top.

With disgust, he splashed out of the bowl. "Why do the women always insist in dousing me with such delicate scents? I am not a delicate man!" He was taller and more ruggedly built than even his father and grandfather. His mother claimed he owed his build to his Scots genes; his father, back in his lucid days, would argue that the Mongol Khans had provided the DNA in question. While Kyber considered Genghis a few too many generations removed to make an appreciable impact on his bloodline, he was certain that neither the clan chieftains nor the Mongol warriors in his family tree would approve of his marinating in flower petals.

He strode to his bathing pool and dove in, eager to rinse off the perfume. The water was crisp and cool, and it braced him, erasing the last traces of mental dullness left from the plum wine the women had poured for him. Surfacing on the opposite side, he pushed on extended arms out of the water. Without slowing, he grabbed a fresh robe off a hook on the wall of mirrors, wrapping it around him as he walked up to a wall—and through it. It was an illusion made by computer—trillions of them.

Nikolai followed him into his private chambers, leaving the mirrored wall rippling like the Lake of Heaven near the palace he maintained in Paekdusan, far to the north. Kyber preferred his summer palace to this grander one in Beijing. There he enjoyed the sharp scent of the forests and the seclusion of the mountains. Yet Beijing was where the seat of the government conducted its business, and where his subjects expected him to be. Out of a royal obligation to serve his people, and out of respect for the long line of courageous ancestors that got him here, he found predictability translated to stability, necessary to ensure the future of the empire. It was why every autumn after Kingdom Day he dutifully returned home.

Kyber burst into the war room, trailed by the security chief. The quartz-glass-and-steel decor, created to his specifications, suited the room's use, lending it the cold, powerful, and masculine atmosphere he desired. Monitors covered the walls, giving views of international news as well as scenes from around the palace, inside and out, from the numerous security computers embedded in the structure.

"Hong," he said, acknowledging the ubiquitous presence of Minister of Realm Affairs Horace Hong before turning to face his security chief. There were few in Kyber's life whom he trusted as implicitly as Nikolai

Kabul. For God's sake, he had his reasons for placing trust in so few. The emperor, his father had almost been murdered while eating breakfast, and every time Kyber viewed the now wasted man, it reminded him that trust didn't ensure long lives for monarchs. It was wisest not to give it at all. "We tore apart that cave searching for Scarlet, and yet we found nothing. Banzai doubted me when I told her there was no sign of her sister fighter pilot, not now or in the past. And yet Scarlet has miraculously appeared—and under our very noses!"

"Not exactly. We found her in Mongolia."

"You're joking."

"I wish I were. Intelligence imagery pinpoints her location in the village of Khujirt."

"Khujirt." Kyber frowned, concentrating. "I know the place. It's near the springs." Old memories slid down behind his eyes—of a vacation to the region as a child. He'd traveled there with his mother, a devotee of hot mineral springs. Kyber recalled his fascination with the remote and rugged scenery, the taiga forest, the ibex and lynx he'd viewed there, and particularly the ancestors of age-old nomadic tribes who raised livestock at the edge of the forests. He'd never forget the day he broke away from his bodyguards to chase after a shepherd near his own age, scampering beside him and his herd of stinking, flea-infested yaks through fields of wildflowers before being rounded up by the empress's angry staff. For a few hours he hadn't been the crown prince; he'd been a boy. "They're farmers. Simple people. Impossible that they revived her. They don't have the technology."

"Difficult, yes, but not impossible. This has contributed to her less-than-ideal condition. Our first observations showed her walking the paths in the area assisted by crutches. Apparently she is now walking under her own power, or mostly."

"But in Mongolia. How did you learn of it?"

"Via a pair of Rim Riders."

"Good! Find out their names. Put them in for a bonus. Better yet, send them to me so that I may praise them in person. Now, tell me how this came about."

"There was talk of a woman new to the area—a badly injured woman. That she was blond, unusual for someplace so distant from an urban center, only intensified the curiosity. Rumors started and spread. Our Rim Riders overheard them, of course, and passed along the information to intelligence as part of a routine report. I saw the mention and thought it was best to investigate. We took satellite pictures over a period of several weeks. But only yesterday could I say I was certain of her identity."

"It's her, Your Highness," Minister Hong chimed in. "Her likeness matches the file photo we have."

Kyber had seen the same archived photo as the men. He summoned a mental image of Cameron Tucker. She shared little in common with Banzai, physically. In fact, she resembled more a hothouse flower than a warrior.

All the more reason to stay well clear of her.

Kyber opened a closet. Since his duties later that day would take him outside, he donned black leather body armor trimmed in furs. Nikolai was dressed in an identical way, as were the rest of the soldiers and palace security. All that separated Kyber in appearance from his men was the platinum armband he wore around his upper right arm. The snake was a symbol of the Han Empire. Other than that one small concession, of which he was proud, he abstained from the fanciful trappings of royal garb. He left that to his mother, Corrine, who loved to dress the part, going as far as outfitting Kyber's father daily, even as he lay in the far reaches of the palace with no more awareness than a vegetable.

Kyber buckled his belt. "Why have we not known of the existence of the second pilot until now?"

"Outside involvement," Nikolai guessed. "Someone took her before we could."

"Why were there no signs of tampering in the cave?"

"If the cryopod was hidden in one of the more heavily damaged areas, it's possible our search party overlooked it in their haste to rescue Banzai. In the gap between their departure and return, someone with the knowledge and motivation could have gone in—and gotten Scarlet out."

"And brought her to Mongolia? Who dares to meddle so brazenly in realm affairs, Niko? Tell me who they are!"

"They're farmers—"

Kyber gave an incredulous snort. "And I am Winston Churchill."

"All we know so far is that they're indeed working on a communal farm. Collectives like these are quite common in the area, as you know. This one is small. Approximately a dozen people living there as permanent residents, others coming and going. Besides farming, they maintain a local hot springs and a pay-as-you-go temple."

Kyber made a sound in his throat. "Paying for divine intervention. If money could buy God's answers, I'd be a god myself." And his father would be conscious and alive, relations with his younger half brother D'ekkar would not be what they were now, shattered by scandal.

And Banzai would be warming his bed, not Tyler Armstrong's.

"So far, I haven't found any connections between them and the Shadow Runners—or any other rebel organization."

Shadow Runners, Kyber thought with a growl. The radicals with whom D'ekkar had become involved while in prison. They were antimonarchy, antitradition—antieverything, it seemed. Having never once stated clearly their objective—besides wanting to make trouble—the Shadow Runners had so far done little more than irritate him like a splinter not yet worked close enough to the surface of the skin to be plucked out. Yet he wasn't complacent enough to dismiss them. If they ever became better organized, the group could prove to be a problem.

"I'm relieved to hear rebels aren't openly behind this, Nikolai, but now that the woman is mostly healed, why has she remained in such a godforsaken place? Is she hiding from me?"

He'd meant it as a joke, but Nikolai replied, "Most likely, Your Highness."

"She hides? *From me?*" Kyber heard outrage creep back into his voice as his mood darkened. "Has Banzai woven lies of exploitation at my hands? I treated her with the care befitting the cultural treasure she is—better than she apparently deserves. The only crime I'm guilty of committing was not bedding the woman when it was clear she needed it."

"We have no evidence of any communication with Banzai. Tucker has been in Khujirt for some time. It is possible, though unlikely, that she was taken from the cave even before Armstrong discovered Banzai."

"Armstrong." Kyber poured himself a hot coffee and inhaled the fragrant aroma. "I should have executed the man while I had the chance. A bad habit I have, Niko, preferring to play with my prey before killing it, no different from the cats inhabiting the alleyways in the Quarter." The disreputable Serpent Quarter, where he'd like to be at the moment, disguised as his shadowy alter ego, Kublai, enjoying a drink in total anonymity. "You say you have images? Show them to me."

Nikolai slipped a computer from his thigh pocket and unrolled a thin screen. Kyber took the device, scrolling through photos as he sipped coffee. The images were crisp and clear, though taken from a great distance. They were of a woman, tall and slender. He saw a glimpse of blond hair under a hood in one, and there, a better view of her struggling with the crutches on a rutted trail. Another showed her trying to stand after a fall, her frustration and determination obvious. Raw willpower.

A powerful feeling of solidarity filtered through him, and he couldn't pull his attention from the image. He knew the torment that gripped her, because he'd been there. He knew what it was like, driving on when all you wanted to do was lie down and wallow in self-pity. The bleak days after the near-assassination of his father, the emperor, had been riddled with such struggles for him. He wasn't sure if he'd come through it all stronger, or only colder. Banzai's appearance in his life had been a welcome diversion from the day-to-day realities of royal life, but now she was gone. He'd be smarter this time. No woman warrior from the past would be allowed into his life or—curse the very thought—his heart.

"These last images were what decided it for me," Nikolai said. "They were taken yesterday by one of our transport crews. Since they were flying over the area, I thought, Why not get some close-ups?"

"Close-ups, indeed . . ." Kyber paused at an image of Scarlet standing in the middle of a dirt road, her head thrown back, her face directed at the sky. Her hair had come loose from its braids. Floating in an ethereal cloud, the golden strands framed an expression of wonder that captivated him. So unself-conscious in her hope and unfettered joy was she that he had to pause to catch his breath.

Women had spurred him to do many things over the years for the sake of happiness—his and theirs—but none had ever left him winded.

Scowling deeply, he thrust the computer back at his security chief. "I do not want her near me, making my life difficult, distracting me! I am, as you know, a very busy man." He stalked to a screen depicting a wintry street below his bedroom balcony. A cheering crowd braved an unseasonably early onslaught of sleet, awaiting his morning appearance. They loved him, his people, as they had loved his father before him. He ruled with a heavy hand, yes, but like little children his subjects appreciated knowing their limits. Within those limits, they had the highest level of education, the longest life span, and the lowest suicide rate in the world.

"I have an empire to rule." He touched a panel that allowed his image to appear on the giant screen above the street. The roar that followed rumbled through the speakers embedded in the walls. "And a people to inspire!" He raised his hand and the cheering increased a thousandfold.

"And a pilot to bring within the confines of the palace."

Turning, Kyber spoke dryly. "Nikolai, you are one of the few people I allow to nag me."

The man acknowledged the remark with a curt bow.

Kyber sighed. The inevitable was upon him: Lt. Cameron "Scarlet" Tucker would have to be brought to the palace. Here he was, telling his staff he did not want anything more to do with the legendary pilots. Yet, he had no choice but to involve himself once again. The reason? Simple. While he didn't want Scarlet, he didn't want anyone else to have her, either.

He turned. "Very well. Bring her to the capital." Oh, how it pained him to say the words. "If for this reason alone: to keep her from the Shadow Runners."

"The Shadow Runners?" Nikolai rubbed his precise goatee. "You've never considered them a serious threat before."

"No, I haven't, but several new factors give me pause, Niko. The Shadow Voice is broadcasting everywhere, touting democracy as the solution to the world's ills. Should the uprising in the UCE succeed, the Shadow Runners may think they can accomplish the same here. They couldn't, of course—the situations are entirely different—but that wouldn't become apparent until much blood was shed. That's why I'll have her brought here." And not out of the fierce sense of competition and hatred of the UCE that had driven him to want to possess Banzai. This time he was taking personal feelings out of the equation and replacing them with duty—the duty he owed his subjects in assuring them a safe and stable future. "I will not stand for rebels disrupting the empire, and since that means giving them no chance to use Scarlet for their purposes, so be it."

"And this will give the UCE no chance to use her for theirs, either," Nikolai said.

"That will *never* happen." Despite his change of attitude about the newest pilot, the humiliation of losing Banzai to Armstrong still stung.

"I'll be keeping too close an eye on her for that to happen, Your Highness," Minister Hong assured him.

Nikolai nodded. "We'll fit her with a standard prox-beacon implant, which will allow her free travel within the security of the city walls while preventing her from leaving."

"No extra work for us," Hong said cheerily, "and added security for the woman. No more and no less than we do for citizens found guilty of certain crimes. You won't have to interact with her at all."

"Good," Kyber grumbled. "I don't plan to."

Nikolai appeared positively pleased with the turn the conversation had taken. "And thanks to your famed benevolence, the American will have top-notch medical care and excellent food."

"And religious services she doesn't have to pay for," Kyber muttered. "I warn both of you—do not send her to me. If she requests an audience, do not grant it. No private dinners. No special favors. She lives here and that is all. You, the staff, the servants—you will see to her general welfare here in the palace. As for me, a weekly report will suffice. No more detailed than what you'd offer the cabinet, Horace."

Minister Hong nodded. "Your wish is my command."

"Now, you have your duties to attend to, Hong, yes?"

"I do indeed." The minister was well acquainted with Kyber's protocol of consulting his chief of security in private after significant events. With a bow and a flourish, he departed.

Nikolai clicked his heels together. "If you will excuse me, I must assemble a team to retrieve the pilot."

"No need. I've already assembled the best team we have."

Nikolai went still. "Your Highness?"

"There is only one team that can do this mission justice, giving it the level of secrecy it requires."

"Sir, you're not thinking what I think you may be. . . ."

"Of course I am. This time the team is us."

"Us." Nikolai, to his credit, didn't sputter.

"I trust no one else to the task. Cameron Tucker must not fall into rebel hands—our rebels or the UCE's. We were careless with Banzai and look what happened. Don't faint on me, Niko. We're going not as our real selves, but as Kublai and Nazeem, Rim Riders and," Kyber added with a wink, "bounty hunters for the emperor."

At the mere declaration, he felt his muscles thrum to life, much as they did during the punishing rounds of sword practice he accomplished each morning before dawn while the palace still slept. It was during that quiet, necessary time that he fancied he connected with the warrior ancestors of his past, the entire long line of Hans, whose honor he somehow felt compelled to uphold. It hit him that he'd become bored at the palace and needed to get out. Going after Scarlet was the perfect excuse. Although he'd had every intention of retreating once more from world politics after his distasteful brush with Tyler Armstrong and the demon spawn's father, he had to admit that running this mission for the sake of the empire sounded far too intriguing to pass up. Besides, it would give him the opportunity to see what was happening in the remotest fringes of his vast holdings.

It had been a number of years since he'd ridden the Rim and surveyed the borderlands. Too long. *Rulers rule best if they do not isolate themselves from their people*, his father had taught him. It was why, Kyber guessed, his father had turned the other way when, as young men, Kyber and Nikolai often rode posing as bounty hunters. In the years since taking the reins of power, Kyber had continued to sneak away from the palace in disguise. He'd learned of the Shadow Runners that way, of his brother's involvement in the group, and many other useful things. It was how he hoped never to be fooled, as his father had been, by a plot that should have been uncovered before its execution. From that dreadful day forward, Kyber swore he'd always know as much as the troublemakers did, so that no one would take advantage of him. And that, he vowed, included taking charge of delivering this latest American pilot to where she could do no harm—to herself or any sovereign nations. "Come on, Niko, where is that smile? We'll take care of this on our own, as we used to in the old days."

"You were only a prince then. You're the emperor now."

"Acting emperor. Nevertheless, I'm safer in disguise than I am within the confines of this palace." His mouth twisted. "Ask my father."

He threw open the door to the war room. "Pack your bags, Nikolai, and stop pouting. My horse will thank you for the chance to stretch his legs, as will yours. Trotting in circles in the arena would bore a stallion to tears, I imagine. How can you not draw a comparison to our personal state of affairs?"

Nikolai's expression didn't change. "If the farmers indeed turn out to be rebels, and they learn who you are, assassination would not be out of the realm of possibilities," the chief advised in what sounded like a last-ditch effort to dissuade him.

"Ah, but risk is what gives a man his joie de vivre, yes?" Nikolai looked ill, and Kyber smiled all the more. "Admit it, my friend, hasn't your life lacked a certain spark lately?"

Nikolai pursed his lips. "I am too busy with my duties to ponder what sparks I lack."

"A shame indeed. How badly I have overworked you. You need a break. I command it! A mission into the hinterlands of our country is bound to be the tonic you need to approach your job in a fresh new way."

Nikolai made a sound in his throat, but Kyber could tell by the glint in his eye that the man was warming to the idea. He shook his head at his rattled chief. "Niko, you are what, thirty-five now? Only a half decade older than I, but already a lonesome and sometimes melancholy veteran who misses the excitement of the old days, when we would ride the Rim in the name of the empire. You need this as much as I do."

Nikolai at last cracked a genuine smile. "Those were the days. I will never forget them."

"You don't have to. Neither of us has to. We can live them again, and for a mission vital to the security of the realm."

"Critically vital, Your Highness."

Kyber smiled. His chief was coming along. "I'll brief Horace. He'll deflect any public or in-house queries as to our whereabouts."

Flexing his arms, Kyber inhaled deeply. He would anticipate this nightfall as no other. He could almost hear the antiquated creak of the massive city gates as they rolled open to allow him past. Lately he had been feeling as if he were fighting a current in everything he did. There was an intangible, nagging sense that his life needed to take a different direction. What that course was, exactly, he didn't know. Now, with the decision to retrieve the second pilot, it felt as if he were finally sailing in the right direction.

"Yes, Niko," he said with robust enthusiasm. "Tonight we will ride, you and I. And we will bring home our prize."

Chapter Eight

After Zhurihe disappeared, Cam forced herself to go on with her life. For most of the hours of the day she no longer needed crutches. She accomplished her chores, never forgetting to put herself through the daily torture of physical therapy. And she never stopped thinking of the aircraft she'd heard.

Yaks grazed alongside sheep clothed in gray dreadlocks. Cam's brightly dressed cofarmers tended the flocks. For existing in a world bereft of most modern technology, the people she lived with appeared remarkably sturdy and well fed—well fed even if none shared or could understand her craving for Southern food: her grandmother's pralines and fried chicken, her uncle's fried catfish, and . . . well, fried everything. Oh, and peanuts in Coke! She lost herself in a memory of stopping at vending machines near the base gym every afternoon on her way home from school, where she'd buy a bottle of Coke and a packet of peanuts, poking the nuts down the mouth of the bottle and licking the salt from her sticky fingers. . . .

Cam sighed. A couple of yaks raised their heads to stare at her curiously. "Y'all have to try it," she insisted, but the animals went back to grazing. The grass was matted and brown from a recent snow, the first of the season. The snow should have been ten feet deep by now at this northern latitude. Global warming in the midst of supposed nuclear winter? It was just one of the many pieces of the puzzle that didn't make sense.

"Cam! *Cam!*"

A young woman ran toward her, black braids flying. Cam's spirits soared. Zhurihe had returned, bless her heart! Her eyes stung. The girl was her only friend in the entire world. Sometimes the gut-wrenching loneliness hurt more than Cam's healing muscles and bones.

But when Zhurihe arrived, Cam could see that her friend was upset. "You must run!" The girl grabbed her arm and tugged. "Go!"

To keep her from passing out from hyperventilation, Cam complied, throwing a gaze up at the sky, half in fear and half in joyful anticipation of seeing another aircraft.

"Not a plane." Zhurihe gasped, running alongside her. "I heard that they were coming, and now I see them with my eyes. Horses. They're coming up the road. Rim Riders!"

Sure enough, in the far distance along an undulating ribbon of road, a cloud of smoke told of approaching riders. Rim Riders. Minions of the barbarian emperor.

Dread chilled Cam to the bone. Rim Riders, she'd found out with a little research among the farm's other workers, patrolled the backwoods of the barbarian emperor's realm the old-fashioned way. At the monarch's orders, they exacted frontier justice when they thought it necessary and hauled off alleged troublemakers for handsome bounties when it suited their fancy. They were favored by the emperor, and he indulged them, making it dangerous—and stupid—to cross them.

Zhurihe no longer had to push Cam along; she was hurrying under her own power now. Much faster, though, and her muscles would begin to cramp. In the past, the pain could be so intense that she lost consciousness. "Zhurihe, this is my max speed."

"But they are coming, coming *now*."

Cam felt a little sick. She didn't feel like ending the day as the emperor's new clothes. She picked up her pace, despite the consequences. "What do they want from us? The food? The livestock?"

"No." The girl's eyes flicked wildly in her direction. "They want *you*."

At the top of a wooded rise above the farm, Prince Kyber pulled his horse to a standing halt. Beast reared back, ejecting steam from his flared nostrils. "Easy, easy now." Eyes narrowed, Kyber surveyed the farm below. Its inhabitants belonged to a cult that reviled technology. The scene before him could easily have been taken from three or four centuries earlier. Why some preferred to live this way eluded him, but as a prince, he allowed it in the name of tolerance. His subjects could do as they wished, as long as it wasn't at cross-purposes to his goals.

Most of the people from the collective were in the fields, he surmised from what he'd observed along the way. A single man sat at a tollbooth, where a usage fee for the hot springs would be collected. Having received advance word of their arrival—the primitive system of lookouts in this area was unmatched—a gatekeeper would have rushed to man the entrance; Kyber wasn't surprised in the least to see the welcoming party of one.

He urged his mount forward, Nikolai cantering along at his side. "Good day," the chief called out to the gatekeeper.

"Good day to you, Rim Riders." The man's eyes tripped over the sight of Kyber's face.

Kyber expected no less. The lenses masking his eye color might not warrant a second glance, but the intricate facial tattoo that covered more than half of the exposed skin certainly would. The pigment existed on the cellular level, nanocomputers that he could turn off and on at will. To further disguise his appearance, he wore his hair loose. Long and thick, it fell around his shoulders. He felt so comfortable in his role as Kublai, Rim Rider, that sometimes he couldn't help wondering if this was closer to what he really was than the outwardly civilized ruler. There were enough barbarians, European and Asian, in the family tree to support the claim, at any rate.

"We would like to have a look around," Nikolai announced.

The gatekeeper's nervousness was mute but obvious to Kyber. He was hiding something. Fortunately Kyber already knew his little secret.

The gatekeeper stepped aside. "You may water your horses there." As was typical of a citizen of this region of ancient horsemen and open steppes, he gazed at the horses with covetous admiration. "Fine animals."

Kyber grunted. "Touch them and I will slit your

throat." Good cop, bad cop—the routine he used with Nikolai often worked well.

The gatekeeper's Adam's apple bobbed. His gaze flicked from Kyber's unhappy expression to the weapons he wore, the armor and rugged riding boots. "We do not steal horses here, Rim Rider."

"What do you steal, then?"

"We—"

Kyber thrust his arm out and snatched the gatekeeper's collar. "You are innocent, you say?"

He sputtered, clawing at Kyber's leather glove.

Nikolai stepped to Kyber's side. "Perhaps he knows nothing, Kublai."

Kyber pretended to let his temper flare. It was easy to do; he was furious that these borderland people would choose to consort with rebels rather than support an empire that had performed countless benevolent acts in the region. Their duplicity and brazen disregard of national security left a red haze of anger over Kyber's vision. "Is this true? Have you nothing here that doesn't belong to you? Is there no one amongst you who must lawfully be reported to your magnificent and generous emperor who loves you?"

At that, Nikolai made a small sound in his throat.

The gatekeeper's face had gone from pink to purple. "I have done nothing," he choked out.

Kyber smiled thinly and set him down. "We shall see, gatekeeper."

"Let us partake of the pleasures of the spring first," his security chief suggested. "We have had a long many days of riding. We have been out on patrol for many weeks." In truth, they'd traveled by magcar three-quarters of the way from Beijing, circumventing the Gobi Desert and leaving the vehicles in a secret location at the border of the forests for the few days it would take to complete this round-trip. A full journey on horseback would have taken weeks, a luxury neither man could afford. If not for the nature of this particular task, fetching the wayward pilot, Kyber would not have abandoned his duties at all.

"Come this way, please." Robes filling his arms, the gatekeeper led them toward the shrine.

Kyber frowned. "We said the springs."

"Ah, but you must purge your sins first, Rim Rider. It is what we require of all pilgrims before they take their pleasure in God's water." It was a delaying tactic; Scarlet wasn't anywhere near the shrine or the gatekeeper would not have brought them there.

"In that case, a quick prayer." It was a small peacemaking effort, and nothing more, to acknowledge local custom. As much as he wanted to strangle the man for his disobedience to the realm in sheltering a woman he should have reported to his district overseer, so too was Kyber reluctant to start rumors of abuse traceable back to himself.

Offerings, old and new, littered the ground near the entrance to a large round tent constructed of thick hides lashed together with yak sinew. Kyber and Nikolai's smiling guide waved them forward. "Please. Go inside."

Nikolai's hand moved out, slightly, his fingers spread. A signal to hang back, to be cautious. The back of Kyber's neck prickled.

Kyber's own hand slid over his pistol. For the first time he felt the danger of the situation, of moving freely out of reach of his enviable security forces. *You have no heirs. To whom would the crown pass if you died this day?*

D'ekkar. Kyber almost snorted. No one outside the royal family and its closest advisers knew that it was fact, not a rumor, that D'ekkar Han Valoren wasn't the emperor's blood son. Since Kyber had no heirs, his half brother, the bastard son his mother bore her lover, was technically in line for the throne. The thought of Deck ruling in his place was enough to keep Kyber alive through anything the troublemakers here might throw at him.

Nikolai moved aside the tent flap. The odor of incense rushed out. Kyber had only to inhale once before his body reacted: dizziness, then lingering, distinctly agreeable buoyancy. It would take only another few breaths for him to want to lie down and lose himself all day in the sensation.

He jerked backward, pulling his chief with him, and whirled on the gatekeeper. The man cowered. This time he wasn't sorry for intimidating him. "The incense is drugged!"

"It is only mildly hallucinogenic."

"Mildly, my ass. It nearly took my wits with the first breath!"

"It will heighten your pleasure."

"When I want to take my pleasure, I do so with women—not narcotics!"

Nikolai's eyes were a bit glazed, but his manner was as crisp and efficient as ever. "Do you wish us harm, good neighbor? Do you not respect the emperor to whom we owe our allegiance?"

"No! No harm. None at all. I sought only to bring you closer to God."

"More like closer to unconsciousness," Kyber muttered

as his head cleared. "It would seem as if you are hiding something—or someone."

"Please. Only my family and I live here."

"No one else?" Nikolai asked as Kyber flexed his gloved hands, cracking his knuckles.

The gatekeeper's mouth worked nervously. "People, they come and go in these lands. Lost souls. You know how it is."

"Female. Tall, slender, blond," Nikolai went on. "With an odd accent."

"And pretty. A pretty woman." Kyber punched a fist into his palm, and the gatekeeper jumped. "Would you know of anyone fitting that description?"

Nikolai made a soft clicking sound of warning at the same time a flash of brightly colored clothing caught Kyber's eye. On the road leading to the springs, a lone figure hurried along, her gait uneven. She had a blanket thrown over her head.

Kyber's pulse jumped. Scarlet. He was sure of it. "Who is that?" he bellowed.

The gatekeeper's words tumbled out. "My daughter . . . she brought home a friend. She was ill—ill for many weeks, this one, but she's a hard worker. She didn't do anything. We didn't . . . I swear—"

Nikolai grabbed for his weapon. "You there—halt!"

Another woman, this one smaller, had unhitched the horses. She slapped them hard and sent them galloping away before she herself ran off, braids streaming behind her.

"Horse thief!" the gatekeeper yelped. "You must go after your steeds."

"That was no horse thief; it was a well-timed distraction." Kyber drew his neuron fryer and aimed it at the gatekeeper. "And the oldest trick in the book." He fired.

The man crumpled and fell.

"You won't remember anything of this. Trust me." Hastily, he shoved the cooling weapon back in his pocket. "You take care of our friend, Niko, and I'll go after the woman."

As the chief dragged the body into the temple to leave it "napping" on one of the pews, Kyber ran down the hill leading to the springs. *Stay put, my little American. I'll soon be joining you.*

He stopped at the shore. Steam rose in billowing puffs from the water. The faint scent of sulfur floated in the air. He unbuckled his weapons belt and peered at the craggy outcroppings of rocks for a sign of the woman. She was nowhere.

A feeling he didn't like slithered down his back. Where did she go? Would he lose her, too, and feel once more the humiliation of defeat? He stripped off the heavier pieces of his body armor and his shirt, then discarded his boots. He took out his breather, wedging the device between his teeth. It would allow him all the time he needed to search the springs

Chapter Nine

They're coming for you! Zhurihe's warning clanged like a fire alarm in Cam's head. *Tell no one who you are. You don't want the emperor to learn of you.*

Hidden behind a couple of boulders and a shifting wall of steam, she watched the bigger of the two Rim Riders strip down to his tight black pants. Hollywood had made a cliché of depraved tyrants who kept legions of muscular, badass minions on the payroll. Cam was *not* happy to see it was true. Dark swirls of tattoo covered more than half his face, but his body was clean of any ornamentation aside from an impressive set of abs. This man knew how to fight; his musculature told her that. And maybe he wasn't quite as stupid as she'd thought. Zhurihe's little horse-stealing stunt hadn't fooled him.

The only thing worse than a brute was a smart brute. She had the feeling this wasn't going to be as easy as she'd thought.

He cupped his hands around his mouth. "Show yourself!" His baritone carried over the water. When she didn't answer, he tried again. "Don't fear me. You've been held here illegally. I have come to rescue you."

Rescue her? It was the last thing she'd expected to hear.

The Rider tipped his head and listened to the silence that was her response. Then he tried again. "No tricks, I promise you." His voice had lost its edge.

She ducked down lower in the water, waiting to see what he'd do. "Ah, why do you make me come after you?" he asked almost tiredly. Then with the barest of splashes the man dove into the springs. For a big man, he had a lot of grace.

Hot water licked at her chin. Hefting a rock in her hand, she waited. The healing springs had stolen her aches and pains, and without gravity sabotaging her muscles and bones, she felt agile and light. And ready. No wonder Zhurihe had sent her here: the water evened the odds.

She wasn't as sure anymore if he meant her harm or not. Until she knew for sure, she wanted to keep him at a distance.

This needed to be a hit-and-run, then.

Summers spent swimming with her brothers in an assortment of swimming holes had taught her a thing or two. You were least prepared when you surfaced for a breath. When the Rim Rider did, that was when she'd act. Conk him on the head with the rock and make a mad dash to shore. In the forest she knew of a hundred places to hide. She'd be slower on land, more clumsy, but if all went as planned, she'd have one hell of a head start.

She waited where her legs could find purchase and give her leverage to strike. Only the Rim Rider didn't pop up for air. Wind rippled the billowing steam. A few birds warbled. Where was he? What the hell had happened to him?

She blinked mist out of her eyes. If he'd surfaced, she'd have seen it. It meant he was still under the water. After all this time? What was he . . . superhuman? No one could hold his breath for this long.

There! A shadow moved under the water. Long and dark, it glided beneath the surface. Cam almost swallowed her heart.

Powerful arms propelled the bounty hunter through the water as easily as a fish. As he stopped to search the boulders along the rim of the pool, his long black hair fanned out, undulating with his movements. He pushed off again, his stomach flexing. A set of six-pack abs warned her that he'd be no easy man to escape. All the more reason to cork him on the first try. A head start was going to be very important in this match.

She readied her rock for striking. *Closer, sugar, come a little closer to me.* The second his head came above water, she'd whack it like a coconut and run like hell.

If his head came above water. What was that in his mouth? It looked like a thin harmonica except for the fizzy stream of bubbles exploding from it in regular intervals, the approximate space of time between breaths in a normal human being. He was breathing—underwater, and without bulky scuba gear!

Now, that wasn't fightin' fair. With his ability to stay underwater indefinitely, she'd have to alter tactics. Instead of surprising him as he surfaced, which, of course, he wouldn't, she'd wait until he swam to the other side of the springs; then she'd scramble to shore.

Cam focused intently on her target. She considered herself expert at anticipating an adversary's reaction. It was why she'd won nearly every air-to-air battle she'd ever flown. Could a water-to-water battle be that much different?

With a hearty inhalation and a prayer, she pushed quietly out of her hiding place and launched herself through deeper water to an outcropping of boulders, a good intermediate hiding spot from which she could reach the beach.

One . . . two . . . three . . . four strokes underwater, followed by a long, silent glide, she surfaced inside the ring of boulders. Mistake. Here the angle of the sun made it difficult to see more than a couple of feet below the surface. She was trapped. If she struck out for shore, she'd be doing it blind. Where did the Rider go?

Adrenaline zipped though her veins, pumping up her heart rate. He was coming for her; she knew it on a gut level. Almost as if she'd conjured him, the Rider exploded out of the water with a loud splash and grabbed her by the wrists.

Cam used his hold on her as a brace. She thrust her knee upward, making solid, satisfying contact with wet pants.

A muffled grunt. His grip relaxed—to his credit, it was for only a fraction of a second, but it was enough. She yanked one dripping-wet wrist free, arched sideways, and tore the mouthpiece from the startled Rider's mouth.

She clamped her lips around the breathing device. "Fair's fair," she mumbled.

A heartbeat later she was swimming through the depths of the spring for all she was worth. Her lips formed a seal around the harmonica-shaped gadget just as light-headedness set in. *This had better work.* She sucked in a breath—of air, not water. She was breathing! With no air tanks. No gear. She had no clue how the thing worked in a world that was supposedly devoid of technology, but there was no time to wonder about it now. She'd head for the far shore, jump onto dry land, and run like—

Something yanked her backward. The mouthpiece popped loose. She made a bubbly, underwater sound of dismay, her hair floating around her face, and shoved the breathing device back between her teeth. Twisting, she saw the problem.

Her eyes widened. The device was connected to the bounty hunter by an almost invisible cord. And as fast as his arms could propel him, he was swimming through the water after it—*and her.*

Options . . . she needed them now. Tug-of-war was out. She could drop the mouthpiece and run. Or . . . she could tangle the rope around the hulk of a submerged tree stump rising out of the sandy bottom to buy time enough for a head start.

Her insides screamed to hurry. She wrapped the slack in the cord around the massive roots, two, three times—and a couple more for good measure. Then, wedging one end of the breather under a root, she snapped the fragile device in half and shoved away.

The Rim Rider swam after her—only to be jerked to a halt. He saw then what she'd done, how the rope was knotted and tangled around the gnarled wood. A hiss of bubbles swirled around him as he fought to free himself. Jerky movements further revealed his shock.

You underestimated me. Big mistake.

Cam burst to the surface, treading water. The man's companion wasn't anywhere she could see. She stroked to the shore. No more grace. No more speed. On dry land she moved like an arthritic elephant.

How much of a head start did she have on the Rim Rider? The water steamed quietly. No sign of him yet.

She stumbled over the boulders bordering the shore. Once she was outside in wet clothes, it didn't take long to start shivering. If she was going to hide, she'd better do it somewhere warm and dry—and fast.

Lose the Rim Rider first, she thought. Had he made it to the beach yet? She turned around. He hadn't even made it to the surface.

Lord Almighty. Was he still tangled in the rope? *Serves him right.* The surface of the water was unblemished. Calm.

Don't fear me. The memory of his attempted dialogue came with a flicker of self-reproach. Tying him up had been impulsive, spurred by battle lust and, yes, sheer competition. *You've been held here illegally. I have come to rescue you! No tricks.*

In retrospect, the Rider had acted more like a cop on the beat that the evil minion Zhurihe said he'd be. Cam thought of the breather and the aircraft. Zhurihe had told her there was no tech left in this nuclear war–ravaged world. What if she'd lied?

What if she'd lied about the Rim Riders, too?

What if the Rider was right and these farmers were the kidnappers?

What if the idiot was drowning?

Cam made a loud groan and reversed course, swearing under her breath the entire way back to the springs. She slipped and slid in her waterlogged shoes, shoving branches and evergreen vegetation out of her path. Okay, if the hulk was already unconscious, all she'd have to do was cut him loose and shove his carcass to the surface.

CPR? *Don't even go there.* If her luck held, he'd start breathing on his own once she draped him over the closest rock.

She dove into the hot depths, swimming down, down, down, until she reached the ancient mangle of the stump. *Simple: cut him loose and run.*

There was the cord. She grabbed it. Attached to the other end was an undulating banner of black fabric. The Rider's pants!

Bubbles gurgled out of her mouth. He was gone! He'd cut himself free like a wolf that gnawed off a paw to escape a trap.

She spun around, her hair swirling across her eyes. Looked up. Looked down. He was nowhere. And she was running out of air.

Up to the surface she went. As if competing for Olympic gold, she stroked away from the center of the springs, pushing her body to the limit in her half-panicked haste to get away. He hadn't underestimated her—*she'd* underestimated him! She'd made the same miscalculation that others had about her all her life. And now it was painfully obvious she was about to pay for her mistake.

Water sprayed over her face as something lunged at her. Blindly she struck out with a fist and made contact with something wet and very solid. Thick arms closed around her waist, forcing her half out of the water. The Rim Rider.

They wrestled, splashing violently. He had the advantage of size. From behind, he hauled her close. It was then she remembered a very important fact: he was buck naked.

Her elbows drove backward into his ribs. This time, however, he had the advantage of surprise. Powerful legs kept them both afloat as he bent her right arm behind her until he'd drawn out a shuddering swear word.

Rim Riders were bounty hunters for the warlord emperor. By definition, bounty hunters turned in fugitives for pay. If they planned on delivering her to the emperor for payment, it meant they probably wouldn't kill her. On the other hand, far from anyone's scrutiny in the wilderness, these men could do a lot of things between now and their delivery date. "Try anything with me, and I'll fight you," she gurgled, water sloshing over her mouth. "I'll fight you until all you've got left to play with is a body that's not worth the effort."

"Don't waste your breath on the absurd!" His sharp indignation at her fear of assault left her almost embarrassed for having brought it up. "Now, will you cease your wrestling?" he asked, and gave her arm a push.

She wondered how many additional versions of "screw you" she could transmit with her eyes.

He jerked on her bent arm. Cam's mouth drew back in a grimace. She didn't like losing, and she'd capitulated too few times in her life to be any good at it.

"Well?" The pressure increased another notch.

Pain shot into her neck. "Give," she choked out.

Gasping, they treaded water, their legs colliding. His skin somehow felt hotter than the water. She wanted to swim away, to put distance between the Rim rider and her unnerving awareness of him, but not at the expense of an arm.

"Relax, then," he ordered, his body pressed close.

"I *am* fucking relaxed!"

He laughed—deep, masculine, and heartily condescending.

She kicked him in the shins with her heels. He flipped her in front of him, keeping her arm in a vise behind her back. His foot shoved hers away before she had the chance to crush his balls with her knee. This minion was expert in unarmed combat, much more than she. It was like salt in the wound after how neatly he'd turned the tables on her.

Immobilized by the painful armlock, she gritted her teeth, struggling to fill her lungs with air. The fight had taken most of her strength. "Okay . . ." She relaxed only enough to convince him to relieve the pressure on her arm.

He waited before loosening his grip this time, making sure she got the message. "Are you quite over yourself yet?"

Asshole. She glowered darkly at him. His face was inches away from hers, giving her a close-up view of the design etched into his golden skin, miniature snakes intertwined until she couldn't tell where one began and another ended.

"You look as if you are plotting my demise," he drawled.

"Actually, I'm just trying to imagine you with a personality."

Irritably, he pushed her along toward shore. As they transitioned from swimming to sloshing toward the beach, the water sank lower and lower on his torso until he emerged sleek, hard-muscled, and completely, utterly unself-conscious about his lack of clothing.

Well, he did have one small strip of something covering his privates, a scrap of black underwear with a small blade strapped to the hip, but it didn't leave a whole lot to the imagination. He was a big, solid man in top physical form. He didn't go hungry too often; that was obvious. The emperor took good care of his minions.

The other Rim Rider thundered down the road on a stallion, black and equally magnificent as the one galloping behind him. "Kublai!" the newcomer called out.

Her captor's name was Kublai? As in Khan? The bounty hunter was named after Genghis-the-infamous-barbarian's grandson. *Oh, boy.*

The Rider tossed Kublai a towel. Turning his back to her, Kublai pressed it to his face. Steam rose from his bare shoulders and hair. His broad back steamed, too, the muscles working as he wiped himself dry.

A cold wind blew down from the mountains. Now that death wasn't imminent and she was out of the warm water, Cam started shivering. It was not going to be a good night; she could tell by the groans and creaks settling into her bones, and the trembling in her overworked muscles. "D-do I get a towel, or do I have to w-wait for sloppy seconds?"

Kublai swiped the towel over his chest one last time and threw it at her. "Sloppy seconds."

He stalked away without seeming to give a hoot that he'd left her staring after him. "Throw her some clothing, Nazeem, before she freezes to death."

"Maybe that w-would be more c-c-convenient for you,

Rim Rider. Then you won't have to worry about bringing me anywhere."

He scoffed at her offer. "The emperor demands that you be brought to him. No more, no less. And that, pretty one, is what I intend to do." He turned his back to her to dress in rugged midnight-black riding gear.

Nazeem handed her a coat, shirt, pants, boots, and long underwear. "Change," he said.

She started walking back to the farmhouse. "No," Kublai ordered. "You will dress here."

She was about to tell them they were dreaming when both men turned their backs. It was too damn cold to argue. Besides, having grown up surrounded by brothers, she was used to changing with men around.

She stripped off the sodden peasant wear. A few pieces of soggy hay fell on the ground. She hoped they didn't have hay where the men were taking her. Or goats.

The full-body underwear the men had provided turned warm even before she'd pulled it completely on. It was too good to be true. The heat reached deep into her aching bones and stopped her shivers. "Stupid question, but are these clothes supposed to get hot?"

"Once the nanofabric regulates your body temperature, it won't be quite so warm," Kublai said over his shoulder. A small clasp now held the front portion of his wet hair away from his forehead, keeping it off his face. The rest swung over his broad shoulders, glossy and black. The man had hair that was not only nicer and thicker than hers, but longer, too.

"Nanofabric. As in tiny computers?" She'd heard the term *nano* before, but that was back in the days of technology.

"Billions of them. They are embedded in the material of your innerwear, and react to air and body temperature to regulate comfort."

Cam's emotions bungee-jumped from elation to despair and back again. "There *is* technology . . . ?"

"Beyond your wildest dreams. Just because the technology-reviling fools who live here choose not to make their lives easier doesn't mean the rest of the world doesn't."

The rest of the world was still around, too! She wanted to sigh and weep and scream and laugh. "They said nuclear war destroyed everything. . . ."

Kublai's eyes flashed like heat lightning. "They lied to you. The war was between India and Pakistan only. Thank God the world of my forebears came to its senses before it spread farther. It was both the darkest and the brightest time in history."

Cam slid her hands into her wet hair as a sickening sense of betrayal replaced her initial elation. Zhurihe had lied to her. Why?

"We're riding to the capital city," Kublai told her. "The journey will take many days. Again, you need not fear me: I don't want or need your body to play with."

"Thank you for sharing that."

"To accomplish my mission with the least amount of trouble, I can keep you bound and gagged the entire time, or you can follow a few simple rules and stay free. There will be no trickery, running off, kicking, biting, punching, faked seduction, or refusing food."

"That's all?" she queried sarcastically.

"And there will be no stealing a blade to slit my throat in the middle of the night."

112

"Hmm. That's a lot to remember. Maybe you ought to write it down."

He barked out a laugh, but this time it was a fraction less pompous than before. The minion had a learning curve; he remembered his shins. "Why, you're a sarcastic one."

"Just one more service we offer."

One dark brow lifted imperiously. "Now, what are they?"

"My services?"

"The rules! Repeat them to me."

She had the strangest feeling that she was supposed to cower when he bellowed like that. She had the equally strange sense that it startled him that she didn't. "Let's see . . . no running, no tricks, no kicking, biting, punching, or faked seduction—who do you think I am, Mata Hari? No refusing to eat, either, although I don't think that'll be a problem. In exchange, I get to go around without cuffs or a gag. And now for your end of the agreement. In return for my cooperation, you will not hurt these people, to include but not limited to: raping, pillaging, burning the house and livestock, poisoning the springs, toppling the shrine—or committing aforementioned atrocities to the village up the road. That's a deal breaker, by the way."

He uttered a loud sound of outrage and insult unidentifiable as any word in the English language. "Of course I would not commit such acts. Do you think I am a barbarian?"

"Aren't you?"

He threw her a glance hot with astonishment. "Do you always say what you think?"

"This bothers you, I take it."

"I don't yet know you well enough to say," he growled.

"And you won't." It came out sounding like a challenge, but it was too late to take it back.

"Such confidence, pretty one." His eyes were so brown and so dark that she couldn't tell where the pupil ended or the iris began. They grew even darker. "We've a long ride ahead of us."

The Rim Riders were taking her to the capital city. Before, she hadn't wanted to go. Now her view had changed. Where there was technology, there was information—information that might lead to Bree.

Kublai brought his fingers to his mouth and whistled for his horse. It was big—at least eighteen hands tall, with a massive neck and chest, muscular hindquarters, and a long, flowing mane and tail. With no visible effort, the Rim Rider pulled himself up in the saddle. In the colors of late afternoon, he resembled a mythical warrior. There were several races in his ancestry, and he appeared to have inherited the best of them. She'd have to be dead not to notice that he was an exotically handsome man. As his stallion pranced in place, Kublai extended a gloved hand toward her.

"I'm riding double with you," she said. It came out too flatly to be a question, too doubtfully to be a statement. She'd be seated in front, wedged between his thighs, surrounded by acres of hard, leather-clad flesh. The man had enough of an effect on her. She didn't need to drown herself it.

Kublai seemed to take note of her dismay. "Unless you'd rather ride with Nazeem."

It was all but impossible to hide her relief. Nazeem, at

least, didn't have a body of which she remembered every detail. Every visible detail, that was. "Nazeem it is."

Nazeem made a muffled noise that sounded suspiciously like laughter. Again Kublai thrust out his arm, his big gloved hand upturned, fingers fanned out. His ever-so-slightly-almond-shaped eyes were dark, impossibly dark. They broadcast his unhappiness at her snub. "You will ride with me," he decreed. "By order of the emperor."

"By order of the emperor?" That was the last response she'd expected. And he didn't seem to be kidding.

Kublai gave her his hand. With a strong tug he pulled her up. She dropped down in front of him, landing hard in the saddle. Her spent, sore body screamed in protest. "It would seem to me that if your emperor has time to micromanage who rides on your horse, he doesn't have enough to keep him busy," she muttered.

She heard the Rim Rider's voice, low in her ear. "Saying what you think again, eh?"

I can't help it, she wanted to shoot back. Provoking him was irresistible. He was too full of himself, too sure of himself, and too arrogant. Even if she was his captive.

Locking an arm around her, he kicked the horse into a full gallop. "The mighty emperor has far more important matters than you to take up his time, Scarlet."

Scarlet? Cam nearly swallowed her tongue. He knew her fighter-pilot call sign!

Of course. Why else would the emperor dispatch a pair of Rim Riders just to pick up a stranger? The emperor wanted her because of who she was. How could she be so dense and not have seen it in the first place?

If the Rim Riders knew of her existence, did they know of Bree? Hope surged inside Cam, hope as she

115

hadn't felt in all the weeks and months spent recovering. What if the Riders had already picked up her friend and leader?

What if they hadn't?

She didn't voice the question. As an air force pilot in a capture situation, she knew never to volunteer information. Since neither Rim Rider had brought up Bree, there was a good chance they didn't know about her. If Bree was in hiding for whatever reason, Cam didn't want to give her away.

Options . . . There were two necessities she could see so far. One: keep quiet about Bree. And two: stay with the Rim Riders until they reached their destination. If the warlord emperor or anyone else had Bree and planned on doing her harm, Cam sure as sugar was going to find out.

As they rounded the bend on the road, Cam threw one last glance back at the farm before it disappeared from view. No Zhurihe. The little liar hadn't shown up to say good-bye. There was anger in that thought, yes, but regret, too. She'd never again see the girl who could dry her tears and kick her butt with equal skill. *I hope you had your reasons, Zhurihe.*

Cam returned her attention to the road ahead, and her thoughts to a future that was as much a mystery as ever.

After a few hours of hard riding, the men found a place they deemed appropriate for a break. A fast little stream cut through an alpine meadow, brown and dry with small patches of snow.

Cam could only partially appreciate the stark beauty. A long ride on horseback was draining for anyone. She was far from ready for such grueling physical activity, and her body was all too happy to let her know about it. The demons were back. Wreaking havoc with her muscles, they played Tarzan on her hamstrings and "Dueling Banjos" on her biceps. She tightened her stomach to brace against the pain.

Kublai slid off the horse first. Then he caught her around the waist and lowered her to the ground. Her leather clothes slid over his leather clothes all the way down until her boots landed on the grass. He took a look at her face and said, "You're in pain."

"A little."

"A little? I think not." He let go of her to open a saddle pack. Cam's legs buckled, and she grabbed hold of the saddle to avoid grabbing hold of the Rider.

"I'm angry with you." Kublai steadied her with a firm grip on her arm. "You should have said something."

She hadn't said much of anything the entire ride. "Would it have changed the plan? I thought we had to reach a certain place by nightfall."

"We do. And, yes, it would have 'changed the plan,' as you say. I would have given you this sooner." He opened a gloved fist. A flat pink oval lay in his palm. "Pain blockers."

"No, thanks," she said. Her body protested the decision, howling: *Yes, yes, yes!*

Shut up, she told her shrieking muscles.

For once the demons took her side. *Painkillers will dull your reactions*, they warned. *You won't be able to think.*

Cam realized Kublai was regarding her strangely. "Internal argument," she explained.

"Take this orally and the pain will ease. It's very power-

117

ful." The pill sat in his hand. She stared at it, tempted, sorely tempted; then she shook her head.

"It's not poison," he said dryly. "My orders are to bring you to the capital, or I'd have killed you already."

"Nice," she shot back sarcastically. "Love you, too."

"Do you now?" he retorted, in what was unmistakably a bedroom voice.

She'd have to be a nun not to react to it.

And like hell if she was going to let him know. "Do you often have this much trouble separating fantasy from reality, Kublai?"

"Do you often have this much trouble exchanging stubbornness for common sense?" he shot back.

"Ooh, touché." His comeback was swift, decisive. He was as good with words as he was in the water.

"Take the pain blocker. It will make the ride easier— and my life easier—if you do. We have many hours to go before we stop for the night."

"I don't want to be doped up on painkillers. I want to be alert. I want to know . . . what's happening to me," she added with an honesty that surprised her.

"Ah. I see the problem now." He held the oval between two fingers. "This isn't your twenty-first-century medicine. We've come a long way since then. Taken orally, this pill will distribute smart medication throughout your body, targeting pain receptors in your central nervous system without dulling the senses."

"Really?"

"Really."

With each new miracle Kublai revealed, with each small act of kindness, he moved farther from the mental image Zhurihe had placed in her head about Rim Riders. Cam's initial belief that Rim Riders were a terrible threat was based on information Zhurihe had given her. Now Cam knew the kind of lies the girl was capable of perpetuating. Kublai wasn't a captor. He was an escort; maybe even a liberator. By bringing her over the mountains, he and Nazeem were handing her the kind of freedom Zhurihe had either refused to or couldn't provide.

Unless the emperor planned to steal it away when Cam reached the other side.

Her stomach gave a twist at the thought. There were so many uncertainties. Best not to let herself get overconfident. It could prove to be a mistake—a fatal one.

Warily, she took the pill from his fingers. For so long she'd endured the arthritislike pain and the aches in her muscles. All Zhurihe and her people could offer were herbs that helped, but never for long enough periods, and often left her feeling drugged or sick to her stomach.

"Put it under your tongue."

Cam took the plunge, hoping she wouldn't regret doing so. It had no taste at all, the pill, and it dissolved within seconds. Then it happened: a soft, plush blanket fell over the demons, blunting their blows.

"Wow," she said almost reverently. If she had a doubt that anything he was telling her about technology was true, it was erased in that instant. He let go of her and she took a few steps. The stiffness was still there, the rigidity in her joints, but, despite the grueling ride, she felt . . . well, human. And clearheaded, too.

Meanwhile, Nazeem walked away, seeking privacy as he spoke softly into something that looked like a cross between a handheld computer and a cell phone. *Hmm.* Calling the emperor to let him know she was coming to dinner? Or that she *was* dinner?

She gazed out at the peaceful meadow, now that she could better enjoy the scenery. Kublai was unloading the packs from the horses. "I'll walk them for you," she offered, taking the animals' leads. "They worked hard. I'll take them around the meadow a little before they drink and graze."

He stepped in front of her, snatching away the leads. His tattoo, hard expression, and black leather gave him a most forbidding appearance. "Do you think me stupid?" he said in a low voice.

"You think I'm fixing to steal them?"

"It's not easy to trust the woman who tried to drown me."

She turned up her hands. "I didn't think you'd drown."

"You tied me to a tree stump. Underwater."

"It was the only thing I could find."

He made a derisive sound. "I'm glad you didn't find my blade first."

"This is all moot. I came back for you."

"And I, pretty one, had already cut myself loose." He walked away with the horses.

Rendered speechless—something her brothers had wished their entire lives they could achieve but hadn't—Cam watched the Rider lead the horses away through the tall, dry grasses.

She limped after him. "Do you think *me* stupid?" she called after him, imitating his outburst from a few moments earlier, his ever-so-proper British accent and all.

He stopped and looked over his shoulder with such shock that she had to fight bursting into laughter. "It's insulting enough that you think I'd steal your horses. Even more insulting that you think I'd ride off with them in the middle of nowhere. Where would I go with no map? Or maybe you know something I don't; maybe your horses of the future come equipped with GPS."

Amusement flickered in his eyes. "They do not."

"See? I'd be pretty stupid to run away. Mongolia isn't exactly the center of the world."

"Close enough," he said.

"You almost sound as if you believe that."

One of his brows lifted in that familiar, imperious, holier-than-thou expression so at odds with his *Scorpion King* exterior. "I do."

Shaking her head, she wrapped her hand around the leads. "I'll walk the horses."

He didn't let go. His big leather-clad hand gripped the leads next to her bare one, chapped from the cold.

"You still don't trust me," she said.

"I have my reasons."

She wasn't sure what she saw in his eyes, but whatever those reasons were, they were big ones.

He reached across with his other hand and gently pried her fingers from the leads. Then he nodded, as if dismissing her, and resumed his trek through the grass.

Leaving her staring after him, he led the horses away through tall dried grasses. She'd never met anyone so self-assured, so serenely arrogant. So full of himself! Rather than repelling her, though, he fascinated her. All great fighter pilots possessed a deep-down, unshakable sense of confidence; there was no time for doubt in war.

That same self-possession and unflinching self-assurance she strove for in herself she sensed in the Rim Rider. Or it could just be an enormous ego begging for a little deflation. It wouldn't take long to tell.

She shambled after him. "Y'all don't mind if I come along?"

He cast a questioning glance in her direction. "'Y'all'?" He said it just as she had, all drawled out and Southern.

"It means 'you all.' You and the horses." She rubbed her butt. "I think I need to be walked as much as they do."

He said nothing. She took that as a yes.

Kublai's boots made even thuds on the hard ground, a counterpoint to her lighter, irregular steps. In silence they walked the horses around the meadow, letting them cool down before finally bringing them to the stream to drink.

Cam crouched at the edge of the water and dipped her fingers in. "This is like ice." She shook the drops from her skin and tucked her hand under her arm to warm it. "But if this is Mongolia in the middle of winter, something's not quite right with the weather. It's much warmer than I would have guessed. Is this normal?"

"It's actually somewhat colder than usual."

"Really? What happened while I was gone. Global warming?"

"There was a definite climatic shift toward warmer weather since your day. There's been some reversal, though, of late, in the last twenty-five years or so. Welcome news, because of the coastal cities lost to the rising seas."

Cam stared down at the clear water running over pebbles on the bottom. "I'm not sure if I'm ready to hear about all the changes in the world. I feel enough of an outsider as it is. But I have to. I have to know, or I'll be lost. I've spent enough months in the dark."

"I can tell you all that you feel comfortable learning this afternoon on the ride."

She smiled up at him. "Thank you."

He remained stone-faced.

She stood, wiping her hands on her pants. "How many days is it going to take to get to Beijing?"

"Three."

"That's all?"

"On the other side of this range, transportation awaits us that will take us to the capital."

"So we're not going to enter the city gates on these magnificent animals? Too bad." She smoothed her palm over the stallion's flank. "It'd be quite an entrance. These horses are gorgeous."

"Yes, they are. They're a breed exclusive to my country. Hansians are found nowhere else." His tone had warmed dramatically. She'd stumbled upon his passion, she thought.

"I know horses. Grew up around them. Thorough-breds. We didn't actually keep them on our property—my father was in the army and we had to move around a lot—but most of the relatives on my mother's side were involved with racing. We went back to Georgia every summer." She stroked her hand down the gleaming flank of Kublai's stallion. "Those were the best days. . . ." She realized she'd been rambling. This Rider didn't give a damn about her childhood summer vacations.

"Go on," he coaxed gruffly.

Startled, she swung her gaze around. It was tough to tell his expression with the dark swirls of snakes obscuring his face, but his eyes held no derision. "About your horses—their heads and ears look Arabian. I know it can't be true. Arabians are small, and these horses are enormous."

"Hansians have the speed and size of Thoroughbreds, the heft of Clydesdales, the brains of quarter horses, and the beauty of Arabians."

Kublai's Hansian, Beast, lifted its head. Water dripping from its lips, it swung its nose around and nuzzled Kublai's boot, then his hand. He murmured something soft to the horse, treating the animal with clear affection and respect, the horse responding in kind.

The horse moved on to graze. They followed. "Now I wish I'd brought you a horse of your own," he remarked.

"And knowing you and your trust issues, you'd have tethered me to yours."

"This is true."

His certainty made her smirk. She shook her head. "It still would have been riding. I sure missed it. I never had time for it anymore. I was either flying or stationed overseas, or both. I should have made the time." She stopped before she became too maudlin.

"Ah, but you rode the wind, yes?"

"Say again?"

"The wind. You flew. A different kid of creature, yes, but still a thrill nonetheless. Or so I surmise. I've never flown a fighter craft. In truth, I haven't wanted to. Something about the tight confines . . ." He cringed. Was Kublai claustrophobic? It might explain why he loved being out here in the wide-open spaces. "But I can well understand why someone would yearn to fly. And I admire those who do it."

His compliment startled her. She narrowed her eyes at him, expecting his comment to turn into another jab, but as with their conversation about the horses, his interest seemed genuine. "And you miss the flying," he continued in his stiff, Rim Rider way. "Yes?"

"Yes." The wall she'd erected around her emotions threatened to come crashing down. But she'd managed to hold it together after describing her family's love of horses and those long summers in Georgia; she could do the same while talking about the F-16. Swallowing, she cleared her throat and nodded. "Nothing matched flying the Viper. Nothing."

Kublai's dark eyes flashed. "The Viper? This was the designation of the craft you flew? The viper is the symbol of the royal family."

She took in the snakes coiled on his face. "What a coincidence." She stored the fact away. She'd need the emperor's aid to find Bree. Any common ground would help her cause.

A cold wind swooped down from the nearby hills, rustling the dry grasses. Kyber gathered up the horses and they trekked back to where Nazeem waited. "We'll be traversing the mountains this afternoon," he told her.

"They told me there's nothing but chaos beyond those mountains. Gangs and mercenaries."

"They told you wrong."

In the new and less threatening atmosphere of their tenuous détente, she admitted, "I always wanted to see what was beyond the mountains. Only I didn't picture doing it quite like this."

A smile played at the edges of Kublai's mouth. He helped her up into the saddle and pulled himself up after her. He wrapped his arm around her waist and said in her ear, "I can show you many more things previously unknown to you."

"I doubt that."

"Such is the naïveté of the inexperienced."

She choked out an outraged laugh. This morning they'd been ready to kill each other. A minute ago they'd been carving out a tentative peace. Now they were flirting. And yet all day this repartee, this heat, had never been far below the surface. She wasn't sure what to make of it. Was this just his personality? Or was the flirtation, the natural and friendly opposition, hinting at a desire for more physical forms of interaction—was it something they brought out in each other?

Maybe she didn't want to know. All she had to do was get through the next three days. After everything else she'd been through, how hard could that be?

Chapter Ten

Daylight this time of year was short in the far north. Darkness had already consumed the forest when, after an all-day ride, Kyber decided that enough distance had been placed between the American and the farm to warrant making camp.

A generous fire crackled. Nikolai busied himself preparing the meal, something the prince had once admitted in secret that he thoroughly enjoyed. A pot of curry stew made in the palace kitchens hung over the flames. It bubbled, filling the quiet air with its fragrance.

With two mugs of hot coffee, Kyber made his way to where he'd left Scarlet. She sat propped up against a tree, her arms wrapped around her bent legs as she stared somewhere he couldn't see.

He crouched down in front of her. She didn't look at him, but her fingers flexed. "Thanks again for the medicine," she said. "It's a miracle."

"It's called science, Scarlet."

She made a sound of agreement and her eyes shifted to him. "Cam," she reminded him. "That's my name. Scarlet's my fighter-pilot call sign."

He thought of all the weeks he'd called Bree Maguire "Banzai" and she'd never once corrected him.

"Cam is short for Cameron," she offered helpfully when he didn't reply.

"I guessed that."

"Sorry. I suppose it's not that much of a mental leap. Even for a barbarian." Firelight outlined her profile. Under her eyes were shadows, but her mouth curved in a slight smile.

"Barbarian? Who was the one who employed civility to teach you recent history and the current state of world political affairs all afternoon, eh?"

"Politics told from the narrow perspective of an emperor's minion."

He had to laugh; her jibes were so sharp. "How do you know it's not the truth?"

"You make it sound perfect here. No place is."

"You have your opinion, Scarlet. . . ."

"The right one, yes. Anyway," Cam went on, seemingly oblivious to his disbelieving expression—or perhaps fully cognizant of it and enjoying the hell out of goading him, "you did sound educated in your descriptions of the world. Opinionated, biased, yes, but not barbarian-like at all. And it's Cam. You called me Scarlet again. A minute ago."

He suppressed a smile as her eyes slid in the direction of his hands. "One of those for me?"

He'd completely forgotten he carried the coffee. He handed one to her. "No 'sloppy seconds' this time."

Her mouth gave a mulish twist as she took the mug,

cradling it in two very feminine hands. Feminine, yes, but he well knew what unladylike things they were capable of doing.

She took a sip. "Mmm. That's good coffee."

"I have nothing but the best," he started to say, fully prepared to regale her with the matchless offerings of his palace kitchens, then clamped his mouth closed. He didn't want to be Kyber tonight. He wanted to be Kublai.

He liked being Kublai. It gave him a certain freedom of behavior.

He settled on the ground next to Cam. Sipping coffee side by side, they fell into silence. He wouldn't call it fully companionable, but neither did it have the wariness of their earlier encounters. A day of sharing a saddle and conversation had a way of enforcing familiarity.

She inhaled the fragrance of the coffee and closed her eyes. "Good java," she repeated. "So I guess you're not as much of a barbarian as I thought."

He could see the mischievous tilt to her mouth. "If that's what it takes to convince you of my civility, I suppose I'll take the vinegar with the honey."

"Oh, I never said you were civilized. Just that you weren't a barbarian." Her blue eyes twinkled in the firelight. "Civilized equals boring."

He did a double take. He could read her remark a dozen different ways, but somehow he knew she'd meant it for what it was: flirtation. He caught her gaze and held it. "All men, even the civilized, carry the beast within them." He lowered his voice until it skated along the mellow edge of pillow talk. "The question is, To what degree? In only the most primal encounters would it become apparent."

Cam didn't look unsettled by his suggestive banter. "Hmm. An interesting theory that begs intensive research." She kept her eyes on him.

"Provided both participants have the stamina," he warned.

True heat arose between them. He saw the moment she felt it. Her thumbs, he noticed, had stopping rubbing back and forth over the rim of her coffee cup. She noticed him watching her and placed the mug on the ground.

"A barbarian's hands will always give him away," she commented.

He couldn't stop himself from glancing down. She caught him, and he found himself wishing he hadn't looked. "How is that?"

"The fingernails. That's how you can tell brutes and barbarians from civilized people. Yours are clean."

"And yours, dear Cam, are not."

She brought her hands to her eyes. "Mercy," she breathed, her speech taking on that delightful accent he'd never heard before meeting her. "Look at all that dirt. What would Mama say, bless her heart?"

"Who's the barbarian now?" he asked smugly.

"We spent all day on horseback. Unlike me, you wore gloves."

They returned to sipping coffee, each, he suspected, thinking themselves the victor. "A minute ago you used the turn of phrase 'taking vinegar with the honey,'" she said. "It's a very Southern figure of speech. As in the Deep South of the United States. Excuse me, the former United States. The UCE now." She spat out the name as if it tasted bad. "The imperial power that owns everything below Canada in the west, and the Middle East—how convenient—on the other side. How the U.S. ever agreed to this arrangement is something I can't comprehend. In Central, do they still call the South the South?"

He shook his head. "My knowledge of the colony of Central doesn't go to that depth."

"Well, I hope they do." She stopped and drank more coffee. Then she studied him, as if pondering his features—not easy, given the tattoo. "And you? You mentioned your people are Scottish and Chinese?"

"Scottish and Korean, actually, with a smattering of nearly everything else."

This time when silence returned, it was several degrees more companionable. It was a novel experience indeed, for he, lacking female siblings, couldn't remember viewing a single interaction with a female as such. Many other things, certainly, but not companionable.

He had to say he quite liked it.

With the return of silence, though, the sadness was back in Cam's expression. "You didn't harm them," she said after a while. "The people at the farm."

"I scared them a little—I admit it freely. But then, they did break the law, after all."

"They told me Rim Riders had roughed them up before."

"What? When did this occur? What were their names?"

"I don't know. I didn't ask. Are you the head Rim Rider or something? Did they break the code of Rim Rider ethics?" She looked something between amused and concerned.

"Head Rim Rider . . ." He shook his head.

"I take it that's a no?"

He set his mug in the dirt next to hers. "Rim Riders patrol the borderlands in the name of safety and security. At times we act as bounty hunters. But to hurt the locals . . . that is not tolerated—by Prince Kyber," he added quickly. "The prince, the acting emperor, is a mostly benevolent monarch. Certainly some transgressions occur at the hands of his soldiers, but the incidents, I believe, are rare and punished if discovered. The emperor doesn't want his legacy to be one of resentment and hatred. Such opinions can fester in the citizenry and grow over generations like a cancer, until they reach the level where they can destroy a very empire. Case in point—the UCE. Their bureaucrats mistreat the hands that feed them—their colonists—and now those hands have formed a hostile fist. There's an important lesson there: Never underestimate the power of your people."

The sorrow always visible to some degree in Cam's eyes grew even more pronounced. "I wish they hadn't felt compelled to lie to me," she said without his having to ask. "That family I lived with."

He regretted her pain. Yet he had to admit it helped his cause. Once he brought her to Beijing, he wanted her to stay there, not run off searching for rebel family members out of a misplaced sense of belonging. Fortunately, having wounded her with their lies, they'd all but solved that dilemma. "Betrayal never fails to taste bitter," he said.

"It's happened to you?"

"Regrettably, yes. I've experienced it on both sides."

"You betrayed someone?"

"Yes. Through ignorance."

She waited for him to explain. And, to his shock, he

did. "I have a brother. A half brother. He's the bastard my mother bore her lover."

Cam winced. "Sorry."

"We didn't know, growing up. We thought we were full brothers. My entire family did. Except for my mother, who held her secrets close. Of course, secrets die only when taken to the grave. My father learned of her infidelity and confronted her. To keep him from telling others, she paid someone who claimed to have invented a secret elixir that would excise my father's memory, selectively." An "elixir" created by a medicine salesman who turned up with links to various rebel groups and that joke of a leader, Beauchamp of the UCE, though the latter had never been proven to Kyber's satisfaction. Palace security was thought to be impenetrable, but no one had anticipated a killer-for-hire waiting for the kind of opportunity that the queen had inadvertently provided.

"Thinking he was eating nothing more than breakfast one day, my father ingested a protein, an engineered prion, which brought on not the selective loss of memory, but irreversible disintegration of the brain." Kyber looked into the dark woods. "It began as a vague sadness in a man who was nearly always happy. The lethal march continued over the weeks as his brain cells died by the millions. None of the physicians who examined him could find the cause of his symptoms. He began to hallucinate. He forgot things, had difficulty making decisions. Muscles jerked in his arms and legs. And then one day he was gone." Kyber took a breath. He still mourned the tragic loss of the man he had so admired, sometimes filled with doubts as to whether he'd ever live up to the man's standard.

133

"I'm sorry," Cam said.

"The elixir killed the man, but not his body."

"He's in a coma, then."

"For years now, yes."

Cam made a small sound that conveyed much. "How difficult that must be for your family."

"You cannot imagine. My half brother emerged as the leading suspect."

"Mercy . . ."

"I had him arrested, sent off to the dungeons." He turned his hands over in his lap. "What choice did I have? Only my mother knew of my brother's innocence, and yet she kept this to herself until it was announced he was to be executed for his crimes. The emperor eventually cleared my half brother of all charges at my mother's behest, but the sad matter tore a rift in my relationship with my brother that has never been healed. Apparently he was beaten badly in custody. I . . . didn't know this."

"You wouldn't have had the power to stop the beatings, even if you did know."

The twist to Kyber's mouth was both wry and remorseful. *If only she knew that you* did *have the authority.* Kyber wondered what his father would have done if placed in the same situation. Would he have been more conscious of the climate of brutality that existed in the prison? "My brother remains bitter, and I suppose I cannot blame him. I am just as embittered about his association with . . . certain shadowy groups that led to his being accused in the first place."

Kyber fell silent. He'd actually told her about the near-assassination of his father, an event that affected him still. What was the phrase he'd heard on the Interweb? Spilling one's guts? Yes, that was precisely what had occurred just now. And it left him feeling rather spent. Aside from sporadic comments made during security-based discussions with Nikolai, he'd never confided to anyone his personal thoughts on his estrangement from D'ekkar. Kyber could not have done it. Kublai, it seemed, could.

He didn't worry that what he'd revealed tonight would cause Cam to make the connection that he was, in fact, Prince Kyber. Only four souls knew of the events: himself, his mother, D'ekkar, and Nikolai. It was not public knowledge. Yes, the citizenry understood that there had been an assassination attempt, but they didn't know why or how, and never would.

Kyber picked up his mug of coffee, sipping to settle himself, half wishing it were a glass of wine.

The hush continued as they brooded over their pasts and battled their demons.

"I heard the emperor eats peasants alive and makes overcoats from their dried flesh," Cam said out of the blue.

Kyber choked on the coffee he sipped.

"That's what I was told." Cam shrugged, though he had the feeling she was far more serious than the casual gesture implied.

"By the same people who told you nuclear war destroyed the world?"

"So it's not true."

"Definitely not!"

From where he stood by the fire pit, Nikolai threw Kyber a questioning glance. Kyber lowered his voice.

"The emperor . . . he is actually a prince, acting as emperor in his father's place."

"And the father?"

"Incapacitated by an assassination attempt years ago."

"Mmm," she said. "I think they must have meant the prince, then."

Kyber winced. "Is the rumor rampant in these parts?"

"I heard it from only one person."

"Who?" he demanded.

Her lips compressed. She wasn't going to tell him. And he knew better than to force it from her.

"Thanks, Kublai," she said after a bit.

He shook his head. "For what?"

"For letting me vent. For answering my questions all day. For . . . being a friend." She looked at him then, her open, welcoming expression bringing to mind the photo Nikolai had shown him of her standing in the middle of a dirt road, her head thrown back, her face directed at the sky. Now, as then, her blond hair fluttered around her face as light as air. And now, as then, it was what her eyes revealed of the woman within that made him catch his breath, not her more obvious physical attributes. "I guess I needed one tonight."

"A friend . . ."

"Yeah. You're a pretty good one to have, I'd say."

Women had called him many things, but never *friend*. "Do you always say what you think?" he teased in a quiet voice.

"I take it that bothers you," she guessed, knowing he referred to the conversation from the morning, after the springs. When he said nothing, she smiled at him from behind her mug of coffee. "You're supposed to say you don't know me well enough to say."

"I don't know if that particular response still applies."

They shared a look that was as surprising as it was arousing in its intensity. Then, as if succumbing to second thoughts, Cam took sudden interest in Nikolai's dinner preparations.

If only Banzai Maguire had been as easy for him to read as Cam, he thought. She'd betrayed him, Banzai—quite shocked him with her departure, if the truth be told. He'd never thought she'd go. Perhaps she'd had her reasons: her inability to believe anything he told her, her obsessive patriotism for a nation long dead, and her infatuation with the UCE supreme commander's son. Yet from the start he'd never been able to discern a true sense of her. Her deepest thoughts had been a mystery—and were still.

Why would Banzai have been any different from the other women you've encountered in your life? he asked himself.

True. He loved women; he savored the time spent in their company. He collected beauties like flowers to sprinkle about the palace, and they often artfully arranged themselves here and there to surprise and delight him, winning, as he suspected was their motivation, a visit to his chambers. While he understood their bodies well, the workings of their minds was a different story altogether, a mystery he had to admit he'd had little desire to unravel. In a rare turnaround, he'd put in the extra effort with Banzai, and look where it had gotten him!

Yet now, in a single day in Cameron Tucker's company,

he'd learned more about her than he had with Banzai in three months.

Or, with his mother in a lifetime.

Enough! Nothing can come of this! When the journey ends, so must your relationship with Cam. Kyber's mood darkened with the sudden return to reality. As soon as he delivered her to the palace, he'd have to walk away from Cam. What choice did he have? Seeing her as Kublai would put at risk the ruse he'd played for most of his adult life. Nor could he meet her face-to-face as the prince. The risk of her recognizing him was too great. *Is that not what you said you wanted, to stay well clear of her?*

It was indeed.

"Dinner is nearly ready," he grumbled rather abruptly. He pushed to his feet and offered Cam a hand for assistance up, releasing her as soon as she found her balance. He didn't care to feel the heat of her palm pressed to his any longer than he had to. As quickly as he could, he left her side, exchanging her presence for that of the fire. Those flames, he knew, would be far more easily extinguished.

Chapter Eleven

On the second full day of travel, they pushed the pace hard until well after dark. "We are behind," was all Kublai would say. The worry in his manner was disturbing to Cam, but he wouldn't go into detail. "You will be safe only within the walls of the city."

There were those who wished to do her harm; that was all he would tell her. She was beginning to see him more as a bodyguard than anything else. And hearing that others were looking for her heightened her fears for Bree's welfare. She'd wanted, so many times during the day while riding with Kublai, to bring up the subject of her friend's possible whereabouts, but each time, her POW training reared its head and cautioned her into silence. Better to wait and see if the men mentioned Bree instead of the other way around. But the wait was killing her. It was hard not to think that Bree was either dead or in hiding. Why else would these two Rim Riders not have brought her up? Cam was prepared to accept either circumstance; the not-knowing was what wore her down more than anything. That, she realized, and her body's woes.

The pain meds Kublai gave her helped, but her muscles were trembling and cramping from the rigor of riding. By the time the men chose a campsite and stopped for the night, Cam was slumping in the saddle. She'd been strong and athletic all her life. Being this weak and not being able to do anything about it was embarrassing.

Kublai dismounted and led her on horseback into a clearing. The rocking of her horse lulled Cam half-asleep.

"Come." A deep, rumbling voice roused her from her exhausted stupor. Strong hands reached for her and helped her down.

Dinner was a mostly silent affair—comfortable, companionable silence that came from two days spent traveling together. Cam scraped the last of some stew from the bottom of her bowl. "Delicious again, thank you."

Feeling much like a wounded animal, inside and out, she shook out her bedroll and spread it on the ground. One of the travel bags served as a headboard. She leaned back, her legs sprawled out in front of her. Then she let go of a huge sigh.

"Hurting, eh?"

Her eyes opened halfway at the sound of the familiar sexy baritone. "A few hours off the back of a horse will do wonders, I'm sure."

"Tomorrow, when we arrive at the capital, you'll have access to the best medical care in the world. Before you know it, you'll be completely well."

"Can't wait." She winced at the spasms clenching the

length of her legs. "Mercy. I sure hope I don't have to relieve myself again before bedtime, because I have the feeling I'll have to crawl there."

"I'd carry you."

She smiled up at him. "You would, wouldn't you? My mama would have liked you. She said that Southern men were the only true gentlemen. With you, I think she'd have made an exception."

She felt rather than saw Kublai smile. The next thing she knew, something was tugging at her boots. She lifted her head. Kublai had crouched down in front of her, his broad shoulders blocking the firelight. He loomed above her, a black silhouette limned in orange. "What are you doing?"

"Removing your footwear." One by one, he set her boots on the dirt. Then he reached for her pants. Her eyes opened wider. "Now what are you doing?"

"Taking off your pants."

Cam swallowed a squeak. She'd been having fantasies about the Rim Rider all day. Her attraction to him had been growing steadily, with him pressed against her back as they rode, and all it took was a glance at the man to confirm that he, too, had been entertaining similar fantasies about her. That, at least, made her feel better. She didn't want to think it was one-sided. But this undressing business . . . well, it was a little sudden. She appreciated spontaneity as much as the next single girl, but she was feeling a little incapacitated at the moment. Leg cramps and romance didn't exactly mix.

"I thought you would appreciate a massage," he explained.

"A massage . . . Heaven."

"It is said I give the best massages in the kingdom."

She laughed. "Who says that? Your girlfriends?"

"There are no girlfriends," he said, shaking his head.

"You mean just not tonight."

"No. What I tell you is true."

"Wow. Too bad. For them, I mean: the women of the kingdom. Speaking of which, why is it called the Kingdom of Asia if you have an emperor?"

"At first it *was* a king and a kingdom. About fifty years afterward, it changed to 'emperor' and 'empire.' But everyone uses the terms interchangeably. It is our land's quirk, I suppose. It doesn't, however, change the population's limitless affection for their ruler."

"I hope the prince is paying you to do his PR."

"P . . . R?"

"Public relations. Making him look good."

Kublai frowned. "Prince Kyber does not require anyone to 'make him look good.'"

"Sorry. I didn't mean to insult O Glorious One."

"Glorious One." Kublai stared off into the night. "The term has definite appeal."

"Write it down. When we get to the palace, you can drop it in the royal suggestion box."

He knelt between her legs and rubbed his hands together. "I will now knead the muscles in your legs to alleviate the spasms and give you a more comfortable night. If that is acceptable, of course."

Who was he kidding? "That would be nice."

Nice? Sweet mercy. Having the Rim Rider's hands all over her would be much more than that. Why hadn't she thought to complain about her muscle spasms last night?

He reached for her waistband, and she stared at his

hands. It stopped him. "You are wearing your long under-clothes, yes?"

"Yes."

"Then there is no risk of baring too much."

No, damn it.

Gently, carefully, he unfastened her pants and pulled them off. A small light he'd brought with him provided a cozy glow, but the thick, damp darkness of the forest pressed in all around, as if trying to snuff it out.

His head was bent down, and she couldn't see his face as he placed his hands on her legs. "I will touch you now."

Please, she thought. *All over. I'm dying here.*

He began by stroking his palms over her legs. Cam swallowed and tipped her head back as his thumbs circled, pressing into her skin, finding the sore spots and soothing them away.

"You have incredible legs," he said. Then, seeming to correct himself, he amended, "Strong legs. Yes, they are very strong."

So, he liked her legs. She tried not to smile. "Actually, they used to be much stronger. There's been a lot of atrophy. I stumble all the time. I know I shouldn't complain—I should be happy to be alive—but I hate the clumsiness. Lately I've been wondering if my balance will ever come back."

"They will do much for you, the palace physicians."

"I hope so. It's been the hardest thing about my recovery to accept, losing my coordination," she admitted, growing more talkative as she relaxed. Kublai's hands were expert. "I should have appreciated it more when I had it. I took so much for granted."

"With our talents, we often do, it seems." He bent to

the task of kneading the long muscles under her thighs, his fingers brushing the edges of her buttocks.

"What are your talents, Kublai?"

He lifted his head to give her the absolutely most intense, sexiest look she could imagine. She had to remember to breathe. "Besides that," she practically gasped.

He threw back his head and laughed. "Do you think me a barbarian still? I don't think your mama would be pleased if I were to regale you with tales of my prowess in bed."

"The best men don't have to brag."

"No," he said. "They do not."

The atmosphere grew even more charged.

"Needless to say, I was going to tell you that swordplay is a talent of mine. No euphemism intended."

She laughed softly.

"I practice each morning without fail. Even when on the road. It is an ancient art—obsolete, most say—a form of martial arts, but I find I crave it. Pushing my body and mind to new levels. The discipline of it all."

"The focus, yes," she said. "That's a lot of it. I used to do gymnastics. All I practice anymore are the rings and uneven bars, but as a girl I had real talent. I wanted to stick with it straight up to an Olympic medal, but genetics slammed that goal into the dirt. All the women on my mother's side are tall, willowy, and blond. I was just another cast in the mold." She smiled. "At twelve years old I sprouted to five-foot-nine. Gymnasts need to be short. Luckily I only put on another inch before stopping." She shrugged. "But as for these legs and my balance, I'm not asking to return to a hundred percent. I'm not asking for miracles. If I can regain some of my lost coordination, and practice something I enjoy, I'll be happy. That's not asking much, is it? There's so little else left. . . ." Her throat thickened as sadness unexpectedly washed over her. What was with her? It took all she had not to crumple into tears, like she used to in the early days after waking.

"You . . . left someone behind."

"I left a lot of people behind."

"Family, I know. But what of a husband?"

She shook her head. "I wasn't married."

"Never?"

"No. Not that I was against it. I hadn't found the right guy yet."

"No lover?" he asked, his hands hard at work. Did he sound hopeful, or was it only her imagination?

"I had a boyfriend, yes."

Cam followed Kublai's gaze to the hand she'd brought without realizing it to the base of her throat. "He gave me a necklace," she said quietly, not believing she was telling this man all the things she'd previously kept private, even from nosy Zhurihe. "It was a pearl on a chain. I picked up a habit of twirling it." The sad part was that the air force had probably emptied her locker once they realized she was missing and likely killed in action, and given the necklace to her family. Or maybe even back to Matt. "Even now, after all these months, I find myself reaching for it though it's long lost. I think it's an unconscious need to grasp something familiar. Does that make sense? Wanting to hold on to something you wish wasn't gone. Like trying to scratch an itch on a limb long since amputated."

Kublai's hands had all but stopped moving. "From time to time, I still look up from reading the sports news to debate the merits of a favorite team with my father. I find myself speaking before I remember he isn't there. As for the loss of your lover, I am sorry."

Cam lowered her hand. "Matt wasn't the love of my life, Kublai. He was only the man I was dating when I was shot down." Matt had been a sweetie, a nice guy. He was a flight surgeon, a military doctor, but as an officer, the major hadn't been on the fast track. When she'd brought him home to test the waters, she could see the disapproval in her mother's eyes. Matt wouldn't ever be a general like her father; nor would he ever fly. "I liked him." A like that had slowly been turning to love. "But fate pretty much ended the relationship before it had the chance to play out."

She thought of Bree next. She couldn't help it. "I had a friend, though. A very close friend. I think, of everyone outside my immediate family, I miss her the most. I wish . . ." She took a breath to steady herself. "I wish I knew what happened to her." She pressed one hand to her mouth. "Oh, God. I'm sorry. I think she's probably dead, and I'm having a hard time with it."

Kublai stared down at her, as if taken aback by the depth of her grief. Except for his father, and the brother from whom he was estranged, he'd mentioned no attachments. No women. No wife or lovers—or girlfriends; he'd told her that flat-out. She'd bet he was one of those men who hated putting down roots, a man who avoided commitments and making promises, because he knew he was true to his word and didn't want to owe anyone anything. If she had to guess, she'd say that Kublai preferred total freedom—from women, from everything. No wonder he was attracted to the life of a Rim Rider, traversing the borderlands on the back of a horse, like the marshals of the Old West. Once they got to Beijing, she'd probably never see him again.

Disappointment bubbled up inside her. She quashed it. It was just as well they went their separate ways. She had a friend to find, and he . . . well, Kublai had the Rim to patrol. Outside of sappy Saturday-afternoon made-for-television movies, men like that never changed, and damned if she'd be the one to try "fixing" him. She didn't view men as projects. Men were people who came into her life because they added to it. The relationship either worked or it didn't, and if it didn't you moved on.

Except when fate forced your hand.

Her fingers traced over the hollow between her collar-bones. Matt's necklace. She forced away her hand—she hoped for the last time. Matt was a part of her life that was over now. Her attraction to Kublai proved that she was ready to move on.

Kublai's hands were back to massaging her legs. "I'm sorry for the loss of your friend," he offered awkwardly.

She made fists in the dirt. "It should have been me. Not her."

"It's always worse to be the last one standing."

She recognized the pain behind that statement. Her eyes lifted to his, so black in the dark night. "Relax," he ordered gently. "Every time I upset you with my crude attempts to comfort, your muscles harden like rocks."

"Your attempts are not crude. They're charming. You're not upsetting me. You're helping me. And yes, I miss my friend. Terribly. I'm hoping to find her or some word of her in the capital."

He was silent for a time as he worked the kinks out of her quads. "She isn't there."

It took a moment to realize what he'd told her. "W-what?"

He met her incredulous stare. "Banzai Maguire," he enunciated, "is not in the capital."

He'd said it! She no longer had to keep Bree secret. "Is she alive? Where is she now? Is she okay? Does she know I'm alive? When can I see her?" In the midst of her torrent of questions Cam started to sit up, and he eased her back down.

Kublai appeared to regret having said anything at all. "I don't know. No one knows."

"Knows what?" Cam felt ready to explode.

"Her whereabouts. Her condition. It's been weeks since she left."

A shudder ran through her. She'd thought knowing would be worse. It wasn't. This was worse. "She left?"

"She ran away. The prince did all he could to try to bring her back, but she wouldn't hear of it."

"Why?" Cam's voice cracked. "Bree always listens to common sense."

Kublai's hands tightened around her legs. "Not when it comes to you, it seems."

Cam's composure all but gave out. "She left to find me . . . ?" *Just as you wanted to search for her.*

Cam laid her head down and stared up at the stars. She was shaking, she realized, from fear and from joy. Bree was seen alive! And, thanks to this Rim Rider, she now had some real leads to follow once she got to the palace. The prince would help her contact Bree, let her friend know she was safe and in the capital, and they'd be reunited.

She'd have her friend back, someone from her own time who knew and understood her. Her best friend.

Life had suddenly taken a very good turn.

Closing her eyes, Cam gave entirely in to the pleasure of Kublai's hands. A delicious shiver coursed through her as his palms stroked up the long length of her legs and back again. There had been men in her past, good men, yet she never recalled feeling anything like this. Not when they touched her, not even in that first giddy kiss.

In the months since waking, she hadn't really thought of being with a man. First there was the grief, and then the relentless pain. But Kublai from the beginning had reminded her that she was a woman.

She came from a long line of proud Southern belles who understood that femininity didn't cancel out strength. Her craving for a man's strong body in no way made her weak. Quite the opposite, in fact. The exhilaration of her attraction to Kublai made her feel as if she could do anything. Like throwing inhibition to the wind.

Kublai's fingers worked down her inner thigh to her knee and back again. The massage had done wonders for her muscles, but frankly, she wasn't thinking about them anymore. Other, more intimate aches demanded attention.

Only the presence of Nazeem kept her from grabbing Kublai by the shoulders and pulling him down to her to kiss his lights out.

His lights? If he kissed her, she'd probably last all of one second before combusting.

"Do you feel well?"

Sighing, she stretched her arms over her head. "Amazingly well." Kublai's voice was the kind you wanted to hear from your pillow at night. The perfect bedroom voice.

"You look flushed," he told her. His thumbs were doing something incredible a few inches above her knees, moving higher by the second. "I'm concerned about a fever."

"I am a little warm," she agreed, breathless. *Warm? Shoot.* She was burning up. She forced a laugh. "It's getting a little hot out here." In Mongolia. In the winter.

His hands stopped, his eyes turning darker still. He knew exactly what she meant. His eyes didn't leave hers as he propped himself on his hands and leaned over her, his hair soft and falling all around them. She wasn't sure what to read on his face—temptation, gladness, doubt, maybe a little craziness, too. She knew all about that craziness. By now she was half out of her mind. "Let me see," he murmured in that rumbling baritone.

He brought a hand to her forehead to check for fever. She closed her eyes to savor the touch; she couldn't help it. His hand slid to her cheek and stopped there.

She leaned into his warm palm and felt him hesitate. Did he finally comprehend his effect on her?

Now he'd probably withdraw his hand and inform her in a medically businesslike way that she wasn't, in fact, running a fever.

He didn't.

His fingers slid under her jaw, putting gentle pressure there until she tipped up her chin and opened her eyes. He leaned over her, his lips hovering inches from hers, his face shadowed. She helped close the distance by lifting her chin a fraction more.

His mouth was a breath away now, so close now that she could almost taste him, could almost feel the softness of his lips, the scrape of his beard, almost invisible in the swirls of the tattoo. He slid his fingers into her hair. His breath whispered against the corner of her mouth. She sighed, her body reacting instantly with an explosion of tingles. "Nazeem," she murmured.

"Nazeem?" His mouth gave a very unhappy twist. He pushed up on his arms. "No, it's Kublai. But I can summon Nazeem to take my place if you like."

"You idiot," she whispered. "I was going to ask if he was asleep, so when I kissed you I'd know he wasn't watching."

"When you kissed me . . ." Kublai looked stunned.

"Um. Isn't that what we were fixing to do?"

He sat back on his haunches and shoved a hand through his hair. "What was *I* thinking?"

"I wouldn't speak for knowing your mind, but it sure as sugar looked like what *I* was thinking."

He spread a hand as if about to explain, then dropped it.

"Kublai . . . with nothing to say?" she teased. "I don't believe it." She propped herself up on an elbow. "Let me guess. Your job description forbids fraternization with the bounty."

"That's it." For a second she thought he was going to snap his fingers. "Prince Kyber forbids any interaction between us. He . . . ah . . . he doesn't want it."

She lifted her brows. "He micromanages to that extent—who rides on your horse, and whom you kiss?"

"Such as it is." To Kublai's credit, he looked very unhappy about the situation.

"Massages are okay, though."

"Why, of course—if needed for the continued good health of the bounty."

"Why do I have the feeling you made that rule up?"

A corner of his mouth lifted in a wry twist. "Because already you know me better than most."

151

"Not nearly as well as I'd like," she countered in a quiet voice.

He reached down and smoothed her hair away from her upturned face, stroking her, his large hand surprisingly smooth. "You always say what you think. . . ."

"You don't, though."

His smile turned rueful. "It's complicated."

"You're married?"

"No." He frowned. "God, no."

Well, his thoughts on matrimony couldn't have been clearer, she thought with an inner smirk. "It's just complicated, though."

"Yes."

Rolling her eyes, she shook her head. "It's always complicated. Everyone likes to say that, but I don't buy it. You open your mouth and words come out—what's so complicated about that?"

"Lie down, Cam."

"Don't get my hopes up again, you tease."

At that he tossed his head back and let out a delighted laugh. It was contagious. When they'd quieted to chuckles, Kublai pointed to her bedroll imperiously, as if he were a king. "Lie down."

"Only if you join me."

"That's the entire point."

She flashed a victorious smile and stretched out on the sleeping mat. She realized how drained her body was when she barely had the strength to roll onto her side.

Kublai settled next to her before she had the chance to grow cold. He moved close behind her, laying a heavy arm over her hips. She inched her butt backward until she'd made solid contact. Even with leather serving as a barrier, he couldn't hide the fact that he was every bit as affected by her as she was by him. A delicious shiver coursed through her as he began to rub the back of her neck, working his way ever so slowly down to the hem of her shirt, where he slipped his hand under the garment, pressing and kneading over the fabric of her computer-controlled underclothes.

"Feel good, pretty one?" His breath felt hot against her ear.

"Mmm. Very."

It didn't take long for fatigue to overwhelm her.

Kublai's touch became lighter and lighter. Then, just as she drifted off, she felt the press of his lips to the top of her head.

He'd kissed her! But he'd waited until he thought she was asleep. Well, she wouldn't ruin it for him by revealing she'd noticed.

I do believe he likes you. That small kiss proved that Kublai's on-again-off-again behavior had nothing to do with Prince Kyber, and everything to do with his confusion about her. Growing up in a house full of men, she'd learned a few things along the way. Kublai displayed all the symptoms of "like"—the mood swings, the cold shoulder immediately after reaching a level of intimacy that violated his comfort level, the inordinate amount of time spent looking at her mouth.

Would she see him again after they reached the capital?

Kublai, she had the feeling, would say no. He'd make up some convenient rule.

If he did, she'd figure out a way around it.

Never underestimate Cameron Tucker. It was her last thought before sheer exhaustion swept her away.

* * *

The next morning it was time to make the switch from horseback to something called a magcar. Soon after dawn, they broke through the woods near the road it used: a furrow lined with silver coils.

Kublai jumped down from the horse first. As always, he caught Cam around the waist and lowered her to the ground. Their eyes met, held. *Last night was great*, she tried to tell him without speaking. The massage was on the surface a simple act, yet one that somehow had felt like a prelude to something more, something better. Maybe she would have found out if she hadn't fallen asleep.

If you hadn't tucked me in my bedroll before going off to sleep in your own bed, gentleman that you are, Kublai.

He averted his gaze and briskly moved her out of his way.

Arms folded over her chest, she watched him stalk off to Nazeem. He hadn't said more than a couple of syllables to her all morning. It was the "morning after" syndrome, except, technically, it wasn't really an "after." Nothing had happened. *Damn it.*

"Hurry along, Cam. We don't want you lost in the woods after three days of riding." Nazeem's voice jerked her out of her thoughts. Waiting for her to catch up, he smiled kindly before joining Kublai, who had just taken down the nanoshield: high-tech, computer-generated masking device that had camouflaged the Rim Riders' sleek, gunmetal-gray vehicle.

"Wow," she murmured. "That's some hotshot car."

All business, Kublai said, "It will get us where we need to go."

"I'm sure it will," she replied under her breath. It was yet another reminder that the journey was almost over. He was back to being the bounty hunter, and she was back to being the fugitive the king had demanded.

Something plunked onto Cam's head, then her shoulder. She lifted her face to the sky. Cold drops stung her face.

The rain that had held off all day was finally coming down. By the time she approached the magcar, raindrops pattered loudly on the tall, dry grass and scrub and the vehicle's hood.

"Open," Kublai said. The doors slid back, revealing a dark interior. "Inside you'll be dry," he advised.

"Sure. Thanks." She settled down into a rear passenger seat. There were seat belts and a dashboard. Overhead lights. It was hard not to be homesick; there was more reminding her of her world in this one vehicle than there'd been on the entire farm in Mongolia. Would she feel the same way about Beijing?

After helping Nazeem stow the horses in a separate rear compartment, Kublai took his place in the driver's seat and started the magcar. They lurched forward, bumping over the ground to the furrow she'd seen. The gleaming coils were now glowing.

"Arrays of permanent magnets," Kublai explained without her having to ask. He always sensed what she was going to say before she said it. "Once on the track, all the magcar has to do is move forward to achieve levitation."

"Levitation?" *Cool.* Cam leaned forward in her seat. The vehicle slid into the furrow with a solid click and rolled over the coils. When it reached the speed of a fast walk, Kublai said, "Here we go," and the magcar surged forward.

The acceleration was incredible, and that was speaking from the viewpoint of an F-16 pilot. Next Cam heard the wheels retract. They weren't riding on the track anymore, but were flying inches above it.

Flying cars. Magical computers. Now, this was the future of *The Jetsons* that she'd always imagined.

The scenery was a blur. Her hands opened and closed restlessly. "Can I have a try? "I may not be able to walk very well, but I bet I can drive just fine."

That broke Kublai's stone-faced silence. "No."

"Please," she wheedled.

His mouth moved in a way that told her he was trying hard not to laugh at the sight of her hands pressed together. "You do not know the way."

"So it's not that I've never driven a magcar before; it's that I don't know what route to take."

"Correct."

She supposed she could swallow that.

They traveled the rest of the way in silence, Cam with her attention riveted outside. Soon the countryside gave way to larger towns and then cities with soaring buildings sporting walls that changed colors and even shapes.

"You look astonished, Cam."

At the sound of Kublai's mellow baritone, Cam blinked and sat back in her seat for the first time in what felt like hours. "You sleep for a hundred and seventy years and things change. I hate to ask it, but are we there yet?"

"We're at the outskirts of the capital."

The faces of the buildings changed in a never-ending show. "Look at that. Giant moving billboards. It's incredible, this place."

156

Kublai made a sound of approval. "The prince does a fine job of urban planning, does he not?"

Nazeem answered with a faint snort. Cam glanced from one man to the other. There was always a curious undercurrent flowing between the two. More often than not, she felt as if most of it flew right over her head.

She sat back in her seat and took in the sheer immensity of the Beijing suburbs, if that was what one called this urban sprawl. "It's frustrating knowing Bree's not here, and that wherever she is, she's wasting her time looking for me. I've got to get the prince to help me. He saw her alive. He'll have an idea where she may have gone. Better than us, anyway."

Kublai's hands tightened on the steering stick.

"As soon as we arrive, I'll request an audience with him."

"Good luck," Kublai muttered.

She frowned at that. "I'm going to find her, Kublai."

"You've been given a new life here. A good life."

"Bree's all I have left from my world. She's my best friend. It's going to take a lot more than this to get me to give up. I'll talk to the prince."

"The prince has more important things to occupy his time."

"Is that what you'd like to hear Nazeem say to someone if you were missing? Would you give up that fast if it were Nazeem who were lost? Why are you discouraging me?"

"Why? You ask me why?" he growled as he drove. "Because the immoral, imperialist scum in the UCE think you belong to them. Because they'll do most anything to get you back within their borders. And because too many are willing to use you for nothing more than their own selfish gain."

Kublai turned to her. His black eyes were hot with anguish, a level of emotion she hadn't expected. "Because if your search takes you outside the capital, you'll be captured or killed. It's not a matter of how, but when."

In two heartbeats his stare had drained her.

No one said anything as they approached the city gates, where two huge-beyond-belief gold statues stood guard.

A soft glow moved over their vehicle, analyzing it before moving on to the next, then the one after. A security check, unobtrusive and efficient, according to Kublai.

The gold statues towered over the magcars. "The first king and queen," said Nazeem, seeming relieved at the chance to distract them all with an impromptu travelogue of the grand city unfolding in front of them.

And Cam listened to him. Listened hard. Kublai's reaction had put everything back in sharp focus. Her mission? To find out where her flight leader had disappeared to.

Bree had been in the palace; that was a starting point. Now it was up to her to find out the rest. Bree wouldn't just run away. There was more to the story. Come hell or high water, Cam was going to find out what had occurred.

First on the checklist? Learn as much as possible about the palace and the people who lived in it—including their purportedly flesh-eating Prince Kyber.

Chapter Twelve

Late-morning sunshine tried to work its way through the clouds. Puddles from the recent rain filled the cracks between ancient flagstones in a courtyard where the delivery was made at long last. Three pairs of boots splashed through the water as Kyber, Nikolai, and Cam strode toward waiting palace officials.

And all of them were keeping Cam far from the eyes of the prince, Kyber thought, fighting to keep his personal feelings on the matter from clouding his better judgment.

He had to hand her over. He had no choice but to avoid her now and in the days to come.

Not only was his mission over, with Cam brought to safety, but she'd seeped into the cracks in his armor as no woman yet had. Perhaps that was the biggest reason he didn't want to have her near him. She had a way of causing him to let down his guard. He wasn't sure what he thought of that effect, only that he preferred not to think of it at all. In fact, the moment he stepped into the palace, he'd bury himself in work, which had long been a solution to unwanted distractions.

Minister of Realm Affairs Horace Hong stepped to the head of the welcoming party. He was the highest ranking of the ministers, and the only one who knew the Rim Riders' true identities.

"Minister Hong will take over from here," Kyber told Cam.

Cam's cautious blue eyes shifted from Kyber to Hong, who greeted her with a pleasant nod. "I will oversee your transition to palace residency. Come, I'll help you get settled."

Kyber thrust out his hand. "Not so fast, Hong. You have the goods. I want my money."

"The goods?" he heard Cam mutter.

Kyber tried to pretend she wasn't standing next to him, watching him with incredulity. "Where is our payment?"

Hong handed him a money card. Kyber pretended to test its authenticity by holding it up to the light before slipping it into his pocket. "Call us when the good prince is next in need of our services, Horace." He hoisted his travel pack over one shoulder. "Ready, Nazeem? The Serpent Quarter awaits. Ah, the Hollow Heart Bar and Grill. Wine, women, and song for two weary travelers." He turned to Cam. "Farewell, pretty one. I wish you good days and memorable nights."

"So that's it?" she asked. Her wide blue eyes searched his face. Her lips were curved and parted slightly. Did she not know that when she looked at him that way, when she touched his arm, she all but begged him to kiss her?

You cannot. You must walk away. Now.

"My job is done."

"You made that part clear. Only I'd expected a little more than being dropped off like a sack of mail."

Did she not know how she affected him? Did she not see how he wanted to take her with him and retreat to his chambers, losing himself in her, keeping her by his side until morning, and all the mornings after? Not for the first time since beginning this journey did he find himself wishing he were as free as Kublai.

Why can't you be with her as Kyber? A thousand reasons, he blustered silently. He was not ready to marry, for one. "Had I known you wanted special treatment, Cam, I'd have had you gift wrapped."

Her nostrils flared, and she released him like a hot stone. "Good days and memorable nights to you, too, sir."

He turned on a heel and strode off with Nikolai. He couldn't get away from Cam fast enough. Nikolai was almost jogging to keep up. The chief knew better than to attempt conversation as they headed toward a private entrance into the palace, where Kyber would retreat to his quarters to bathe away the dust of the road—and the awareness that Cameron Tucker was living within the same walls as he.

The prince's minister ushered Cam into the palace proper. She slowed to take in the sight of the almost cathedral-like grand hallway. Despite her weariness, the grandeur took her breath away—and almost made her forget Kublai's brushoff.

The floors, the walls, even the ceiling were all made out of solid cream-colored marble. More statues like the ones guarding the gates of the city stood here, two rows of grim soldiers, fifteen feet tall, at least, and made of gold. "The Hall of Ancestors," Minister Hong explained.

Leaded windows framed a view of towers and turrets. Cam had slowed to take a look outside, limping badly, when the minister clapped his hands twice. "Hydro-cart."

A robotic, supercharged wheelchair glided out of a dark alcove and stopped in front of them. "Is that for me?"

He took the handles in his hands. "If you don't mind."

If he was nice enough to offer, she'd be polite enough to accept. She sat down.

"I'll be bringing you to your private quarters, where the palace physicians await you," Hong explained. "Once they examine you and prescribe your course of treatment, you are free to move about at will."

"I can leave the palace?" Kublai had sounded so worried about her safety.

"In fact, I encourage it. See the sights. Experience the city and all it has to offer. I shall make myself available to escort you anywhere you like. All you have to do is ask."

"Thank you." She smiled at the minister over her shoulder. He was somewhat older than Kublai, and a nice-looking man. And he seemed awfully accommodating.

"Breakfast is on the way from the kitchens, as well," Hong said as he walked behind the wheelchair. The thing was running under its own power, apparently.

"I'm not very hungry." Now, *that* was a first.

"I will request that the meal be put aside and a light snack be brought to your room instead."

Mercy. This treatment was top-notch. She wasn't sure what she'd expected from Prince Kyber, but it wasn't this.

But all the politeness in the world couldn't replace a face-to-face meeting. "Minister Hong . . ."

"Horace, please."

"Horace. I would like to meet with the prince as soon as possible. This afternoon, preferably."

Hong made a small choking noise similar to Nazeem's. "It will not be tonight. I assure you of that."

"Tomorrow, then?"

His voice sounded tight, as if he were clenching his jaw. "It is difficult to arrange an audience with the prince. He is a busy man."

"Look, he sent Rim Riders all the way to Mongolia to bring me here. I think he wants to see me."

"I will endeavor to arrange it."

"Thank you." She closed her hands over the armrests. "I would have thought the prince would have been waiting at the back door, the way he was so anxious to get me back to the palace."

"The prince waits for no one."

"I'm getting that impression. He probably doesn't have time, what with all the micromanaging, ordering who rides on whose horse and all that."

Horace probably thought her irreverent, and not as respectful as she ought to be about royalty. "I'm an American," she explained.

The man made another sound in his throat, the kind that meant nothing and everything at the same time. "On the subject of the prince," he began.

"Yes? Yes?"

"If the reason you wish to speak with him is on the subject of Banzai Maguire, the UCE may be in a better position to assist you in your queries."

163

The UCE? Hmm. She hadn't thought of that. She got the impression everyone here hated the UCE. As for her, the jury was still out. She didn't yet know enough to form an opinion. What did anger her tremendously was the United States for becoming the UCE. How could the government have allowed that to happen?

"Though . . ." the minister went on thoughtfully, "Prince Kyber doesn't care to reach out to other nations for help."

To Cam, it sounded as if the Kingdom of Asia were as isolationist as the UCE was imperialist. Yin and yang. What a world!

Horace wheeled her through a set of massive double doors, three feet thick, at least, and carved with scenes from Oriental folklore. Doors off to each side looked like they led to bedrooms. Bedrooms upon bedrooms. Enormous paintings hung from the walls. By Salvador Dalí, she realized, recognizing *The Persistence of Memory* immediately, the painting of the melting clock. Prince Kyber, the richest, most powerful man in the world, would not fill his walls with prints. The paintings had to be real. Money, it was obvious, was not a factor in the interior decorating.

Horace stopped at one of the bedroom doors and stuck his fingers into a recess in the wall. The door slid aside to reveal a large room both comfortable and high-tech.

It contained everything Zhurihe had told her no longer existed. Cam's lingering hurt at the girl's lies stung even more now that she saw the proof of her friend's deception.

A smiling woman dressed in white physician's clothes

met her at the door. "Welcome, Miss Tucker," she said. "I am Dr. Park. Your physician."

Cam's heart lodged in her throat. *Speak of the devil.* "Zhurihe?" Minus the braids, it was her! No, Cam thought, taking a closer look; this woman was a good twenty years older, and with more elegant features, but, mercy, they could be twins.

The woman's smile was kind. "My first name is Dae. You may call me that if you like."

"Whatever you prefer, ma'am," Cam said. "It's . . . it's . . . it's just that you look like someone I know."

"Perhaps you have already met one of us." The woman turned. "Min, come. Meet Miss Tucker."

The new woman also wore the white clothes of a physician and was, like Dr. Park, an older, taller, more beautiful and sophisticated version of Zhurihe. "This is Dr. Park. Min Park."

"The pleasure is mine, Miss Tucker." The sister wore her black hair long and loose. She tossed it over her shoulder and bent her head in greeting. "As a psychiatrist, I look forward to assisting you in your recovery."

"Thank you," Cam said, almost robotically. This was too weird, the resemblance to Zhurihe.

The Parks brought her to a comfortable chair. Other women worked in various capacities around the large bedroom, assisting the doctors, cleaning up. Dressed in plain gray scrubs, they were even closer in age and appearance to Zhurihe. They were shorter than the Park doctors, but unlike Zhurihe, their eyes were dull, their mouths slack. Were they mentally disabled? Was that why they worked at menial tasks?

"Is there anyone here named Zhurihe?" Cam asked the doctor.

She thought she saw one of the worker girls lift her head. By the time she focused on the group again, all of them were bent to their tasks. Cam narrowed her eyes, suspicion pricking her. Did one of them know who Zhurihe was? Did they recognize the name? She decided to keep an eye on the girls.

Dr. Park shook her head. "I can have the staff do a search for you. In what sector of the city does she reside?"

"She . . ." Cam thought of all of Zhurihe's questionable activities and nixed the idea. "She lives out of town. Do you have any sisters who live outside Beijing?"

Dr. Park made a small frown and shook her head. "We all reside here. Inside the palace. Seven living, all told."

"Are y'all sisters? The younger ones look like a set of quintuplets."

"No." Dr. Park lowered her voice, hinting at embarrassment. "They're clones, not sisters."

Clones. Mercy. "Clones . . . of you?"

"The emperor said he wanted more of me—and so he had more made."

"Prince Kyber manufactures clones?" That was almost as bad as eating peasants, in her opinion.

The doctor shook her head as she took readings from Cam and fed them into a handheld computer. "It was his father, the emperor. Price Kyber is acting emperor."

That's right. The emperor was in a vegetative coma.

"He made six copies of you. . . ." The thought boggled.

"There were nine altogether, each with varying degrees of capability. Min, the first clone, is brilliant. Her hand—eye coordination wasn't quite perfect enough for her to become a surgeon, but her talents are well suited for the field of psychiatry."

Min nodded, smiling at Cam's wide-eyed wonder. *A clone. Imagine that.*

Again, Cam peered at the group of gray-clad server clones. The one Cam had noticed looking at her was busy pouring liquid into a larger jug. Her hand was small. All her fingers were wrapped around the pitcher's handle except the pinkie she held straight out. Just like Zhurihe!

Cam narrowed her eyes. Coincidence?

"My second genetic copy became an excellent medical technician," Dae explained. "The fourth, fifth, and sixth, with decreasing levels of abilities, were fit to be servants only, as you see."

Cam glanced at the Zhurihe look-alikes and counted. "Where are the other three?"

"They are no longer with us." Dr. Park was taking a scan of Cam's heart. Her head was forward, hiding her expression from view. "They were put down in childhood. Inadequate brain function."

"Put down?"

"Euthanized."

Cam stared at the servant girls, who appeared oblivious to the conversation. What kind of place had she come to? "You kill people for low IQ?"

"They were not people," Dr. Park said, pleasantly, as if talking about something as harmless as flower arranging. "They were clones."

Her dismissal of these humans, no matter what their genetic makeup, was horrifying. Yet Cam sensed no evil in the doctor. Had she any right to judge a culture in which she was a stranger, an outsider? Sure she did. To ignore something was the same as supporting it. She didn't know how or when, but she vowed to do something, anything, to change the attitude toward clones.

Both doctors moved toward Cam, and the tests began.

After several rounds of therapies that actually left her feeling better, Dr. Park lifted a device Cam had learned administered medication like the needles of her time, only much less painfully. "One more thing to do, and then we are done for today, Miss Tucker. Tomorrow we will meet and discuss the results of the exams. From there, we'll design a program to increase your muscle mass and strength."

"And coordination? My balance isn't very good."

"Do you not feel the results our initial treatment already?"

Cam opened and closed a hand. "Maybe, yes, a little."

"You will notice even more as the day wears on. Now, hold still, please." The doctor gently moved Cam's head to the side, lifting her hair away from the back of her neck. Cam winced as something sank into her nape. "Ow. That one burned." She rubbed the skin. There was a small lump. "What was that for?"

"It is a prox-beacon. Harmless, really."

A flicker of alarm went through her. "What does a prox-beacon do?"

"It assures the prince that you will remain within the city walls." The woman flashed a kind smile. "He really is quite worried about you."

"Enough to make me a prisoner. Tell me more about what you put in me. Will it reveal my whereabouts? My thoughts?"

Park's laughter was almost musical, this physician who didn't object to copies of herself being put to sleep with no more thought than one swatted flies. "If that were the case, every husband and every wife in all the empire would be requesting one for their spouse. A prox-beacon simply causes discomfort should you move outside the protected area."

Cam frowned, rubbing the lump on her neck.

"Please," the doctor urged. "You will irritate the incision. Once the swelling goes down, you will forget all about it."

"Until I try to scale the city walls and get out," Cam said irritably.

"I am certain that if you need to depart the area, the prince will be happy to deactivate the beacon."

"How does one . . . shut it off?"

The woman was too smart to fall for that. "One comes to a suitably equipped medical office. It is not really a single beacon, you see, but thousands of microscopic alarms that remain in the vicinity of your neck and skull."

She wiped her hands and stood. "One of my attendants will see to your comfort, as I must leave to attend to my other duties."

Like wounding baby animals.

"Joo-Eun!" the doctor called out to the group of slack-jawed gray-clad girls.

Three of them glanced nervously at the one who kept her head down, the one with the uplifted pinkie and the interest in Cam. *Hmm . . .* Clone status notwithstanding, each person was an individual with her own mannerisms and quirks. No matter how closely the Park clones resembled each other, after only a few minutes observing them

Cam had already noticed traits that set them apart. In Joo-Eun, especially.

"Joo-Eun, please," Dr. Park said with a hint of impatience.

The girl raised her head, her braids swinging. Just like Zhurihe's.

But really, how could they be one and the same? How could Zhurihe live in two different places? Then Cam thought of the magroads and flying cars and realized it was possible to get back and forth in a day or so if one didn't go by horse.

Yet when the girl met Cam's eyes, it was with a stare that was so vacant Cam found herself wondering if anyone could fake something like that.

"Joo-Eun is simple," Dr. Park explained. "Unfortunately her difficulties seem to be getting worse over time. I don't know how much longer she . . ." The doctor sighed. "Never mind. You may have to repeat your instructions several times if she seems not to understand. Remember to speak clearly." She turned to the girl. "Prepare Miss Tucker's bath, please, Joo-Eun. Stay with her to see to her needs."

Reluctantly, the girl left the others. In a shuffling walk, she did as she was asked, her eyes downcast and her face averted. It pricked Cam's sympathy. Bless her heart, she was a ghost of the vibrant Zhurihe.

Something definitely drew her to this simple girl. Was it just her resemblance to her former friend?

Or *was* she her former friend?

The moment the other women left the room, Cam pushed out of her chair with more control over her body than she'd had since waking in this future world. She felt lighter on her feet, almost graceful. She was practicing walking when Joo-Eun returned from arranging towels and clothing next to a large, round in-floor tub.

The girl bowed, bent over nearly double as she backed toward the door. "Will that be all?"

"I thought your instructions were to stay."

The girl's mouth made the tiniest of twitches. "As you wish."

"But you never did stay, did you? You'd always leave— for days, and even weeks at a time. Why was that?"

The servant remained silent.

"Could it be you were doubly employed . . . here in the palace?" Cam walked closer to the fidgeting girl. "And on a farm in Mongolia? Were you spying on me, or on him? Or both of us?"

Meekly, the girl shook her head. A flicker of guilt kept Cam from interrogating the servant any further.

Pushing her hair off her forehead, Cam turned away. "Sorry. Go. Just go." It was sensory overload, too much to absorb in one day. Her longing for closure with Zhurihe was making her think this servant girl was her, and now she'd gone and frightened one of Prince Kyber's servants.

In the hush of the luxurious bedroom, Cam heard the door swish closed, and, a fraction of a second later, a squeak of a sneeze.

Her head jerked around. Zhurihe! No one else sneezed like that. No one.

Cam pushed on the door. It didn't budge. Then she remembered one of the conversations she'd had with Kublai on horseback. Nearly everything operated using voice commands. "Open!" The door slid aside and Cam burst into the marble corridor. "Zhurihe!"

The girl took off running at full speed. What had happened to the shuffle?

"Zhurihe!" Cam bolted after her. Although the medicine had done wonders for her, she didn't have the stamina to catch the fleeing servant. Cam jogged to a stop in the middle of the empty corridor, her chest heaving.

The plot thickens, Cam thought. The girl was Zhurihe; she was sure of it. What she was doing here in the prince's palace as part of an army of clones was something Cam was bound and determined to find out.

Chapter Thirteen

Kyber sat on his throne, one knee bent, the other leg stretched out in front of him. From the dais, he received briefings from his cabinet ministers on all that had transpired in his absence.

And he was bored as hell.

His thoughts drifted to Cam. How many times had she asked to see him? He'd lost count. It worried him, to say the least. He'd already learned that Cameron Tucker was not a woman easily discouraged. Several times now he'd considered giving in to her requests, granting her an audience. Would she recognize him? Perhaps not visually, but she'd know his voice. As Prince Kyber, he'd have to see her eventually, and endure the questions about Banzai that he'd be unable to answer to her liking. Yes, as soon as she no longer affected him, he'd throw the doors to his reception room wide-open.

A particularly vivid replay of Cam falling asleep in his arms invaded his mind. He blocked it. He'd never had difficulty putting other women out of his mind, Banzai Maguire included.

Propping his elbow on an armrest, Kyber supported his heavy head with two fingers as the minister of culture approached. "How was the summit, Your Highness?" she asked brightly.

A summit on education: that had been his cover story. "Very good, Minister. Much was accomplished." More than he'd ever intended.

"Was the weather fine?"

"Yes." *And the company was even better.*

"Excellent. I'm pleased to hear it."

He checked his watch. Why hadn't Dae Park reported to him yet regarding Cam's latest tests? He'd like to throttle the rebels who had woken her from stasis without the proper training. He would have the physician message him immediately after the meeting with his cabinet. No, better to have Dae report to him in person. . . .

"Thank you, Your Highness."

Kyber blinked as the minister of culture took a few steps backward and curtsied. It hit him that he'd just conducted an entire conversation without remembering a single word. Not since he was fourteen had a woman so captured his thoughts. That the episode in question was the morning after he'd lost his virginity, being distracted had been expected. It wasn't now.

All the more reason to control his thoughts, to stay away from Cam until his objectivity had returned. Thoughts led to action, and he would not, could not, take action regarding her. Not when it came to his heart, that was. He knew that once he took Cam as a mistress, he'd want more. And if he wasn't mistaken, so would she.

He wasn't ready for more. Visions of his mother and the upkeep she'd required of his father over the years haunted him. Marriage—bah. Merely thinking about the complications of it all gave him a headache.

Stifling a groan, he pushed himself upright on his throne. The thing was damn uncomfortable. Why didn't he insist on a regular chair? *Because Father ruled from this throne.* Yes, and since he wanted to prove as good an emperor as his father, he'd taken nearly all the man's customs as his own.

A throne does not a ruler make. Cam had told him that while on their journey. He missed their hours-long, rambling conversations, never tired of listening to the exotic flavor her accent gave the boring words he'd long known. She spoke "Southern," she'd explained to him during one of those two days of riding. Kyber smiled. Her speech was the verbal equivalent of honey.

Minister Hong walked up to the dais, clearly pleased by the warm reception that had nothing to do with him. "We have the latest images from the UCE—the colony of Central, where the tax protest is taking place."

Kyber sobered. "Display them."

The wall ahead pixilated into riot-filled streets. Protestors threw rocks, and police dressed in riot gear fought the protesters back. Kyber sat up straighter as the image of several police throwing off their riot gear to join the protesters sank in. What would it take to push what was happening in Central to a full-fledged revolution? Not much, he thought. A lasting spark. A defining moment. And then it would be over. "It's gotten worse over there since I've been away. Much worse. Ideas, Niko?"

"I believe the unrest is feeding off UCE government

reaction. Every move Beauchamp makes to quell the trouble worsens it. The curfews, the arrests, the travel restrictions—it's exacerbated it all. However, the government insists they're firmly in control."

"Beauchamp," Kyber spat. "He wouldn't know a lie from a lily pad." Yet, watching the images change to different crowds and different cities—all in Central—he didn't see any telltale signs that the government *had* lost control.

The anger and passion of the protesters was near to boiling over, though. Flags waved, and plenty of them, but they weren't the flag of any country he knew. What had Cam called it—the Stars and Stripes?

The image switched to another protest, this one more massive than the others. "New Washington, DC," he grumbled. "Fort Powell. I remember the reports from some time ago of abuses practiced on the political prisoners held there. And the UCE had the gall to accuse the Kingdom of Asia of violating basic humanitarian practices?"

As the scenes played before his eyes, the streets of the UCE capital besieged by chaos, in his mind's eye he envisioned the stately, tree-lined streets of downtown Beijing teeming with angry citizens. "Let us make damn sure *that* doesn't reach here."

That raised heartier-than-usual murmurs of agreement from his cabinet.

Kyber lifted a hand, his finger drifting until he found his minister of defense. "Realm Admiral Moon. Beef up security at the borders, and all around the Rim. Send out extra Rim Riders and report any irregularities to me."

"Done, Your Highness."

"Take those measures and double them."

Moon dipped his head in answer.

The worse the situation in Central became, the higher his concern. At all cost he must keep his Shangri-la intact. To do that, he must let the chaos outside the borders play out as fate intended. As for the chaos reigning inside his palace walls . . . well, that was another matter entirely.

"He refused to see me?" Cam fisted her hands, wanting to growl. *What a jerk!*

Then, somehow, she managed to politely thank the palace staffer who'd brought the news that Prince Kyber was too busy to meet with her. Again! As furious as she was at the apparent brushoff by the prince, she refused to take it out on the staffer. Even if it was the sixth request the prince had refused. In two days. No, three, if she counted the day she'd arrived here. And if she was back-dating, that would make it ten requests, not six.

The man took a step back, bowed, and left.

Cam swept her hair away from her face, holding it there with two hands as she walked to a panoramic picture window. All her pleading for an audience with the prince in the name of Bree's safety had gotten her nowhere. It didn't make sense. Prince Kyber clearly wanted her here, and now that she was living under his nose, he wanted nothing to do with her. He wouldn't even give her five minutes of his time!

She was almost ready to take Minister Hong up on his offer of contacting the UCE to see if they could help her. The only thing holding her back was his warning that Prince Kyber didn't take kindly to reaching outside his neatly sealed borders for any help. She wasn't at the stage

177

yet where she could afford to piss off the prissy prince. She needed him. She needed to be nice. But if his rudeness went on any longer . . .

It was after five, and the sun had set. The orderly peace of evening had taken over the streets outside the palace. People went to and from stores, picking up items on their way home. The children were plump and happy, and unlike in the China of her day, many families had more than one—and that included girls.

But something marred the apparent perfection: Bree's disappearance. The prince had ignored Cam's every attempt to learn why.

Could Kublai help her?

Lord, she missed him. She missed his deep voice and hearty laugh. His teasing, too. He gave back as good as he got, and she respected that in a man. Yeah, he had a tendency to be condescending, and a little pigheaded, but it was part of his roguish charm. And they'd shared that moment of attraction. . . .

Where did he live? She had no idea. Then she remembered something he'd said the day he exchanged her for the bounty money. The Serpent Quarter—a pub called the Hardened Heart. No, Hollow, the Hollow Heart. That was where he drank. And if he was like most men of his type, he'd be heading there now for a few drinks with his friends.

How difficult would it be to find him? She'd been given a cash stipend, and hadn't used a cent. She'd buy him a drink in exchange for his views on the prince's irritating attitude.

Yes, she thought, her heart giving a little skip. Kublai had an opinion on everything. Plus, he seemed to know the prince, certainly better than she did. He had to be Prince Kyber's number one fan, if nothing else. There was a very good chance that Kublai could convince Prince Kyber to see her.

Cam went to her computer and entered *Serpent Quarter* in the location finder. There it was, approximately four square blocks in the northernmost corner of the palace district. She brought up the map on a flexible, portable computer screen as thin and as light as a piece of paper. She rolled it up to shove in her pocket, then hesitated.

Wait. She had a better idea.

She'd bathe, get prettied up. Mama always said that when wanting to impress a man, always make sure you looked your best.

Especially, Cam thought with a smile, when you were hoping he'd do you a favor.

Kyber emerged from his bathing pool to find a woman stretched out nude on his bed. He halted in the middle of scrubbing a towel through his hair.

Smiling at his attention, the woman arched her back, lazily lifting an arm and running long, delicate fingers over her abdomen to the gold rings she wore in her nipples. The jewelry made small, bell-like tinkles in the suddenly silent room.

How did she get in here? was his first thought. Then he remembered that a woman was always brought to his room in the evenings unless he requested otherwise, as he had the past three nights since returning from the Rim. He didn't always make love to the women before dismissing them; sometimes he merely kept them around for the pleasure of their attentive company, which was slightly more interactive—and usually more entertaining—than that of the palace felines and ferrets.

He walked closer, close enough to discern the scent of her body from the light aroma of her perfume. "I know you," he said. "You were the manicurist." She was the lovely young woman who had tended to his feet and hands the day he and Nikolai left to find Cam.

Her fingers circled the nipple ring. "Yes. My name is Anjali. They said you were interested in seeing me, Your Highness."

Yes, he thought. He had been.

Ten days ago.

She rolled onto her stomach, her elbows tucked, lifting her hips invitingly. Any other time, Kyber would have gone to her without another word and buried himself inside her body.

When he didn't, she peeked over her shoulder. "Would you like to come to bed?" Her dark brown eyes had turned even darker with sexual arousal.

He took a robe from the back of a chaise and draped it over her. Her rear end dropped to the mattress. "Do you not want my company?" she asked, her mouth forming a perfect pout.

Kyber sat heavily on the edge of the bed. "It is not you, my sweet." What was it then? "I shall pass this night alone." *As you have all the nights since arriving home from the Rim?*

Instead of kissing the woman good-bye, of all things, he reached out and ruffled her silken curls. "Go on. Get dressed."

Then, with a sigh, he drew the towel around his hips

and walked to his balcony. The weather was cold, and so he left the French doors closed. Outside, street globes cast citizens running their errands in a soft white light.

He wanted to be out there, not here.

Normally he did not assume his alter ego, Kublai, so soon after a trip to the Rim. It was a risk anytime he left the palace without a retinue of bodyguards, even if the disguise he wore was convincing. Yet the draw was strong, tonight, to escape who he was. Who he was required to be.

He stood for a while, watching his citizens go about their mundane chores. One woman caught his eye. Graceful and standing a full head taller than most of the other women, she hurried across the central square. She didn't wear a hat, as was fashionable, and it allowed the breeze to toss her shoulder-length blond hair.

Something inside him unknotted. She looked like Cam. . . .

She *was* Cam!

He opened up the doors. Cold air rushed over his damp body, and he welcomed it. He'd worked himself to exhaustion so he wouldn't dwell overly much on her presence in the palace—or her repeated requests to see him. But, heaven above, he missed her. He dreamed of her. She'd made him laugh. She'd given him hell. He'd never in his life encountered a woman who could do both. *Go after her.*

Kyber pressed his lips together. After the debacle with Banzai, was he so willing to be played the fool again?

Cam is not Banzai.

He gave his head a shake. No, he couldn't see her. Not until he was sure his emotions were under control.

But Kublai could.

His hand tightened around the door handle. It was madness. It was ill-advised.

You don't know where she is headed, or why.

Hmm. Excellent point. The streets of Beijing were mostly safe, even at night, but a pretty woman out alone? There was always the risk of untoward behavior. He would not tolerate that, or even the risk of it.

Kyber took a breath and stood straighter. For the sake of national security, he would call on the services of his number one bounty hunter to act as bodyguard. No one took better care of Cam Tucker than Kublai.

Throwing his towel to the floor, he went in search of clothes appropriate to the mission.

It was full dark now. Though they contained technology beyond anything in the twenty-first century, the street-lights designed to resemble lanterns cast the Serpent Quarter in a charming glow—atmosphere it probably needed to lend an aura of intrigue. It was one of those areas that by day would appear seedy, but by night glamorous, in a 1940s *Casablanca* sort of way.

It took a while to get used to the billboard buildings. That was the only term Cam could think of to explain it. Entire sides of buildings could, in the blink of an eye, explode in a rainbow of colors, or melt into three-dimensional scenes, or, as was most common, burst into news and advertisements. They were like old Internet pop-up ads you couldn't run away from. But as she walked deeper into the Serpent Quarter, the buildings became older, and the perfectly paved streets more rutted. Atmosphere, she reminded herself.

She ignored the constant barrage of media lighting up almost all available flat, vertical surfaces. Hunching her shoulders against the chill, she drew her leather coat around herself and turned the collar up. She probably should have worn one of the hats she had seen in her closet. All the women had them—ranging from jaunty little caps to enormous flying-saucer affairs. And they weren't plain old hats, either. They glowed, and played music, or the news, or looked like mini versions of the media-playing buildings. Capitalism was alive and well in this kingdom; she wouldn't doubt some of these women were being paid to carry advertisements as fashion statements.

Cam stopped on a street corner to consult her map. There were streets, but no traffic on them other than pedestrian. Cars were restricted to the magroads and electric freeways. Above her head, a virtual air force of sleek jets crisscrossed the sky, taking off and landing vertically from the tops of nearby buildings.

"Headed out for the evening?" asked a pleasant male voice.

Cam spun around. The man looked familiar. She squinted at him in the glow of the streetlight. "Minister Hong?"

"Horace." He smiled and placed his hands behind his back. He wasn't in his official government outfit but an elegant suit. And it was not the kind of clothing one would wear to the Serpent Quarter, if she actually knew what kind of clothing one wore to an area that looked like . . . this.

"Horace, yes. What a surprise to see you here."

"And you. Do you have plans to stay out for the evening?"

"It was getting a little boring in the palace." As an afterthought, she added, "Waiting for Prince Kyber to decide he wants to see me. Are you sure you can't get me in to talk to him?"

Hong flashed white teeth. "Why don't we discuss it over a drink?"

Why don't we not, she thought. Hong was a handsome, elegant man of Chinese ancestry; he'd been nothing but polite to her, but there was something about him tonight that made her want to walk in the opposite direction. Very fast.

She fought the urge to check her watch. If the Rim Rider was in the bar, she didn't want to miss him. And now it looked like the kindly minister wanted to tag along. "I can't. Another time?"

"I know of a place you'll enjoy."

She really wanted to escape. Mama's manners lessons were becoming a more distant memory by the minute. "Another night, Horace. I had my heart set on something."

A rock bounced off Hong's shoulder. He glanced at Cam in surprise, flicking at his suit as if chasing away a fly. "Did you just get hit with a—," she began. Another small rock sailed over the street and plunked off the side of his head. "Are you okay?"

"I am. I—" This time he ducked in time: a rock bounced off the side of the building.

She took him by the arm. "You'd better get out of the street before—"

Another rock bounced off his chest. People were staring at them. Cam pulled the minister down behind a closed produce stand. He was dabbing at his head. "Has this ever happened before?" she asked under her breath.

"Never."

"Someone's definitely aiming for you. Is there a group that might have a problem with a government decision you may have made?"

"The prince makes the decisions. We only act on them."

Why didn't that surprise her? A rock tore through the canopy of the produce stand. "That was close, Horace. Stay here." She peered out from behind the stand, waiting for the next rock. When it came, she was going to see who was throwing it.

She waited, intent and alert, her fighter-pilot instincts turning on. Almost on schedule, another rock zinged past. Judging by the sound of a muffled "oomph," it found its target.

And she had found hers.

Someone—it looked like a child, a boy—ducked around the street corner. Cam took off after him.

The rock thrower popped into view for another launch. Cam jumped him, grabbing him around the waist and pinning his skinny arms. "You ought to be playing baseball." The rock in his hand dropped onto her toe. "Ow. What are you doing? Do you know that's Minister Hong? He's very important. He could arrest you."

The boy couldn't be more than seven or eight. His eyes grew huge at the mention of arrest.

"Tell me why you were throwing rocks, or I'm going to call the police." She wasn't sure how that was done around here, but she'd figure it out.

The boy struggled. "I didn't do it. I didn't."

"I saw you with my own eyes."

"It wasn't my idea. It was hers! She paid me to do it."

Cam followed the boy's frightened gaze—and couldn't believe what she saw: a teenage girl with two long braids darting away at the other end of the alley.

"Zhurihe!" Cam released the boy and took off after her.

The girl jumped a low fence. Cam leaped after her. She turned down another alley. Cam stayed on her tail. "Zhurihe! Wait!"

The alleyway narrowed. A pile of ceramic pots blocked the other end. Zhurihe jumped over the pots, toppling them. She scrambled to her feet seconds before Cam reached her.

Cam stumbled over the fallen pots. Liquid splashed onto her clothes. It smelled sour, almost rotten, and now it was all over her. *Well, this night was a total waste of makeup.* After more than an hour spent getting all prettied up in hopes of seeing Kublai, she'd ended up taking a bath in kimchi!

"Zhurihe! Stop, please." The girl sprinted once more onto the main sidewalk. "I know it's you. I won't hurt you."

They darted in and out of crowds of pedestrians, some who watched with curiosity, others with amusement. Zhurihe threw a wild glance over her shoulder—and collided with a large man. Down she went.

Cam was on her in a second. "Gotcha!" She locked her arms around the squirming girl, squeezing her tighter when she struggled. "My sister—she always runs away," she gasped out to the shocked man. He seemed more concerned about getting away than worried that Zhurihe and Cam looked nothing alike.

Cam wrestled Zhurihe into an alley between two old buildings. They spun, fighting and breathless, bouncing off the brick walls. The efforts Cam had spent sweeping up her hair were for nothing, too. It spun tangled and wild, whipping around her shoulders. "Did you think I wouldn't notice you in the palace? Did you think I wouldn't recognize you?"

Zhurihe's struggles had lessened some, but Cam suspected she had a lot of fight left in her. "And what's with the clone army, *Joo-Eun?* Dr. Park told me you were simple, and getting simpler by the day. You'd better be careful who you fool. Not everyone will take the lies as well as I do. I think Dr. Park might want to weed you out of the gene pool, like she did with the others."

Zhurihe made a sound of such raw pain that Cam loosened her grip. Zhurihe spun away from her, cheeks red from tears and exertion. Cam knew she should be furious with the girl for all the lies, but the expression on Zhurihe's face broke her heart.

"I'm sorry," Cam said. "I shouldn't have said that."

Zhurihe bit her lip, appearing to fight to compose herself. "But you are right. They could make the decision to kill me with no more authority needed than that required to put down a pet. That's all we clones are to them—disposable workers and pets. Experiments, all. Prince Kyber, the entire cabinet—they have the power to change it but they don't. I have the power to make them notice us, and I will."

"Cloning is still new then."

"Yes, but there are thousands of us, and more every day. We are feared and valued. We are freaks and wonders of scientific accomplishment." Zhurihe turned her head.

187

Her breathing ragged, she ran her hands up and down her arms. "With the human race now the creator of life, who needs God?"

"We need God to make sure we don't kill people like you," Cam said quietly.

Zhurihe's chin came up. "You called me a person."

"Isn't that what you are?"

The girl's distraught expression changed to the smile Cam had once counted on to lift her flagging spirits in the bleak days after waking from stasis. "You're also a liar, Zhurihe, and a cheat. A controlling, mean little wench. Maybe you clones are more human than anyone thinks."

Zhurihe's lower lip trembled.

"You hurt me, Zhurihe. You told me everything was gone when you knew this was here."

"I knew if you thought this existed, you'd want to come here."

"And there's something wrong with that?"

"You would have wanted to find Banzai Maguire."

Cam's heart stumbled at the mention of the name. "What do you know about her that I don't?" Her temper flared. She snatched the girl by the collar and half dragged her close. "You know how much she means to me. If you lie this time, Zhurihe, I'll . . . I'll—"

"I know nothing more than you do—I swear it, Cam. This time you have to believe me. She disappeared after leaving the kingdom. Before that, I helped her free Tyler Armstrong from the dungeons. They escaped, and almost died trying."

"Almost died how?"

"Assassins. UCE. It happened in New Seoul."

So, they made it only as far as the former South Korea

before running into the bad guys. Not good. Cam had suspected Kublai was exaggerating in order to keep her close to the palace, overstating the dangers elsewhere in order to force her loyalty to this nation as opposed to the others. Now she saw she may have been wrong.

She'd also been wrong about Zhurihe—very wrong. Her hand twisted in the fabric of the girl's collar. "All those times you were leaving me on the farm, you were working double shifts at the palace. Going back and forth by magcar, right? Bree likely knew you by your palace name—Joo-Eun."

Cam tightened her grip on Zhurihe's collar. The girl wheezed in the affirmative.

"And the entire time you were fixing to help her leave, you were consoling me, telling me that she was dead— and probably telling her the same thing!" Cam pushed her away in disgust. "I can't figure out whether you're a pathological liar or a spy."

"I am neither! I wanted only to keep Bree safe. And you, too, Cam. I have my reasons."

"As selfless as you think your cause is, it doesn't give you the right to play with other people like chess pieces!"

"But I—"

"Shut up, Zhurihe. Just shut up." Grief and resentment threatened to take over. Cam took a couple of steadying breaths. Frowning, she demanded, "And why the hell did you pay that boy to throw rocks at Minister Hong?"

"I wanted him to leave you alone."

They regarded each other warily. "Is Hong dangerous?"

"Stay away from him. Don't listen to him. He's not to be believed."

"How do I know you're not lying again?"

"Trust me."

"I'm supposed to trust *you?*"

Zhurihe's face turned white. "Have to go." She spun on a heel, braids whirling, and ran off into the night.

"Zhurihe! Wait!" Cam started to chase after her when a heavy hand landed on her shoulder, holding her back.

"It's not polite to keep a date waiting, pretty one."

Kublai! She spun around and there he was, standing in front of her: all six-foot-two, tattooed, irresistible bit of him.

Chapter Fourteen

The next thing Cam knew, she was sitting at a dark corner table in the Hollow Heart. Kublai pressed a cold pack to her wrist. "I didn't even feel it," she said. "I think I bashed it when I tripped over those pots."

He wrinkled his nose. "Kimchi." She tried to tug her hand away, but he held fast. "Apply the ice a little longer."

"I want to wash up. I stink."

"I don't mind."

She sighed and let her head sag onto her hand. A lank strand of hair fell over her eyes, and she blew it out of the way. "I haven't had many days worse than this, Kublai. The prince refused to see me for the sixth consecutive time—or the tenth, depending how I count. Then I chase down the boy throwing rocks at Minister Hong and—"

"Minister Hong was in the Serpent Quarter?"

"Yes. And I was as surprised as you are to see him there.

191

Anyway, I chased down the boy tossing the stones and—"

"A child was throwing rocks at Hong?"

"Yes, but someone else told him to do it, and—"

"Who did?"

"She . . ." Cam stopped short of giving an immediate answer. There was the question of Zhurihe's double identity, something she hadn't fully puzzled out yet. Until she had a better idea what was going on, she'd best not share too much and risk putting Zhurihe's life at risk. Kublai was loyal to the prince. If he were to learn of deceit going on in the palace, namely Zhurihe's deceit, it could get the clone killed—if Dr. Park didn't get to her first. As many wrongs as the girl had committed so far, Cam didn't think she deserved to die for them. Her instincts told her that while Zhurihe couldn't be trusted, she wasn't evil. "It was an older girl," she said finally. "A teenager, and she kicked my butt."

"I think it was the other way around."

Cam made a sound halfway between a huff and a snort. "Let's just say she had the advantage of being younger."

"And not having been in biostasis for a hundred and seventy years."

Leaning on her hand, she smiled up at him. "You give good pep talks."

His thumb moved over her arm, tracing the line of the ice pack. "You're Rim Rider material, you know that?" he said.

She leaned closer. "You might find Rim Riding with me more fun than going with Nazeem."

He watched her with that enigmatic expression of his. "Fun wasn't the first word that came to mind." He reached for the strand of hair that kept flopping over her eyes and tucked it behind her ear. The filmy white embroidered blouse she'd somehow not stained in her pursuit of Zhurihe slipped lower, baring one shoulder. His fingers dipped from her hair to her bare skin.

She couldn't breathe the entire time those fingers circled over the rounded part of her shoulder. That touch went a lot deeper than what was obvious. One lingering, almost regretful caress, and that magical contact vanished.

She exhaled through her nose. *Breathe deep; that's it, Cam.* "How did you know I was in the Quarter?" she asked when she could speak.

"I saw you walking here, crossing the square near the palace."

"And you followed me? You saw Hong, the rocks?"

He shook his head. "I'd lost sight of you, and came here, hoping you might remember the name of the pub. When you didn't show, I went looking for you."

"I wasn't sure you'd want to see me. I got that impression when we split at the palace."

"But you came looking for me nonetheless."

"I needed a friend."

His lips compressed. "And I, too."

"Listen to us, a couple of morose . . . well, I can't say drunks because we haven't touched our drinks." Two tall glasses of beer sat bubbling between them. "Let's just say a couple of gloomy souls." She folded her arms on the table and leaned forward. "So, when are you riding out again?"

The candor in his expression faded, like someone had pulled a curtain across his soul. "I'm awaiting the prince's word."

Cam made a face. "That makes two of us. He won't talk to me. All I want is five minutes of his time to see what he can tell me about Bree's disappearance."

"Maybe he has nothing to tell you."

"If so, I want to hear it from him. I did find out something on my own, though. Bree got as far as New Seoul, and survived a brush with the bad guys."

Kublai almost rose up from the table. "How did you learn that?"

Cam leveled him with a steady gaze. "My sources are confidential."

"Sources? What sources?"

"No one who's trying to hurt anyone, okay? She's a palace staffer who picked up on a little gossip, that's all. God, Kublai, you're so loyal to the crown, sometimes it feels like I'm talking to the prince himself."

Kublai picked up his glass of beer, downing half of it at once. "I shall take that as a compliment."

"Shoot, you even resemble him."

Kublai gulped more beer.

She compared and contrasted his tattooed features with the portraits she'd seen throughout the palace. Every time she gazed up at the larger-than-life paintings—of a gray-eyed prince dressed in royal regalia, stiffly posed with his parents and brother in the gardens, sitting happily astride a magnificent Hansian—she thought of the Rim Rider. "So, how's Beast, your gorgeous horse?"

"He doesn't care to be confined to the city. He's more than ready to ride out again."

"A little like his rider, I bet."

Kublai's expression softened. "A little, yes." He seemed

to have forgotten what unease her mentions of the prince had caused.

"Well, he's an amazing animal. Give him an apple for me next time you ride him. I miss him. It must have been all those days I spent on his back. All that power between my legs. No euphemism intended."

Kublai's mouth spread in a smile. "Too bad."

She laughed, a soft, wicked laugh. "Let's talk power between the legs, then. I need the distraction. I'm a woman, so I don't have the body parts you do—"

"Thank the good Lord," Kublai said, throwing a glance to heaven.

"—but the concept is still valid. Take horses and jets, for instance—lots of similarities. You ride, and I fly." She sighed. "I meant that in the past tense. I flew."

"You'll never stop being a pilot, as I will never stop being a horseman. It's ingrained in us. It is part of who we are."

"I like to think that, too. But I read that modern warcraft are spacecraft. They don't fly in the atmosphere very often, like the one I saw in Mongolia, because they're not tactically efficient there. I'm an air-to-air pilot. If that doesn't make me obsolete, then what does?"

Something flashed in Kublai's eyes. He pushed aside his empty glass to check her bruised wrist. The skin was reddened but it wasn't throbbing anymore. He discarded the ice pack and threw a money card on the table, pulling her to her feet by her good hand. She laughed as he tugged her along. "Where are we going?"

"The Royal Museum. I have a surprise for you."

"A plane! You're going to show me a plane in a

museum. Is this supposed to make me feel that I'm not outdated, outmoded, and outgunned? Tell me it's not a biplane. I didn't fly those, you know."

"Stop guessing or I won't take you."

She laughed at his gravity. "I used to have patience for surprises. I don't now. I guess it's been so long since anyone surprised me . . . with a good surprise."

"This will be a good surprise," he assured her.

Hands clasped, they walked quickly through the rain-slick nighttime streets. The TV walls of the buildings splashed garish color across the pavement. "But won't the museum be closed? It's late."

"A minor technicality."

"Great. All I need is to get arrested my first week in Beijing."

"You won't be arrested. Trust me."

"Connections, Rim Rider?"

"You could call them that."

The museum building loomed ahead. It was shaped like a giant diamond. Opalescent, it glowed from within. Cam was skeptical. "How are we going to get in if it's closed?"

"You said you are a gymnast, yes?"

"I was."

He shrugged as he brought her around back. "That's all the skills you'll need."

She made a face. "That leaves it wide-open."

"Have faith," he said. "The effort will be worth it."

Lack of confidence had never been one of Kublai's traits.

On the back lawn, he crouched down on the wet grass. "Here is where we must sneak."

"Oh, great."

"Follow me."

They scurried, bent over, to one of the opaque facets of the diamond. Now that she was closer, she could see handgrips leading all the way to the roof, a good fifty feet above their heads. "You're kidding, Kublai."

"Ready?" he asked, his eyes alive with mischief.

Cam looked up at the roof. Well, this couldn't be worse than anything else that had happened to her, and it sure took her mind off the horrible evening. "Ready."

They clambered up the diamond. At the top they were treated to a stunning view of the city—including the palace. "Beautiful," she murmured. "It looks like a jeweled sand castle."

"On a bejeweled beach." For once he didn't sound boastful. He truly loved this city, and it showed quite frankly in his face.

He went to work breaking and entering. After slipping a blade from his pants and counting a specific number of facets, he found the seam he needed. With the pointed tip of the blade, he followed the line down and around the facet.

"Isn't this wired with alarms?"

"Not this facet."

"You've done this before."

His gleaming smile was her answer. Carefully he lifted the facet and placed the heavy piece so that it lined up with the intact facet below. "Let's go."

To the tune of *Mission Impossible* playing in her head, she followed the Rim Rider though the opening. They dropped to a catwalk below, shimmying to a ladder that took them down to the ground floor. "Alarms?"

"Disabled."

"How?"

"If I tell you, pretty one, I will have to kill you."

She laughed. "Don't tell me then. I want to see whatever it is you're going to show me."

He took her by the hand and led her through a maze of rooms filled with treasures until he found the room he wanted. Before he'd allow her inside, he slipped behind her and covered her eyes with his hands. "Are you ready?"

"Ready."

"Really ready?"

"Kublai!"

He dropped his hands. Cam stared at the incredible sight: a mint-condition F-16 Viper.

"I thought you would like to see it," he said.

She shook her head, rendered speechless by the fighter, silver and sleek.

"I ride and you fly," he murmured. "I have told you much about the Hansian breed. Now it's your turn to tell me about the Viper."

Awed, she walked up to the jet. Coming up on her toes, she brushed her fingers across the fuselage. "It's real. . . ."

"Would you like to go inside?"

She brought her hand to her chest. "Be still, my heart."

He waved at the ladder hanging on the side of the jet, a climb she had made countless times. She grabbed hold of the rail with both hands and pulled herself up into the cockpit, slipping down into the seat. "Yes," she whispered. "Yes."

Kublai watched her from the top of the ladder, his

pleasure evident, despite the tattoo that so often masked subtler expressions. Cam ran her fingers over the controls. Then she jerked her hand back. "The lights in the instruments are on." She swerved to meet Kublai's gaze. "There's power?"

He nodded. "You could even start the engine, but I wouldn't recommend it. In the room behind us, there's a display of ancient tapestries."

"You're serious."

"Of course. Korean tapestries, dating back to—"

"I mean about the engine starting! It's nearly a two-hundred-year-old airplane, Kublai."

"The fossil-fuel cells have been replaced with a nuclear drive, but other than that and a few other changes, it is as fully functional as it was when you flew it."

"I could have, you know—I could have flown this very one." Cam savored the sensation of being in the cockpit again, one hand resting lightly on the stick, her other on the throttles.

"What aircraft, as an opponent in a dogfight, was the toughest challenger?"

"Hmm." She slid her fingers around the connectors where her oxygen hose and G suit plug-in would have fitted. "It's hard to pick any one aircraft as the toughest challenger. A mediocre aircraft flown by a great pilot will almost always defeat a great aircraft flown by a mediocre pilot. But if I had to pick a couple, I'd say the F-18 and the F-15, the Hornet and the Eagle."

"Have you flown any other jets besides this one?"

"Only in pilot training. I've had chances to fly in the F-15, F-18, and F-14. Nothing equaled the Viper, though." Quietly, she admitted, "What I wouldn't give to fly it now."

"I know," Kublai said, even quieter.

Cam turned. "Thank you. For doing this for me. For bringing the memories back—good memories. I feel lost sometimes."

"I know. I've been there." The way he looked at her gave her chills.

"The loss of your father," she murmured. He nodded. She lifted her arm to cup his face in her palm. "You know what it's like to have to keep going."

"When all you want to do is lie down and wallow in self-pity. To be honest, I don't know if I've come through it all stronger, or only colder."

She shook her head. "Oh, no. Not colder. Wary, yes; I see that in you. But you're not cold, Kublai. You're anything but."

It seemed as though he wanted to say something but stopped himself.

"It's those complications, right?" she teased.

He was already halfway down the ladder before she finished the sentence. She hoisted herself over the edge of the cockpit and climbed down after him.

He took her hand. "We'd better go."

"Not yet." Coming up on her toes, she caught his face between her hands and placed a tender kiss on his mouth. Kublai froze. She meant to pull away and let him recover, but she couldn't, not quite yet. Again she brushed her lips over his, tasting him as she'd long wanted to, feeling the firm softness of his lips, the sandpaper roughness where he'd shaved. "Is this so horrible, Kublai? Is this so bad? Come on; the prince isn't watching."

"Not so. It was all captured by the security cameras. He'll be watching it in the morn."

She jerked back, her gaze going to the ceiling.

"Kidding," he said. Then, to her shock, he drew her back to him. "If you call that a kiss . . ."

He folded her in his arms and took over where they'd left off, tasting and tugging on her lips, as if fighting the temptation to kiss her fully, yet drawing inexorably closer to doing it until, finally, something seemed to give way.

The instant his tongue slipped between her parted lips, the kiss went from tentative first taste to explosive decompression. Desire scorched through her. Kublai was rough enough to take her breath away, gentle enough to let her know he was aware he held a lady in his arms.

Mercy, what a kiss. She put her whole heart into it. She never did anything halfway, never held back, and she certainly didn't hold anything in reserve now.

It seemed to her that Kublai could tell, too. He gave a drawn-out groan, his arms molding her to his body. It had to be the most luscious kiss she'd experienced—ever. And it didn't surprise her. She'd wanted to kiss Kublai for too long to have been mistaken about what he could do with that mouth of his.

They moved apart only after the choices had narrowed to stay conscious or keep on kissing and end up on a hospital ventilator. Breathless, she made fists in the fabric of his shirt. "Yowee," she said, grinning.

He chuckled, his hands running up and down her back. She searched his face and saw nothing but happiness there. No regrets, no reservations. Sobering, she ran a hand over his thick, clean hair. "You can tell a lot about the nature of a man by the behavior of his horse," she murmured. "And by the way he kisses."

"The same can be said about the nature of a woman." He took her chin between his fingers and touched his lips to hers in a tender, lingering kiss. His uneven breaths told her just how hard he worked to hold back from doing more. Shuddering with some inner effort, he drew her into a powerful hug.

"We're done for tonight, aren't we?" she mumbled against his chest. Did he hear the disappointment in her voice?

She pushed away. "Make it easy on me, Kublai. Tell me to get lost."

"Never!"

"It would be better than this. When you turn on the affection, it makes me think you want me, too. And then it's this again. On and off. I feel like I'm forcing you into something you don't want. Tell me to go away, and I won't bother you anymore."

He caught her hand and pressed it to his lips; it was a gesture she'd expect more from a nobleman than a bounty hunter who trolled the wilderness. It reminded her how much she didn't know about him. And that there was a good chance she never would. "I do want this, Cam. I do want you." His dark eyes were on fire, giving her no cause to doubt him.

"Then prove it," she whispered. "Or forget about it."

"I want you to know who I am before we make love. And to be honest, I don't know quite how to make that happen."

"How hard can that be? Just be yourself, and I'll get to

know you." He got that distressed look again. She smiled. "You're so old-fashioned, Kublai. Such a gentleman."

"Circumstances can make a man resemble something he is not," he argued ruefully.

"Well, I respect that you're being honest with me."

Now he looked truly pained.

"You okay, Kublai?"

He opened his mouth to say something, but stopped. Instead he took her hand.

They retraced their steps to the roof. After replacing the loose facet, they walked back to the street. Kublai seemed filled to bursting with something he wanted to tell her, yet she didn't have a clue as to what it was.

They crossed the large, windswept square in front of the palace that was by day filled with adoring subjects hoping for a glimpse of the acting emperor, the prince who'd kept his distance—and his knowledge—from Cam since the day she'd arrived. "I need him, Kublai," she said in frustration. "I need the prince."

The Rim Rider stopped and faced her. A cold, damp wind blew their hair across their eyes. "And he needs you."

The intensity in his expression puzzled her. "Will you help me, Kublai? You're the only one who can. You got me into the museum. Get me into the prince's area of the castle. Then he'll have no choice but to see me. And to help—something he's withheld from me."

"He has not withheld his help!" He glanced around and lowered his voice. "He brought you here. He's given you shelter in the palace."

"He has, and I am grateful, but he ignores me. Bree

Maguire was here in the palace. I'm her wingman; it's my job to stay by my flight leader's side. Whatever information he knows about her whereabouts, I want it."

"I don't think he has anything to tell you."

"Then let him at least say as much to my face."

The big Rim Rider closed his eyes for a moment, as if struggling with a tremendous decision. Then he brought his lips to her ear and breathed, "I will do it."

"Thank you," she whispered back.

"And I'll better the offer, pretty one. Not only will I bring you to the prince's private chambers; I'll introduce you to the man himself."

Chapter Fifteen

Inside the walls of Fort Powell a battle of wills raged. "Who is the Voice of Freedom? Where are those broadcasts coming from?"

When Bree didn't answer the shouted questions, the interrogator pressed his fingertips into the skin of her jaw until he drew out a gasp. "You're only making it harder on yourself, Maguire."

"I told you—I don't know who the Voice of Freedom is."

"Then maybe you can help us with another matter. He's been talking to you all along. He's fanning the flames of revolt in Central, yet somehow he's remained hidden from us, escaping our most technically advanced traces of his transmissions. How does he do it? How are the broadcasts accomplished? An easy question, Banzai. Answer and we are done here." He brought his face closer. "Answer me," he whispered. His breath washed over her mouth and nose, smelling faintly of smoked meat. She twisted away, afraid she'd retch. Shock, pain, and the drugs they gave her kept her skating constantly on the edge of throwing up. How long had she been in this place? Days? Weeks?

The interrogator squeezed her jaw, forcing her to look at him. "Who is the Voice of Freedom?" he asked for the hundredth time.

"If I knew the answer, do you think I'd be here?"

He slapped her. Her head snapped around. Only a small explosion of pain this time. Had she grown so accustomed to being hit, and was her numbness a blessing in disguise?

"You're going to die, Maguire."

Her chin came up. "Not at your hands."

"Overconfidence around here is a mistake. Too bad no one told you that." His face was so close now that she could see the individual hairs where he'd shaved. When he smiled, his mouth filled her field of vision. "Let's try a little more time on the cable."

Bree's heart sank. *Not again. Please.* The broken wrist she'd suffered during the pirate attack had been healed in typically accelerated, twenty-second-century fashion. Though still tender, it wasn't what made the torture so excruciating; it was the almost-dislocation that hanging from the cable caused her shoulders, a position so agonizing that she never lasted long. God willing, she'd pass out just as quickly as last time.

"It doesn't have to be this way, Captain. Declare your allegiance to the UCE, say you'll be our great nation's loyal servant. Ask for mercy, and you shall have it."

She thought of Ty. *I'm fighting for you, babe. For all you wanted and never got to see.* "I'll never ask for lenience from a nation that knows none," she whispered.

"String her up!"

Bree heard the heavy footsteps of one of the guards, a bulky woman in her forties with a salt-and-pepper mustache and the coldest eyes Bree had ever seen. The commandant, Bree called her. The interrogator walked away, and the commandant took his place. Quiet and oh-so-methodical, she clamped cuffs around Bree's wrists and connected them to a cable hanging from a meat hook in the ceiling.

The guard yanked on the cable. It whizzed through the pulley and jerked Bree's arms above her head. Hand over hand, the guard pulled on the cable until Bree's feet swung an inch or two above the floor. There the guard left her to casually tie up the slack on a hook somewhere out of reach.

Bree hung, sweating and shaky. The pain moved in, dull at first, then consuming her shoulders and back in molten fire. *God, help me get through this.*

"'I am an American soldier,'" she whispered. "'I serve in the forces that guard my country and our way of life. I am prepared to give my life in their defense. . . .'"

She prayed a lot lately, sometimes to God and sometimes to her country. Reciting the Code of Conduct was one way of bringing some semblance of comfort, of distraction, to the nightmare that was Fort Powell. She'd lived by those articles as an air force officer, and, by God, in the memory of every man and woman who ever fought to be free, in America and around the world, she'd live by them now. . . .

She blacked out, came back, bouncing between excruciating pain and hallucinations. Her dreams splintered, and she was back in the cell again. Her head had sagged back as she hung in the restraints. What were those brownish spots splattered across the ceiling? Old blood they'd forgotten to clean. Or maybe they left the stains on purpose—for its effect on the prisoners here. It worked, she acceded, because every time she glimpsed the spatters, she wondered what had happened to the person, if they'd hurt as much as this. If they'd felt as abandoned as she did now.

Forsaken . . .

Without warning, her throat constricted. Her nostrils flared, and she wished she could take back the tear rolling down a sweaty cheek. "Where are you?" she entreated the Voice. "We're supposed to be in this together."

We must all hang together or assuredly we will hang separately. Benjamin Franklin's quote had been one of the Voice of Freedom's favorites.

A horrible sound of frustration tore from her throat. "If that's what you believe, then why am I the only one hanging?" The sense of abandonment, the pressure, the fear—it all threatened to collapse in on her. "Talk to me! Tell me if we're still in this. If I'm doing any good from in here. Damn it, give me a sign."

Her voice carried from the concrete chamber, down the long, underground hallway to a six-foot-thick titanium door built to withstand far more than the roar of the protests inside. Or out.

She drifted in and out of consciousness. When she opened her eyes again, Ty was there, watching her from the shadows. Was he real or just imagined?

She made a soft cry of joy, her chest swelling with love. "Oh, my God. You're alive."

Ty's pirate rags were gone, and he wore the uniform of a UCE officer. The flag on his upper arm was as foreign as the expression on his face. "We chose the wrong side, Bree. But we can go back."

"Go back? To where?"

"To the side of virtue. Of peace and stability. We belong to the UCE, Bree. Come with me. We'll command a future that is the *right* future."

"I don't want to be in command."

"I meant it figuratively. I want what you want: a home, a family, and peace."

"None of it means anything if you don't have freedom, Ty. Nothing."

He shook his head as if giving up on her.

"Aren't you going to help me?" The alternative was too painful to contemplate.

"Help you, Bree? I don't know you." He turned and walked away. . . .

She closed her eyes, tears streaming down her cheeks. The turning point. She could capitulate now and swear allegiance to the UCE. She could deny who she was so she could stay alive. Then she and Ty could escape this hell and have their future.

But what kind of future would it be?

A coward's future.

As sharp as her grief was over losing Ty, she sensed that part of her life was over—the personal, *human* part. It didn't matter what she wanted anymore. *You belong to the people now. The people of Central.* What was, and would someday be again, she hoped, the United States of America.

When she opened her eyes, it was darker. One small bulb lit the cell.

Someone cut her loose from the ceiling cables. She crumpled onto the cold cement floor. Impatiently, she was hoisted to her feet. The ringing in her ears surged. One, two steps, and everything went completely dark. . . .

The lights came on then, half blinding her. She blinked and found herself standing on a stool next to a gallows. Around her was a turbulent crowd.

Gradually, her awareness expanded to include uniformed strangers seated in what appeared to be a courtroom. She wasn't on a gallows but sitting on a chair in the center of a dais, bathed in a circle of light. The crowd wasn't real but an image displayed on huge monitors that dominated the walls.

Escape. Was it a possibility? Could she make a run for it? She didn't see any guards, but at knee level a field wavered—a virtual cell, and almost as impenetrable as the real deal. Whoever had brought her here felt handcuffs appeared too tacky.

She tried to focus, somehow sensing that the proceedings around her were critically important, but her mind kept wandering. It was getting harder to ascertain what was real and what was not.

"Banzai Maguire."

She jerked her head up at the voice. Ty? He stood before her, dressed in the unmistakable uniform of an executioner. Lifting his black hood, he revealed his face inch by excruciating inch. She knew that mouth, how it could appear so cold and yet kiss her with such aching tenderness.

He threw the hood off his head, and Gen. Aaron Armstrong met her stare of shock.

He no longer wore executioner's garb but a UCE uniform. Medals covered half his chest. Five stars sat on his shoulders. *He has Ty's blue eyes*, Bree thought distantly. And they were cold, so very cold.

Didn't Ty's gaze turn cold when he was afraid?

Yes, but this man acted anything but scared.

Armstrong's voice boomed. "Such are the charges against you."

"What charges?" Had she blacked out again? Frantically she reviewed the past few moments and remembered nothing of a trial.

"High treason against the government of the United Colonies of Earth."

"I never swore allegiance to the UCE."

"Confess your crimes, Banzai Maguire, and you will be spared. Spared death."

She answered Armstrong with as much pride as her degraded condition would allow. "I will never swear loyalty to a nation that knows no freedom."

"Then days from today you will die."

She shared a long, penetrating look with Armstrong that was gut-wrenching in its intensity.

"Don't you have anything to say for yourself?"

She drew herself upright, the rope falling loosely around her neck. Rope? When did the dais become a gallows? It didn't seem real. And yet, it didn't seem like a dream, either. "Yes, I have something to say."

Infinitely calm, as if she'd been practicing for this moment all her life, she swept her gaze over the rapt faces of the audience, meeting as many of their eyes as she could. "Like Nathan Hale before me, I only regret that I have but one life to lose for my country."

The crowd filling the monitors roared. She felt its

211

thunder. They must be outside the building. The people weren't cheering, though, she realized; they were booing. And it seemed they were booing Armstrong!

Bree swayed in place, tears of pride stinging her eyes. The citizens of Central had given her back her strength when all seemed lost. She thrust a fist in the air. "We have it in our power to begin the world anew!" she shouted to them. "America shall make a stand, not for herself alone, but for the world!" Her voice rang out loud and clear.

She caught one glimpse of the crowd going wild before the giant monitors went black.

The light above her dimmed, throwing the audience into darkness, so that she could no longer tell if they were there. She stood on a stool, not the floor, she realized. Lifting her gaze slowly to meet the eyes of her executioner, she felt a knowing smile curve her lips. "You may kill me, sir, but you will never kill the revolution." She drew in a breath and shouted, "Freedom!"

With a snarl, the general cut the rope and kicked the stool out from under her. The rope yanked tight and snapped her neck—

Bree's inhalation was long, loud, and hoarse. Her arms jerked out, hands flying to her throat. She sucked in wild, gasping breaths before she finally convinced herself that she wasn't suffocating; that she wasn't hanging from a gallows, a horrified crowd below her.

She had just experienced many things, and she couldn't tell how much had been her fevered imagination. All she knew was that she was lying on a bare mattress in a brightly lit prison cell. Alone. And for the first time in all the days she'd been in Fort Powell, she thanked God for it.

Chapter Sixteen

A heli-jet rose from the roof of the justice building. Nosing over, it accelerated, reaching the White House within minutes.

The general disembarked. Head down, he stalked across the rooftop to where security guards waited to take him down to Beauchamp's little smoke-filled corner of hell.

He never made it that far. The president of the UCE stormed across the roof. "Stay back," he barked at the young officers who tried to follow him, and continued his ugly march to meet the general.

"Mr. President." The wind of the heli-jet's vertical engines whipped Armstrong's trench coat around his legs. "For a man who just got his wish, you look quite upset."

"Upset?" the president bellowed. "I am much more than upset!"

"The top rebel has just gotten her comeuppance, and this bothers you? Surely you're not forming a soft spot for

213

the terrorists crying for the overthrow of our legitimate government."

"You televised the tribunal, Aaron! What were you thinking?"

"That many in the population were long overdue a peek at the consequences of treason."

"Maguire couldn't keep her eyes open. It was clear to anyone watching that she was drugged and weary."

"That was my entire point. No one ever said the consequences of inciting rebellion weren't graphic to watch."

"She passed out on you—twice!"

"She was awake for the important parts," Armstrong said. "She heard and understood the charges levied against her. She had ample opportunity to renounce all association with the rebellion. She chose not to."

"And now it's set off riots the likes of which we have never seen!" The president swept a hand out to the side, drawing the general's attention to the streets of New Washington. Contained more or less in several pockets, as far as his eyes could see, were thousands upon thousands of demonstrators.

"Are you going to let them run wild, Mr. President? You are the leader of this great land. Do something."

"I will," Beauchamp growled back. "But I need your word you'll not incite the masses any further with lame-brain ideas of scaring them."

Armstrong smiled. "It worked, though. They're scared."

"Aaron!"

The general held up his hands. "You have my word. I will not frighten the rebels. I'll let them do as they wish."

Beauchamp scowled. "That isn't what I'm asking of

you, and you know it. Permissiveness will kill us all."

Armstrong matched the man frown for frown. "I'm relieved to hear it. For a moment there, I thought you were going over to the other side."

"Other side." Beauchamp made an ugly sound in his throat. "I will do anything to keep this great nation alive and well. I expect the same of you."

"Have I not already proved my conviction in a speedy resolution to this trying moment in our history?"

Beauchamp let out a gust of air. "Yes, Aaron, you have." The president turned away, running a hand over his face. He looked weary now that his fury had passed somewhat.

Exhaling, he waved in the direction of his office. "Come now, and let us discuss the details of the upcoming execution, wherein you will assure me that the only stage time allowed Banzai Maguire will be when the coroners carry her dead body to the morgue."

Bree sat up on the edge of a thin mattress that had no sheets. Disoriented at first, she used the sounds of the twenty-four-hour-a-day media barrage in her cell to find her bearings. The shows that played along an entire wall of the cell were relentless noise; television shows, documentaries, war footage of UCE victories, a constant stream of information.

Technology in Fort Powell typified most places in the twenty-second century, dependent on computers that were small—microscopic, in most cases—and integrated so well into the building and various other devices that no one noticed or even thought about them. It was how the lights went on or off, how the walls could change color, how the floor stayed bacteria free—and how these videos streamed into the cell around the clock, emanating from screens that weren't only in the walls of the cell, but *were* the walls. In fact, the entire prison was so integrated with its computers that disabling security or anything else critically important would be impossible without taking down the computer itself—which, according to everything Ty had once told her about safeguards and remote backups, couldn't happen.

Bree rubbed her neck and then her eyes. How long had she been out cold? It felt like days. Maybe it had been weeks. She knew she wasn't aware of half the things that happened to her here.

And what horrible dreams this time. The tribunal. The cheering crowd. The hanging. It had seemed so real, parts of it. She'd dreamed of Ty again, too. Dreamed that he was alive and had changed sides.

Swinging her feet off the cot, she dropped her face into her hands. What did the dreams mean? Were they her own doubts surfacing about Ty's loyalties? Or were the drugs designer hallucinogens that could tailor a person's thoughts, twisting them to continue the interrogator's work while the subject slept? Or did the visions reflect some events that had actually happened? Or *would* happen?

A chill went up her spine. Her thoughts were so confused that she didn't know what to believe. The drugs. God, how she hated the drugs. They were making her paranoid, making her distrust the man she loved.

The man who left you here, all alone.

"Stop it!" She hunched over and moaned, hating her own weakness even as she retreated into it. . . .

Hair tangled, Bree lifted her head and stared numbly at the show playing on the wall, this time Interweb news.

"In other news, it seems the UCE's favorite bachelor is back in action. . . ." A woman with short silver hair and makeup, even silver lips, animatedly addressed the camera. "Tyler Armstrong is back on the party circuit, according to sources close to the supreme commander's son."

Bree's head jerked up.

"After an apparent terrifying experience with brain-washing at the hands of cult figure Banzai Maguire, Tyler, we've now learned, has accepted an invitation to sexy actress Lee-lee Sweet's Christmas bash. Welcome back, Ty."

Lee-lee? Ty had never mentioned anyone named Lee-lee.

The image cut to a news clip of Ty walking into a theater, maybe at a premiere. He was dressed in a dark, expensive-looking, understated designer suit; his hair was cut shorter, and in his left ear a tiny jewel sparkled. He didn't look anything like the grubby, battle-worn man she'd fallen in love with. His arm was wrapped around a woman—a gorgeous, slinky, scantily clad woman. Miss Sweet, apparently.

Bree leaned forward, eyes wide, and watched Ty stop for a photo op with paparazzi and reporters like a seasoned veteran of the party circuit. To their delight, he drew the actress close. Hey, what was up with his hand? It was sliding way too close to her breast.

Bree's head felt ready to explode.

"Can their on-again, off-again romance be on the mend? After a brush with death, it looks like this time bachelor Ty may finally be ready to settle down."

Bree started searching for a remote to shut off the program before it hit her that prisons didn't have remotes—or even regular TV. At least, not Fort Powell. It ran twenty-four hours a day, designed, no doubt, to drive her crazy. And in this particular case, it might do exactly that.

She shoved off the bed as the feature continued: Ty Armstrong pictured with various celebrities; socializing on someone's yacht; at the beach with that wench Leelee. *None of it's true. It's a brainwashing trick.*

Then why did it hurt so much?

That's what they want. Don't believe anything they say. It was all designed to break her down.

She paced, as if she could outrun her heartache and the lump forming in her throat. *You know Ty. Certainly better than he knows you.* She'd been revealing bits of herself, piece by piece, but Ty, he was an open book, so giving, so willing to love her and to patiently wait for her to feel the same.

Because he wants you to believe the lie. He's working for his father. Has been all along. He's on the fast track, the closest thing UCE has to royalty. The sky's the limit when it comes to his future. Do you think he'll give it all up for you?

"*We'll be leaders of the future, Bree. . . .*"

"Stop," she ground out, squeezing her eyes shut. The drugs in her system were arguing as loudly as her common sense. *You have to trust him. If he's really alive, he'll come for you.*

Try to believe that, she pleaded with herself. But she hurt so badly inside that she wanted to die.

And that's exactly what they want to happen.

"Yes, they do. Or at least go crazy." She continued talking out loud, sounding more and more like the raving lunatic the UCE no doubt wanted her to be.

Two guards appeared at the door to her cell. A shudder ran through her weakened body. *Not the interrogator again. Not this soon.* She needed time to regroup, to be ready for him. She feared her weakness—that she'd break before making it through another round of endless questions. And the torture . . . *Please, let me be strong.*

The guards were new. She hadn't seen them before. Nor had she seen anything like the hot meal they brought her on a tray. Salisbury steak—or something that resembled it—with mashed potatoes, gravy, and peas.

The guards used a code to unlock the cell door. It slid aside, and they walked in. Bree stared at the tray of food, salivating. The other guard dropped a stack of clothing on her mattress: a prison-orange jumpsuit, slippers, and underwear. A change of clothes! As hungry as she was, she almost craved the feel of clean clothing even more.

She narrowed her eyes at the guards. "What's the catch, guys?"

"It came to the supreme commander's attention that there were inconsistencies in your care."

The supreme commander? As in "Ax"? Ty's father?

Was it an act of kindness, or were shifting politics to blame? Or, in this case, thank. "Inconsistencies, huh?" She rubbed a hand down one of her sore arms. "Is that what they call it?" They'd fixed her latest bruises, like they did her dislocated shoulders—twice. They kept breaking her and patching her up. How much more her body could endure, she wasn't sure, and hoped they were.

Incredibly, the guards turned to go without exacting

any kind of payment. She went to the bars and called after them, "Tell the general thanks."

They kept walking. She couldn't believe it. They were really going to leave her in peace to eat this glorious meal, her first real food in who knew how long?

Immediately she stripped and changed into her new clothes. Swathed in crisp, clean-smelling fabric, she returned to her meal. At first, sitting on her bed to eat, she stared at the food. The simple fare was the treat of a lifetime. Deprivation had a way of making a person appreciate the smallest things. Anticipating what she knew would be the greatest culinary experience of her life so far, she buried the tines of her fork in the mashed potatoes.

"Can you hear me?"

Bree jumped back. The plastic fork flew out of her hands and clattered across the floor. She stared at her potatoes. "Did you say something?"

She squeezed her eyes shut, shook her head. "No. It's the drugs talking."

She retrieved her fork and took aim at the peas this time. "Just shut up and be eaten."

"I know you can hear me. I can hear *you*, Banzai Maguire."

Bree froze, her heart thumping. The transmission came from somewhere in the vicinity of her collar. It wasn't a vegetable trying to get her attention. It was the Voice of Freedom.

Chapter Seventeen

General Armstrong strode up the front path to his residence. It was late, after midnight. Behind him a heli-jet lifted off from the expansive sweep of front lawn, scattering fall leaves that the groundskeeper had missed. Roosevelt, the family's border collie, raced to the general, barking excitedly and letting the slumbering household know he had arrived home.

Oddly without emotion, Ty watched his father approach. He was the only one in the household awake. How could he sleep? He'd spent the past week in a private hospital, while Bree was God knew where and in what condition. He couldn't imagine crashing into anything but a fatigue-induced coma until he had her back safe and in his arms.

General Armstrong bent over to ruffle the dog's ears, amusedly accepting Roosevelt's slobbering kisses. So much about the man was crisp, efficient. Cold. And then there were these touches of humanity—petting the family dog, kissing his wife, playing touch football with the young boy that Ty once was. Armstrong was like a puzzle where none of the pieces fit. They had once, perhaps, but something changed over time. Lately Ty had seen less of what made the general a man, and more of what made him a monster.

His father threw open the front door and caught sight of Ty standing in the foyer. There the general halted, his gloved hand tightening on the doorknob. "Tyler."

"Father."

"You're home, then."

"They released me this afternoon. I guess there are only so many scars you can heal with a derma-strip."

"I would have come to see you, Tyler, but—"

"Visitors would have been too stressful, they told me. Your orders—or theirs, Father?"

The general compressed his lips. "I've had a lot on my plate this past week. I'm certain you're aware of why."

"Quite."

"You were on my mind, Ty. I called you—"

"I didn't take calls."

"So I gathered."

The men regarded each other in tense silence, both quick to hide any weakness, any vulnerability. Every muscle in Ty's body was as taut as a stretched spring. If his father had tried to kill him, could the man actually stand there as if it hadn't happened?

Discomfort flickered in his father's eyes. Belatedly becoming aware of the changed dynamic, Ty stepped aside to allow the older man past. He was taller than his father now, more muscular. He got the uncomfortable feeling that his father had just perceived him as a physical threat. A trace of embarrassment filtered through him with the realization. Yeah, he was angry as hell, and a hundred other variations on outrage and anguish, but beating the shit out of his old man was not, as yet, high up on his list of priorities. He wanted answers first.

Ty watched his father put away his hat and coat, stripping off his gloves last of all. One of the most powerful—and hated—men on Earth taking off his outerwear just like any other parent who'd returned home after working late at the office. It added to the unfolding incongruity of the scene.

Lean, chiseled, and without a single trace of softness, the general turned to Ty, hesitating. Strangely, he appeared weary, besieged; maybe a bit lost.

Did he want to embrace his son? If he made the move to do so, would Ty reject him? That was what Ty guessed his father was thinking, and it was exactly the kind of discomfort and doubt he'd anticipated while waiting for his father to arrive home, waiting mysteriously without any guards to watch him, waiting as a free citizen and not under house arrest. He'd never expected to be welcomed home in this way, as if he'd done nothing wrong, as if he'd caused no major international incidents, had not chosen to protect a woman known as Banzai Maguire knowing full well her very existence could bring about the downfall of the nation he'd sworn to defend at all cost. At the very least, he'd expected the general would react with powerful disappointment at his actions—anger and shame. Instead, Ty saw only sorrow and determination battling for dominance in the man's expression. The discrepancy put the fear of God in his bones. Fear for Bree, and what had happened to her.

"Now that you're here, we must talk," his father said.

"No shit."

The general's cheek gave a small twitch. He'd never cared for swearing. Incredible that he was so proper, sticking firmly to a code of manners and good etiquette at home and in social situations. Considering what he'd accomplished over the course of a forty-five-year military career, it was a miracle that he'd maintained such standards, but there it was.

Before Ty realized what was happening, the general had crossed the foyer and entered his library. Ty followed him and stopped in the doorway. The absurdity of the situation continued to soar. His father was acting almost normally. Ty was only one week back from the Indian Ocean. There should have been more shock, more emotion, but after showering and shaving, and a battery of medical tests, all Ty had to show for it was a suntan and the hole in his heart where Bree had been.

It left him feeling disoriented, to say the least.

Ty swallowed twice and walked into the library. As if it were any other evening, the general poured two glasses of scotch over ice. He lifted one to his mouth without offering Ty the other. That, it seemed, he'd have to retrieve for himself.

Fine. He needed the drink, so he took it, taking a hefty swallow.

"I must say, you have made things difficult for me, Tyler."

"That's all you're going to say? That I've made things difficult for you?" He couldn't take another moment of this careful dancing around the issues. "You leave me to rot in Kyber's dungeon, which I escape, and I nearly die

224

evading an assassin who I can't help but wonder whether he was sent there on your orders. And all you tell me when I get home is that we have to talk?"

His father's eyes were glacial. "Do you really think I would try to kill you? My own son?"

Ty reached for his collar and tore through the buttons, one-handed. The shirt fell open, exposing the ugly scar below his collarbone. "What would you call this? A bad shot?"

The general blanched. In all the years of living with the man, Ty didn't remember ever once seeing him turn pale. "Ax" Armstrong had earned his nickname for his decisive, incisive, and often bloody strategies of fighting terrorism and keeping order in the UCE's colonies. Some said he was a dove clothed in hawk's armor, using the largest military in the world to further his personal vision of peace. Others claimed he was ruled by personal ambition, waiting for the right moment to oust President Beauchamp, in office since before Ty was born, and turn the UCE into a military dictatorship. Ty had long since decided that the less he knew about his sire the better. Now that had changed. He had to know more. He had to know *everything*.

"It's an exit wound." Ty seethed. "Your assassin shot me in the back." He took a mighty breath, trying to hold on to some semblance of calm. "At night," he continued in a quiet, distinctly deadly tone, "as I lay in bed, holding the woman I love. The woman you wanted dead."

His father regarded him stiffly, lips pressed together. His pale eyes were as cold as ice.

"And now you 'want to talk.'" Ty emptied the leaded crystal glass of scotch and threw it into the fireplace, where it shattered explosively. He stormed to the library door, fully intending to leave. Yet he stopped, his breath ragged as he leaned an elbow against the doorjamb, his hand buried in his hair. "Did you or did you not order my assassination, Father, or designate me an unavoidable casualty? I have to know."

"I am guilty of many things, Tyler. Some that I regret. But I would never stoop so low as to send an assassin to hurt my own child."

Ty didn't answer. He couldn't. He doubted he had the wherewithal to speak. His insides felt shredded. It made it difficult to converse like a normal human being. He'd come home in emotional disrepair from many a long military mission, often with the horrors of war fresh in his mind, but never had it been like this. It was because of Bree, he knew. Without her, it was as if half of him were missing.

And his father thought all they needed to do was talk. *Christ.* He dropped his hand and started to leave.

"Tyler."

He halted, teeth clenched. "What do you want?"

"I've placed you on administrative leave from your duties with your unit."

"So I hear. Why not go a step further and put me under house arrest?"

"Because I trust you'll have the wisdom to make the right choice in the days ahead."

"And what choice is that, sir?"

"Your country, above all else."

"Country? For all I know, it's not there anymore. You've kept me completely in the dark all week, blocked incoming calls, blocked me from accessing the Interweb."

226

"The Interweb has been pulled down."

"Pulled down. How?" He got over his shock at something he couldn't fathom happening and narrowed his eyes. "When?"

"Today. Too many images have come across the wires lately. Disturbing images. It's not good for the country, Ty. And then there's the matter of the Shadow Voice. Drastic measures were needed to silence it."

Drastic measures was an understatement. Ty couldn't imagine the country without use of the Interweb. Everything would be thrown into crisis. Everything *was* in crisis. "You also blocked my use of the phone. You took away any means for me to communicate while I was in the hospital. I was in an information vacuum."

"It was for your own protection, Ty."

"Bullshit. What don't you want me to know?"

Ty recoiled at the it's-going-to-hurt-but-the-UCE-has-no-choice expression on his father's face. "Good God. You're going to execute her. . . ."

"Banzai Maguire committed a number of very serious crimes. She must be punished accordingly."

"She's an innocent in all this. Essentially a pawn."

"I don't believe she is," the general said quietly. "She had ample opportunity to back away. That she did not is telling. She understands the choice she made, Tyler. In fact, today she declared her guilt publicly—"

"Publicly?" Ty tried to imagine the circumstances but couldn't.

"Yes. At her sentencing."

"Don't you think the public knows what a forced confession looks like?"

"She gave it quite freely."

Had she? Had Bree capitulated? Ty knew what torture could do to a man. He prayed that wasn't what forced Bree's change of heart.

"And now she must face the consequences of that decision," his father finished.

A chunk of ice lodged in Ty's chest. "I won't let it happen," he said, looking up slowly. "I won't let you kill her."

"Not me, son. Your country. The high court. The people's will."

"The people's will is for her to stay alive!"

His father sipped his drink. "We shall see."

"Yes, Father. We shall see."

They regarded each other with an intensity that imparted upon the cozy library the atmosphere of a gore-strewn combat zone.

When Ty spoke again, it was in a voice far more controlled. "I will do everything in my power to thwart you."

The general's expression was just as cold. "And I will do everything in my power, which is considerably more than yours, Commander, to make sure that you do not."

And so the gauntlets were thrown.

"Forget about the administrative leave." Ty buttoned his shirt. "I'm resigning my commission. Effective now. I'll let you handle the paperwork."

"Only fools let a fit of pique change the course of their lives." Ty spun around at the sound of his mother's voice. She stood in the foyer, clutching her robe around her. Her eyelids weren't swollen from sleep but from tears. Never one to hide her emotions, she fairly thrummed with anger. Ty braced himself, having inherited her infamous temper. "You loved serving your country, Tyler. I never saw you happier than the day you joined up to fight in the war. Nor," she added quietly, "your father."

She and the general exchanged a long look fraught with a thousand undercurrents, a thousand varied meanings, things to which only they, a long-married couple, were privy.

Then his mother shifted her attention back to Ty. "You left medical school to become an officer. You had many a chance to return to school in the years since, and yet you didn't. It means that you love being in the service. Don't be so quick to give it all up because of a misunderstanding."

"A misunderstanding?" Ty choked out a laugh. "I think it's gone a little beyond that."

"A woman's love, then?"

She was perceptive. He fought the urge to assure her that the seeds of what he'd become had been planted long before he'd met Bree face-to-face, long before he knew the woman of his fantasies would become the cornerstone of his existence, bringing true meaning to his life. "I am giving up my commission because my belief in our system of government no longer exists. Without utter faith in the UCE, I can't call myself an officer of its military without putting those who serve with me at risk. I won't do that to my men."

"You are still a citizen of the United Colonies of Earth," his father reminded him.

"No, sir. Not anymore. I, sir, am a New American."

I am not a Virginian but an American! The famous prerevolutionary statesman Patrick Henry's impassioned declaration had never seemed more apropos.

"Chico's in town," his father said. "Perhaps it would do you some good to talk to him."

Ty couldn't believe what he was hearing. As boys, he and Chico had grown up on a variety of military bases, their fathers both high-ranking officers. They'd joined up at the same time; both had had fast-track careers. He considered Chico, Juan Granados, a friend, but the man lived and breathed UCE policy, as Ty once had, and was by-the-book enough to be named commander of Fort Powell.

Where Bree was likely being held prisoner.

A startling sense of divine intervention burst in Ty's mind. He made damn sure his father didn't see his reaction. He'd pay a visit to Chico, no question. But it'd be with more than career counseling on his mind.

Ty started to walk away, leaving his parents to stare after him, but thought better of it. Slowly he turned to face them, the couple who had given him life. "I don't know what will happen," he said quietly. "None of us do. But know that I love you," he said, keeping his eyes pointedly on his mother's to avoid the general's hooded gaze. *Yes, even you, Father.*

Only then did Ty stride away. He'd lost much in a week: his innocence, his faith in his country, and perhaps any chance at a future. But not his woman. No, not Bree. Ideologies aside and risk be damned, he was going to find her and free her. Something told him there wasn't a minute to waste.

Chapter Eighteen

Bree hunched over her cooling dinner, by all appearances whispering to her vegetables. "When are you going to get me out of here?"

"I'm working on it," the Voice replied.

Bree bit off a sound of dismay. She'd begun to think of the Voice as all-powerful. Invincible. Now she couldn't help picturing *The Wizard of Oz*, when Dorothy discovered the wizard was really a little old man hiding behind scary props. "You'd better do something fast. Things aren't looking so good."

The Voice made a *tsk-tsk* sound. "Ye of little faith . . ."

Her voice attracted the attention of one of the military guards who had brought her dinner. "Shush!" she whispered.

The blond-haired guard stopped outside the bars to stare. How was she going to explain the talking? She threaded her fingers together so he'd miss how badly her hands were shaking.

The sergeant checked his six, looked right, looked left. Extreme wariness and curiosity rolled off him in waves. "So, here she is," he said. "They say you can catch bullets with your teeth and can make yourself invisible."

Had he been drinking? She turned her hands up. "I guess the invisibility potion didn't work too well."

"You've escaped capture so many times, it was the only way anyone could explain it."

"Yeah. I'm a legend now, huh?" She glanced around the stark cell. Some legend. Yet that was her duty, her role in all this, wasn't it? To be a force for change. To be the legend. To make them all *believe*.

"And the legend's growing." The guard checked his six again before continuing, his voice hushed. "Your name alone is all they need to unite volunteers in every Central town. Sheep, we call them. Sheep easily scattered if we shoot the shepherd."

She folded her arms over her chest. "You mean me."

"Yeah." The guard's gaze was intense. Although he stayed on the other side of the bars, his surly attitude made her a little nervous; not only because she had the Shadow Voice on the line, but because as the days went on, she'd seen fewer guards. If this one wanted to try something unpleasant, he could very well get away with it. "They found you guilty. High treason."

"For what? For loving my country? For wanting liberty?" She stood straighter. "For being willing to die for freedom?"

"It's a capital offense. They're going to execute you for your crimes."

Heat consumed her face. She'd long assumed death

would be her sentence. Knowing it proved more difficult than suspecting it, though. "I'm not afraid."

"You ought to be."

"Don't be afraid of death," she said in a quiet voice. "Be afraid of the unlived life. My great-grandmother Michiko used to tell me that. She was four-foot-eleven, but she put the fear of God in every man in my family— all of them over six feet tall. She would have gone off to fight in World War Two if they'd let her. Instead she spent the war in a Japanese internment camp, even though she was born and raised in Omaha. It's 2176— 1776 was the year the thirteen colonies declared their independence. Now I'm here, a hundred and seventy years after I should have died in a missile attack. Coincidence? Maybe. I believe fate brought me here for a reason, and a lot of other people do also. I matter in a bigger way than anyone in the UCE chain of command ever wanted to admit, or they wouldn't be trying so hard to kill me."

Uncertainty flickered in the guard's eyes then, a hair-line crack in his armor that she hadn't expected.

Her chin lifted. "I'm not afraid of dying for the country my great-grandmother loved, because its existence was synonymous with freedom. I want it back, that promise of freedom. And I think the people in the UCE do, too."

The sergeant regarded her, his lips pressed together tightly. It surprised her that he didn't argue. Was he not fully committed to doing the UCE's dirty work? Had she given him cause for second thoughts? Bree wasn't sure. If she wasn't sure, then the guard might not be, either.

The guard turned away from the cell, took a few steps, and stopped. He turned once more to ponder her before disappearing where the corridor cut a sharp corner.

A shuddering breath escaped her. Bree let her eyes close for a moment, her hands shaking. Even if it all ended badly, which it looked as if it might, she could then die knowing she'd made some impact on a single soldier, however small. Pebbles hit ponds and made ripples that spread out in ever-expanding circles. One changed man like this guard could change others. Now all she had to do was hold tight to that thought when things got really scary.

She returned to the center of the cell. "You still there?" she asked the Voice in a hoarse whisper.

"Well done, the way you used the situation to our advantage."

She bristled. "I meant what I told him. It wasn't propaganda."

"And that is what separates you and me from those who would like to see our efforts fail."

"You seem to know a lot about me, yet I know nothing about you. Are you a woman? A man? Are you inside the UCE, or out?" Silence. She sighed. "When this is over, can I at least meet you?"

She could almost feel the person behind the Voice smile. "You already have."

Her eyes opened wide. A hundred faces riffled through her mind like cards in a shuffled deck. She'd met the person behind the Voice? When? Where?

"What do I do in the meantime?" she almost whispered. "It hasn't exactly been a vacation in here."

"Stay strong. Know that the colonists support you."

"I need to do more than stay strong. I need to do something concrete."

"Look above when things grow darkest. Get as high as you can. Look to the sky, and you'll know. I can't tell you more."

"Look to the sky. Got it." Then an idea hit her. "Are you able to transmit my voice to the public? If I can somehow motivate them from inside prison, then maybe I can shift the political climate in favor of sparing me."

"The climate already favors you. The entire Interweb was taken down after and because of your address to the public the other morning. Opinion is running so heavily in your favor that the government fears spontaneous combustion. General Armstrong ordered the UCE guard into New Washington and all the metropolitan areas. Civil disobedience, you see, and all because of you." The Shadow Voice chuckled. She'd never heard the person laugh before. "Ah, it was beautiful, just beautiful."

"What are you talking about? What address?"

"At your sentencing. You don't remember being there?"

They found you guilty. High treason. So that was what the guard meant.

The flashback of a dream hit her: wall-sized monitors showing a turbulent crowd; Bree facing down General Armstrong by quoting Nathan Hale.

"I thought it was a dream. . . ." Part of it *was* a dream, thank God. "I hallucinated that I had a rope around my neck, that I was hanged." She rubbed her throat and tried to work saliva into a suddenly dry mouth. "The guard just now said they gave me a death sentence. I assume an execution. Is there a timetable for the grand event?"

She wasn't sure if what she heard coming from her collar was static or throat clearing. "Your execution is scheduled for nine tomorrow morning."

Tomorrow? It felt as if the floor dropped away from under her feet. "What time is it now?"

"Nineteen hundred."

Seven P.M. Fourteen hours to go—and counting.

Standing in shock next to her bed, she stared down at the tray of cold food. It looked like her surprise dinner had just turned into a last supper.

The minutes ticked relentlessly toward Bree's execution. If only there were more time.

A somber drizzle fell as Ty Armstrong hurried through downtown New Washington on foot. The streets were filled with people. It seemed the entire civilian population was outside. If not for the national state of emergency and a brutally enforced curfew, the rest of Central would be here, too. Without an Interweb, news traveled the old way, via word of mouth. Ty had learned that UCE police had used chemical irritants to disperse the crowd from outside the Supreme Court Building, where they'd virtually camped out since Bree's sentencing had taken place. Now they were flowing away from the capital— and Fort Powell, his destination. Time was of the essence, and he had to fight his way through a never-ending stream of anti-UCE protesters.

Avoid the UCE troopers at all cost, he thought. If he was arrested, his chances at saving Bree fell to nil. Clad in all-black riot gear, the police were tasked to defend the capital. He hadn't yet heard that they'd shot at the protesters, but the atmosphere grew tenser by the second. It was only a matter of time before one of the troopers cracked, regardless of orders received, and fired into the crowd.

When that happened, Ty hoped he was far from the action. Nothing must slow him down before he fulfilled his objective: getting to Bree before his father did.

She understands the choice she made, Tyler . . . and now she must face the consequences of that decision.

His father's words haunted him. Something in the man's eyes had left Ty cold. Now he knew why. Ty had watched a recording of the sentencing so many times that he'd all but memorized it. It was easy to understand why Bree's appearance had roused such a furor. She'd looked worn out, drugged, though they'd been careful to erase any visible signs of torture. And the way she seemed to drift in and out of the proceedings, spent and dazed, hadn't broken only Ty's heart, but those of millions of colonists.

Murder would come easily to him, Ty decided, should he ever cross paths with those who'd made her suffer.

He wondered whose idea it was to televise the sentencing when they could have easily chosen to have closed proceedings. Perhaps it was a last-ditch effort on the part of the president to soothe the angry colonists.

How beautifully it had backfired.

Beauchamp, Ty had never cared for. Even as a boy he'd felt uncomfortable in the president's company. The politician had a way of sucking all the air out of a room. Yet he'd commanded higher approval ratings than his father for all the years they'd worked together. Ty knew it was because his father made no excuses for what he was; he didn't try to soften his edges or play politics. He simply did his job, brutal as it often was. Beauchamp, on the other hand, was as changeable as spring weather in Montana. Ty was pleased to see the president make such a spectacular public-relations blunder. Only, why did it have to be with Bree?

Bree . . . hang tight. I'm coming.

Ty checked his wrist computer. In less than five hours Bree would be executed in front of a firing squad—unless he did something about it. Soon they'd be coming to get her, to prepare her for the event. Then the guests would arrive to watch the happening—guests that Ty was certain included his father. Ty needed to be out long before that.

Other than the blade he wore on the inside of his wrist and the laser-guided semiautomatic he hid inside his trench coat, he had his hands to do his work—and those of a childhood friend and few wartime buddies.

He'd saved his share of lives while serving in the navy. It wasn't anything he'd set out to do; in the course of battle, things happened. "I owe you, man," many a grateful soldier had told him. "If you ever need anything, anything at all, just say when and where." What he'd started with Ahmed, he'd continued here on his home shore, calling on those debts one by one. No one had turned him down.

Ty hunched his shoulders against the dampness and kept up his punishing pace toward the fort. A group of teenagers waving American flags collided with him. They spun away, but not before he glimpsed the unease in their faces. He knew what he must look like by now, after a couple of days living on the streets, but it must be worse than he thought. Better to disguise him from his father's henchmen, he thought.

After leaving his parents' home the night he'd learned

of his father's plans to execute Bree, and wanting to avoid the lonely familiarity of his small flat in the city, he'd slipped between the cracks and disappeared. He was good at it, disappearing. As a SEAL specializing in covert ops, he had the skills needed to assimilate into a culture, any culture, especially his own.

Ty took a side street he knew led to the fort's rear gate. Rubbing a hand over the stubble on his jaw, he paused to ascertain the best place to await his contact. When he was on active duty, he could pass in and out of the gates with ease. However, a man in his situation—and with his intentions—didn't dare enter in the usual way: submitting to a DNA scan that would set off alarms from here to his father's office. Luckily, he had help.

Ty didn't wait for more than a few minutes before he heard someone approach from behind.

"Yo."

Ty turned slowly. A hulking man whose family hailed from the colony of Northern Mexico stood in the shadows. He wore the uniform of a UCE major. "Chico," Ty murmured back.

They grasped each other's hand. Neither said a word, but Ty was certain gratitude was written all over his face. He hadn't known when he'd contacted him if Chico would support him or his father, and would have respected his decision either way. But Chico had seemed almost relieved. "It's time to choose sides. For the sake of my wife and kids, I want to make sure I'm on the right one."

"Then get me inside. You run the place."

"I can get you in," Chico had said. "But I can't promise you'll get out."

Ty didn't care what happened to him. It was Bree he wanted out safely. That was where the other blood debts came in. As a backup to his and Chico's high-risk plan, Ty had called on one debt that would ensure Bree's swift transport in a private magcar straight to the collection of another debt: a safe house in the form of a cattle ranch in the deserts of southwest Central, the Arizona region, with an ex-SEAL and his family. If the revolution came, Bree would be safe. If it didn't, she'd be safe, too. Where Ty factored in after tonight didn't matter.

And that was the way he needed it to be.

"Your father's coming for the execution," Chico said. "By heli-jet. He's going to land on the roof. I've got to meet him or he'll know something's up. It's bad enough as it is, most of my guards calling in sick. I've got a skeleton day shift reporting to work in a couple of hours, if that. But Armstrong will bring his own people. No matter what, stay away from the roof."

Ty nodded gravely. The last thing he wanted was a run-in with his old man in the midst of stealing away his prize prisoner.

The men walked to a late-model magcar parked in the street outside the prison gates. A folded uniform sat in the center of the backseat next to a chewed-on stuffed bunny. Chico's private car. If the car was ever searched, DNA evidence obtained would confirm that Ty had been there, solidifying Chico's guilt. Chico didn't have to take such a personal stake in this. Leaving a uniform somewhere Ty could find it would have been good enough. But he'd done more, so much more.

"*Viva* Mexico," Chico murmured in response to Ty's thankful gaze.

Now it was clearer why Chico was willing to put so much on the line. If the UCE unraveled, other colonies besides Central would have a chance at freedom. Chico wanted his birth colony to be free.

Ty changed clothes in the backseat of the car, cloaked by the dark, wet night. When he climbed back out, he stood for Chico's intense inspection. Chico checked for the presence of a transponder embedded in the uniform. The transponder would get him through the gates. What happened once they were inside the prison would depend on how much of what Chico had promised actually materialized.

It had better, Ty thought. Options were few, and time was short.

"You need a shave," his friend told him, a trace of a smile playing around his lips. "What happened to the picture-perfect SEAL I knew?"

"He found some buried treasure." Ty stroked his chin. "Do I need to clean up?"

"Don't sweat it." The prison chief reached into the car and retrieved two helmets, one for each of them. With a dark face shield capable of night imaging, it would hide his features. Ty could see his own dark and sinister reflection reflected in Chico's mask.

"Ready, man?"

Ty replied with a curt nod. They were going in.

Bree jackknifed up in bed, blinking in the darkness until her vision was as clear as it was going to get. Her heart pounded as if she'd just finished a 10K race. Impending death had a way of getting the blood going.

What was she doing sleeping with so little time left?

The drugs . . . They'd given her something strong after dinner, and it had put her out cold. She hadn't wanted to waste what could be her last hours sleeping; she'd begged the hated guard she called the commandant not to knock her out, but the cold woman had. How long had she slept? What time was it?

Why was it so quiet?

Bree concentrated, listening. The hall was as hushed as her cell. No one else was imprisoned in this section, but usually she could hear the guards—talking, coughing, laughing, and generally making a racket, even at night. Now there was no sound at all except for the faint hiss of air. Where was everyone?

"Hey," she whispered to her collar. "You with me?"

The Voice didn't reply.

"Hello?"

Nothing. She jammed a hand through her lank hair. How could she justify waiting any longer for the Voice of Freedom to get back to her when her life was on the line?

She pushed off the bed and went to the door, clinging to the bars. It was quiet. Too quiet. Then she heard a thumping noise coming from the section of the hallway she couldn't see. It grew louder. A guard. *Damn it.* And he was running full speed, by the sound of it.

The guard turned the corner and lumbered to a stop outside her cell. One look at the shock of salt-and-pepper hair and breasts the size of watermelons told Bree who it was: her nemesis the commandant, the terrifying guard who had so efficiently assisted in the mechanics of her torture.

"You must come, come now," the guard grumbled. It was the same greeting she always used when coming to fetch her for the interrogations. Surely they weren't going to try to fit in a torture session this close to her execution. Unless the guard had come to *escort* her to the execution.

Like hell would she go easily. Bree stepped back from the bars. This revolution, like any other, was going to have its share of martyrs. Given a choice, Bree would rather not be one of them. If she had to be killed, she wanted it to be in action. She wanted to go out in a blaze of glory.

Bree took a couple of steadying breaths, pumping her arms to get the blood flowing to them.

The door slid open, and the guard stepped inside the cell. "You will come. Come now—"

"Make me!" Bree threw a punch. Her fist impacted under the woman's hairy jaw. Pain shot up her arm from her knuckles.

Bree rubbed her knuckles as the guard took a single staggering step backward and growled—actually growled—like a childhood version of a monster. But then, lowering her head, the guard launched her big body forward.

Bree thrust a leg out and tripped her. The impact spun her around as the commandant crashed to the floor. A pistol attached to the guard's belt flew across the cell, ricocheting off the back wall like a hockey puck.

Pushing up on thick arms, the guard swept her gaze around to find her lost weapon. Surprise registered on her face, then desperation. Before she could snatch back the gun, Bree whirled in a roundhouse kick, knocking away her hand. Then she used her momentum to swing around for another go.

The kick caught the guard on the side of the head. A grunt of pain and the woman went down again. Down, yes, but still not out. How many freaking times was it going to take for David to topple Goliath?

Bree hefted the pistol into her hands and aimed. The surveillance viewers embedded in her cell and all through the corridor were recording every second of this, she thought. By now, someone in a far-off room could have already thrown the alarm switch.

Her body fidgeted, screaming at her to run. If she didn't get the hell out of this section soon, more guards would be on the way. She hadn't seen a single one besides this woman, but it didn't mean they weren't there. However, armed or not, no way could she leave the place dressed in a fluorescent-orange jumpsuit that screamed, *I'm an escaped prisoner.* She opted to delay five more minutes to trade clothes with the commandant.

Bree aimed the gun at the woman's head. "Take off your uniform."

"No! You must come with me now."

"I don't think so."

The guard was halfway to her knees. The whites of her eyes had turned almost red with rage, and she foamed at the mouth like a rabid dog.

Bree aimed. "Sit. Stay!"

A sound rumbled ominously in the guard's throat.

Bree released the safety on the pistol. The guards didn't carry stunners; they packed the real thing. These guns had one setting: kill. "I have no problem blowing your head off," she warned. "Take off your clothes and give them to me." Bree stared down the sight of the pistol. Sweat ran down her forehead and made her eyes sting. She swiped at her face with the back of her hand. "The weapons belt first. Slide it to me."

The big woman unbuckled her belt, her eyes never leaving Bree. She stood there, the belt dangling from her hand.

"Slide it!" Bree snapped.

The belt scraped over the floor. Bree kicked it outside the cell, into the corridor. "The rest. Now!"

The commandant tugged off one boot. Then the other.

"Faster!"

The commandant continued to undress at a maddeningly slow speed until she finally sat on the floor in a massively constructed bra and panties: regular boring white panties. Bree was almost disappointed not to see the jockstrap she'd expected. "Give me the uniform!"

Finally the commandant threw the wadded-up clothes at Bree. The guard was a large woman. The size difference suited her needs perfectly. She couldn't get rid of her prison jumpsuit—it was how the Voice of Freedom contacted her. The guard uniform would have to go on top of it.

Bree backed out into the corridor and removed the handcuffs from the commandant's belt. She slid them across the cell floor to the woman. "Put them on."

The guard glowered at her, dangling the handcuffs from an index finger.

"A battle of wills is pretty stupid when someone's got a gun pointed down your throat," Bree said calmly.

The commandant seemed to think so, too. She opened the cuffs.

"Lock one on your wrist and the other on the bars. That's it. Good."

The woman was now locked to the bars inside the cell. Bree had the key.

She closed and locked the cell door. "*Hasta la vista,* baby," she said, and took off running.

The halls were empty, eerily so. Where were all the guards? The prison was large, the floor plan like a maze. *Which way out?*

What was it the Voice had told her to do? *Look above when things grow darkest. Get as high as you can. Look to the sky, and you'll know.*

Look above? Bree did, and saw only the ceiling. *Get as high as you can.* Bree's heart jumped. The roof! That was where she needed to go.

She remembered a ladder she'd seen leading up fire-house-style to the next floor, and returned to it. She didn't know where it led, but it went up. That was a good start.

She clambered up the ladder. Once on the next floor, she flattened herself against the wall, peering up and down the corridor. No one was around.

The ladder continued up to the next higher floor. She took it and repeated the drill five more times before she hit a brick wall—literally. But carved in the brick wall was a heavy porthole-shaped door. And it was open.

Bree hesitated before going through it. Was it a trap, leading her onto the roof and certain capture? Or was someone like the Voice facilitating her escape?

What are your choices? You can backtrack and try to get out another way. Or you can trust in the Shadow Voice and see what waits on the roof.

What was the worst that could happen to her, anyway? Execution? The way she saw it, that was already on the schedule for today. She gazed moodily at the lightening sky. And not too far off, by the looks of it.

"Freeze!" someone shouted from the floor below. "Stay there. Do not move."

Bree peered down through the ladder opening, her pistol gripped in two hands. Two armed UCE prison guards dressed in riot gear were climbing the rungs.

Bree yelled at them. "Throw down your weapons, or I'll shoot!"

"Bree!" One of the guards lifted his face mask. "It's me—Ty."

A strangled sound that said far more than she was able to verbalize slipped from her throat. His hair was cut short again, but it looked as if it had been days since he'd shaved—or slept, judging by the shadows under his eyes.

She wanted to run to him, to throw her arms around him. *No.*

She steeled herself against all emotion. What if the drugs were still circulating in her system? The last time she'd had this dream that Ty was wearing the uniform of a UCE officer, he'd walked away from her, leaving her to die. "I'm getting out of here, Ty. Don't try to stop me."

"Bree, no. Don't go out of the roof. General Armstrong's heli-jet's due to arrive any minute. He's come to watch your execution."

She inched toward the open porthole. "I'm supposed to go outside."

"On whose orders?" Ty appeared distraught. And who was the man standing with him? He was big and very quiet. A stranger.

"I can't tell you!"

"Listen, Bree. You've got to trust me."

She swallowed, her mouth dry. "I'm not sure I trust anyone right now."

He flinched, as if her words had hit him like physical blows. "I don't know what they did to you in here, if they turned you against me, but I'm here to get you out. There's a supply truck waiting downstairs in the depot. We'll get in the back and get the hell out. Up here, we're trapped. If you go out on that roof, we're dead."

Her aim didn't waver. She wanted so much to believe him. Then she thought of Lee-lee, and it took all she had not to pistol-whip the man.

Thwap, thwap, thwap. She jerked her attention to the open roof door. One thing that hadn't changed much in 170 years was the sound of a chopper.

"Goddamn," Ty's friend muttered. "He's here already? Two fucking hours early! I'm going out to meet him. Whatever you do, stay hidden—and keep her hidden—until I get everyone down from the roof and inside."

His friend departed, presumably for a different way out to the roof. Ty turned back to Bree. "That's my father in the heli-jet. He'll have a security detail with him that won't be interested in getting you anywhere but out in front of a firing squad."

"Who's your friend?" she asked.

"He commands this prison."

"But he's helping you help me."

"He's on our side, Bree. Ninety percent of the guards working here are. They saw your trial. I saw it, too. Before, you fought with missiles; now you fight with passion. You've inspired the entire colony, Bree, and much of the world."

"Everyone keeps saying this. But I'm just me, slogging my way through something I know nothing about."

"People don't follow status, Bree. They follow courage.

If you're willing to lead them to freedom, they'll follow you. And so will I."

Her eyes filled. "Ty . . ." Her throat squeezed tight.

He fought a visible struggle to get hold of himself as well. "I love you, Bree. Trust me."

No one could fake the look in his eyes, the way he gazed at her as if there were nothing in the world more important to him.

She sat back on her haunches, her pistol dangling from one hand. "Where the hell were you?"

Ty was up the ladder with her gathered in his arms before she had a chance to blink. She shoved against him, pummeling his breastplate with her fists. "They beat me. They interrogated me. I waited for you. Why didn't you come—why?"

Cognizant of her gun, he grabbed her wrists. "I'm here now," he soothed. "I'm here. I'm not leaving your side. I'm getting you out of here. Out and far away, baby."

She fell into his embrace, closing her eyes, pressing her cheek to his leather breastplate. He rocked her gently, and she breathed in his scent. Ah, how she loved him. "I guess we're even now. I got you out of Kyber's dungeon, and you're getting me out of this hellhole."

"Not unless we get moving." He jerked his chin toward the orange jumpsuit peeking through her guard uniform. "You should get rid of that."

"I can't. The Voice of Freedom contacted me using some kind of transmission device in the collar. Except that the Voice never seems to be around when you need her."

"He's a she?"

"Well, is she a he?"

"I don't know."

"Neither do I. I decided to pick a gender and stick with it. Less confusing."

"What did he say, the Voice?"

"That she was working on getting me out of here."

"That explains this, then." Ty waved a hand at the open porthole to the roof. "All the doors to the place are unlocked. The security system's been hacked into somehow, but they can't trace it. They don't know who did it. What was supposed to be impossible has happened. Key areas of security are disabled, but not all of them."

"When did it start?"

"Right after I got here."

"You've got to be kidding me."

"I'm not. The few guards who showed up for work today are outside guarding the exits."

"Not all," she muttered. "One's handcuffed to my cell."

His mouth tipped crookedly. "Why am I not surprised?" He reached for her collar to help fasten the clips to a breastplate, helping hide her jumpsuit. She could feel his body heat. She could smell him. Every cell in her body reacted. She could block out so many things, but never him. Never Ty.

Her eyes lifted to his, and she saw how dark his eyes had become. A jolt of attraction shot between them, but this was neither the place nor the time to do anything about it.

He grabbed her by the upper arms. "We've got to go, Bree. We've got to do it now. Chico's busy distracting my father. If the security system comes back up, it's going to get ugly for us. Let's get out while we can."

She shook her head when he tugged her toward the

ladder. "No, not down. Up. The Voice told me to look to the sky and I'd know what to do. I think she means the roof."

"That's suicide!"

"Is it?" She pushed away from Ty and went to the circular door. Crouching, her weapon drawn, she peeked around the door frame. The heli-jet sat in a painted circle in the middle of the roof. Wind rushed past, pushed by the spin of the vertical engines. In edgy, tense silence, they watched a severe-looking man dressed in a crisp black trench coat and a high-crowned, General Patton–type hat trimmed in patent leather storm away from the craft. He had sharp cheekbones and a hard mouth, and looked as impossible and arrogant as she knew he was. It was easy to see why many said the Ax had designs on the UCE presidency, wanting to install a military dictatorship in its place—with him in charge, of course.

Ty's friend Chico and another officer escorted the general off the roof. The heli-jet pilot followed a few moments later. The whine of the engines faded as they spun slower and slower.

"That's it," she cried, turning to Ty. "That's what the Shadow Voice meant. The heli-jet. We're supposed to hijack it. The Voice must have known somehow that it'd be left here, unguarded."

"It's ideal. The craft has weapons and stealth tech—the best the UCE has, and probably even more equipment than I'm guessing. We'll be invisible to anyone tracking us." Ty's face lit up. "I'm going to fly my father's heli-jet to his house."

"His house . . . ? I think we need a better idea."

"No. It's the house I grew up in—in Montana. It's

locked up tighter than Fort Powell ever was. Better than that, no one would expect we'd have the gall to go there, particularly my father."

"Okay." Bree's heart was beating hard. "We've got the plan, the means, and the motivation. But do you know how to fly that thing? I don't."

"I've got a couple of thousand hours flight time in heli-jets. Haven't flown in a while, but—"

"I don't care! Let's go!"

Guns at the ready, they burst through the door and into the cold, predawn air. Hands clasped together, they bolted for the heli-jet.

A voice pierced the silence. "Freeze!"

Bree swung her attention around to the source of the sound. Behind her was a UCE guard, his arms extended, a rifle aimed right between her eyes.

Chapter Nineteen

Outside the palace, Kyber crouched. Dressed in black, he knew he was almost impossible to see when he stood, swinging a cablelike rope over his head. His heart thumped hard, and he knew it wasn't from the jog through the shadowy palace grounds. He would soon show Cam that there was nothing more he could do for Banzai, but oh, so much he could do for her.

"Kublai, on second thought, this isn't such a good idea," Cam said. "If we get caught, I'll probably get a scolding, but you'll get fired. Or worse."

"Impossible, pretty one."

"Lack of self-confidence has never been an issue for you, has it?"

Only where you are concerned, he wanted to say. With a grunt of effort, he threw the rope to the balcony high above.

It hooked around the railing. Kyber tested it. "It's good. Now you simply hold on and the rope will carry us up."

Her mouth twisted as she gazed skeptically at the rope dangling from the balcony. "And if he meets us at the top? The flesh-eating prince?"

"He does not eat human flesh!" Kublai lowered his voice. "No more than I . . ." He drew her close and kissed her, a hungry, deep kiss. She giggled, a muffled laugh against his mouth, until the heat took her, too.

Sometime into the embrace, driven by a sixth sense, Kyber pulled away from Cam to find his bemused chief of security walking up to them. Nikolai peered at them as if his vision had somehow failed him. "Kublai?"

At least the man had the wherewithal to remember to call him by his alias. "Nazeem, greetings. Out enjoying the pleasant evening, too, I see."

"It is a rather . . . warm night for this time of year, I see." The smile was in Nikolai's tone rather than on his face. "I suspected you might be out strolling in the gardens, so I thought I'd have a look."

Kyber knew what the chief really meant was that the prox-beacon embedded in Kublai's clothing showed him sneaking about the palace gardens at night, and the chief wanted to make sure the clothes were still on Kyber's back and not some intruder's. Had they not been on Kyber, he'd have alerted palace security immediately and raised a barrier around the gardens, preventing escape.

Cam appeared quite happy to see the chief. There had always been a quiet respect between the two. "Are you on your way out? Nice suit."

"Thank you." The chief ran a hand down the crisp, dark gray collarless outfit he wore daily. It was a far cry from his dusty Rim Rider wear. He looked to have wanted to return the compliment, but couldn't seem to form one that would suit Cam's disheveled, though rather adorable, appearance. Her white shirt was dirty and snagged in several places, and dark stains on her silk pants confirmed her collision with a wall of kimchi pots. "So, what are you two doing at this late hour?" he asked casually.

"Breaking in, if you can believe it," she confided.

"Oh, I can believe it," the chief said with a stern glance in Kyber's direction.

"You Rim Riders are definitely the kingdom's bad boys."

Nikolai lifted a brow at Kyber. The man had an impressive range of nonverbal communication, and it was clear he didn't approve of their lies extending beyond their now-ended mission as Rim Riders. *I hadn't intended for it to be so, either, Niko.*

But he'd rectify that tonight. "She wants her audience with the prince, Nazeem, and I intend to give it to her."

"I see. With all due respect, Your H—" The chief stopped himself before he blurted out the royal title. Before he began again, his gaze settled on Cam, warmed, then cooled as he returned his attention to Kyber. "I hope you know what you're doing."

With sudden and unaccustomed qualms, Kyber hoped so, too.

Nikolai turned to Cam. "A pleasant evening to you."

"And to you," she replied.

He hesitated, then said, "Yours is a true heart; have the courage to follow it."

Cam watched the chief go, her puzzlement obvious. "Why do I always get the feeling that your communication with Nazeem exists on two levels—the conversation I hear, and the one that's really taking place?"

"Do you really want to know?"

"Well, yes."

"Because I'm really the emperor and he's the chief of palace security."

Cam snorted. "I knew I shouldn't have asked."

Kyber tugged on the rope. That was the dress rehearsal, he thought. He hoped the live performance went better.

He placed the rope in her hands and hooked the supports under the soles of her shoes. Gripping the rope, he stepped behind her and did the same. "Up," he commanded, and their feet shot off the grass.

They slowed as they reached the balcony. "Vault over the railing," he told her. "On my count, one . . . two . . . three."

They flew over the railing and landed in a heap on the floor of the balcony. "He had to have heard that," she whispered loudly, her blue eyes wide with alarm.

"He's not in his chambers," Kyber said briskly.

"How can you be sure?"

"You'll see." He opened the French doors that led to his private bedchamber. A floor of rough-hewn wooden planks bore the muted sheen of hand-waxing, reflecting the fire crackling in his fireplace. His rooms were decorated differently from the rest of the palace, more to his personal taste, both as an ode to his barbarian ancestors and to conjure the sense of freedom he experienced when on the road as Kublai.

"Wow," Cam whispered. "This is beautiful. The rumors may color him evil, but he's got great taste."

Kyber smiled.

"Look at that bed—fur blankets! What I wouldn't give to spend a night under those."

"Wish and you shall have it, pretty one."

She flashed him a look. "And risk him coming back here and catching us? No, thanks."

He faced her, clasping her hands in his. "I'm the prince," he said in a low voice.

Cam rolled her eyes. "You used that joke already."

"It's not a joke."

Her expression grew serious. "Okay . . ."

"I am Prince Kyber of the Hans, acting emperor of all Asia. I rode out to the Rim in my alter ego, Kublai, because I didn't trust anyone else to the task of bringing you safely back to the palace. It turns out I cannot even trust myself, at least not around you. I never planned for this to happen. I never planned to develop feelings for you."

She merely stared at him, dumbstruck.

He took advantage of her shock to reverse the effects of the nanopigment on his skin, and watched her expression grow even more incredulous as the tattoo faded. Then he removed the colored lenses masking his true eye color and placed the disks in a dish on his bedside table.

"My God. You're the *prince!*" Then she covered her eyes with her hands. "Sorry, this is taking some time to sink in."

"I expected it would."

"I mean, I meet a cute guy, a nice guy—under unusual circumstances, I admit. We click. Having been through a traumatic experience with a capital T, I yearn to have wild and crazy sex with him, even though I've known him for less than two weeks, but it doesn't matter like it would usually matter because there's a connection, you see, and of course there's the trauma, which is my excuse for this behavior if I can't find any others. So, I pressure him into taking me home and I find out that he's a prince. Not any prince—the heir to one of the wealthiest and most powerful empires the Earth has ever known." Her hands flew to her temples. "So, this is what you meant when you said things were complicated."

Her sarcastic humor amused him. He was surprised she was taking this as well as she was.

Then Cam's mouth tipped irritably. "You never answered my requests to see you. I asked a dozen times, Kublai."

"Kyber," he corrected patiently.

"Kyber. You ignored me. You blew me off."

He struggled to make sense of her twenty-first-century slang. "Your requests for an audience—I handled them poorly, I know."

"I was pissed. I still am!"

"I didn't know what to do, Cam. Never in my life have I chosen a direction that's left me so unsure of the outcome. I was comfortable as Kublai, but the thought of being myself around you made me falter."

She gave a soft whistle. "You're saying what *you* think."

"Ah, and that, too—this saying whatever comes to mind. It comes from too much time in your company, I suspect."

"But it feels good, right?"

Like repeated kicks to the solar plexus, he thought. "As for your requesting to see me, I knew you'd ask about Banzai's disappearance, of which I know no more than you, and that only made it worse."

The affectionate smile she wore faded. "You're serious about that last part. You really don't know where she is."

"No. And not from lack of trying. I didn't want you to suffer the same fate, which is why you're here now. My goal was to treat you entirely different from Banzai, allowing you the freedom to come and go from the palace, so that you wouldn't feel restricted and thus be tempted to leave."

"Bree can get prickly about that. Feeling confined."

"Yes," he said. "She can."

Cam quieted, turning her gaze away to study her hands, which she'd clasped in front of her. She had a way of carrying herself that was naturally regal. If he hadn't known better, he'd have guessed she was born to royalty, and like him a victim of a childhood of etiquette lessons and lectures on personal appearance. "It's wonderful to find such a steadfast protector," she said finally, looking up. "But why are you so protective over two pilots, two American pilots, whom you've never met?"

"Why?" He thought on it. "Why . . . I don't know why, exactly. Perhaps because you were found here in my kingdom, both of you. And because it was the actions of a group who once ruled over a region here that caused you to be shot down—and I felt compelled to atone for it." He thought some more. "And because it seemed like the right thing to do."

Cam touched his hand. "That's so selfless. So admirable."

"And because I hate the UCE with every last molecule of my being. Imperialist pigs. Bastards. You cannot trust them. They do not deserve you or Banzai."

He brushed past her, driving his hands through his hair. "And so here we are, Cam. I hope I can salvage the mess I've made of this." Why? Since the question was being asked, he might as well answer it, if only to himself. He wanted Cam in his life—in what way, exactly, still baffled him, but he wanted her all the same. "When it comes to lying, I've learned all too well that the longer you dig the hole, the deeper it gets. I brought you here because I want to end the dishonesty."

She closed the distance between them with a few steps. "It's done, Kublai—*Kyber*. Mercy, it's going to be difficult getting used to that name, but you got over Scarlet, so I can do this, too. And I'm sure you've heard it before, but your eyes are the most arresting shade of gray. Let's not belabor this. We're mature adults with a heck of an evening to look forward to, so let's do that and forget that you lied your pants off, and that I can't trust you farther than I can throw you." Her hands came up at his expression, which was surely one of intense dismay. "Kidding."

Chuckling with relief, he gathered her close, smoothing a hand over her tousled hair.

"You're still Kublai the Rim Rider to me," she murmured. "Just with a few more responsibilities."

"A few," he agreed dryly, and she smiled up at him.

"The prince of Asia." She shook her head. "It's a little overwhelming."

He slipped a hand behind her head and brought her close for a thorough kiss.

"So was *that*," she whispered, her eyes still closed and her chin tipped up.

"Come." He took her by the hand and led her into his sitting room, enjoying her pleased reaction to the massive rugged fireplace, where an enormous white wool rug commanded a place of honor. "Here, Cam, I will make thorough and delicious love to you—"

He stopped short. Cam crashed into him from behind. Peeking around his back, she joined him in staring agape at the rug, where a nude woman slept, sprawled on her stomach.

The woman rolled over and sat up sleepily. "Your Highness." Undisturbed by Cam's presence, she struck a come-hither pose.

Would nothing go his way tonight? First Niko, then this concubine. He didn't dare glance at Cam's face for fear of what he'd find there.

"Out," Kyber said to the concubine. "Out now."

"It's okay," Cam pleaded under her breath as the woman gathered her robe and slippers. "She was probably told to come here."

"I am sure she was!" Hadn't he ordered the staff to cease sending women to his chambers? Maybe he'd forgotten. Since returning from the Rim, he'd noticed his mind had been in disarray. And he knew precisely whom to blame.

As the woman hurried from the room, Kyber combed his hands through his hair and faced Cam. What next? "Never a dull moment," he offered somewhat sheepishly.

"I can see that." The color was high in her cheeks—he couldn't tell if it was due to embarrassment, anger, or both. "If I sleep with you, are you going to keep sleeping with them?"

He practically stuttered, something he didn't believe he'd done once his entire life. "I haven't given it any thought."

Cam spoke slowly in that Southern drawl of hers. "Did you think I'd be so impressed by all the wealth, all the luxury, and the attention of a handsome prince that nothing else would matter? That I wouldn't care if you kept your life just the way you liked it, having sex with these women whenever you weren't having sex with me?"

He started to reply in the negative, but his own inner voice stopped him. Hadn't some part of him wished Cam wouldn't care? That he wouldn't have to change a thing, and he could keep her in his life?

Hurt flickered in her eyes. She replied before he could. "You can't even answer that one simple question. You know what? The Mongolians were wrong about you. You don't eat human flesh; you break women's hearts."

"I didn't think a heart could break unless it was given."

She gave him a scathing look. "You're right. I haven't handed over the whole thing yet, but I've given up a pretty big chunk. It happened the night you gave me that massage. You were there for me. You didn't ask for anything in return. You were kind and generous and funny, and . . . Oh, forget it."

She turned on her heel and strode back to the open French doors. Then, realizing it would make for a quicker escape, she veered toward the hallway door.

And collided with him. "Cam . . . wait. I didn't mean any offense."

"For a man with dozens of women at his beck and call, you know surprisingly little about them."

"You're right."

She appeared as surprised as he was that he'd admitted such a thing.

"I don't have a lot of experience with women—not in an adult relationship as equals. Wait, that's not correct; I have absolutely no experience with such matters."

"How old are you?"

He prayed it wasn't a trick question. "Thirty years."

"And, uh, what have you been doing all this time? Ruling?"

"More or less. Providing for my people, hunting down assassins, throwing my brother in jail, only to learn that my mother betrayed us all."

She blanched. "The story about your father being poisoned is true. Only he was the emperor."

"Of course it's true. I know it may be hard to believe, but the only untruth I've perpetuated with you is that of my identity."

"Don't dress it up with fancy words. Perpetuating untruths is lying."

He took her hand in his and plunged to one knee. "I have to build your trust all over again, I see."

"Kyber . . ." Cam appeared uneasy with his stance of contrition.

"Let me begin with the concubines. Yes, they're at the palace for all the reasons you suspect. For my entire adult life I have indulged in their services." Even during Banzai's stay at the palace, he realized, when he thought he fancied the pilot, he'd called a concubine to his chambers every night. "The staff sends them here because they know no different, Cam, but I haven't so much as touched one since I returned from the Rim."

"No kisses?"

"No kisses."

She lifted a brow. "Massages?"

He could feel a smile playing at the corners of his mouth. "No. Nothing. By now the staff no doubt believes me afflicted with a rare personal ailment."

Whose symptoms include focusing on one woman, he

thought. *Wanting her company only.* Perhaps he ought to get treatment for this malady, lest he begin to entertain thoughts of monogamy and commitment overly much.

"I have not been with a woman since I met you, Cam. I have not kissed a woman, touched, smelled, or tasted one, since I returned from the Rim. I haven't wanted anyone else but you. Now, will you please let me make love to you, so that I can get you out of my system? Lord knows I've waited long enough." He climbed back to his feet as she threw back her head and laughed.

"You're irredeemable," she accused. "Impossible." He caught a glimpse of her blue eyes sparkling before she leaned forward and kissed him full on the mouth. "And in rebuttal to what you said, it's been me who's been waiting, me who's had to put up with your relentless I-want-you, I-don't-want-you behavior, me who's—"

He swept her off her feet. "You who will not have to complain about a lack of intimate attention after this night!"

He carried her, laughing, toward the white rug, then stopped, remembering the woman they'd found there. Turning, he strode with Cam in his arms to his bed. And then he remembered the manicurist who'd last stretched out on those covers. He realized then that he didn't want his first time with Cam to be where he'd been before with other women. That ruled out the baths, the balcony, and the swimming pool, too.

Cam appeared bemused by his indecision. "Can't decide where to drop me?"

"No, I have decided." He strode with her in his arms, uncaring of the amused stares of the few servants out and about this late hour in the residential wing.

"Where? The museum?"

He snorted. "No. Though it'd be an apt location for a relic like you."

"A relic!" she protested.

"A sexy, beautiful relic."

He laughed at her delighted outrage. He couldn't remember a time since his father's sickness that he'd felt this lighthearted. He certainly couldn't recall feeling this way with a woman, as if they were actually . . . friends.

He carried Cam all the way to the kitchen wing, through the double swinging doors out to the small herb garden, and on to the door of a soaring glass building.

"A greenhouse?" Cam asked with clear anticipation. "I like it. It'll be hot and humid. Just like home."

"Not the greenhouse, though it would be suitable." He wanted something more than suitable, however. He wanted a place as special as the woman.

Behind the greenhouse was a long, low-roofed building over 150 years old. He carried Cam inside. Like the greenhouse, it was heated, moist and warm, but not uncomfortably so. "This place was a favorite of mine when I was a boy." He lowered Cam to her feet and watched her take in the scents and sights: the lush landscaping, the thousands of blooms in every shape and color, and the thousands of slumbering butterflies that clung to the stems and leaves.

"By day they fill the air," he said. "Their wings make a soft, incessant sound, like a sea of dry, rustling paper."

"This is incredible." Cam spoke in hushed tones, as if loath to disturb them. "I feel like I've stepped into a storybook—a fantasy story."

He locked the door securely behind them and led her

deeper into the butterfly preserve, following a path he could find with his eyes closed. The thick foliage opened to a small meadow with precisely cut grass, as soft to the touch as his fur blankets. There were chairs to sit on and watch the butterflies, but he chose the lawn.

There he turned to gaze down at Cam's upturned face. He ran his fingers down her skin. Then he took the butterfly he held between his fingers and let it flutter its wings against her cheek. She laughed softly and closed her eyes. "Butterfly kisses."

He set the butterfly free, replacing its light caresses with his own. With his fingers he explored the contours of her face and throat, savoring her, learning her. Had he taken her the night of the massage, it would have been swift and hard and driven by hunger. Tonight, though his desire was powerful, he was determined to take his time.

Turning her head into his exploration, she took his fingertip in her mouth and suckled gently. Heat flared in his loins and a soft groan escaped his locked jaw.

They ended up on the grass, though he didn't quite remember at what point in their kiss the repositioning happened, or who initiated it.

Their clothes came off, his heavier Rim Rider gear and her gauzier blouse and pants. And then she was stretched out on the grass, her curves glowing in the muted overhead light.

He snatched an unwitting butterfly out of the air and held it, wings fluttering, over Cam, letting the tiny creature beat its wings against her bared body. She laughed, her toned stomach muscles flexing. She was long, slender, and athletic, her breasts small, her hips narrow: to him, the most heartrendingly perfect woman he'd ever seen.

"You're beautiful, Cam," he told her, pressing his lips to her throat as he inhaled her scent.

"So are you," she whispered back.

He chuckled. "I have been called many things, but never that."

She flattened her hands on his chest. "Well, you are," she said huskily, smoothing her palms over the contours of his torso, his ribs and abs, and then trailing her fingertip from his navel and lower. There, in her quiet yet uninhibited way, she took hold of him, and caressed him along his entire length.

Teeth clenched, he drew in a breath. A feather-light sensation contrasted with her firm stroking and caused him to open eyes he hadn't realized he'd shut. He looked down at her hand. She'd been holding a butterfly, letting it flutter against his overheated, sensitive skin. The pleasure-pain almost overwhelmed him. He felt himself move in her hand. Much more of this touching and . . .

He took Cam's wrist, moving away her hand. With the single-minded intent of pleasuring her, he pressing her down to the grass, whispering in her ear as he moved over her, drawing out sighs with intimate compliments and erotic promises. For so long he'd been the recipient of such attention. Now he was able to give the gift of what he'd learned.

And he did, sliding lower on her long body until he found what he wanted. Gently spreading her thighs, he opened her to his attention, stroking and suckling her most sensitive places. He took his time with her, learning what pleased her, ignoring her pleas for completion until the last of her long, shuddering climax faded away.

"Sweet heaven, Kyber," she whispered. "Oh, mercy."

He smiled down at her. Sweat glistened on her body, and her face was flushed. "Do you expect me to move after that?"

His laughter was deep. He grabbed her wrists and tugged her up to him. "I expect you to do far more than move, pretty one." He pulled her legs over his hips until she sat astride him. The heat of her body astonished him. Fully inside her, he cradled her face in his palms and kissed her.

Cam sighed into his mouth, holding fast to his shoulders as her hips began a slow, undulating motion, sending thick, aching pleasure radiating outward. He didn't know whether to moan, groan, or laugh out loud with the joy of making love to this woman, this woman who had chosen to be with him not out of duty or trade but out of desire, who had the attitude, grace, and patience to take everything he threw at her, intentionally and otherwise, and the moxie to give it right back. He could be a forceful, intimidating man. He liked that she didn't allow him to ride roughshod over her.

They swayed together, their skin moist with sweat, their scents mingling. Gradually all the barriers and reservations fell away, and they gave in to the heady wonder of the act itself.

Cam said very little. For a woman who was so talkative out of bed, she was so very silent in it. But what she didn't express with words, she did with a full range of sighs and moans and facial expressions that vividly reassured him that she felt this lovemaking as intensely as he did.

"Cam," he said on a harsh breath. Her hands covered his buttocks and urged him toward his release.

He expelled an explosive breath, threw back his head.

His peak was unbridled and prolonged. He heard the butterflies waking and taking flight all around them. The air stirred, rustling, an explosion of powdery wings feathering against his heaving body and Cam's. Wrapping her arms over his shoulders, she held him close, murmuring his name and sweet endearments, kissing him until he'd settled somewhat back to earth.

For the longest time, Kyber held Cam, even after his wits had more or less returned. With his lips buried in her damp hair as she sagged helpless against him, he couldn't help pondering the difficulty of going back to the concubines and their favors now that he'd finally learned, after countless women, the definition of the term *making love*.

Chapter Twenty

The "afterward" with Kyber wasn't anything like Cam feared. She'd half expected him to retreat from her, moody and silent, in reaction to the intimacy.

He did anything but.

After making love a second time, they dawdled in the meadow of sleeping butterflies. Her body was wobbly and exhausted, but this time she liked the reason.

Kyber stretched out on his side in the grass next to her in all his naked glory. "The first time I ever saw you was in a picture," he said, running his fingers down her cheek. "It was one of several taken by a craft flying over the collective where you were recovering."

"Aerial photography," she murmured. That explained the plane she saw in Mongolia.

"You were struggling with crutches on an uneven dirt road, trying to stand after a fall. Such determination I saw in your posture. Raw willpower. It affected me somehow, seeing that in another person." He dragged his thumb over her parted lips. "I felt a sense of solidarity with you, even though I didn't know you, and never expected I would."

"And I never expected that aircraft would bring me to you," she whispered.

A noise interrupted them. "My beeper," he grumbled. He pushed off the ground and wrestled a small computer out of a heap of clothing. As he lifted the device to his eyes, his face formed immediately into a frown.

Her sixth sense alerted her to danger. She sat up, her bare breasts bouncing slightly. "What is it?"

"An emergency."

Her heart skipped a beat. "Does it have anything to do with the people who want to kill me?"

He showed her the computer. "The source of these images is the Interweb."

The small screen displayed an angry, surging crowd locked behind gates.

"Isn't that the UCE?"

"It is."

The images showed UCE soldiers walking with a woman, pushing her along. A bolt of recognition shot through Cam. Then horror. "That's Bree!" she cried.

"Yes," Kyber said grimly.

Cam stared at the screen, horrified. "She's under arrest." Bree's posture was defiant, but she limped and favored her right arm. "What did she do?"

It was the announcer who answered her question and raised a dozen new ones. "After the most comprehensive manhunt in history, the traitor known as Banzai Maguire is now in custody."

Traitor? Bree? "How can she be a traitor if our country doesn't exist anymore?

271

"In light of the current national state of emergency, President Beauchamp has called for swift justice," the announcer said in a Central UCE accent. "Charged with multiple counts of treason, Banzai Maguire will await trial at Fort Powell under the highest security. High treason is a capital offense."

Cam lowered the computer. "This is bullshit."

"It's the way of the UCE," Kyber explained, taking her hand and raising her to her feet. "Imperialist scum, they are. You will soon see. They're the scourge of the earth."

"I don't mean the UCE; I mean you!" She ripped her hand from his fingers. "Why didn't you tell me Bree was in trouble?"

He appeared startled by her ferocity. *Too bad.* Her job was to fly on Bree's wing, and now her flight leader was in big-time trouble. Tact and social graces didn't factor in.

"Cam, I didn't know of Banzai's whereabouts. I told you that. It was the truth. She was last seen in New Seoul. After that she left the kingdom by sea or by air with her lover."

Lover? Cam stared at Kyber's mouth. She couldn't believe what had come out of it. Bree had a lover? *Good for you, lady.* What was the name Zhurihe had mentioned . . . the man Bree had saved from the dungeons? Tyler Armstrong. That was him, Cam thought.

"Somewhere along the way, Cam, just as she was warned, UCE forces caught up to Banzai and captured her."

Cam jammed her legs into her stained pants, tugging them up to her waist. "Bree hasn't done anything wrong." Or had she? "At least, judging by what you've said, I don't think she has."

"She's been consorting with rebels, and that brings with it danger. The Shadow Voice, or the Voice of Freedom, depending whose side is doing the calling, is an anonymous rebel advocating sociopolitical change. It's been using Banzai Maguire for months now as a symbol to motivate the colonists to rebel."

"Well, it looks like it's working."

"Yes. The UCE is dancing on the razor's edge of losing control of its colonies."

Cam remembered what she'd learned by accessing the computers in her room: A tax placed on the Interweb in Central, the most powerful of the UCE colonies, had brought about some longtime resentment. Taxes in the UCE didn't seem to be anything new, but this was the first time someone other than the colonists themselves had benefited from the money. And the bureaucrats hadn't asked. They'd demanded. They'd been trying to fund ventures in foreign states. Like in prerevolutionary America, when the universally hated Stamp Act led to full-scale rebellion— and the birth of the United States, Cam thought. Central was the United States of America all over again, and the UCE was an overextended motherland in dire need of funds, just as England had been. Was the UCE stupid, or just greedy? Couldn't they see that history was repeating itself, that the Revolution was repeating itself?

With one difference: Cam's best friend, Bree Maguire, was at the center of the firestorm.

Dressed, she and the prince retraced their path back to Kyber's bedroom. Outside the French doors that faced the central square, the city looked like a kaleidoscope. "Oh, my Lord," Cam whispered. All the media screens on all the buildings around them showed the same image.

Kyber moved next to her. "It's a broadcast we've allowed past our filters."

"Your kingdom censors the news?"

"In a time of crisis, we practice self-preservation," he retorted.

Kyber stalked to his desk and a bank of computers, taking and sending communication to what Cam assumed were members of his cabinet and staff. She avoided looking at the disturbing pictures on the screens. It wasn't easy. The images surrounded the palace. She'd have nightmares tonight.

She turned to Kyber, who sat at his desk with a stunned expression on his face, and asked, "Isn't there anything the Kingdom of Asia can do for her? It's not right what the UCE is doing, setting her up as an example."

"No. It's not our fight."

"We share the same planet, Kyber. That puts us all in the same basket."

"Look at the people out there, Cam. The citizens of this country. They're well dressed, well fed. Do they look unhappy? Yet there are forces afoot who would challenge the Hans because they don't believe autocracy is a legitimate form of government. Some around the world may look at what's happening in Central and decide they are repressed, too. Some, even here, may try to fit the square peg of democracy into the round hole of this country."

"It sounds like you view democracy as a threat."

"It's not so much that democracy itself is a threat, but that it won't form a strong enough glue to bind us together, we the many different people and cultures of Asia. Yes, we have a single language, but without a strong hand, a *royal* hand, keeping us together, this vast land will fly apart into chaos and war."

Once more she gazed outside the huge French doors at

the square below that was by day filled with adoring subjects hoping for a glimpse of the acting emperor, the prince who until tonight had kept his distance from her.

She needed Kyber. She needed him now.

She turned. "You're the most powerful man in the world. Talk to the UCE president—to Beauchamp. Help free my flight leader."

"Our differences run deep, Cam, his country and ours."

"Good God, Kyber. Can't you put that aside to right a terrible wrong?"

His expression darkened. "Maybe I should explain why he has every reason to despise and mistrust us. Once this empire was a league of Asian nations linked by an economic trade agreement: the Asian Economic Consortium. Years of the West's outsourcing high-tech jobs to us brought wealth and power that no one anticipated. The newly formed UCE wanted those riches. They wanted us. When the UCE tried to tax what we, the consortium, gave to the world, my ancestors declared independence— and bled mightily to achieve it. The Bai-Yee Wars. The fighting ended generations ago, but the circumstances surrounding it remain a polarizing force in the world. Did you know that to this date, the UCE has never conceded defeat? The peace treaty still sits in an airless case in the very Royal Museum we visited tonight with a blank signature line above the words, 'The United Colonies of Earth.'"

"It's horrible what happened, I agree, but it's the past, Kyber. It's unhealthy for anyone to remain stuck there— an individual or a nation."

Something she said must have hit a button; she saw a flicker of pain in Kyber's gaze. Saw him flinch.

"If you don't do something about this, I will. I don't know what yet, but I can think outside the box."

Kyber pushed to standing, his knuckles bearing the lion's share of his weight. "The same people who captured Banzai will be coming after you next. Nowhere but within the gates of this city are you safe. Leave, and they will find you—and then they will kill you."

"You make it sound as if I'm fixing to run off half-cocked! If I operated that way, I'd have crossed the mountains in Mongolia for here months ago. I'm going to think this through."

"You may find you'll not want to make your existence known when you see the stakes against Banzai."

"You underestimate me," she answered coldly. "When I fight, I don't base tactical decisions on my emotions."

"Banzai did."

"I am not Banzai."

"No, you certainly are not," he said in an intimate tone of tenderness that she felt clear to her toes.

"Isolationism helps no one," she pleaded, quieter.

"We will remain behind our borders as we always have, geographically, socially, and politically."

"Because of the Bai-Yee Wars."

"That and more."

"How do we know that what was best decision back then is still the right choice now?"

Kyber's gaze turned inward, as if her words had touched a chord, maybe something he'd never considered. Then, just as vividly, she saw him seal off that line of thought.

She walked to where he stood at his desk, taking up a strategic position directly opposite, the thick, gorgeous slab of mahogany between them. "My father was a three-star general. He always told us that being endowed with great power, as he was and you are, brings even greater responsibility. He wasn't a particularly religious man, but he had a plaque he hung in every office he ever occupied. It was a passage from the New Testament. 'From everyone to whom much has been given, much will be required, and from the one to whom much has been entrusted, even more will be demanded.' The world needs you, Kyber," she said quietly.

"I don't need the world."

"You can't hide behind your borders forever."

"Can't I? It has worked exceedingly well for all the years since this kingdom declared independence."

She rubbed her forehead to soothe the headache forming there. "You've never cared for the UCE or its policies. Now's your chance to see them defeated. If you were to openly choose sides in this, the way France did in the first American Revolution, you could swing the entire battle in the colonists' favor—and in your favor! I know we Americans may not have won our independence if it weren't for French support."

"I will not send my soldiers to foreign soil."

"Who said anything about sending troops? You have the power to influence the outcome simply by choosing sides."

He recoiled at that, and she threw up her hands. "You have an instant aversion to any involvement outside your immediate areas of personal concern, do you realize that? No wonder you want to stay behind your borders. Anything more would mean participating fully, committing yourself with an unknown level of personal risk. Even in your private life, you avoid that."

He shot her a dark glance. "Did you think I fell short of participating fully when we made love just now?"

"No," she replied softly.

He made a low sound of satisfaction, maybe relief.

"And that's what made it so wonderful, Kyber."

Their eye contact grew heated and she forced herself to ignore it. "I do know, however, that you'd rather be with concubines than in real relationships, because you told me so. Real relationships could lead to marriage, an empress of your own. A family. People you could lose and grieve for, which is something we both know too much about."

She leaned over the desk as he leaned toward her, furious, his knuckles white on the dark wood. Had her little speech penetrated his thick, rock-solid skull yet? Shaken his status quo? Bombarded the wall he'd built around himself?

She hoped so. Bree's life depended on it.

"Do you know what I think?" she asked, grasping at straws, her heart in her mouth. "That when your father became incapacitated and it all came crashing down around you, you weren't ready for it. You held on to the mind-set of that cocky young prince whose father took care of the kingdom while you rode the Rim, fancy-free. No one's required you to move past that state of mind: your staff, your cabinet ministers. They also loved and miss your father. Knowing you'll keep everything exactly as it was during his rule makes them comfortable. Plus, you're the emperor, and they don't want to risk angering you."

"Unlike you, pretty one," he said in a tone so deadly it put butterflies in her stomach.

She showed him with her posture that he couldn't intimidate her. "Say anything you want about borders and isolation and hundred-year-old wars, but I think the real emperor lives in a back wing of this palace."

He growled. "My father is in a vegetative coma."

"Coma or not, it sounds to me like he's still leading this kingdom."

Kyber listened to her with a mix of outrage, fury, and dawning horror. Then, as clear as day, she saw him close himself off to her and her accusations. "Go! Leave me."

"Somehow I knew that's what you'd say," she whispered.

"Leave now!" The lost look in his eyes contradicted his fierce demeanor. Her heart twisted at the anguish she'd caused him, but she'd had no choice.

Refusing to scurry off like the concubine, she walked to the door, then paused there briefly to say in a soft, careful voice, "I see in you the potential to be a modern-day superhero, a leader for the ages. Yet something is holding you back, holding you back in many things, personal and public."

He remained sullen, solemn, and all alone in front of his French doors. It didn't look like he was listening to her, but she knew he was.

"You have the throne. Now become the incredible leader you were born to be. History is giving you the chance to take part, Kyber, a chance at real glory. All you have to do is grab hold of it."

And all she had to do was make sure he realized it, and helped save Bree in the process.

Chapter Twenty-one

It was a standoff on the roof of Fort Powell. Bree said nothing as she stared down the barrel of the guard's gun. Sweat formed on her forehead, trickling down her temples. She felt Ty's anguish. They'd been so close . . . so close.

Yet there was something about this guard that stopped them, something familiar. "It's the guard who spoke to me last night," she whispered out the corner of her mouth. "He . . . he asked me if I was afraid of dying."

She'd said no, of course, but that was big talk when you weren't looking down the barrel of a shotgun.

"No one leaves with her." The blond guard waved his weapon at Bree. "Move away from him."

Bree hadn't breathed since the standoff began, it seemed. "You asked me last night if I was afraid to die," she said.

The guard's eyes shot back to her.

"Now I have a chance to live, and you won't give it to me?"

He appeared genuinely confused. "This guard's not taking you to die?"

"He's not a guard."

"I'm rescuing her," Ty said. "Or at least, I'm trying to."

"Is it true?" the guard asked Bree.

She nodded.

"He's not making you say that?"

"No."

The man lowered his gun. His uniform was soaked with sweat. "I knew Nessie had gone after you, to bring you to Armstrong. I found her handcuffed in your cell."

The commandant's name was Nessie? Bree swallowed and didn't say anything.

"So I figured you'd escaped. I wanted . . . I wanted to make sure you did."

Clearly distraught and still struggling, he threw his weapon to Bree. Shocked, she caught it. "You'll probably need it," he said.

Without another word to explain his unexpected actions, he walked away.

She exchanged a let's-get-the-hell-out-of-here glance with Ty. They ran to the heli-jet. "You're flying it, right?" The last time they'd escaped like this was when they'd fled Kyber's palace. Then, she'd driven and he'd done the shooting. Same with the cattle truck they'd hijacked afterward.

"Yeah. I'm driving this time. Now strap that cute ass of yours to the seat and let's get going."

"Sit down, strap in, and shut up. Works for me." She jumped in.

He jumped into the pilot's seat, and Bree sat at his right. His hands revealed little hesitation as he started up the aircraft. With a rush of vertical acceleration, they lifted off the roof.

Below were thousands of people. Every square inch of cement was filled. "We should let them know," she said. "Let them know I got out."

Ty's face was rigid. Cold. She wasn't exactly immune to the fear either. "Bree, it's a mob."

"I know," she said quietly. "And I'm the reason they're here. They don't want me to die."

"If it were up to me, I'd whisk you far and away as fast as I could to safety." Ty turned to look at her, searching her face with sad eyes. "But you're not really mine," he almost whispered. "I think I always knew that."

She shook her head. "What do you mean?"

"You belong to them, not me. You always have. All I want to do is to hide you, but that's not my right. Like the Voice of Freedom said, you belong to the people."

"You're the man I love. No matter what I have to do for the revolution, that won't change. I'm going to be your wife one of these days. We're going to get married. That is, if we ever get a minute when no one's trying to kill us."

Ty didn't smile, but his mouth softened. He lifted a hand to softly drag his fingertips down her cheek. She turned her head and pressed her lips to his palm, covered in a black leather glove.

Then, with obvious reservations, Ty pushed forward on the stick. The heli-jet plunged. Something hard glanced off the windshield as they swooped over the crowd. "They're throwing rocks!" Ty swore and jerked the craft out of the way. "The engines are vulnerable to foreign-object damage. We can't stay down here."

"Put it down then."

Ty appeared aghast. "Put it down?"

"This heli-jet's small. It'll fit in the street. Land it. They'll move out of the way."

"You're crazy."

"That's why they call me Banzai."

It was obvious Ty didn't share her cheer.

A clear circle opened in the center of the mob, the protesters moving out of the way, if only to keep from getting crushed. After the heli-jet touched down, Bree slid her window back, letting in a hurricane roar of screaming mouths and waving hands. It was a mob gone mad.

A rock bounced off the front glass as Bree tore open her black uniform to reveal the orange jumpsuit underneath. "Is there a way I can talk to them? A speaker?"

Ty pressed an icon on the control screen. "Do it."

She pumped her fist outside the window. "We have the power to begin the world anew!" she shouted, using the same words as at the sentencing. They had watched; they'd remember. "The time has come, the time for deliverance. We will make a stand for freedom, not for us alone, but for the world!"

The mob's cries lowered in volume. "It's her," she heard someone close to the heli-jet say. "It's Banzai Maguire!"

The shouts spread. "Maguire, it's Maguire." A ripple of voices spread outward from the epicenter.

"What do we do?" someone shouted at her. "The UCE military's cracking down. We'll be overpowered."

"They're scared, Ty," she said under her breath to him. "Overwhelmed. They're at a crossroads. The UCE is cracking down and they're losing hope."

"Then give it back to them. *Inspire* them."

She spread her hands. "How?"

"Just tell them what's in your heart. Tell them what's in *their* hearts, but that they don't know how to say."

Shaking with nerves, she turned back to the rapt crowd. From their signs, so many of them were there to protest her imprisonment. "An army," she said softly at first, then loud enough to register on the speakers and carry far and wide. "An army! Look at you—you're an army for freedom, thousands strong. Millions more of us are banding together all over Central to defy tyranny and win freedom. I know you've heard of my talents at escaping every trap set—including this one—"

The crowd laughed and cheered.

"But it's because of people like you. I've been helped by people who love freedom as much as I. By *people like you!*

"Know this: some of the stories of me are legendary, I hear, but I'm scared, too. I know many of you fear for your lives and your families, but remember—the UCE fears *us!* As the Continental Army of so many centuries ago prevailed against overwhelming odds, *so will we!*"

The cheering had become deafening, but the heli-jet's speaker cast Bree's voice far and wide. "Today we face what may be the most important choice in our lives. Do we declare ourselves free, fight and win this war—possibly dying for that victory—or do we go home? Everyone would be safe, then. No one would get hurt."

By now, she was half hanging out the heli-jet window. Only Ty's grip on her waistband kept her from tumbling out.

"Do you know what I say to that? 'Don't be afraid of death; be afraid of the unlived life!' I'd rather die fighting for freedom now than die decades from now, warm in my bed but embarrassed to tell my grandchildren that I chose safety over their futures. This is what the Founding Fathers fought for so many years ago. They were victorious, but what they won has again been taken away. Benjamin Franklin said, 'Those who give up essential liberty to preserve a little temporary safety deserve neither liberty nor safety!' It's our turn to fight. Who's ready to tell the UCE where they can put their Interweb taxes?"

The crowd roared. She couldn't believe it was happening, that she was able to inspire them. Ty had told her to say what was in her heart; she'd done just that and it had worked.

People surged all around the heli-jet. She knew Ty worried that they'd accidentally damage the craft and kill any chance of escape. She needed to tell him to launch, but she heard shouted questions: "How? When? Where?"

"Find your leaders," she told them. "They're out there. You know who they are. Organize and prepare. And then march on Washington, DC, the *real* capital, and show the UCE our determination to fight!"

"March on old Washington?" Ty asked, incredulous. "Bree . . ."

It's under control, she mouthed. "I'll meet you there," she yelled. " 'Some may cry peace—but as for me, give me liberty or give me death!' "

The crowd went wild. Ty pulled her back into the heli-jet. "Strap in. We're out of here—now, or we're not going to get out of here at all."

He started up the jet engine. The crowd moved back far enough to allow the craft lift off. As they rose into the air, American flags waved all around them, an enormous field of Stars and Stripes.

The heli-jet's nose dipped as it accelerated. Then, with a burst of speed, Ty and Bree left the chaos of Fort Powell behind.

Bree shuddered and relaxed against the seat. "Holy Christmas. Is it time for your medication or mine?" she joked.

"It's not over," Ty warned her, pushing the heli-jet to its max speed.

She rolled her head to look at him. "It never is."

After a few moments had clicked by, she frowned. "By the way, who the hell is Lee-lee? Lee-lee Sweet?"

"How do you know about her?"

"They played the Interweb in my cell twenty-four-seven. There was a show on celebrity couples. You and Lee-lee starred."

Ty groaned. "She's an old girlfriend."

"How old?"

"Real old. Three or four years ago, I went through a period of doing the party scene after I lost those men in the Raft Cities. I returned to the navy when my leave was up, but never returned to the parties."

The slow burn of jealousy faded. She'd only half believed those images anyway. "Good. I was worried that while I was rotting in jail, you were whooping it up with hot babes."

Ty snorted. He reached across the cockpit and squeezed her hand. "I'm done with the Lee-lees of the world. I love you, Bree. I love you as I've never loved before; you know that."

"Banzai Maguire!"

Bree sat ramrod straight in her seat. A voice boomed out of her collar. To Ty's expression of disbelief, she said, "It's the Voice of Freedom."

"Who are you with?" it demanded. "Who are you speaking to?"

Ty brought a finger to his lips and shook his head.

She nodded. "Thank you for shutting down the prison. How the heck did you do that?"

"As much as I'd like the credit, I didn't do it. Someone hacked into the system. Impossible, and yet it happened."

"Someone else is helping us?"

"The Trojan Horse, too, was thought to be a gift."

"Good point," Ty muttered, his eyes on the sky ahead.

"Now tell me where you are, Banzai." The Voice of Freedom sounded almost panicky.

"We're—"

Ty's hand landed on hers and squeezed. He shook his head.

Why? She mouthed the word.

He typed on the cockpit keyboard: *If we trust the wrong person now, it's all over.*

But it's the Voice of Freedom, she typed back.

We think it is.

Bree stared straight ahead. Ty was right. They couldn't risk trusting an unknown. And even if it was the real Voice of Freedom, she/he/it had gotten her into one mess after another. The Voice's intentions were good—the best—but its execution left a lot to be desired. "I left a motivated crowd behind in New Washington," she replied. "They're gathering now, organizing. Without an Interweb for communication, the process will be slower, but it'll happen. You can handle that, okay? Look, I've got to go. I'll contact you when I get there."

"Get where? You left before my plans for your protection were fully realized."

You snooze, you lose. "Listen, I can't trust too many people right now. I'm sure you understand."

The tense silence told her that the Voice did indeed understand, but was royally pissed off.

"I'll call, okay?" Bree promised.

But the Voice of Freedom, it seemed, had already hung up.

Less than four hours later they touched down on the helijet pad at Ty's family ranch in Montana. The trip had been inexplicably easy, uneventful. No other aircraft had come up on their wing; no radar had tracked them. They'd heard nothing on the radios directed at them. Ty was certain it meant that forces loyal to his father would be waiting for them, but when they arrived at the ranch it was deserted.

"Don't question good fortune," he told Bree, ushering her inside. The house smelled familiar, a little like cinnamon, a little like pine. There was no time to waste on a tour. That would come later . . . if it ever did.

He led Bree downstairs to the basement. "This is the command center. It's dedicated to security."

"There's enough gear and gadgets in here to supply a small country's military."

"My father wanted to be prepared in the event Beauchamp ousted him from office. No one can get into this place once I throw up the shields. Not even my father himself—unless he calls in an air strike, which he won't. He loves the place too much." Ty's fingers danced over the huge rectangular monitor, typing in codes. "My father made me memorize the security commands when I

288

was a boy, in case he was incapacitated and needed me to shut out the world—or, more accurately, the UCE."

He wiped his hands. "Done. Now I'll show you around."

His tour ended some time later at the bedroom he'd occupied as a child. Bree stepped through the door, gazing with the softest of smiles at the model airplanes dangling from his ceiling. He'd told her so many stories about this room, and now she'd arrived; Banzai Maguire was here in his bedroom. A frisson of wonder went through him. "It seems surreal to me that you're here," he said quietly.

"Me, too." She thought for a moment. "Hey, do you still have that book—the one where you saw my biography?"

He reached for a thick text and pulled it from his bookshelf. "This is how I first learned of you." He flipped to a dog-eared, much-read page and handed her the military textbook.

"That's me. . . ." Bree's eyes glittered with sudden moisture as she gazed at the small photo of her dressed in an air force flight suit and posed in front of an F-16. "This is the picture that led to everything."

"A revolution."

She brought her hand to his cheek. "And more."

"Believe it or not, my father gave me this book. See what came of it? We will never give our children books."

She laughed. "Not if they're going to go through what we have."

Their smiles faded simultaneously. They'd been through a lot, and it wasn't over yet.

"Come here, Sleeping Beauty." Ty pulled her close and

pressed his lips to the side of her throat. "I want to make love to you so badly, Bree, I can taste it—can taste *you*. . . . " He bit her earlobe, and she gave a tiny yelp.

"Almost every single time we've gone to bed together, someone's tried to kill us. Do you know that?"

He lifted his head. "No one can get in here."

"Your father can't override what we've done?"

"Once the codes are input into the main computer, it locks out all overrides. My father designed it that way."

That seemed to appease her.

For about a second.

"I'm not getting into bed, or in the shower, or doing anything until I know that every window, every door, every air vent, every gopher hole is locked!"

He couldn't blame her. The two times they'd shared a real bed had ended in disaster—once with their near murders, the second with their capture. Affecting a gallant attitude in the finest tradition of knights in shining armor, he took her hand and proceeded to lead the symbolic leader of a world-class rebellion on an inspection of every window, every door, every air vent, and every gopher hole on the ranch.

They ended their search in the kitchen, a large room with panoramic views of the mountains yet cozy in the tradition of ranch homes. "We haven't checked the pantry yet," Ty told Bree.

She leaned back against a nearby counter and smoothed her hair away from her face. "Well, we looked in every other nook and cranny, let's do it."

Ty lifted a finger and beckoned. "You do it."

Casting him a confused glance, she pushed away from the counter and walked through the door he'd opened.

She took in the sight of the sealed compartments holding food and other perishables and shrugged. "Well, we won't starve."

She started to walk out, but he stopped her. "I figured you'd smell it. But the containers are more airtight than I thought."

She wrinkled her nose. "Smell what?"

He grinned as he threw open the first of several bins holding a treasure trove of—

"Junk food," Bree breathed. "Be still my heart. Chocolate . . . and chips . . . and—look at all this stuff!"

Ty tore open a candy bar and broke off a piece, handing it to Bree. "I don't know what brands you know, but plan on digging through it all until you find some favorites."

"My hand's shaking," she joked, bringing the candy to her nose first to inhale the aroma and then tasting it as if she wanted to savor the experience. "Mmm . . ." She closed her eyes as she chewed.

It aroused Ty, watching her delight in the candy the way he wanted to take his enjoyment with her body. Even with the world in chaos and the entire UCE military looking for them, here in this temporary refuge, he'd make sure their lovemaking progressed at the same leisurely pace as Bree's snacking. He'd waited so long for her—for this. He'd be damned if he was going to rush the experience.

Ty rested his hands on her hips and kissed the side of her throat. "Want more?" Her skin was hot, damp, and tasted like her.

"Mmm," she murmured again, this time at the feel of his mouth. "What other candy do you have?"

His chuckle was low and deep. "Why don't you come with me, little girl, and find out for yourself?" Taking her head in his hands, he kissed her.

"No one tried to kill us," Bree said later as she snuggled next to Ty in bed. Empty bags of chips and candy littered the night tables.

He gathered her close, grinning. "You damn near did, though."

Dressed in bathrobes, they cuddled in the big feather bed in the ranch's master suite—in Ax Armstrong's bed, Bree thought, unable to wrap her mind around the absurdity of it all.

The Interweb remained down. On the entertainment monitors was local news: sporadic, pieced-together rebel broadcasts that popped up and were quickly taken down in favor of UCE-run propaganda. "Rebel forces following the Voice of Freedom's urging are gathering in huge numbers at the sight of the old capital." The man who read the news resembled a bus driver more than a carefully coiffed anchorman. "Minutemen, local militia, and continental army regulars, contact your local leaders for further instructions. . . ."

A new image appeared, overriding the guy reading the news. It was Beauchamp, the UCE president. He sat behind a desk in what Bree recognized as the Unity Office.

"I hate that man. . . ." Bree clutched her robe to her chest as if she could contain the thundering beats of her heart. Ty rubbed her back.

"Greetings, my fellow colonists. I come to you with a plea for help in our darkest hour. There are those among us who would bring our great nation to its knees, forsaking peace for irresponsible violence. Have confidence that your leaders have the situation under control. Troops are being sent to reinforce the blockade around an uprising at the old capital."

"They set up a blockade," Bree said with dismay. She closed her eyes. "I don't know if I'm ready to hear that lives have been lost because of what I've set in motion."

Ty gathered her close. "Death before tyranny," he reminded her.

"We need to join them, Ty—to join them at the capital. We can't stay here where it's safe."

"I know. . . ." He kissed the top of her head. "We'll have tonight. Tomorrow we'll return."

"I ask you tonight to remain in your homes," Beauchamp went on. "For your safety and those around you, observe the curfew at all times. All attempts at movement into the old capital will be seen as hostile. Supreme Commander Armstrong is standing by with the full power of our ground forces to quell the aggression."

"If my father moves his army in, it'll be a bloodbath," Ty said grimly. "We need to get other nations involved in this. The Euro-African consortium."

"Better yet, the Kingdom of Asia. They're the true power."

"Run by a man who won't lift a pinkie finger to do anything past his own borders, who hates the UCE as much as the UCE hates him."

"I know the last time I saw him I zapped him with a neuron fryer. I don't expect him to be friendly to someone who escaped him and was hostile. But," she sighed, "if only Kyber would agree to help. Think of what

France's participation did for the colonists in the American Revolution."

"That would place Prince Kyber in the role of Lafayette," Ty said dryly.

"It's not *that* far-fetched." God knew this revolution needed a Lafayette, the young Frenchman who left behind a comfortable life as a noble to fight for Gen. George Washington. "I know what you think of him, but Kyber's a good man—under all that ego. He has principles."

"Only as they relate directly to his personal well being."

Bree shook her head. "He'd do it. I know he would, given the right motivation." She had no idea what that motivation might be, but she sure as hell hoped it found him before time ran out.

Chapter Twenty-two

The eyes blinked. The lungs breathed. The heart beat. It was a nervous system on autopilot, Kyber thought, watching his father from where he sat next to the emperor's bed.

Coma or not, it sounds to me like he's still leading this kingdom.

Cam's words had angered him. Then, as the night wore on, tossing and turning alone in his enormous bed, he had found that her words began to haunt him. It had reached a point where it was impossible to stay away. He had to come here to find out the truth.

Say anything you want about borders and isolation and hundred-year-old wars, but I think the real emperor lives in a back wing of this palace.

Kyber turned his hands over in a rare gesture of helplessness. "I need your advice, Father."

The room was silent but for the gentle breaths of the comatose emperor.

"The world is knocking at our door. Do I answer? Or do I leave it closed?"

Something urged Kyber's gaze to the night table. On it, the empress had arranged the items his father had most cared about in life: a gold pistol, assorted holophoto images, an egg-sized emerald . . . and an ancient-looking book with pages edged in gold. Curious, Kyber drew it onto his lap, opening it. A Bible. His father had been a practicing Catholic, and so discovering the Bible didn't surprise him. What did was what he found on the book-marked page: Luke 12:47–48. "'From everyone to whom much has been given, much will be required, and from the one to whom much has been entrusted, even more will be demanded,'" he murmured. They were nearly the exact words Cam had recited only hours before.

He lowered his head and closed his eyes. Responsibility. Duty. It had been important to his father; that, he knew. And all Kyber had done was flee it. *When your father became incapacitated and it all came crashing down around you, you weren't ready for it.*

Was he now?

He knew the answer to the question he'd never dared ask. He knew because of how he'd lived his life since becoming acting emperor. His father would never recover. Kyber had avoided marriage because he wasn't ready to become full-fledged emperor. To have an empress of his own would solidify his taking of the throne. The throne he hadn't wanted. Yet.

Kyber fell to his knees at the bedside, his hand clasping his father's cool, frail one. "I have failed you not in my actions but in my inaction. I was a boy who wasn't ready to become a man. I've been humiliated into seeing this,

Father. Shamed into taking responsibility. This means accepting not only my role as ruling monarch in your place, but taking our kingdom's rightful place in the world." He was careful to use a tone of respect. "We've grown too comfortable behind the walls of isolation. Comfort breeds complacency. While life has stayed relatively stable in our land, the world has changed. Instead of ignoring it, why not have a hand in fixing it? Responsibility means accepting my role—and our country's role—in world affairs. And that I vow to do." As well as accepting responsibility in all the other areas of his life as a man.

Cam, he thought. *Yes, pretty one, you.*

He gazed down at the fallen emperor's slack face, once so full of life. "You were my hero, Father. You always will be. If I prove to be half the leader you were, I'll know I have succeeded. Not by following in your footsteps, but by making my own."

He stopped himself at the almost imperceptible squeeze of his father's fingers. The doctors had told him his sire didn't show enough brain activity to be able to listen, let alone communicate. But Kyber was certain the man had just squeezed his hand. A glitch in the autonomic nervous system? Perhaps. A blessing given? Kyber could only hope.

Emotion pressing behind his eyes, Kyber stood, gently replacing his father's hand atop the bedsheets. *The king is dead. Long live the king.* "Change of command," he murmured.

Then, buoyed by a sense of destiny, he left the chamber.

In the smoky presidential briefing room, two men sat, arguing. "My back's to the wall, Aaron," Beauchamp told his general. "We need a distraction for our beleaguered land."

Armstrong spread his hands. "But start a war with Asia in order to create a diversion? That's like blowing up your house in order to kill a termite. We need our strength and attention here, on this front."

Beauchamp grumbled. "I disagree."

"I ask you again, let me see if I can first break the spirit of the rebellion. Clear me to march on the troublemakers massing at the old capital. I'll employ conventional ground forces for maximum effect and minimal collateral damage—after all, you'll be stuck rebuilding it all when I'm through."

The president appeared torn. "This is what I wanted to avoid. All along I've been against using force against our own people."

Beauchamp didn't mind killing his people as long as he wasn't the one doing it; he'd have happily seen them die in a foreign war. "If my plan works, you won't have to take on the Kingdom of Asia, which would all but drain our coffers, not to mention cost countless lives."

The president took a hearty hit of his cigar. His face practically disappeared behind a cloud of smoke. "All right," he said grudgingly. "I clear you to march on the old capital. But if in the space of two days you are not successful, the UCE will take steps to launch an attack on the Kingdom of Asia. It's not as daunting as it sounds, Aaron, if we first soften the target." He gazed at the glowing tip of his cigar before glancing up. "Beginning with their king, courtesy of the dependable Minister Hong."

After hours of wandering outside in the gardens, where she'd found the solitude she needed for planning and soul searching, Cam returned to her bedroom in the palace to find the most beautiful bouquet waiting for her. *Kublai*, was her first thought. Then: *There is no Kublai.*

And she doubted she'd left Kyber in the flower-giving frame of mind.

Besides, not enough time had elapsed between her leaving the prince and these flowers arriving. She found a card amongst the flowers. The small rectangle glowed as soon as her fingers touched it, like a tiny TV screen. A face appeared. Minister Hong!

Stay away from him. Don't listen to him. He's not to be believed.

Zhurihe's warning seemed at odds with the charming and apologetic gentleman on the card. "Cameron," Hong said. "I owe you an apology as well as my thanks for chasing down our little rock thrower." His smile faded. "Beware the deceit you find in the palace. It exists to undermine Prince Kyber and all of us in the cabinet. Terrorists, all. No matter how kind they seem, stay away. Any association with them will drag you into the mire of their activities. There is only one way to affect change, and that is through legislation and laws."

Stay away from him. Don't listen to him. He's not to be believed. Zhurihe's warning kept coming back to haunt her.

Hong smiled. "As I said earlier this evening, I would like to get to know you better. Dinner, perhaps?" The minister smiled. Then his image gave a small bow before signing off.

Cam became aware of a presence in the room with her. Gasping, she spun around. A slack-jawed Park clone had brought a tray of tea and small snacks, and was arranging it on a low lacquered table in her sitting room. She had yet to get used to the way palace servants came and went and never knocked. "We've got a few things to talk about, missy." Cam marched toward her.

Nervously, the girl regarded Cam. Her eyes were dead. There was no fire in them. This was not Zhurihe.

"Sorry." Cam's heart was beating hard. She swallowed. "I thought you were Joo-Eun."

"*I'm* Joo-Eun."

Cam's head jerked around at the sound of the soft voice near the door. Zhurihe stood there. "Why did you run away from me in the alley?" Cam demanded. "It's getting really irritating, having to chase you down."

"Kublai came. I knew he might recognize me."

"Did you come here to apologize, too? That seems to be the theme for tonight." Well, princes excluded. "Those flowers are from Hong. What did you bring me?"

Cam had intended sarcasm, but Zhurihe replied frankly, "A warning."

"What—to stay away from Hong? You did that already."

The girl walked up to her and took her hand as she had so many times during Cam's recovery. "I paid that boy to throw rocks at Hong in order to protect you from him. He wants you to develop fond feelings for him so that he can turn you against the prince."

"I would never let myself be used like that."

"Trust no one. Only your heart."

The way she said it told Cam the clone knew about her and Kyber. "What else, Zhurihe?" The girl seemed ready to explode with something unsaid.

"Bree has escaped. I know where she is, and what you can do to help her."

Chapter Twenty-three

"And so it begins," Bree murmured. The heli-jet sped toward a white-domed building rising out of miles of marshland. So many thousands of colonists were in those marshy fields that the land itself was hidden by their bodies. They'd erected scaffolding around the dome of the old Capitol building.

Ty and Bree landed and joined the group of militia leaders at the top. Looking down, Bree surveyed the crowds below, her hands clasped behind her back.

"Banzai Maguire!"

A voice emanated from her left pants pocket. She pulled out the torn-off collar from her old prison garb. "It's the Shadow Voice," she alerted Ty. "The Voice of Freedom."

Everyone standing with her pressed close to hear what the Voice had to say, the force responsible for taking over where she'd left off, bringing over a million militiamen and women to the site of America's old capitol.

"The Ax is on the move," it said.

Bree exchanged a worried glance with Ty.

"General Armstrong has gathered a massive conventional force—soldiers, tanks, ground-based weaponry. They're moving into position all around us."

"We're surrounded," Bree repeated in a whisper. With little in the way of real weapons and soldiers other than their pistols and their hearts, this revolution was comprised of sitting ducks.

Black-clad rebels took positions on the scaffolding encircling the Capitol's roof. Ex-SEALs and former Special Ops, Ty informed her. With shoulder-launched missiles, they hoped to keep the revolution's leaders alive as long as possible.

They waited all afternoon for a glimpse of the approaching army. And then they saw it—massive, a dark horde of loyalist soldiers. She was dismayed to see there were so many of them. The crowd below had fallen into tense murmuring. "If his point is to intimidate us," she muttered. "He's doing a bang-up job."

"If my father's aim was to scare us, he'd be doing more than marching," Ty argued. "Something else is going on."

Bree just wished she knew what the hell it was.

Cam stood before the floor-to-ceiling window in her bedroom, her hands clasped together and pressed under her chin. It was late morning in the kingdom, evening in Washington, DC. What would happen when their morning came? Cam didn't want to think about it, but she had to. Her friend was trapped in the shadow of an advancing army.

And Cam needed her to stay trapped for a little while

longer. *Sorry, Bree, but that's the only way this is going to work.*

Passion drives the rebellion in Central, Zhurihe had remarked during their conversation. *Saving Bree will require tapping into that passion.*

But how? Cam had been pondering the question ever since the girl left. A symbol—she needed one to push the boiling emotions in Central to overflowing. And the perfect symbol sat in Kyber's museum—polished, pretty, and operational: the F-16.

Already, she had the beginnings of a plan, a fantastic plan, but, damn, not yet the details of its execution. Her idea would require penetrating one of the most heavily defended world powers on the planet with an antiquated fighter. She could fly low, under the radar, so to speak. The jet was so old-fashioned that maybe it would escape notice.

Cam shoved her hands through her hair, holding it in two fists off her forehead. "God, it'll never work," she whispered. "It's insane." Maybe insane was too kind a word. Did she really think she could penetrate UCE defenses?

People have long underestimated you. Have you now taken over the job?

Cam dropped her hands and stiffened her spine. People had faced worse odds than this, much worse. Especially Bree. If her friend could escape Fort Powell, then Cam could fly over Washington, DC.

To accomplish that, though, she'd need Kyber along for the ride—not physically, but figuratively. He had the power to make her hatching idea happen. *Go to him.*

The problem was, after their argument she had her

doubts he'd talk civilly, let alone help her, but she had to try. Too much was at stake to do otherwise.

Squaring her shoulders, Cam turned away from the window and left her room for Kyber's. When she entered the corridor, she wanted to walk, walk with the grace and composure taught to her by her mother, but the little girl in her, the unrepentant tomboy who'd stuffed newts in her pockets instead of dandelions, urged her to run.

She arrived at Kyber's massive double doors breathless. Would he still be sleeping? Would he speak to her?

Do you want to speak to him?

Cam swallowed and pushed aside her qualms. Just as in combat, there was no room for self-doubt now. "I would like to see the Prince," she told the door guards, who were stationed in the usual spot. The men shook their heads.

"He is not here," said the first guard.

A rush of desperation chased off her disappointment. "Where can I find him?"

Maybe the bodyguards read the anxiety in her eyes and took pity on her, or maybe they sensed the heart-churning emotions left from her hours making love to their leader. Whatever the reason, one of them answered, "He is in the gymnasium. Shall I escort you there?"

She backed away. "Thanks, but I already know how to find it."

She bolted off. "Open," she said impatiently as she reached the gymnasium. The door slid aside. The guard within retreated to an inconspicuous but still effective spot as she flew inside.

Kyber stood with his back to her. Wearing nothing on his upper body but the platinum armband high on his left biceps, Kyber wielded an enormous sword. When she'd seen similar heavy swords in museums, she'd often wondered how anyone could fight with them, let alone lift them. Yet, as she watched in fascination Kyber maneuvering the mighty blade, she finally understood that it was possible. He handled the weapon with sheer physical strength and grace. It seemed to her more than a mere workout, though. His face was taut with concentration, his skin gleaming with sweat as he put himself through a series of seemingly choreographed moves.

Cam recalled what Kyber had told her that night while still in the Rim. *Swordplay is a talent of mine. Euphemisms not intended.*

Then, she'd laughed at his joke; now she watched in admiration. He'd made light of his ability. The boastful prince—downplaying a talent? Hard to believe, but the truth was staring her in the face.

It is an ancient art, obsolete most say, a form of martial art, but I find I crave it. Pushing my body and mind to new levels. The discipline of it all.

Swordplay was how he achieved his focus. And now she was here to shatter it.

She spoke softly. "It looks like both of us had a sleepless night."

Kyber stopped, mid-swing, like an ancient warrior caught in freeze-frame. Then he slowly turned around. Something inside Cam softened as they made eye contact, but she made her voice hard. "I doubt you feel like talking to me, but I have something to discuss. It can't wait."

Kyber laid down the sword on a platform behind him. Then he returned his attention to her. Something

305

seemed different about him. Changed. Not being able to discern what it was made Cam even more nervous. "I've come up with a plan to help Bree," she said. "I want you to hear me out before saying anything."

A muscle in Kyber's jaw moved, but he remained silent.

"Passion is fueling the rebellion in Central. The only way I can help my friend, and help the revolution, is to fight in kind. To fight with passion." She made a fist. "Symbols inspire passion. Bree was able to inspire the colonists because she's a symbol for freedom. I need a symbol, too. I think I've found one, but it's yours, not mine. That's why I need your help." She held up a hand. "Wait—don't say anything yet. Let me finish. Passion started this war," she said fervently. "The same kind of passion will end it." How closely that came to describing her relationship with Kyber, she thought.

She could smell his skin, feel his body heat. Her entire body reacted. She couldn't stop the arousal he caused in her, but she could ignore it. Or, at least, try to. "The symbol I have in mind is that F-16 in the museum. What better way to inspire the colonists to fight, and to inspire Bree to lead them than with a flyover using a fighter jet from her time?"

While Kyber obeyed her request for silence, she remained unsure of what she saw in his expression. But she didn't let it dissuade her from vocalizing her idea and trying to win him over in the process.

Cam rubbed her hands together to bleed off some of her nervous energy. "First we give it a patriotic paint job—stars and stripes—and send it out on its first official, operational mission in one hundred and fifty years to remind the colonists what they've lost—and what they can win back if they stand up to oppression. I think it'll work, Kyber. By firing up the masses, building on what Bree has done, but more explosively, we can speed the fall of the UCE, and without mass death and destruction. There's historical precedent for it. Look at how the Iron Curtain fell in Eastern Europe back in the twentieth century. Communism ended there without war. We can do the same in Central. I *know* we can."

She waved a hand at him. "Okay. You can talk now."

The ends of his mouth twitched. "Are you certain?"

"Yes. I'm done."

Squeezing her sweaty hands behind her back she awaited his answer. She'd never seen his eyes this intense. The look on his face sent a shiver through her.

"We will need more than a patriotic paint scheme to achieve the desired result," he said.

She narrowed her eyes at him. "What are you saying?"

"I agree with your strategy. It needs more developing, yes, but I believe that with the right execution, it can work."

Her heart started thumping hard with joy. "You're in? I thought I was in for a fight, most likely a futile one."

"Let's just say that my sleepless night was unexpectedly constructive."

He smiled at her astonishment and pleasure before regaining an expression of grim determination. "Peace with the UCE government in this matter is akin to an alliance with them, and that I will not have. I also do not want my kingdom to appear to be involved in the revolution in an overt, militaristic way. Not only would it be seen as an act of aggression by the UCE and the Euro-

African Consortium, it would likely cause the new nation of Central to feel indebted to me, should the revolution be successful. They'll chafe at the perceived obligation, causing a new rift where I hope to close an old one. And, speaking of closing rifts," he said, softer. "It appears we have one of our own."

Cam shook her head. "Not anymore," she whispered and walked into his arms.

As powerful as their desire was for each other, they slept in Kyber's huge bed and didn't make love. If Cam's mission was to come to pass, Kyber insisted, sleep would help keep her alive.

During those few hours of rest, Kyber's teams of engineers and mechanics worked nonstop on the F-16. By the time Cam and Kyber arrived in the hangar, the aircraft was undergoing the final stages of its transformation from museum piece to a symbol powerful enough to cause a spontaneous change of government in Central and save Bree at the same time.

Kyber folded his thick arms over his leather breastplate and murmured to Cam, "There have been many improvements installed on this craft—the best stealth tech money can buy, structural strengthening and an upgraded fuel system to allow you to fly at supersonic speeds from Beijing to Washington, but I think the most important one of all will be your ability to nanowrite."

Cam nodded. "Agreed." Instead of bombs and guns, she'd unleash a futuristic version of skywriting: three-dimensional images with sound. She'd fill the skies above the Capitol with nanites—microscopic computers programmed for a patriotic super show of stars and stripes, the old national anthem, while Kyber worked things from his end: transmitting a taped address on the Interweb, where he'd publicly declare his support of the colonists of Central as well as ask for the cooperation of the other world leaders.

"This kingdom has never chosen sides before," he reminded her. "By not doing so, we are in fact supporting the wrong people. That, I will not stand for."

As the retrofitting of the F-16 for enhanced operation neared completion, Nikolai and Minister Hong joined Cam and Kyber. "We are ready to proceed when you are," the chief told them.

"I'm ready now," Cam said. "Bree's in trouble and time's running out for me to help her."

"You will have quite the craft with which to offer that help," Hong said. In his typically elegant fashion, hands clasped behind his back, he observed the jet with an air of vague disdain.

"What is it, Horace?" she teased. "Is it not as cool as your twenty-second century craft?"

He smiled charmingly. "Not even close."

She smiled back just as charmingly. "We'll have to agree to disagree, then. The Viper is as good as they come—and then some."

As Nikolai and Kyber murmured between themselves, Hong continued to walk around the fuselage, a strange expression coming over his face as he appeared to inspect the aircraft for abnormalities. Was he nervous, too? It was contagious, she thought. Her mouth was dry, and her heart was racing, but she worked at appearing calm so as not to upset Kyber. He was worried about her. If his doubts grew enough, he could pull the plug on the entire mission.

A commotion broke out near the entrance to the hangar. "Stop him—stop!" A small figure—a woman, judging by the sound of the voice—swathed in dove-gray raced toward the plane. Arms held straight out, she aimed a pistol at the minister. "Throw down your weapon," she yelled.

His eyebrow lifted. "I believe you are the one with the weapon."

"What's going on here?" Kyber asked.

"He's going to kill you," the hooded woman cried. "And then destroy the plane."

Hong rolled his eyes, seemingly unafraid of the gun aimed at his head. "Oh, please. Who *is* this woman?"

Something about the man seemed too cool. *Don't trust Hong.* Zhurihe's warning clanged in Cam's head. She grabbed Kyber's arm. Who was this woman? And . . . "What if she's telling the truth?"

Security rushed in. Kyber ordered irritably, "Take her away."

"But what about Hong?" Cam demanded.

Kyber shook his head. "Hong is—"

"Going to kill you!" the stranger shouted.

"Put down your weapon," Nikolai shouted back.

"Then he's going to make sure your F-16 crashes!"

Rolling his eyes, Hong started walking toward where Cam stood with Kyber. A gunshot rang out.

Hong staggered, his face paling in shock and surprise. Cam watched in horror as the woman lowered her smoking pistol. She'd shot Hong in the back.

Kyber and Nikolai ran to the Minister. "No!" the woman shouted, lifting her pistol. "Your Highness, beware of Hong! Stay down! Stay down!"

Cam saw Hong reach inside his coat, as if feeling for his injury. But instinct overtook her. She shoved Kyber away as Hong pulled a gun and aimed it at the prince.

Kyber took her down with him, grasping her arm and pulling. They hit the floor hard, Kyber using his body as a shield. He rolled with Cam away from the sounds of gunshots as security forces swarmed into the hangar. The gunfire continued.

Suddenly, the scene was silent.

When Cam next looked up, police surrounded Hong, but it was clear to her the Minister was dead. The gray-clothed stranger also lay in a pool of blood. Cam got up and walked closer. It was a young woman with two long braids.

"Oh, Lord. Oh, mercy." Cam fell to her knees. "What's happened, Zhurihe? What are you doing?"

The girl shuddered as if in great pain. "Hong was acting on orders. I had to stop him."

"Whose orders?" Kyber demanded as he appeared behind them.

"Beauchamp," Zhurihe said, panting. "The UCE."

"How do you know this?"

"I'm a clone," the girl answered in a self-deprecating tone. "I'm stupid. Unaware. And I enjoyed cleaning his quarters when I knew he was receiving the president's messages."

Cam heard the creaking of leather as Kyber crouched down next to her. His face reflected his shock and deep concern at what Zhurihe had just confessed.

311

The girl looked up at Cam. "Hong was why I wanted to keep you out of the palace. You thought I sought only to lie. I did lie, but this man was the reason. It was to keep you away from him. I knew Hong sent the assassins after Bree and Ty, paid for by Beauchamp." Zhurihe winced and shuddered. A drop of blood appeared at one corner of her mouth.

"Where are the medical people, Kyber?" Cam asked. She looked up at him.

He stood and shouted, "Where is the emergency medical staff?" transferring Cam's question to his police.

Shaking her head, Cam cradled Zhurihe's face in her hands. "But why," she whispered. "Why did you do all this? And at such personal risk?"

"I didn't want Hong to succeed, because I hate the UCE."

"That seems to be a universal sentiment around here," Cam muttered.

"I'd also come to hate the prince for not caring about the rights of clones."

"Not caring? I . . ." Kyber exhaled. "The act of doing nothing has cost me much."

Cam rubbed her hand over his broad back.

"But I saw you changing, Your Highness," Zhurihe whispered. "I saw in you a possible ally, someone who would do great good for *all* peoples. I saw Cam's trust in you. And what with your love for her, I saw a chance to establish through marriage an alliance between this kingdom and others that would prove stronger than any treaty."

Cam and Kyber exchanged a quick, startled glance. Love? Marriage? Cam felt heat flare in her cheeks. They'd only just met.

"Most of all, I wanted to matter." Zhurihe's breaths stuttered. "As a clone . . . an insignificant clone . . . I wanted to prove we could . . . make a difference in this world."

Cam took the dying girl's hand. "You do matter. You'll always matter. And know you changed the world today, Zhurihe."

The clone's mouth gave a wry twist. Then she seemed to let go. Cam knew the moment Zhurihe died, for the spark went out in the girl's dark eyes.

Lovingly Cam smoothed her hand over the girl's face, closing her eyelids.

Then she demanded angrily, "It's a little late now, but why didn't anyone come? Where were the doctors?"

As she asked the question, medical people finally entered the hangar. "She's dead." Cam stood, shaking. "What took you so long?"

A physician turned to Kyber, clearly at a loss. "We were told it was a clone."

Kyber took Cam into his arms. He said nothing to the doctor. Like Cam, he realized it was too late.

"*Why* aren't they seen as people?" she asked.

"The topic spurs debates all over the kingdom," he said, low in her ear. "In your time, people debated whether or not those still in the womb were people. This is no different. As our machines become self-aware, we will undoubtedly debate their humanity, as well." His voice turned thoughtful. "They will be important, those debates. What decisions we make will ultimately define us as a civilization."

"When this war is over, I'll take up Zhurihe's fight," Cam said with determination.

Kyber pressed his lips to her forehead.

"And it may never be over unless I get my butt in that jet."

She saw the anguish on his face. "No," he said. "I cannot do this. I cannot send you off to do this alone. I'll . . . go in your place."

"You don't know how to fly an F-16."

"Then I'll find another way."

"We don't need another way, Kyber. You're already in this up to your ears—with all your forces behind us, your public broadcast in support of the rebels, your denouncement of the military buildup in Washington . . ."

"Hmm," he grumbled, appearing unconvinced.

"You're an Emperor, I'm a fighter pilot. This is what I do best."

So many emotions filled his gray eyes. She felt each as powerfully as if it were her own. "This is what I do," she said, quieter. "And this"—she waved her hand toward the hangar entrance, where supporters looked on from behind ropes—"is what you do."

With a sound full of pain he drew her close. She knew she had to hurry, to reach Bree before things got worse at the Capitol, but, stunned by Zhurihe and Hong's deaths and apprehensive of the mission yet to come, she savored her few moments in Kyber's embrace.

"I want you to be part of my life, Cameron Tucker," he murmured. "To be part of my future."

She shook her head. "Was that a proposal?"

"It can be if you're ready. Otherwise, call it a statement of my intent. I have fallen in love with you."

"Oh, Kyber. I don't know . . . ," she whispered. "I don't want to promise anything I can't deliver. I'm flying off to maybe die, Kyber. Maybe it's just me, but I don't feel good about making any promises until I know I have a shot at coming back. I left a man behind in my first life. No, I didn't feel about him the way I do about you, but he loved me. I never came back."

Kyber's voice was gentle and deep. "And here I thought I was the one afraid to make a commitment for fear of loss."

"Not my loss—yours! You'd be the one hurt. I'd be . . . well, dead."

"Don't forget, pretty one, loss is a subject I know as well as you. But if you wish, I'll wait for an answer. You must return first." He gripped her shoulders. "Which you will."

She nodded. "And meanwhile, you can make sure you really want me as your wife. It would be a political position as much as a family one. For so long, your country has been so against the UCE. It'd be a new nation, but the people are the same. I wouldn't want my involvement to embarrass you or make you unhappy. I'm going to do whatever I can to see that democracy returns to my homeland." He answered with a nod, but she knew he wasn't happy—not only about her reluctance to give him an answer, but also with the prospect of her flying off to fight. "This is *what I do*," she reminded him in a quiet voice. "What I need from you right now is your protection, your satellites tracking me, helping make sure I don't get shot out of the sky before I get there, all while we try not to do anything to inadvertently start World War Three."

"Four," Nikolai corrected as he walked up to them. "We've already had three."

"Then let's not have any more," she said.

Not seeming to care that his chief of security was nearby, Kyber swept her into a kiss. Only with clear reluctance did he let her go. "Come back to me, pretty one," he said as she backed away, their hands still clasped.

"I want to," she whispered. "More than anything."

She let her fingers slide along his palm to his fingertips before breaking contact. He dropped his arm slowly, then watched as she strode at long last to the gleaming Viper.

Inside the cockpits with a flick of her finger, Cam brought the powerful engine to life. A thousand memories of all the missions that came before this, of all the reasons that she was here today, collided. Usually she was calm and in control of her emotions when preparing for a mission, but after she'd witnessed Zhurihe's needless death and knowing Bree was in mortal danger, it took all Cam had to keep focused.

The engine, with its futuristic supercharge, sounded otherwise normal to her experienced ears as she taxied toward the open hangar door. Kyber stood with Nikolai just outside, his face lifting to see her. Cam raised the shield on her helmet, extending her hand as if she could somehow touch him. "My exasperating, egotistical, handsome, generous, compassionate, and very sexy Prince Charming," she said tenderly. "Remember that piece of my heart I told you about, the part I said was yours? I wanted to say, before I left, that I love you, Kyber. I love you with my *whole* heart."

In perfect synchronization, Kyber and Nikolai lifted their hands to their ear comms. She saw each man smile—smiles that were totally different. Nikolai's was one of teasing pleasure directed at his boss. Kyber's was one she'd remember for the rest of her life. Everything she needed to know was there for all to see in his face. She knew it reflected what he carried in his heart. Their relationship was new, but for one so young it had *forever* written all over it. It was said that wartime romances proceeded at an accelerated rate. She believed it.

Cam snapped her sun visor back in place. Her oxygen mask went over her face next, making it impossible to tell whether she was a man or a woman. Fitting, she thought. A good soldier was a good soldier, regardless of body parts.

By now she knew the men were jogging up to the tower. From there Kyber would keep in contact with her throughout the five-hour flight—five hours at an amazing supersonic speed, possible only with structural reinforcement and gas tanks filled with synthetic fuel. Up over the pole she'd fly, down through Canada and the Great Lakes before soaring toward the Eastern seaboard, where Washington, DC, waited—the real Washington, DC, not the futuristic fake designed by the UCE. And then she'd do her part in all this, and hope to heaven it worked.

As she lined up on the center of the runway, miles of black pavement stretched before her. This was it. *Hang on, Bree. Here I come.* She took the throttle in her hand and pushed it forward. The engine wasn't rumbling anymore; it was roaring. The instant she released the brakes, she was riding a rocket.

Passing one hundred knots . . . one-fifty . . . rotation . . . lift off. She aimed the nose at the sky, and all she saw was blue. Throwing back her head with the joy of being in the air again, she whipped the throttle to the right and spun in a vertical roll, a victory roll, before turning on a dime and heading northeast.

Susan Grant

Seconds later, a horrible and sudden pain filled her skull, stealing her breath and almost her sight. She cried out softly. Her hand hit her helmet visor in her haste to hold her head.

"Oh, God," she panted. The pain spread, duller now, not as sharp, flowing down her neck and lodging in her jaw. It was like having someone pulling on all her molars while hammering nails into her brain.

She raised her visor, sweat forming on her face.

"Cam . . ." In her headset, Kyber was calling her. "You've veered off course."

She jumped, startled. She had changed heading and hadn't realized it. *Pay attention.* She made a correction back to course, and hoped she had the wherewithal to keep it there.

"Cam! What's wrong?"

"I don't know." Her tongue felt thick. Maybe it was because her mouth was so dry. "I feel . . . sick. Head hurts." She blinked, trying to clear her blurry vision. "I'm dizzy, too."

Pain lanced through her skull and lodged behind her eyes. She wasn't breathing ambient air but oxygen. Was the system contaminated? "What do you show for life-support status?"

The radio was silent. It was quiet for so long she worried that it had malfunctioned. But when Kyber answered, she knew by the tone of his voice that something was wrong. Very wrong. "It's not the oxygen, Cam."

"What then?"

"The prox-beacon. You're wearing one."

"Shit!" Her shock, anger, and fear imploded. "The beacon," she gasped out. "I forgot all about it." Dr. Park had

318

implanted the thing when she arrived, but since she'd never left the city walls there had been no reason to remember the otherwise harmless microscopic computers.

"Cam!"

She realized Kyber had been shouting at her. "Can it kill me if I ignore it?" she gasped out.

There was silence again. Sweating profusely, she lifted her visor and mopped her brow. "Can it?" she snapped.

"Dr. Park says she doesn't believe so."

Now *that* was a definitive answer.

"But you need to come back around and land immediately."

"We're out of time!"

"You can't fly like that for five hours."

Can't I? she thought, gritting her teeth. If Bree had done time in Fort Powell, then sure as sugar Cam could fly a mission with a supersized hangover. She had to.

Chapter Twenty-four

Armstrong's army covered the horizon in three directions—everywhere but east, toward the sea. If the UCE Navy was out there, Bree had the feeling they were about to find out. Communication with rebel forces around Central confirmed that other, smaller armies were taking up positions in other Colony cities. Yet she knew the truth: when the slaughter came, it would happen here.

Bree swallowed and stood straighter.

"Look. *There.*" Ty grabbed her arm and pointed her in the direction of the rising sun. Driving along the beach toward the Capitol was a hulking, futuristic tank. A huge painted-on UCE flag, a white globe on a blue square in the upper left corner of a solid red field, left no doubts as to who owned it. Sand spewed out in its wake as the vehicle raced directly toward the Capitol.

Bree heard the commands all around her: almost everyone with a gun or a missile was aiming it at the tank. Those who weren't were keeping watch for any surprise attacks from the other directions.

"That thing has the power to wipe out this entire building," Ty explained.

"The hatch is opening. Someone's poking his head out—no . . . I can see him now from the waist up," she observed, peering at the incongruous sight through her binoculars. "He's not wearing any protective gear. And he's waving a white flag."

Ty's gaze spun back to the tank, his eyes narrowing in surprise.

"Stand down, stand down," went the calls all over the building as others saw the tank approach.

"Is it a trick, I wonder?" Bree said, passing the binoculars to Ty.

"Possibly." His mouth thinned. "But in all previous engagements, combat and otherwise, my father has never used subterfuge as a shortcut to victory."

His father? Sure enough, now that the tank drove closer, she could see quite clearly that the man standing waist-high in the hatchway was Supreme Commander Aaron Armstrong. "What technique did he use to achieve victory?" She was almost afraid to ask.

"Frontal assault with superior firepower." He thought for a moment and said. "But who says we're the ones he's trying to kill?"

Cam fought against blacking out by keeping her eyes on her instruments and her mind on the mission. She was coming over the North Pole. The most dangerous part of the trip loomed ahead as she crossed from Tri-Canadian airspace into the UCE's.

Her flight suit was soaked with sweat. She was hesitant to drink her water because she didn't trust her stomach. There was something singularly unpleasant about barfing in the cockpit and then having an airsick bag ride shotgun with you for the next five hours.

Kyber was obviously watching her vital signs. "Cam," he said. Whenever she didn't check in every five minutes, he'd call her. By the sound of his voice, he was devastated about forgetting he'd ordered the prox-beacon implanted.

"Yeah," she whispered.

"Give me a status report."

"Same story: it hasn't gotten worse, the pain. Tell Dr. Park it reaches one level and stays there." And what a level. She felt horrible. "I think all the months of recovering in Mongolia with no drugs helped prepare me for this."

"It's said that everything difficult that happens in life prepares you for something else."

She winced at a particularly deep twinge at the base of her neck. "I wonder what this is preparing me for."

"Why, marriage to me, of course."

She laughed. "Ow!"

"What is it?"

"I laughed and it hurt like hell. No more jokes."

"Who said I was joking?"

"Kyber!"

"Sorry."

She knew he was only half-sorry. His relief at being able to engage her in conversation took precedence.

The F-16's threat warning system light illuminated. "What the hell?" Cam stiffened in her seat, her heart lurching. A swell of adrenaline drove her concentration into absolute focus.

"What is it?" Kyber demanded.

Her voice was calmer than she felt. "I've got an RAW—a radar alert warning. I thought y'all said traditional radar wasn't used anymore."

"Where are you?"

"Over Canada."

"That's why—because of the plagues, some of the technology they use is backward."

"If they come after me, I'm in trouble." Radar alone didn't pose a threat. It was, though, a way of opponents' taking aim. When she got close enough, they could lob stuff at her—bad stuff, like missiles.

She mopped her brow. Her neck felt fused to her spine. If she craned her neck, she would likely knock herself out. "Missiles," she muttered. "I don't know how I'd fare flying evasive maneuvers."

"Outrun them."

"Of course," she whispered. This was no ordinary F-16. "I'm going faster than any twenty-first-century weapon." She was flying at Mach 3, in fact, nearly triple the speed of sound. If a twenty-second-century jet came after her, she couldn't engage, though: a normal dogfight would rip her wings off, even with the structure shored up for this faster speed.

To be safe, she picked up her speed even more.

"Careful," warned one of the royal engineers sitting with Kyber. "Don't push it beyond where we know you can hold together structurally."

"Will do." She tried to keep calm as she rode out of the

range of the Tri-Canadian radar. Once clear, she realized that she was about to arrive in UCE airspace. And as soon as she did, she'd have a lot more than radar to worry about; she was sure of it.

"Time to go down." She pushed forward on the stick and headed for a lower altitude. By the time she reached the Atlantic seaboard, she was screaming over the water low enough to leave water spouts in her wake—and her head hurt so bad she could barely see. "I've got to try to make it," she whispered to herself. "Bree needs me."

She doesn't know you're on the way.

Cam managed a smile. *She will soon.*

No air defenses stopped her as she entered enemy airspace. It made sense: the Viper was old and slow. Yet she couldn't shake the strange feeling that someone had left the door wide open for her. Now all she had to hope was that it didn't get slammed in her face as she reached her target.

Ty couldn't name the feelings gripping him as he watched his father approach. None of them, however, were good.

He'd told Bree that he wasn't sure what his father's intentions were today. This could be the beginning of a grab for power. He'd always sensed that his father didn't care for Beauchamp. Maybe the man had decided, now that the rebellion was begun in earnest, to embrace it. He'd offer to use this army, in fact the entire and far more efficient and deadly UCE forces, to aid the rebellion, hoping to gain favor and in the end power. Many had claimed over the years that "Ax" was ruled by personal ambition, waiting for the right moment to oust President

Beauchamp and turn the UCE into a military dictator-ship. Was this that moment?

The tank rolled to a halt. The general disembarked.

Bree grabbed a voice amplifier: "An assault on one of us is an assault on us all. . . ."

Armstrong halted, looking up slowly. It was dead silent on the roof of the Capitol. No one spoke. He appeared to square his shoulders, as if he were frightened himself. In his other hand was a small device. A weapon? Ty lifted his binoculars to his eyes to better figure out what his old man was attempting to do.

Along the scaffolding, the ex-SEALs and Special Forces soldiers aimed their weapons at the general. Any of them could take him out—and would have a good excuse to do so. Yet calm reigned. An almost eerie air of presentiment hung over the entire Capitol and the acres of marshland surrounding it, and especially in Ty's heart.

The general found Bree in the crowd. Holding her steely gaze, he brought his hand to his mouth and spoke, the device amplifying yet distorting his voice: "I am well aware of the toil and blood it will cost you to come to me, Banzai Maguire, but come to me you must. Hear my words; heed my call. I am waiting for you."

"Holy Mother of God," Bree coughed out. "The Voice of Freedom is your father."

Chapter Twenty-five

"I told you he was a he," Ty muttered as they waited for the general to be escorted to the rooftop.

"As far as I'm concerned, the Shadow Voice could have turned out to be the Easter bunny and I wouldn't care at this point."

In truth, Ty shared Bree's sentiments. The war was far from over. The UCE army still loomed on the horizon, and Beauchamp still held office. But no one could argue that they'd acquired a miraculous ally in General Armstrong.

In his cold, efficient way, typical of the man when he was nervous, Ty knew, Ax marched to where Bree stood with Ty.

Bree stepped forward to meet him. "What happened in Fort Powell? What did I say to the guard?

"'Don't be afraid of death,'" he replied carefully. "'Be afraid of the unlived life.' A quotation of your great-grandmother's."

"Correct." Bree let out a shaky breath. "Answer me this, sir: about my torture—did you authorize that?"

"Never. Beauchamp's people had control of you at first. I'd gotten you out of the Raft Cities, so he felt he wanted a piece of you. It was a bit of a power play between us, but I finally convinced him to let me take over your care. Remember your hot meal the night you spoke to the guard? That was when I took charge of your treatment. Though I am fully guilty of taking advantage of your condition once I learned of it. I made sure your trial was televised so all of Central could see the poor shape you were in."

"As the Voice of Freedom, how did you transmit . . . everywhere?"

The man shrugged. "Simply by using the technology available to me in my position as top military leader. And no," he said, looking at Ty. "Your mother didn't know."

"What about the assassin?" Ty asked.

His father's eyes darkened. "Beauchamp sent him—I knew nothing of it!"

"I worked with that soldier. Lopez was his name." Even after all this time, Ty could hear the anguish the incident caused in his own heart.

"The lure of power and money can change men."

"Not you, Father?"

"I am only human. I want what's best for this country. I've done many things, kept many secrets, and it's all been in the name of freedom. I am tired, Ty. I would not mind walking away from this when all is done. If that's what the people want of me."

Ty ran his hands through his hair as a thousand mental pictures flipped through his brain, and he took incidents

327

that had happened with his father and saw them in this new light.

"You had nothing to do with the prison security system failure?" Bree asked.

Armstrong shook his head. His forehead creased. "That remains a mystery. Even the president blamed me."

"And Chico? Did you put me in touch with him intentionally?"

"Yes. Glad you picked up on that. You were always a bright boy." His father's eyes twinkled with subtle humor.

Chuckling, Ty let a sudden rush of emotion take hold of him. He moved forward and offered his hand to his father. Their grip was powerful, hinting at the love between them. They weren't quite ready for more than a handshake yet, however.

"Now what, General?" Someone whom Ty recognized as a militia leader shouted. "Are your troops in on this, too?"

To Ty's dismay, his father's face fell. "Now's the time for us to see. I couldn't reveal anything of myself until I knew I could do so here. As far as they know, I'm their general, loyal to the death to the UCE."

Ty saw Bree cast a wary glance to the army surrounding them on three sides.

"I can also say with confidence that a majority would defect if given reason to do so. The only reason the soldiers have stayed with me is out of personal loyalty."

"Do you mean if you say the word, they'll change sides?" Bree asked.

The general exhaled. "There are no guarantees. As peacefully as we pray this situation ends, this is, in fact, war. While, yes, I believe many of the troops will fight for us and not Beauchamp's UCE, there's no guarantee any of them will in fact do so."

"But what do you think, father?" Ty asked. "What does your gut say?"

"My gut says most are ours. And those on the fence, as soon as Beauchamp takes the reins, they will come over to our side."

Our side. Coming from his father, Ty thought the words had a nice ring.

The general extended his hand to Bree. "Banzai Maguire," he said with a blend of affection and admiration, "you should stand with me, so that when the images reach the far corners of this colony, this soon-to-be new nation, they will see us together as equals."

"I would be honored."

Bree stepped toward him, grasped his hand, and walked with the general to the edge of the roof. A soldier in the general's path aimed a camera at them. Touching a small handheld screen and communicating directly with his army, Armstrong said, "My brave soldiers, I order you to stand down. Stand down. A peace treaty has been negotiated here today. A peace treaty, fate willing, for all time. There are two kinds of men in the UCE: those who yearn to be free, and those who are slaves. I offer today the chance at freedom for all who desire it. For those who don't, know this: a new nation will soon be born, retaken from our past. It will be a glorious new future, but you will not be part of it."

He stood straighter, taking off his hat. Ty noticed that his short black hair was damp with sweat. So the Ax was not immune to nerves, after all.

Taking in a mighty breath, the general bellowed, "To

President Julius Beauchamp and his servants I say this: Central's future is yours no more! Central is free!"

Bree let out a whoop, and spontaneous cheers broke out all over the building.

Almost immediately, Beauchamp himself answered, using the Capitol's speaker system, which he had electronically usurped. "Mine is the legitimate government! Armstrong wants the power for himself!"

"No! We will hold free elections for our next leader. He or she will be a citizen *chosen by the people*. I know good people, worthy people, are out there. Many of them. As for me, I am happy to retire from my public life."

The soldiers' cheers became thunderous.

Bree left Armstrong's side. Jostled by the celebration, she found Ty and moved into the circle of his arms. He drew her close. "When we were in the heli-jet, you said I didn't belong to you," she said. "You said that I belonged to the people. I don't think that's true anymore. I've done what I came here to do. I'm yours, Ty. Yours always."

He crushed her to his chest. He didn't even kiss her; he merely held her close in a long, tight hug, as if he never wanted to let her go.

Shouts of warning tore them apart. The lookouts' high-powered imaging screens revealed a disturbing sight coming from the one area his father's army didn't occupy: the sea.

"They're Beauchamp's private guard," the general said grimly. "Marines."

Everyone on the Capitol turned to watch as the soldiers rolled ashore. More ships plowed forward behind them. They were trapped, all of the rebels, and it seemed about to be slaughtered.

"New target—at a hundred miles, sir!" one of the lookouts manning an aviation tracker shouted.

Bree's disappointment was clearly etched on her face. "They're coming by air now, too," she said wearily. So much for this day ending peacefully, without massive bloodshed. "What else could go wrong? We can't afford any more letdowns. Hundreds of thousands of soldiers, and too many likely on the verge of giving up and going home."

"No," the lookout said. "It's only one. And it doesn't have the signature of any of the warcraft I know—space or atmospheric."

Several other Spec Ops guys joined the lookout in analyzing the new threat. Their eyes went from the aviation tracker to their handheld computers and back again. "Impossible," one said. "It . . . can't be."

"Let me see." Bree exhaled noisily and pulled herself along the scaffolding to where the men huddled around the monitor. Ty followed.

Upon seeing what so confused the men, Bree made a small sound that encapsulated disbelief, incredulity, bewilderment, and joy all at the same time. "That jet," she told him. "It's an American F-16!"

Chapter Twenty-six

Eyes narrowed against the pain in her skull and neck, Cam flew a few hundred feet off the water. "Keep it level, keep it steady. . . ." She found that if she talked to herself, she could focus better. And focus was what she needed this low to the deck. She was flying so fast that a sneeze could slam her into the water. At this speed she'd be dead in an instant. There was no room for mistakes.

She raced over the seas—the Atlantic Ocean, the same waves she'd splashed through as a girl visiting the Georgia shore in summer. She was here to protect those waves now. *Waves . . . Amber waves of grain . . .* She jerked alert.

I'm hallucinating.

She shook her head, then cursed her stupidity when agony gripped her neck, radiating into her jaw and sinuses. Backing off the throttle, she slowed down, but she kept the plane above Mach 1 because, boy, that sonic boom would rattle a few glasses—and maybe a general or two.

As she rolled in toward shore, the final run, the scene startled her. There were far more infantry on the ground than she'd expected. And no smoke or fire, no signs of a battle under way.

"It's the strangest sight, Kyber. Hundred of thousands of people. Everyone's just standing around, staring each other down. Wait. There are more. Coming in by sea, troop carriers unloading what look like futuristic marines."

"Yes. We see them on the satellite. A private force, my intelligence people say. Beauchamp's."

Well, she thought, she'd get down extra low in that case, and blow their socks off. She roared over the advancing marines, knowing the thunder she caused as she rent the air was deafening.

She arced in a gentler curve as she slowed, wheeling over the Capitol building, where Bree was said to be. Despite her suffering, the poignancy of seeing Washington, DC, spread out below was intense.

It almost made up for all the crap she'd had to deal with today.

Almost.

"Here it goes," she whispered, and brought her finger to the trigger for the nanowriter. The entire plan hinged on this working. *Please.* She hit the screen icon and banked in a gentle turn, making a large circle over the Capitol.

It was painful to do, but she craned her neck to see what she'd painted in the sky. The sight took her breath away. The montage of images showed reenactments from

American pre-Revolutionary history, mixed with scenes from the centuries before the UCE. The Interweb was down—Kyber had told her that—so Cam could only imagine, and hope, that images of world leaders declaring their support of the revolt in Central had a tremendous impact on those on the ground.

"There is troop movement," she shouted into the radio. "I see soldiers running." Running toward the Capitol and Bree, she realized, her heart pounding. But even from a thousand feet in the air, she knew they were deserting their UCE masters, not attacking. "It's begun," she murmured. "It's truly begun."

Yes. Grinning, Cam rolled over on a wing, intending to take a victory spin around the Capitol, when her weapons warning system went crazy. *Nee-nee-nee-nee-nee-nee*. This was no measly radar warning. The alarm said it all: Beauchamp's marines had lobbed a missile.

Except, not at her. It was streaking through the air from the sea and headed straight for Bree's position.

Using the Han Empire's air-to-air add-on, Cam blew it out of the sky. It went up in a harmless but beautiful bloom, illuminating all of Washington.

"Incoming!" someone shouted.

Ash and bits of the blown-apart missile rained down on the Capitol. It gave a whole new meaning to *rockets' red glare* and *bombs bursting in air*.

"Fireworks," Bree told Ty. "You said you always wanted to see them."

Above, the F-16 veered back to sea. Except for missile defense, it seemed to have no real weapons. Whoever it was had truly come in peace and at the risk of their life.

From the top of the Capitol, Ty and Bree had a birds-eye view of the miraculous sky show. "Prince Kyber," she said, watching the nanowriting. "He's offering his support to us. And the leader of the Euro-African Consortium. Ty, this is what we needed. This will make the difference!"

"And so will that pilot," the general said, appearing behind them. "We've detected the evidence of defections from Beauchamp's guard. I don't think the 'Star-spangled Banner' persuaded them, but seeing world leaders on the other side certainly has. A brilliant move, that."

The F-16 roared overhead, wings rocking, as if the pilot were giddy with the heady pleasure of flying, and Bree would have given her eyeteeth to be in that cockpit. But she was needed here, standing amongst the militia as their symbol of freedom.

"Hmm. Could that pilot be your missing wingmate, Cameron Tucker?" Armstrong asked. "If it is, she's come at a good time."

Ice cascaded from Bree's head to her heart, followed by a hot hope. "It has to be," she whispered, the realization sinking in. "This has the markings of Cam all over it."

Beauchamp's marines were breaking ranks, and thousands of defecting UCE soldiers took up defensive positions around the Capitol. They could see Armstrong, and responded by cheering when he greeted them with a salute.

Another missile arced into the sky, this one aimed at the F-16. Who was ordering the attacks? It must be Beauchamp himself. Immediately, the jet went into evasive maneuvers, launching countermeasures and racing across the sky.

"Shake it, Cam. Shake it off." Bree brought her fists out in front of her, as if she were the one flying. It looked as if the missile would explode harmlessly over the ocean: more evidence that Cam was flying. Whoever was at the controls of that jet was a fantastic pilot.

But not so lucky today, it seemed. The futuristic missile came around for another go. The antiquated jet had fooled it once, but it wouldn't happen twice. Everyone on the Capitol roof sucked in a collective breath as the missile clipped its target.

Trailing dark smoke, the F-16 banked. Bree's fists came together. "Get out, get out," she said under her breath. This low, Cam couldn't waste time deciding whether to bail out. She had to do it now.

Live to fight another day, Bree prayed. And she was rewarded. The F-16 turned until it faced the ocean, and the pilot ejected. The seat rocketed out and the burning, pilotless fighter flew on, gradually losing altitude before it crashed harmlessly into the sea.

"There he is!" The crowd on the roof pointed at the pilot, who was coming down fast. The wind was carrying the parachuting figure toward the Capitol. Bree had a flashback to the terrible day she'd watched Cam get shot out of the sky over North Korea. She'd never forget the sight of those long dangling legs.

They were the same legs she saw now.

Holy Christmas, it *was* her. It was Cam!

"She! It's a she!" Bree fought her way through the militiamen to the roof stairs, ignoring even Ty who had to run to keep up with her. "It's Cam," she shouted to him breathlessly, taking the stairs two at a time, all while the thought ran through her mind: How the hell had Cam gotten an F-16 to fight with and she hadn't?

Cam plummeted to earth. The force of the ejection had knocked her out, but she'd woken in time to find the ground rushing up. Now she had more important things to worry about than her headache.

Gripping her parachute's risers, she tried to steer away from the buildings. So many had been torn down in this eerie, marshy ghost town of Washington, DC, that it wasn't difficult to maneuver for a clear spot. *Thank the Lord.*

Below her swinging feet, people were running to keep up with her. The good guys this time, she thought, panting to keep the pain from taking her awareness before she landed.

"Kyber," she whispered, though he could no longer hear her. "I made it. I lived through it." He'd be fearing for her safety now, knowing she'd ejected. From halfway around the world she could feel his pain.

Cam hit the ground in a perfect PLF landing. Standing, she unclipped her chute. *Never underestimate Cam Tucker,* she thought, took a couple of steps, then collapsed.

Bree ran to the fallen pilot. "Cam! Cam!"

Her friend lay on her back in the middle of the road in front of the Capitol. Bree's heart stopped. *Is she dead?*

But no. Just as Bree reached her, Cam rose up on her elbows—only to be practically knocked flat as Bree slammed into her, arms open wide.

337

I found her, Bree thought. She'd found her wingman. At last.

The reunion was a fervent reunion of tears, whispers, and laughter.

And then everyone else caught up. "We've got to get her to a hospital," Bree said, seeing Cam's pain-stricken face.

"It's a prox-beacon," Cam explained, clearly hurting. "As soon as it's disabled, I'll be fine."

They loaded her into a nearby truck and set off for the hospital. Ty radioed with the news that Armstrong's armies were driving Beauchamp's forces back. Cam's air show had motivated the entire country. Not much was left of the UCE Guard after massive defections. The same was happening in every city across Central.

"He's going to help," Cam told Bree, half-delirious with pain. "Prince Kyber."

"You convinced him to help us?"

Cam simply smiled. "And more. He doesn't know it yet, but we're going to get married."

In the back of the ambulance, Bree sagged against the gurney. "You're going to have to start at the beginning. . . ."

Cam's mouth curved. "Yeah. You, too . . ."

Chapter Twenty-seven

The war was shorter than anyone imagined it would be, lasting weeks, not months or years. It came to an abrupt and inglorious end when Julius Beauchamp fired a bullet into his mouth. UCE army loyalists surrendered to United States forces without further incident.

After a triumphant journey from his Montana ranch, General Armstrong arrived at the White House—the original White House. Or, rather, a convincing replica built in record time over the old and crumbled foundation.

On December 23rd, 2176, Bree stood behind a podium in front of a cheering crowd. "Ladies and gentlemen, I present to you the man behind the Shadow Voice." She raised her voice above the thunderous applause. "The Voice of Freedom! Aaron Armstrong—our *freely elected* president!"

Choked up, she stepped aside as the tall, lean man took his rightful place in front of those who had put him in office through the first true elections in the United States in more than a century. It was no accident, she thought, that on this very same date, minus approximately four-hundred years, George Washington, victorious commander-in-chief of the American Revolutionary army, appeared before Congress and voluntarily resigned his commission. General Washington not only stunned the world with an action unprecedented in history, but set the standard of military submission to a civilian government that had ended up lasting even after the United States' ill-fated consolidation into the meganation called the UCE. Four centuries later, Aaron Armstrong himself made history by repeating it.

It was a day Bree knew she'd never forget, a day that saw much weeping and laughter, apprehension and hope. It was the day that the old United States, in all its idealistic intent, was reborn.

"'Having now finished the work assigned to me,'" the newly civilian president Armstrong declared, paying homage to General Washington's famous speech, "'I retire from the great theater of action, and bidding an affectionate farewell to this august body under whose orders I have so long acted, I here offer my commission and take my leave of all the employments of public life.'"

The public loved it—and they loved Armstrong. And so began the new age for which they'd all fought.

Chapter Twenty-eight

To the delight of a weary world, Prince Kyber of the Han Empire asked Cameron Tucker to be his wife.

It was clear to everyone that Kyber was smitten with the beautiful, brave, shoot-from-the-hip commoner. The union was so obviously a love match that it smoothed over many a prickly diplomatic problem once thought hopeless, doing more for world stability in one year than all the treaties of the previous two hundred.

At the royal engagement party in the gorgeous grounds of the Han summer palace, Bree decided she'd come full circle by returning to the Asian kingdom. Almost two years had passed since she'd first opened her eyes to this frightening, confusing future world, and yet it seemed millennia ago. She'd changed; the world even more so. And in her opinion, there was no better excuse to party. Once a fighter pilot, always a fighter pilot.

Bree's hand found her husband's, callused not from fighting wars but from building a deck on the grounds of his father's ranch in Montana, where the two of them now lived. As Bree had retreated from the public eye, Cam had launched herself into it. Bree couldn't be prouder.

Dignitaries mingled all around her, but that wasn't what made this party such an incredible event. After so many years separated from the rest of the world, Asia was taking its first cautious steps toward dropping its isolationist veil.

Bree watched Cam make the rounds on the arm of her fiancé, and she had a feeling her friend would be no mere pretty wife of a king. Already a force for change inside Asia's once-impenetrable borders, Cam, it was clear, in no way intended to relinquish individual power. Bree's wingmate was only now coming into her own, and with her fight for clone rights, advocacy for the reopening of all borders and trade, and her lobbying to liberalize the more archaic practices of her new homeland, Cam's impact on the world would no doubt be huge in the years to come.

She walked toward Bree and Ty with a young woman in tow. "I have someone for y'all to meet," she said.

The stranger thrust out her hand. "Jenny Red."

"Ah, Jenny. My pleasure." From what Cam had told her, this was the fiancée of Kyber's estranged half brother, D'ekkar.

Ty shook Jenny's hand, then murmured in Bree's ear, "I'll get us a drink." He obviously didn't want to intrude.

As he walked off, Cam moved closer to Bree, equal parts joy, hope, and surprise lighting her face. "I didn't know if they'd come," she said, smiling warmly at Jenny. "But you did."

Bree hesitated. "Is . . . ?"

"Yes, Deck's here."

Bree followed the other two women to the edge of the dining terrace. In the fountain gardens below, two men of similar build and stance stood facing each other in the shadows.

The women gathered at the railing. Cam seemed a bit nervous. "He's not armed, right?"

"No, but I am." Jenny pulled up a sleeve. A long, thin blade glittered on the inside of her forearm. She moved aside her skirt to give Cam a peek at a second knife.

Cam revealed the tiny pistol she kept hidden in her bodice. "Me, too."

"So I guess we're okay."

"They'll have to behave this time."

The women grinned at each other before turning their attention back to the men. Jenny grew more serious as she watched. Love for Deck was achingly apparent on her face. "He needs this."

"So does Kyber," Cam murmured. "They're family."

"Sometimes you don't really know how much they mean to you until they're no longer around. . . ."

Cam pressed her lips together and nodded. Then, after a moment or two, she said, "Kyber didn't know about it, Jenny. Deck's mistreatment in the dungeon . . . he wasn't told. He regrets it terribly."

"I think Deck knows. Look."

The two men came together in an embrace, awkward at first, then with the intensity of true brothers.

"Mercy." Cam brought her clasped hands to her chin at the same time Jenny smiled, her eyes moist. Jenny squeezed Cam's arm. "We did it, future sister-in-law."

Susan Grant

Cam pulled the woman into a hug. "I hope this means y'all will come here more often."

"I never thought I'd say I hope that, too, but I do. I want Deck to be happy. He won't admit it, but he needs to be part of this." Jenny turned back to Bree and smiled, almost sheepishly, as if she were a little embarrassed by all the emotion.

Don't be, Bree yearned to say. "Happily-ever-afters don't come easily, but when you've got one within your reach, grab it and don't let it go."

344

Chapter Twenty-nine

Roses in red, white, and blue pelted a sleek black sedan making halting progress through the streets of the rebuilt Washington, DC. Barriers of applauding police kept the cheering crowd more or less off the road, allowing the car to proceed. It was a fitting end to the first president's last day in office.

Six years, thought Aaron Armstrong. The term had seemed much shorter than that. "Life is fleeting," the saying went, but he still had to ask the question. Where had the time gone?

A small boy crawled into his lap. "Grandpa," the youngster murmured. Sticking a thumb into his mouth, he lay his head on Armstrong's chest.

The former president rubbed the boy's small but sturdy back. Quietly and together, as if of the same mold, they watched the cheering faces speed by. Beyond the road rose the spire of the Washington Monument, standing

Susan Grant

proud on land reclaimed from the sea. "Patrick Henry Armstrong, someday all this will be yours."

The boy snuggled closer. He'd always liked the rumble of his grandfather's voice.

"But you'll have to earn it," Armstrong explained. "You'll have to win a free election, and be the choice of the people. But you'll do it. I know you will." He gently chucked the child on the chin. "You've got my organizational skills and your grandmother's compassion. And, thanks to your father, you've inherited an Armstrong stubborn streak a mile wide. Your mother's no slouch, either. If it weren't for her, we wouldn't be riding in this car and witnessing this . . . this miracle."

Armstrong felt the swell of emotion. His grandson's little hand patted him on the chest, as if saying, *Don't worry, Grandpa; my future election campaign will go just fine without your interference.*

Armstrong chuckled. How he loved this boy! How he loved all of them. He couldn't arrive home fast enough, where the rest of the family awaited—Maggie, Ty and Bree, and Patrick's brand-new baby sister—busy preparing for a private celebration in his honor. They were who deserved all the accolades, not him, and he planned to spend his retirement years doing just that: making sure they knew they were the reason he took the steps he had, risking all for freedom and liberty, and changing the course of the world in the process. He'd achieved much in his life; he knew that—more than most men could have realized given ten lifetimes. Yet in the end, it was his family that was the most deeply satisfying accomplishment of all. They were the future.

Former UCE Supreme Commander Aaron Armstrong

settled back against the soft leather cushion of his seat and indulged in a well-deserved smile. When all was said and done, he had to admit that the future was looking pretty damn good, indeed.

Chapter Thirty

At the height of summer, nights in Paekdusan were short. Even in the hour after midnight, the sky was more indigo than black. It was in that deep, midsummer twilight that the emperor of Asia and his wife sneaked their horses out of the royal stables to lead them through soft, dew-covered grasses.

"Everyone wants to know when we're going to have a child," Cam said, squeezing Kyber's hand. They walked along under the stars.

"Making heirs is a Han preoccupation," he admitted.

She shot him a private smile. "I noticed."

He slid an arm around her waist, drawing her close. Ah, he loved this woman. How he loved waking with her, living with her, and most of all, ruling with her. "That, my love, is called practice. What I meant is the actual production of heirs. But there's still time for that."

"We've made the kingdom wait long enough, don't you think? It may be time we got started more seriously on the issue of producing little princes and princesses."

Joyfully, he swept his wife into his arms. Their body armor clinked lightly, their wedding bands glinting in the starlight.

"First, one last ride," she murmured, touching a fingertip to his lips. "Then we'll return to do our duty for the empire."

"I cannot fathom any other duty as sweet."

"Me, either."

A breeze off the mountains rustled the canopy of leaves above, and they shared a kiss—long, lush, and heartfelt.

"Don't ever tell Nikolai," Kyber said against her parted lips, "but I'd say that riding the Rim with you is far more fun than with him."

She laughed in that unabashed, musical way he never tired of hearing. And so he drew her into his arms once more for the kind of kiss he knew he'd never tire of stealing.

He drew back after a bit to hold her face in his hands. Gazing down at his wife, he felt his breath catch. Cam literally glowed. Blond hair framed her upturned face in airy wisps, making her look almost angelic. He could feel her joy, her love, as it flowed from her unchecked. It was exactly as she'd appeared in the photo from Mongolia that Nikolai had shown him all those years ago. Though he hadn't realized it then, that was the moment he'd fallen in love with a fighter pilot named Cameron Adele Tucker. Her unwavering loyalty and astonishing courage had touched his heart then as she touched it now.

Kyber's smile was one of plain, unadulterated happiness, for under the stars on that magical midsummer's eve, the road to adventure beckoning before him, he knew, without a doubt, that there was no other place he'd rather be than in the arms of his "Scarlet Empress."

Epilogue

Not long after the birth of the first Han princess, the ailing emperor finally succumbed to the killer proteins that ravaged his body. He passed away, gently and without fanfare, late one night, allowing Crown Prince Kyber to step up to the throne he had unofficially occupied for years.

For the coronation events, Bree, Ty, and Ty's family were put up at the grand palace in Beijing. Even after experiencing the glitter and glamour of Cam's royal wedding to Kyber, Bree wasn't prepared for the all-out extravagance of the coronation ceremony.

"I admit I'm a little starstruck," she whispered in Ty's ear as they entered the grand ballroom for a reception.

His fingers brushed down her back, bared by her low-cut gown. "If it makes you feel any better, I'm a lot starstruck. Though I have to say I like having friends in high places."

A slim hand on her shoulder cut short Bree's laugh.

"Cam!" She gave her friend a hug. Cam was dressed in scarlet from head to toe, in a gown to die for. She looked gorgeous, but most of that, Bree knew, was from being in love—both with her husband and with their new baby daughter. "I have something for you," Cam said.

Bree glanced at her empty hands and frowned. "A Snickers bar? Almond Joy? Cheese Nips?"

Cam rolled her eyes. "You have a one-track mind. Ty, I have to borrow her for a little bit. Sorry, no boys allowed."

Bree waved good-bye to her amused-looking husband. Then she linked arms with her friend as they left the party. "So, what does the empress have in mind?"

Cam's eyes sparkled. "You'll see," she said in a singsong voice.

"I'm suspicious."

"You always are. You always wanted to shake the gifts at Christmas, too. I hated that you hated surprises, but this time, sugar, you have no choice."

Cam broke away to pull open a pair of massive, carved double doors, thousands of years old. They revealed a sweeping balcony open to the glittering city lights of Beijing. Cam lived in this luxury every day, Bree thought. Did you get used to it after a while? Bree preferred her laid-back ranch life—pancake breakfasts and jeans. Cam, though, seemed perfectly at home in this lavish palace. It probably didn't hurt to have the man you adored close by and feeling the same way about you. That, Bree understood. Where Ty was, was home.

Bree's eyes took a few seconds to adjust to the mellow light of hanging lanterns. When they did, she saw a couple of dozen women standing alone or in groups, women of many ethnicities, wearing a variety of clothing that told her they hailed from a number of different lands. They greeted Bree with expressions ranging from friendly curiosity to downright awe.

"It took a bit of doing," Cam explained, "but I finally waded through the red tape to get them here." Her mouth gave a saucy twist. "It helps when your husband is an emperor."

Bree's heart fluttered. "Are these . . . ?" Speechless, she waved a hand at the circle of women.

"Yes. They're the women whose stories came to light in the months after the revolution ended. Each of them has been brought here to receive recognition for their acts of courage and . . . well, basically their guts. Each of them shared in the transformation of the world. There are more, of course, many more, but these were the ones we know about." Cam waved her arm in a sweeping arc. "Presenting . . . girl power at its best."

Bree brought her shaking hands together, lacing her fingers in front of her. Cam lowered her voice. "They want to meet you."

She shook her head. "I want to meet *them*." Even now, after all had been said and done, she felt awkward in her role as hero, always surprised to find those who idolized her. She shunned the public eye and was happiest tucked away in Montana with Ty, even though her reclusive lifestyle threatened to turn her into even more of a legend.

"You inspired me," a very young, pretty woman said, approaching first. She had a quiet manner about her, but without any shyness. Tall but delicately built, with a long dark ponytail streaming down her back, she offered Bree her hand. "Cai Randolph," she supplied confidently at Bree's questioning stare.

Recognition jolted Bree's memory. "Cai, yes." She was the "anchor," the techie half of a Quandem, a pair of elite operatives trained for covert military action. Neural implants allowed the woman to sit back in a control chair and feed information to her partner, whom Bree learned she'd later married. Now *that* was a love story. "You were instrumental in my capture. I do believe you zapped me with a neuron fryer that day. Unless that wasn't you."

"Sorry about that," the woman said a bit ruefully.

"As a rogue hacker, you were even more instrumental in my escape from Fort Powell. You shut down the prison. I simply walked away from my cell and out the door."

"It was the least I could do, once I learned you'd been set up."

"You make it sound simple, while I know it couldn't have been. You were member of the UCE military, acting on orders. In the Raft Cities, you did what you thought was your duty, but once you saw the truth, you followed your conscience. That couldn't have been easy. I admire your courage; I admire you."

Cai, refreshingly humble, acknowledged her praise with a simple nod. She was so young, Bree thought, and so brave.

Another woman approached—shorter, compact, in great physical shape. On the lapel of her red suit-dress, a gold maple leaf sparkled. In contrast, an ankle bracelet woven of leather and clearly of Native American design peeked out from under the hem of her long skirt. "Day Daniels," Bree said.

"Banzai Maguire." Respect filled the Mountie's eyes,

one of which was hazel and one green. "Your revolution came."

Bree nodded. "We looked to the north . . ."

"And we were there to help," Day whispered.

A spontaneous hug overcame them. They gripped each other, emotion running high. And when they finally broke apart, they clasped each other's hands.

Bree saw Cam wiping away a tear then, and she lost it. She was feeling especially emotional. The surprise reunion with these women whose exploits and selfless acts she'd tried to piece together from a number of reports was almost too much. "You are to be admired for your bravery at the border when it all came tumbling down," Bree told the proud Canadian.

Another woman approached to pay her respects. She, too, was very young, though something in her bright, miss-no-detail gaze made her seem older. A slit in her glittery dress gaped slightly, giving Bree a glimpse of a feminine garter—and the deadly blade she'd slipped behind it.

"It's been a long time, Jenny."

"Too long."

They embraced. Bree gave an extra-long hug to the woman who'd married Kyber's half brother, D'ekkar. "You saved the Voice of Freedom from silence when you enabled it to transmit from Australia. To do it, you returned there at the risk of imprisonment—or worse."

"Worse." Jenny cocked a grin. "Definitely."

Bree shook her head. "If you hadn't gotten the Voice of Freedom up and going again, I don't know what might have happened."

"We'd have done it. Somehow, someday." Cam waved

a hand expansively at the circle of women looking on. "Look at them, all of them. Have you any doubt that we would have won in the end?"

Bree smiled through her tears. "Good prevails."

"What you mean is, no good deed goes unpunished."

At that, the women laughed, a sound that lifted Bree's heart. This would be a high point in her life; she knew it with absolute surety. And she planned to enjoy every last minute of it. "Come on, ladies. There are more introductions to be made."

She led the way toward the bar, where Cam gathered up a half case of extremely rare vintage champagne. Bree did the pouring into the proffered glasses. "Drinks all around. We're going to have ourselves a little victory celebration, just us women. And then we can talk. If there's one thing I've learned in my life—rather, in my *lives*—it's that men, God bless 'em, don't have a monopoly on war stories. . . ."

And so it was that New America was born and the world was renewed along with it. As the years passed, the economy stabilized, spurring growth and a gradual return to prewar prosperity.

That's not to say there wasn't unrest; as you well know, our new nation would experience many rocky years. However, because of the revolution, the world was now a better place. A safer place.

Thomas Paine, that brilliant man, the persuasive eighteenth-century campaigner for American independence, once wrote: We have it in our power to begin the world anew.

And so, as best we could, we did.

Turn the page
for a special
sneak preview of
Marjorie M. Liu's

TIGER EYE

Coming in March 2005. Watch for it!

Chapter One

Dela had mysterious dreams the night before she bought the riddle box. A portent, maybe. She did not think much of it. She was used to strange dreams, only a few of which had ever come true.

Still, she was alert when she left the hotel the next morning, stepping into the dry furnace of a rare clear Beijing day. Winds had swept through the night, sloughing away the smog and scent of exhaust and decay. Blue sky, everywhere. Sun glinted off the glass of skyscrapers, cars, diamonds, the aluminum spines of umbrellas shading dark-eyed women, casting sparks in Dela's unprotected eyes. The world trickled light.

The city had changed. Ten years of capitalist influence, spinning a web of glass and advertisements; a modern infrastructure sweeping over the land as surely as the fine Gobi dust imported by the northern winds. A new cultural revolution, here in the city, across China. It mattered to Dela, the form and result. She could hear Beijing's growing song, the soul of the city, the collective soul of its thirteen million inhabitants, etched into the steel.

Dangerous, alluring—she did not like to listen long. There was too much hunger in that voice, overwhelming promise and hope, twisted with despair. A double-edged blade, forged from the dreams of the people living their lives around her.

Just like any other big city, she reminded herself, pouring strength into her mental shields. *Devils and angels, the lost and found.*

Cabs swarmed the hotel drive like fire-ants, fast and red, and Dela jumped into the first one that squealed to a stop. Directions, spoken in perfect Mandarin, slipped off her tongue. One week in China, and her old language lessons had returned with a fury. True, she sometimes practiced with her assistant, Adam, a former resident of Nanjing, but regular life had settled its wings on her shoulders, years without stretching herself, dredging up the studies that had once taken her around the world. Dela thought she might have forgotten all those parts that were not metal, of the forge, and was glad she had not.

The cab wrenched from one clogged lane to another, a hair-raising mish-mash of roaring engines and squealing tires, curving down a tree-lined street where colorful exercise bars lined a scrap of shaded park. Elderly men and women pushed and pulled their way through rotating stress exercises, children screaming on seesaws. Bicycles overburdened with cargo, both human and vegetable, trundled down the crowded street, cars swerving to avoid the monstrously wide loads, as well as the packs of ragged young men darting across the road.

Dela saw a familiar low wall, cracked with age, its carved flowers and barbed wire still unchanged. She tapped the plastic barrier and the driver let her out before the wide entrance, scratched blue doors flung open to admit both foreigners and locals, making their way through a treacherous maze of parked bicycles. Dela saw faces bright with curiosity and greed.

Entering Pan Jia-Yuan. The Dirt Market. Tourist trap, hive of antique rip-offs and bald-faced lies—a treasure hunter's paradise. And Dela was in the mood to hunt.

Dust swirled around her feet as she slipped past crooked old men and women hawking nylon shopping bags to beleaguered early birds, hands already full of purchases. Stepping onto the concrete platform shaded by a voluminous tin roof, she listened to cheap jade jingle: bracelets, statues, necklaces. Pretty enough, and quite popular, if the gathered crowds were any indication. Nothing caught her eye. Potential gifts, perhaps, for acquaintances who would appreciate the gesture. Not good enough for actual friends, few and far between, deserving of special care, something beyond trinkets.

But later. Dela had something else to find.

She combed the shadowed interiors of the open-air stalls, searching until she heard a familiar call inside her mind. *Weapons.* She followed the whispers to their source.

Scimitars and short swords; Tibetan daggers, hilts engraved with piled grinning skulls. Mongol bows, rough with use and age, quivers flimsy with faded embroidery, metal trimmings. Everywhere, dusty tinted steel—but all of it disappointing. The metalwork was poor; these were cheap imitations for not-so-cheap prices.

Marjorie M. Liu

Dela stared at the eager merchants, who smiled at her blond hair, pale skin, and electric eyes. Easy mark. She could see it written on their faces, and their judgment made her feel lonely; a foreign emotion, and unpleasant.

Bad enough they probably think I'm dumb, she thought sourly. Solitude was a gift, but only when paired with anonymity. The disinterested observer.

Dela frowned to herself. *You shouldn't have returned to China if you didn't want to stand out. Buck up, girl.*

She left the weapons stalls, ignoring protests—some of which bordered on desperate—with a polite shake of her head. Those weapons offered her nothing. She knew quality when she saw it, age and history when she felt it. A simple thing, when one worked with steel as much as she did. When it sang its secrets inside her head.

Still looking for treasures, Dela simply wandered for a time, soaking in the heat, the scents of incense and musty artifacts kept too long in shadow. She watched children sell boxed breakfasts of fried noodles and onion pancakes, crying out prices in high voices. She listened to an old man play a lilting melody on a stone flute, and bought one of his small instruments. He laughed when she tried stringing notes together, the hollow stone wheezing miserably. Dela grinned, shrugging.

After nearly an hour of browsing, Dela found something perfect for her mother. Generous rectangles of linen, dyed a vibrant navy, embroidered with delicate stylized flowers—a bouquet of colors, random and perfect. She bargained like a fiend, dredging up every scrap of charm and language she possessed, and by the end of the transaction, both she and the seller were grinning foolishly.

"Aiii yo," sighed the older woman, smoothing glossy silver hair away from an oval face that looked at least twenty years younger than her body. Gold-flecked eyes glittered, but not unkindly. "It has been a long time since I met a foreigner who made me work for a sale."

Dela laughed. "It's been a long time since I met anyone I enjoyed arguing with."

The woman quirked her lips, and for a moment, her gaze changed, becoming older, darker, wiser. "I have something else you might want."

"Ah, no. I think I have enough."

The old woman ignored her, already digging through the tapestries and knickknacks piled at her feet. Dela watched, helpless. She did not have the heart to simply walk away. A good haggle created a bond—certain unspoken etiquette. The "last chance" possibility of a final transaction.

The late summer heat was growing oppressive; air moved sluggishly between the stalls, thick with wares and milling bodies. The scents of dust and grease tickled Dela's nose. Sweat ran down her back. Slightly bored and uncomfortable, she turned full circle, gazing at the throng of shoppers.

A man at the end of the aisle caught her eye. He was of an indeterminate race, darkly handsome, wearing sandals and loose black slacks, as well as a white shirt with the sleeves rolled up. He was crisp, clean, and somehow out of place, although Dela could not determine exactly why.

At first she thought he was staring at her—and perhaps he had been—but now he studied the old woman digging through her wares, and Dela felt inexplicably uneasy. His eyes were cold, measuring, haunted by a simmering intensity that would have been overwhelming if not matched to such an attractive face and body.

When the old woman popped up with a triumphant sigh, Dela stepped close.

"Behind me," she whispered, not caring if the woman thought her strange, "there is a man watching you."

Her gold-flecked gaze flickered; something hard rippled through her face. "I am used to him. He seems to think I have something he wants."

"I don't like him," Dela said.

The old woman smiled. For a moment, her teeth looked sharp, predatory. "Which is why I am going to do you a favor. For one yuan, you may have this riddle box."

Dela stared. One yuan was an incredibly low price for the Dirt Market, where everything was inflated to exorbitant amounts, especially for foreigners. She gazed at the object in the old woman's hands. Loosely wrapped in linen, she saw soft lines, rounded edges. Wood, perhaps, although she imagined the hint of something harder beneath the cloth. No metal. Nothing called to her.

"What is the riddle?" Dela asked.

The old woman bared her teeth. "Choice."

Dela looked at her sharply and reached for the box. The woman pulled away, shaking her head.

"Bought and sold," she whispered, and Dela was struck by the intensity of her stare, more powerful than the gaze of the strange man still observing them. "It must be bought and sold. One yuan, please."

Dela could not bring herself to argue, to refuse. Despite the odd air surrounding the transaction, the vague uneasiness pricking her spine, she fished a bill from her purse and handed it to the old woman.

Another sigh, and the old woman looked deep into Dela's eyes. "A good choice," she said, and Dela sensed some deeper, inexplicable meaning. She carefully slid the wrapped box into Dela's purse—a swift act, as though to conceal. Dela felt uneasy.

You know better, she chided herself. *This 'box' could be full of drugs, and you're the stupid American courier, traipsing around until you get pulled over by the cops, and thrown into a sweaty prison.*

Or not, she thought, staring into the old woman's mysterious face. Dreams and portents, she reminded herself, fighting down a shudder. The stifling air was suddenly not warm enough. Her bones felt cold.

The old woman stepped back, smiling, and suddenly she was just like any other Dirt Market hawker. Eyes sharp, but somewhat glassy. Easy-mark eyes.

"Bye-bye," she said, and turned her back on Dela.

The sudden reversal in attitude, from intimate to dismissive, took Dela off guard. She almost protested, but from the corner of her eye felt the strange man's attention suddenly weigh upon her. An odd sensation; tangible, like sticky fingers on the back of her neck. Impossible to ignore.

Go, whispered her instincts.

Without another look at the old woman, Dela walked down the aisle, away from the strange man and his searching eyes. She did not look back; she moved gracefully through the thickening crowds, slipping between stalls and merchants, ragged men and women rising from their haunches to shove vases in front of her flushed face. Her chill vanished; the heat suddenly felt overwhelming, the press of bodies too much, the sensation of being hunted tightening her gut. Premonition haunted her.

When Dela finally broke free of her winding path, she found herself near the front gates. Heart pounding, she jogged to the street and hailed a cab. A breath of cool air brushed against her sweaty neck.

"My," drawled a smooth masculine voice. "You *are* in a hurry. What a shame."

Dela was used to unpleasant surprises, but it was still difficult not to flinch. The strange man stood beside her, intimately close. Perfectly coifed, breathtakingly handsome.

She disliked him even more. He was too perfect, fake and unreal. Even his voice sounded over-cultured, as though he was trying to affect an unfamiliar accent. There was nothing kind about his smile, which skirted the edge of hunger, conceit. He made Dela's skin crawl, and she stepped out of his shadow, frowning.

A cab stopped in front of her; Dela opened the door to slide in. The stranger caught her hand. His touch burned, and she barely kept from gasping at the strange sensation. His skin felt thin as parchment, ancient, but with such heat—actual fire, to her ice.

Shock turned to anger.

"Get your hand off me," she said, low and hard.

He smiled. "It has been a long time since I had a conversation with a beautiful woman. Perhaps I could share your cab? I know a lovely courtyard restaurant."

Conversation? Beautiful woman? Dela would have laughed, except he clearly expected her to say yes; he even nudged her toward the cab, maintaining his iron grip on her hand, his smile as white and plastic as a cheap doll.

"I don't think so," Dela snapped, surprised and pleased to see his dark eyes shutter, his smile falter. Did he really think she would be so easily cowed, so stupid and desperate? "And if you don't let go of me this instant, I am going to start screaming."

Perhaps it was the cold promise in Dela's voice; all charm fled the stranger's face. The transformation was stunning. He leaned close, his breath hot, smelling faintly of garlic, pepper. His gaze, dark and oppressive, lifted the hairs on the back of Dela's neck. Something fluttered against her mind, bitter and sharp.

Dela clenched her jaw so tight her teeth ached, and the stranger smiled—a real smile, bright and blistering and sharp.

"How interesting," he said, squeezing her hand until her bones creaked. The pain sparked rage, striking Dela's fear to dust. No one hurt her. Ever. Not while there was still breath in her body.

Loosening her jaw, she smiled—and screamed.

It was a marvelous scream, and Dela took an unholy amount of glee in the look of pain that crossed over the stranger's face. Bikes crashed into cars; passersby stopped dead in their tracks to stare. Dela pulled against his hand.

"Help me!" she screeched in both Chinese and English. "Please! This man is trying to rob me! He's going to rape me! Please, please . . . *someone!*"

Dela did not think she had ever sounded so frightened or pathetic in her entire life, but the horrible part was that while she had started out acting, the growing fury in the man's face suddenly did scare her. He looked like he wanted to kill her with his bare hands—as though he would, right there with everyone watching. Her entire arm screamed with pain as his fingers crushed bone.

Soldiers, common enough on Beijing's streets, ran from the gathered crowd of onlookers. Strong young men, they latched onto Dela's assailant, wrenching him away from her. It was quite a struggle; he was very strong and refused to let go of her hand. When he did, a cry escaped his throat; a bark of frustration, anger.

Dela slipped backwards into the cab, fumbling for the door, eyes wide upon the hate distorting that handsome face. The urge to run overwhelmed her, and she rapped her knuckles on the plastic barrier. The startled cab driver did not wait for her destination. He swerved into traffic, car brakes squealing all around, horns blaring. Within seconds, the Dirt Market—and the ongoing struggle outside its gate—was left behind.

Dela rubbed her arms, shuddering. Her face felt hot to the touch, but the rest of her burned cold. She bowed her head between her knees, taking deep measured breaths. The breathing helped her sudden nausea, but her heart continued to thud painfully against her ribs. She managed to tell the driver the name of her hotel, and then held her aching hand, trying to forget the feel of the stranger's fingers squeezing flesh and bone. The hot ash of his skin. The cool tremble against her mind.

A great stillness stole over Dela as she rode the memory of that sensation. She could count on one hand the number of times a stranger had purposely pressed his mind to her own, and while her shields were strong—her brother had made sure of that—Dela was in no mood to test herself against anyone who really wished her harm.

But he didn't know I was different until the end. Which meant the stranger had followed her out of the Dirt Market for another reason, one that had nothing to do with her psi-abilities. Dela remembered his cold dark eyes, how he had watched the old woman long before paying attention to her. What was his need, his purpose?

Through her purse, Dela felt a hard lump. The riddle box. Clarity spilled over her, and she almost examined her tiny purchase then and there. She caught the driver watching her through his rear view mirror, and hesitated. If she really had just purchased something awful like drugs or God-knows-what, she did not want any witnesses when she began poking her nose into Trouble. If that was what the riddle box represented.

He can't find me, Dela reminded herself. *That creep has no idea who I am, and this is a big city.* It was a small comfort.

When Dela arrived at the hotel, she stumbled up to her room, ignoring the strange looks people cast in her direction. She caught a glimpse of herself in the elevator's polished steel doors, and winced. Her blouse had popped open, her face was beet red, and her hair looked . . . well, just plain bad.

"Round one goes to the Evil Minion of Satan," she muttered, holding shut the front of her blouse. A nearby businessman gave her a strange look, and Dela laughed weakly—which didn't seem to comfort him at all.

Once inside her room, Dela turned all the locks on the door and threw her purse on the bed. The linen-wrapped box spilled out onto the burgundy covers, and she stared at it for one long minute. Stared, and then retreated into the bathroom for a shower. Dela couldn't take any more bad news—not just then. She desperately wanted to scrub away the morning, the lingering miasma of the stranger's presence.

Dela remained under the hot water for an indecent amount of time, until at last she stopped shivering. Infinitely calmer, she wrapped thick towels around her body and hair, and returned to the main room. She flopped on the bed with a sigh and picked up the wrapped box. Such a small, innocuous object.

Sometimes a cigar is just a cigar. The box may have nothing to do with that guy crawling all over you. He could have just pegged you as a victim.

True, but what had the old woman said?

He seems to think I have something he wants.

Frowning, Dela carefully unwrapped the layers of fine linen—surprising, to find such quality on an object from the Dirt Market—and caught her breath as the riddle box was finally revealed.

It was exquisite, with the breathless quality of some exotic myth. Round, no larger than the palm of her hand. Rosewood, polished to a deep red that was almost black, inlaid with silver and gold, onyx and lapis. The lid was etched with some foreign, incomprehensible script that looked more like musical notations than words, and the curved sides displayed an elaborate series of images, a story: a magnificent tiger inside a thick forest; the beast suddenly a man, fighting, raging—and then the tiger once again, prone, locked inside a cage.

The detail was incredible, impossibly precise and subtle. Dela had never seen such clarity of pinpoint and line—not even in her own art, and her methods were unorthodox, to say the least. Dela ran her fingers over the carvings, the bright inlays. She felt the tiger's gold-lined fur beneath her fingers, sensing his capture. The sensation of imprisonment made Dela inexplicably unhappy.

She pressed the riddle box against her cheek and closed her eyes. She could finally taste the trace of metal inside her head, but it was faint, faint, an ancient whisper like the brush of a brittle leaf.

Its age startled her, sent a rush of pressure into her gut. Dela rolled the metal inside her mind, listening to its sleepy secrets. Millennia old. Two millennia, maybe more. She felt breathless with awe.

What was that old woman thinking when she sold this to me? It's priceless.

But Dela thought of the strange man, the old woman's cryptic remarks, and his behavior suddenly made sense. She cradled the small treasure in her palms, turning it over in her fingers as surely as her thoughts were turning, twisting. Yes, someone might very well kill for this—or kidnap, assault. But why had the man waited until he thought Dela possessed the box? Why not go after the old woman if he suspected she had it? Surely she would be an easier target.

Dela sighed. She could understand the old woman wanting to rid herself of the box if she thought it would cost her life, but the black market would have offered her more money than one yuan! It didn't make sense.

Dela tried opening the lid, but it was stuck fast. She studied the box, and smiled. A true riddle. It took her fifteen minutes of careful fiddling, using her instincts more than her eyes, but she finally found the two releases, set in an onyx claw and a silver leaf. Pressing them simulta-

neously with one hand, she unscrewed the box lid—
——and the earth moved.

Violent vertigo sent Dela reeling into the pillows, clutching her head. Scents overwhelmed: rich loam, sap, wood smoke. Some essence of a verdant forest, come alive inside her room. Darkness, everywhere, but her eyes were clenched shut; Dela was afraid to open them, scared she would no longer be in the hotel. Dorothy, transported to Oz. Her displacement felt that complete.

Dela slowly became aware of the bedspread beneath her bare legs. The pillows, soft against her face. *Silly imagination*, she chided herself, and turned to look at the box.

It was no longer on the bed beside her.

Something in her stomach lurched, another premonition. She felt a ghost of movement, behind her, and she twisted—

——only to watch, dumbfounded, as sheer golden light spiraled through her room, shimmering in steep waves, a sunset palette of colors stroking air.

The light slowly took form, a gathering pressure of intense pinpricks. Dela blinked, and in that moment, the light coalesced. She felt thunder without sound, an impact to the air that lifted everything in the room, including herself.

The light disappeared, and in its place: A man.